About the Authors

Marie Ferrarella is a *USA TODAY* bestselling and *RITA*® Award-winning author who has written more than two hundred books for Mills & Boon, some under the name Marie Nicole. Her romances are beloved by fans worldwide. Visit her website at www.marieferrarella.com

USA TODAY and award-winning author **Janie Crouch** has loved to read romance her whole life. She cut her teeth on Mills & Boon as a teen, then moved on to a passion for romantic suspense as an adult. Janie lives with her husband and four children in Germany, in support of her husband's US Department of Defence job. Janie enjoys travelling, long-distance running, movies of all kinds, and coffee. Lots and lots of coffee For more: www.janiecrouch.com

USA TODAY bestselling author **Julie Miller** writes breathtaking romantic suspense. She has sold millions of copies of her books worldwide, and has earned a *National Readers Choice Award*, two Daphne du Maurier prizes and an *Romantic Times Book Reviews* Career Achievement Award. She is a multiple finalist for the prestigious *RITA*® Award. For a complete list of her books and more, go to www.juliemiller.org

Heroes in Hot Pursuit

Heroes in Hot Pursuit:
Second Chance Operation

MARIE FERRARELLA

JANIE CROUCH

JULIE MILLER

MILLS & BOON

First Published in Great Britain 2021
By Mills & Boon, an imprint of HarperCollins*Publishers,* Ltd
1 London Bridge Street, London, SE1 9GF

www.harpercollins.co.uk

HarperCollins*Publishers*
1st Floor, Watermarque Building,
Ringsend Road, Dublin 4, Ireland

HEROES IN HOT PURSUIT: SECOND CHANCE OPERATION © 2021
Harlequin Books S.A.

Colton Baby Rescue © 2018 Harlequin Books S.A.
Battle Tested © 2017 Janie Crouch
APB: Baby © 2016 Julie Miller

Special thanks and acknowledgement are given to Marie Ferrarella for her contribution to *The Coltons of Red Ridge* series.

ISBN: 978-0-263-30060-4

MIX
Paper from
responsible sources
FSC C007454

COLTON BABY RESCUE

MARIE FERRARELLA

To
Nancy Parodi Neubert
And
The Successful Return
Of
Happiness

Chapter 1

He *really* did not have time for this.

Detective Carson Gage frowned as he drove down the darkened streets to The Pour House. He had more important things to do than attend his older brother Bo's bachelor party at a second-rate dive bar in the sketchy part of town.

Hell, he would have rather stayed home and spent the evening talking to his K-9 unit partner, Justice. Granted it would have only been a one-way conversation, but the German shepherd was probably more intelligent than half the people who were going to be at the bachelor party anyway.

This whole thing was a joke, the Red Ridge police detective thought. Bo shouldn't be getting married anyway, not to a woman who he'd only known for a total of three months. This was way too sudden.

The whole thing seemed rather strange to him, not to mention ironic. Bo's bachelor party was being thrown at The Pour House, which just happened to be owned by Rusty Colton, who was the father of Bo's last girlfriend, Demi—the woman Bo had been engaged to for one month, then dumped when he took up with Hayley Patton, his current bride-to-be.

More than likely, Carson thought dourly, given who was being invited to this party, the evening was going to end up in a huge brawl—which was why he intended to stay for just one drink, then get the hell out of there.

Besides, he had work to do. His burning obsession was to find some piece of irrefutable evidence he could use to finally put away the Larson brothers, the cold-blooded twins who fancied themselves up-and-coming crime lords intent on building up a vast criminal empire and destroying everything and everyone in their path.

The Larsons were behind at least two murders that he knew of and they were at the center of a rash of drug busts, but because the thugs who worked for the brothers were more afraid of them than they were of the police, he hadn't been able to find anyone willing to testify against the twins.

But he would. Come hell or high water, he would, Carson swore, his hands tightening on his car's steering wheel. All he needed was to find that one elusive piece of evidence that would start the process of nailing the Larson brothers' coffins shut.

Carson picked his way through the streets, driving slowly. The area seemed even more unsavory at this time of night than it was during the day.

"If you *have* to marry this one, why couldn't you just run off and elope like a normal guy?" Carson asked out loud, addressing the brother who wasn't there. "Why all this need for fanfare and hoopla?"

It almost seemed, what with having the bachelor party at The Pour House, like Bo was deliberately rubbing Demi's nose in his wedding.

Yup, fireworks were definitely going to be on the agenda tonight, Carson thought. One beer and he was out of there, he promised himself again. He had no burning desire to break up a bunch of drunken men who should know better, doing their damnedest to knock each other's heads off. Bo had said he was inviting both Coltons and Gages to this party. Gasoline and fire, Carson thought.

He swore under his breath. No, he definitely didn't need this.

With a sigh, he pulled into The Pour House's parking lot. Because he wanted to be able to drive off the lot with a minimum of maneuvering—*and* make sure that his car didn't get dented by some celebrant who had overindulged in liquid courage, Carson decided to park all the way in the back of the lot. It would be a bit of a trek to the bar's front door, but it was between that and his peace of mind, and his peace of mind definitely made it worth it.

So he guided his vehicle all the way to the last row of the lot. The lot happened to back up against a grassy embankment.

Pulling up the hand brake, he sat there for a while, trying to get into the right frame of mind.

It wasn't happening.

With a sigh, the police detective got out of his car and locked it. Carson was about to start walking toward the entrance of the bar when he thought he saw someone lying facedown at the very far edge of the lot.

Carson paused, squinting. That part of the parking lot was pretty dark. What streetlights there were didn't reach that far.

"Looks like someone's already been partying too much," he muttered under his breath.

Some people just couldn't pace themselves accordingly and this guy obviously couldn't hold his liquor, Carson thought. With a resigned sigh, he changed course and headed toward the drunk instead of the bar. If he didn't wake the guy up and get him out of the way, Carson had no doubt that during the course of the evening, someone was liable to run the drunk over.

The lot wasn't all that full yet, he observed. This guy must have got a *really* early start. From what he could make out, the man was half on the edge of the lot, half on the grass at the very perimeter of the parking lot.

Drawing nearer, Carson saw that the man, whose face was obscured because it was turned toward the grass, had one arm stretched out with his index finger raised, like he was trying to draw attention to something.

That's odd.

And then, despite the fact that it was pretty dark there, Carson saw that there was writing on the ground just above the man's head. It looked as if he had written something—

In blood?

Taking his phone out, he hit the flashlight app, then squatted down. Using the light from his phone, Carson looked at the ground just above the man's head more closely.

"It looks like you wrote *Demi C*," Carson murmured, half to himself. The last letter was barely finished.

Demi C? Demi Colton?

Carson's eyes widened. What was this guy doing, writing the name of his brother's former girlfriend on the parking lot asphalt? And where had the blood come from? Had the guy hit his head?

"Hey, fella, wake up. The parking lot's no place to take a nap." He shook the man's shoulder but couldn't seem to rouse him.

Blowing out a breath, Carson rose to his feet and

circled the man's body so he could get a look at the drunk's face.

"C'mon, fella, you can't sleep it off here. You've gotta get—"

The rest of the sentence froze on Carson's lips.

The man he was trying to wake up was his brother. Bo's eyes were wide-open and unseeing.

There was a black cummerbund stuffed into his mouth. And he wasn't breathing.

Chapter 2

Detective Carson Gage's hands were shaking as he urgently turned his brother over onto his back. Any hope of trying to revive Bo disappeared the moment he saw the bullet wound.

His brother had been shot right through the heart.

Irrationally, Carson felt for a pulse anyway. There was none. Swallowing a curse, he sat back on his heels. His brother's skin was already cold to the touch. This was January in Red Ridge, South Dakota, but death brought a different sort of cold with it and there was no mistaking it for a simple reaction to the weather.

"Damn it, Bo, I *told* you playing fast and loose with women would be the death of you someday. Why d'you have to prove me right?" Carson demanded angrily.

He curbed his impulse to straighten Bo's clothing. Bo always took pride in his appearance and death had left him looking disheveled. But the crime scene investigators were going to need to see everything just the way he had found it.

Shaken to the core, Carson got back up to his feet and opened up his cell phone again. He needed to call this in.

It took him a minute to center his thoughts. He was a trained police detective, Carson silently upbraided himself. He couldn't afford the luxury of coming apart like some hysterical civilian who had just unexpectedly witnessed death up close and personal— even if this *was* his half brother.

Taking a deep breath and then exhaling, he put in a call to his chief, Finn Colton. As he waited for Finn to pick up, he looked again at the name his brother had written in his own blood.

Demi C.

Demi Colton. Carson shook his head. When this got out, it was going to throw all of Red Ridge into one hell of an uproar, he thought. As if the feud between the Coltons and the Gages needed more fuel.

The next moment, he heard Finn's deep voice as the chief answered his phone. "Hey, Gage, aren't you supposed to be at your brother's bachelor party right now, getting drunk and toasting Bo's last few hours of freedom? What are you doing calling me?"

Carson enunciated the words carefully, afraid that if he spoke any faster, his voice was going to break. He and Bo weren't close, but they were still family. "There's been a murder, Chief."

"Damn," Finn cursed. Instantly, the voice on the other end became serious. "Whose?"

Carson paused before answering. "Bo's."

"This your idea of a joke, Gage?" Finn demanded impatiently. "'Cause if it is, it's not funny."

"I only wish it was, Chief," Carson answered.

"You're serious," Finn responded, stunned. When no contradiction came, Finn asked, "Where and when?"

Carson looked down at his brother's body. The whole scene seemed utterly surreal to him. "I just found him two minutes ago, lying facedown at the edge of The Pour House's parking lot."

"The Pour House," Finn repeated. "Isn't that where his bachelor party is supposed to be taking place tonight?"

"One and the same," Carson answered his superior numbly. He realized he was leaving the most important part out. "And, Chief?"

"Yeah?"

"Looks like Bo wrote a name in his own blood. Maybe his killer's name."

Carson heard a noise on the other end as the other

man said something unintelligible before going on to ask, "Whose name did he write?"

"Demi C."

This time there was total silence on the other end for approximately thirty seconds as the information sank in.

The city of thirty-five thousand citizens had more than its share of Coltons. There were three branches in total, as different from one another as the seasons were. The chief liked to say that he belonged to the middle branch, the one that was neither rich nor poor and rough around the edges.

But whatever section he gravitated to, the chief was still a Colton and Carson couldn't help wondering how Finn Colton would deal with having to bring in one of his own as a suspect for first-degree murder.

Finally, the chief broke the silence and asked, "You think Bo wrote that?"

"It's in his own blood, Chief," Carson answered. Then, in case there was any further question as to whether or not Bo was the one who wrote the name, he added, "There's blood underneath Bo's fingernail. Looks like he wrote it."

Finn sighed as if the weight of the world had suddenly been dropped on his shoulders.

"Good enough for me," he replied. "I'll have Demi brought in for questioning. Meanwhile, I'll send some of the team to bring in your brother's body." His voice softened, as if he was feeling sympathetic about what Carson was going through. "You can give your statement in the morning if you need some time, Gage."

Finn was cutting him some slack, Carson thought. He didn't want any slack, he wanted to get his brother's killer.

Now.

"I don't need any time, Chief." Somewhere in the distance, a coyote howled. Carson would have been hard-pressed to name a lonelier sound. "I'll stay here with Bo until the detail gets here," he told his boss. "And then I'm coming down to the station. I want to be there when you interrogate Demi."

"Gage, you can't—"

Carson felt the walls going up. He cut Finn off before the chief could officially exclude him. "I *need* to be there when you question her, Finn. You owe this to me, Chief."

There was silence again. An annoyed silence if he was any judge, Carson thought. He fully expected the chief to argue with him, but he wasn't about to back down.

However, Finn surprised him by saying, "All right, you can be there, but I'll be the one handling the interrogation. I don't want to hear a word out of you, understood?"

Even though Finn couldn't see him, Carson nodded his head grimly. "Understood."

Terminating the call, Carson put his phone into his pocket. Silence enshrouded him although the distant sound of music and raised voices coming from the bar sliced through the air, disrupting the night.

"Sounds like your bachelor party's getting underway without you," Carson said to the prone figure near his feet. "Not exactly the way you expected the night to go, is it?" he asked ironically. He squared his shoulders. No, he and Bo hadn't been close, but Bo was still his brother and he didn't deserve this. "Don't worry, Bo. If Demi did this, she'll pay. I don't know what happened, but I promise she'll pay. I'll see to it."

It was getting colder. Carson pulled his sheepskin jacket tighter around him and turned up the collar. But he remained where he was, a guard at his post. He wasn't about to go anywhere until the unit came to pick up Bo's body.

"I know my rights. I'm a bounty hunter, damn it, and I know my rights better than you do," twenty-seven-year-old Demetria Colton shouted angrily at the two police officers who brought her into the small, windowless room within the Red Ridge police station. "Why am I here?" she wanted to know.

But neither of the two police officers, one young, one old, answered her, other than one of them telling her, "The chief'll be here shortly."

"The 'chief'?" Demi repeated in a mocking tone.

"You mean Cousin *Finn*? Is he still pretending to be in charge?"

The two officers left the small eight-by-ten room without answering her. An angry, guttural noise escaped the redhead's lips. Frustrated, she would have thrown something if she'd had something to throw.

"Why am I here?" she demanded again, more loudly this time. Furious, she began to pound on the locked door. "I know you're out there! I demand to be released. You can't hold me here like this, you hear me?" she cried. "I haven't *done* anything, damn it! You let me out of here! Now!"

When the door suddenly opened just as she was about to start pounding on it again, Demi was caught off guard and stumbled backward. Had the table not been right there behind her to block her fall, she would have unceremoniously landed on the floor.

"You're here," her cousin calmly told her as he and Carson walked into the room, acting as if they were about to have a run-of-the-mill, normal conversation, "to answer some questions."

Demi tossed her head, her red hair flying over her shoulder.

"What kind of questions?" she asked defiantly, her dark brown gaze pinning him down.

"Like where were you tonight?" Finn wanted to know, gesturing toward the lone chair on the opposite side of the table and indicating that she should sit.

"Home," Demi bit off, grudgingly sitting down.

"I was in my home—since 5:00 p.m." she added for good measure.

Finn gave no indication whether or not the answer satisfied him. He waited until Carson sat down next to him, then asked, "Alone?"

"Yes," she bit off, then followed that up with a question of her own. "Why?" she demanded. Squaring her shoulders, she drew herself up and raised her chin, always ready to do battle with the world—and her cousin. "Is that a crime now?"

Hearing Carson's chair scrape along the floor as he started to rise, Finn shot him a warning look before answering Demi's question. "No, but murder is."

"Murder," the redhead repeated, growing more furious by the second. She made the only logical conclusion. "You think I *murdered* someone?" she cried, stunned. "And just who is it I was supposed to have murdered?" When Finn didn't answer her immediately, she pounced on him. "C'mon, you can't just throw something like that out and then leave me hanging in suspense, Finn. Just who was it that you think I murdered?"

Unable to remain silent any longer, his hands fisted at his sides, Carson pinned her with a damning look as he answered her question. "Bo. You murdered Bo and then you stuffed a cummerbund into his mouth."

"Bo," she repeated in noncomprehension. And then, for a moment, Demi turned very pale. Her eyes flicked from Bo's brother to her cousin. "Bo's dead?" she asked hoarsely.

It was half a question, half a statement uttered in total disbelief.

Then, not waiting for an answer, what had become known in the county as Demi's famous temper flared, and she jumped up to her feet, her fists banging down on the tabletop.

"You think I killed Bo?" she demanded incredulously, fury flashing in her eyes. "Sure," she said mockingly. "Makes perfect sense to me. The man's dead so let's blame it on the woman he dumped— EXCEPT I DIDN'T DO IT!" she yelled, her angry gaze sweeping over her cousin and her former fiancé's brother.

"Sit down, Demi," Finn ordered sternly. "And calm down."

Instead of listening to her cousin and taking her seat again, Demi Colton remained standing, a firecracker very close to going off in a flash of fireworks.

"*No*, I will *not* calm down," she cried. "And unless you have some kind of concrete evidence against me—" she said, staring straight at her cousin.

"How about Bo writing your name on the asphalt in his own blood?" Finn said. "Demi C."

Demi paled for a moment. "The killer is framing me?"

Finn raised an eyebrow.

Demi gave him a smug look. "Just as I thought. You *don't* have any sort of actual evidence against me. Okay, I'm out of here," Demi declared.

"You'll leave when I tell you to leave," Finn told her sternly. Rising from his chair on the opposite side of the table, he loomed over her.

"*Do* you have any evidence against me, other than my name written in Bo's blood and the fact that I had the bad judgment to have been engaged to the jerk for a month?" she asked, looking from her cousin to the other man in the room.

Though it obviously killed him, Finn was forced to say, "No, but—"

Triumph filled her eyes. "There is no 'but' here," Demi retorted. "You have *nothing* to hold me on, that means I'm free to go. So I'm going." Her eyes swept over her cousin and Carson. "Gentlemen, it has definitely *not* been a pleasure."

And with that, she swept past them to the interrogation room door like a queen taking leave of a pair of disloyal subjects.

Finn shook his head as his cousin stormed out. "Hell of a lot of nerve," he muttered under his breath.

"As I recall, Demi was never the sweet, retiring type. If she was, she would have never become a bounty hunter," Carson told him.

Finn blew out a breath. "You have a point." He walked out of the interrogation room with Carson directly behind him. "Well, check out her alibi, talk to anyone who might have seen her," the chief said, addressing the victim's brother. "I'm open to any further suggestions."

Carson looked at his boss in mild surprise. "I thought you made it clear that I wasn't allowed to work on my brother's case." Although, he thought, since Finn could work on the case in which his cousin was a suspect, he should be allowed to investigate his brother's murder.

"Technically, you're not," Finn said as they walked out into the main squad room. "But I'm not an idiot, Gage. You're going to work this whether I give you my blessing or not." He stopped just before his office. "So you have any ideas where to start?"

He'd been thinking about this ever since he'd found Bo's body. The fact that Bo had written Demi's name seemed pretty damning to him, but he didn't want to discount the slim possibility that someone else had killed his brother.

It didn't warm his heart to have to admit this, but in all fairness, he had to. "Well, it's common knowledge that Demi wasn't the only woman Bo romanced and then dumped. I'd say that there were a whole lot of women who'd love to have seen Bo get what was coming to him. And that includes a number of disgruntled husbands and boyfriends, as well. Why don't we start talking to them?"

That Bo was a playboy wasn't exactly news to

anyone. Finn frowned. "But would any of them actually resort to murder?"

Carson shrugged. Nothing jumped out at him, but this needed closer examination. "Only one way to find out," he told his boss.

"I agree," Finn responded. "Make up a list. Meanwhile, I'm going to have some of the boys go over the crime scene with a fine-tooth comb, see if someone missed anything just in case. Although the ground's undoubtedly been trampled on," he commented.

Carson nodded grimly. "Nobody ever said that solving crimes was easy. I can swing by my place, pick up Justice," he said, referring to his K-9 partner. "See if maybe he can pick up a scent."

"*After* you put that list together," Finn told the detective.

Carson headed over to his desk. Given the hour, the squad room was practically empty. "Will do," he told the chief.

"Oh, and, Gage?" Finn called after him.

Carson turned around, expecting further orders. "Yeah, Chief?"

"I'm really sorry for your loss."

The words were standard-issue, said over and over again in so many instances that they sounded numbingly routine, yet he felt that Finn really meant them.

"Yeah, me, too," Carson answered stoically, then added, "Thanks."

* * *

Carson had just finished making a preliminary list of all the women he could remember Bo having had any romantic encounters with over the last several years when J.D. Edwards, one of the crime scene investigators, came into the squad room. J.D. looked excited.

Temporarily forgetting about the list he'd just compiled, Carson crossed over to the man. J.D., in turn, had just cornered Finn.

"You're going to want to hear this," the investigator was saying to Finn.

The chief, seeing Carson, nodded at him, indicating that he join them. Carson was all ears.

"What have you got?" Finn asked.

"Lots," J.D. answered. "First off, I found this under a wheel near where the body was found." He held up a sealed plastic evidence bag. The bag contained a necklace with a gold heart charm.

Finn squinted as he looked at the necklace. "That looks familiar."

"It should be," the investigator said. "It belongs to—"

"Demi," Carson said, recognizing the gold heart. "That's her necklace."

"And that's not all," J.D. informed them. The investigator paused for effect before announcing, "We've got a witness who says he saw Demi Colton running in the shadows around 6:45 p.m. near The Pour House."

"Six forty-five," Carson repeated. He looked at Finn. "I found Bo's body at seven."

J.D. looked rather smug as he said, "Exactly."

"Who's the witness?" Finn wanted to know.

"Paulie Gains," J.D. answered.

Carson frowned. He would have preferred having someone a little more reliable. "Gains is a small-time drug dealer."

"Doesn't mean he couldn't have seen her," Finn pointed out. He looked at J.D. "How did he know it was Demi? It's dark at that hour."

J.D. laughed. "Not that many people around here have her color hair, Chief."

Finn nodded. J.D. was right. "Okay, that puts her at the scene. Looks like we've got that evidence Demi kept going on about," he told Carson, adding, "Time for that bounty hunter to do some heavy-duty explaining if she intends to walk out of here a second time. Let's go wrestle up an arrest warrant."

Carson didn't have to be told twice. He led the way out the door.

Chapter 3

It took a little time, but Carson and his boss finally found a judge who was willing to issue an arrest warrant at that time of night.

"Do me a favor, lose my number," Judge David Winkler told Finn, closing his front door and going back to his poker game.

Tucking the warrant into his pocket, the chief turned toward Carson. "Let's go. We're not waiting until morning," Finn told the detective as he got back into his vehicle.

Armed with the warrant, for the second time in less than five hours police detectives hurried back to Demi Colton's small ranch house on the outskirts of town, this time to arrest her.

The house was dark when they arrived.

"I've got a bad feeling about this," Carson murmured as he and Finn approached.

Carson knocked on the door. When there was no response, he knocked again, harder this time. Rather than knock a third time, he tried the doorknob. He was surprised to find that the door was unlocked.

Guns drawn, they entered and conducted a quick room-to-room search of the one-story dwelling. There was no one home.

"Damn it." Finn fumed. "My gut told me to keep her in a holding cell and not let her just walk out of the police station like that."

"Looks like some of her clothes are gone," Carson called out to the chief, looking at a cluster of empty hangers in the bounty hunter's bedroom closet.

"Yeah, well, so is she," Finn answered from the kitchen. When Carson joined him, Finn held up the note he'd found on the kitchen table.

"What's that, a confession?" Carson asked, coming around to look at the piece of notepaper.

"Just the opposite," Finn told him in disgust. "It says 'I'm innocent.'"

Carson said what he assumed they were both thinking. "Innocent people don't run."

The chief surprised him when Finn said, "They might if they think the deck is stacked against them."

"Is that what you think? That she's innocent?" Carson questioned, frowning. He supposed that there was a small outside chance that the chief might be right, but as far as he was concerned, he was going to need a lot of convincing.

"I think I want to talk to her again and find out just how her necklace wound up under the wheel of that car," Finn answered.

In order to talk to the woman again they were going to have to find her. Carson blew out a long breath, thinking.

"Maybe her father knows where she is," he said, speculating. "Won't hurt to talk to him. Man might be able to tell us something."

Although, from what Bo had told him about Demi's contentious relationship with her father, Carson highly doubted that Rusty Colton would be able to give them any viable insight into his daughter's whereabouts.

But, Carson speculated, the old man might know something he didn't know he knew. They had nothing to lose by questioning Rusty Colton.

At least they would be no worse off than they were now, Carson reasoned as they drove over to The Pour House.

The bar's door was closed when they got there, but the lights were still on. Carson banged on it with his fist until Rusty Colton came to unlock it. The tall, skinny man had his ever-present mug of beer in his hand as he opened the door.

Bleary brown eyes quickly assessed the situation from beneath unruly reddish-brown hair.

"Sorry, boys, I'm just about to close up for the night," Rusty said just before Carson pushed his way in. Taking a step back, the bar owner regrouped. "Okay then, I'll have to limit you to just one round—although I just might see my way clear to staying open a little longer if you two boys are willing to pay extra."

Small, beady eyes shifted from the chief to the detective. Rusty waited in anticipation to have his palm greased.

He waited in vain.

"We're not here to drink, Mr. Colton," Carson told the man coldly.

He'd never cared for the owner of The Pour House. There was something palatably unsavory about Rusty Colton. Carson had no doubt that the man would sell his own mother if he needed the money.

Annoyed, Rusty gestured toward the door. "Well then, 'gentlemen,' I need to get back to closing up my establishment," he told them.

Neither of the men moved toward the door.

"We were wondering if you could tell us where your daughter is, Rusty," Finn asked in a voice that said he wasn't about to be trifled with. "Demi."

Rusty snorted. "She's a grown woman, Finn. She comes and goes as she pleases. Ungrateful whelp never did mind me," he said, banging down his empty mug on the counter. "I can't be expected to keep track of her."

Carson moved in a little closer to the man. He wasn't that much taller than Rusty, but he was a great deal more muscular and therefore more intimidating. "You keep track of everything when it suits you. Now, let's try this again," he said evenly. "Where's Demi?"

"Well, if you must know," Rusty said, smugly drawing out each word, "she's gone. Long gone. I think you two apes probably scared her and she hightailed it out of here."

That wasn't good enough for him. "What makes you so sure?" Carson wanted to know. "Did she tell you?"

"Didn't have to," Rusty answered, pushing together several glasses on the counter in a halfhearted attempt to clean up. "I stopped by her place during my evening break—I leave Amos in charge then. He's dumb, but nobody's going to try to skip out on paying that big ox," he informed the two men at the bar proudly.

"Get back to the point," Finn ordered. "You stopped by Demi's place and then what?"

"Well, she wasn't home so I decided to dip into that big wad of cash she keeps under her mattress like I do every now and then—only when I need a little something to get me through to the end of the month," Rusty admitted without a drop of embarrassment.

"Except that I couldn't this time," he complained. "It was gone. Guess the little witch must have taken it and hightailed it out of here." He looked quite put out by his youngest daughter's action. "Didn't even think to leave me any, my own daughter," he complained.

Carson exchanged looks with his boss. They weren't going to get anything more out of Rusty.

"Let us know if she comes back," Finn told the man as he walked out.

Rusty grunted something in response, but it was unintelligible and they'd already lost too much time, Carson reasoned, following the chief out.

"Warrant's not going to do us any good right now," Carson bit out, handing the paper back to Finn.

"I'll put out an APB on her," Finn said, striding back to his vehicle. "Maybe we'll get lucky. In the meantime, have the team look into those people whose names you wrote down."

Frustrated, Carson nodded as he got into the car. For now, at least it was a place to start.

Early the following morning, Carson stood by as the chief called a staff meeting of all the K-9 cops and gave them instructions. Articles of Demi's clothing, got from her house, were handed out in order to give the dogs a scent to track.

Others on the force got busy looking into Bo's

past. The latter included interviewing women Bo
had seen, exploring the various gambling debts he
ran up and, since Bo had been an in-demand dog
breeder who'd trained and sold dogs to people and
organizations besides the police department, Carson
started conducting a second background check on
those people. Maybe there was a disgruntled client
out for revenge and the situation had got out of hand
for some reason.

It was time-consuming and grueling and it all
ultimately led nowhere.

Serena Colton absolutely refused to buy into all
the lurid hype surrounding her cousin Demi.

Here, tucked away in her private wing of her parents' vast, prosperous Double C Ranch, the story of
Bo Gage's murder and how *Demi C* was found written in Gage's own blood beside his body sounded like
the fanciful imaginings of a second-rate scriptwriter.
Except that Bo Gage *was* found murdered and Demi's
name *did* appear to be written next to his body.

"I don't believe it," Serena said to her three-
month-old daughter, who was dozing in her arms.
"There's *got* to be another explanation for this, Lora.
Sure, Demi has her shortcomings," she readily admitted, "but she's not a murderer."

Serena sighed, gently rocking her daughter as
she restlessly paced around the very large bedroom.
"You take all the time in the world growing up, Lora,

you hear me? Stay little for as long as you can. And I'll do my part. I won't let anything like this ever touch you," she whispered to the sleeping child. "I'll keep you safe, little one. I promise."

As if to challenge the promise she had just made to her daughter, the sound of approaching sirens pierced the night air.

The sirens grew progressively louder, coming closer.

Worried, Serena moved to the window facing the front of the house and looked out. She was just in time to see the headlights from two police vehicles approaching the house—mansion, really—where she lived with her parents and younger sister, Valeria.

"What could the police possibly want here, and at this hour?" Serena murmured under her breath. Her brother Finn was the police chief and he wouldn't be coming here like this unless there was something very, very wrong—would he? She couldn't help wondering.

As if in response, Lora stirred in her arms. But mercifully, the baby went on sleeping. Although how she didn't wake up with all this noise was a complete mystery to Serena. The sirens had gone silent, but in their wake came the loud, urgent pounding of a fist against the front door.

Her heart was instantly in her throat. The next second, she heard her parents and Valeria all rushing down the stairs to answer the door.

Still holding her daughter in her arms, Serena left her room and went to the landing, hoping to find what was going on from the shelter of the second floor.

She was just in time to see her father throw open the front door. Not surprisingly, Judson Colton looked furious. The tall, strapping ranch owner wasn't accustomed to being treated in this sort of manner.

"Just what is the meaning of all this noise?" Judson Colton demanded even before he had the door opened all the way. When he saw that his own son was responsible for all this uproar, he only became angrier. "Finn! How dare you come pounding on our door in the middle of the night and wake us up like this?" he shouted. "You're not only disturbing me, you're disturbing your stepmother and your sisters as well, not to mention that you're doing the unforgivable and spooking the horses!"

Lightning all but flashed from the man's eyes as he glared at his son and the three men Finn had brought with him. Especially since one of them was holding on to a large German shepherd.

Judson eyed the dog warily. "We raised you better than this, boy," he snapped at Finn indignantly.

"I'm sorry if you're offended," Finn told his father formally. "But this is police business. Murder isn't polite," he added grimly. He and his men had been at this all day. It was nighttime now and he was too tired to treat his father and stepmother with kid gloves.

"Murder?" Joanelle Colton cried, pressing her well-manicured hand against her chest as if trying to hold a heart attack at bay. "This isn't about that man who was found dead outside of that horrid bar, is it?" Finn's stepmother looked from him to Carson. "What does *any* of that awful business have to do with us, Finn?"

"That's what we're here to find out," Finn answered patiently.

Serena had a feeling she knew exactly why they were here.

Carson glanced at the chief. Because this was Finn's family, he needed to absent himself from the immediate search of the house. If there was anything—or anyone—to be found, the chief wouldn't want that to be compromised in a court of law.

"Dan, Jack and I'll search the property," Finn told his father and stepmother. "Detective Gage is going to search the house." He nodded at Carson.

"Search the house?" Joanelle echoed in stunned disbelief. "Search the house for what?" she added indignantly.

But Finn and the two officers he had brought with him had already left the house to start their search.

Taking his cue, Carson, warrant in hand, quickly hurried up the stairs with Justice leading the way.

"Search the house for what?" Judson repeated more forcefully as he followed Carson and his K-9.

"Demi Colton or any sign of her, sir," Carson answered just as he and Justice came to the landing.

He stopped dead when he saw Serena standing there, holding her baby in her arms. At that moment, totally against his will, he was transported to another time and place in his life. He was back in the hospital hallway where a solemn-faced doctor was telling him that he had done everything he could to save her, but Lisa, his girlfriend, had just died giving birth to their daughter. A daughter who wound up dying the following day.

Carson felt an ache form in the pit of his stomach, threatening to consume him even as it undid him.

He struggled to bury the memory again and regain control over himself, just as he had done when his loss had occurred. He'd learned that 99 percent of surviving was just remembering to breathe and put one foot in front of the other.

His voice was gruff and cold as he told the woman standing there, "If you're hiding Demi Colton, now is the time for you to speak up."

On the stairs behind him, Judson cried, "Demi Colton?" He almost laughed out loud at the detective who worked for his son. "You're looking for Demi *here*? Hell, you look all you want, but I can tell you that you're wasting your time. You won't find that woman here."

"If you don't mind, sir," Carson answered stiffly, "I'd like to check for myself."

"Then go ahead and do it, but do it quickly," Finn's father warned. "And see that you don't disturb my daughters any more than you already have. Do I make myself clear, boy?"

"I'd prefer 'Detective,'" Carson replied. Judson Colton merely glared, then turned and went back downstairs.

Finn's stepmother had another sort of complaint to register with him. "Must you bring that mangy creature into my house?" She looked disdainfully at Justice. The canine was straining at his leash.

"Justice is part of the police department, ma'am, same as the rest of us," Carson informed the woman without missing a step.

Rather than cringing or stepping aside, he saw a slight smile grace Serena Colton's lips as she looked down at Justice.

"My father's right, you know. You're wasting your time," Serena told him. "I haven't seen her since yesterday. Demi's not here."

"I need to verify that for myself," Carson told her shortly. "Why don't you go downstairs and wait with the rest of your family?" he suggested.

Carson could feel Judson Colton watching his every move.

"I'd rather stay up here, thank you," Serena answered. "She didn't do it, you know," she told Carson. "Demi's not capable of killing anyone."

Serena was entitled to her opinion, he thought, even though it was naive. "You'd be surprised what people are capable of if they're pushed hard enough," Carson told her.

"There is a limit," Serena insisted.

"If you say so," he replied, complete disinterest in his voice.

His attention was focused on Justice who was moving around Serena's room with growing agitation. Suddenly, Justice became alert and ran up to the walk-in closet. He began pawing at the door.

Carson looked over his shoulder at Serena, disappointment clearly registering on his face. "Not here, huh?"

"No, she's not," Serena insisted, crossing the room to her closet.

Carson waved her back. Taking out his weapon, he pointed it at the closet door and then threw it open. Justice ran in and immediately nosed the hot-pink sweater on the closet floor. The German shepherd moved the sweater over toward his master.

Picking it up, Carson held the sweater aloft and looked accusingly at Serena.

"I said I saw her yesterday," Serena pointed out. "Demi must have dropped her sweater here when I wasn't paying attention. I never said she wasn't here *yesterday*, only that she's not here now—and she isn't," Serena insisted.

Drawn by all the commotion and the headlights from the police vehicles when they drove to the house, Serena's brother Anders, who lived in a cabin on the property and worked as the Double C foreman, came into his sister's bedroom.

"Serena's right. Demi was here at the house yesterday afternoon, but she left and she hasn't been back since. Trust me, I can't abide that little bounty hunter, and I'd tell you if she was here. But she's not," Anders said with finality.

"And neither one of you would know where she went or might consider going if she was running from the police?" Carson pressed.

Serena and her brother answered his question in unison.

"No."

Chapter 4

"Here." Carson shoved the hot-pink sweater over to Anders. "Take this and put it somewhere, will you? The scent is throwing my dog off."

Anders frowned at the sweater Carson had just shoved into his hand. "Sorry. Hot pink's not my color."

Carson wasn't amused by the foreman's dry wit, not when he was trying to find his brother's killer.

"Just get rid of it for now. As long as that's around, Justice can't home in on anything else Demi might have left behind that could wind up proving useful."

Muttering something about not being an errand boy under his breath and looking none too happy about having Carson on the premises, Anders took the sweater and marched out of Serena's suite. Wadding the sweater up, he tossed it into the linen closet that was down the hall and shut the door.

Carson looked back at his dog. Now that the offending piece of clothing was gone, Justice became totally docile.

"C'mon, boy, keep on looking," he urged his German shepherd partner. "Seek!"

Responding to the command, Justice quickly covered the remainder of the upper floor, moving from one area to another, but nothing seemed to spark a reaction from the dog. Nothing caused him to behave as if he had detected any telltale scent that indicated that the woman he was hunting was hiding somewhere on the floor or had even left anything else behind.

Serena kept her distance but still followed the detective, shadowing him step for step. For now, Lora was cooperating and went on dozing.

Coming back through the adjacent nursery, Carson made his way into Serena's oversize bedroom. His eyes met hers.

"See, I told you she wasn't here," Serena told him. When his face remained totally impassive, she heard herself insisting. "You're looking for the wrong person, Detective. Demi didn't kill Bo. There's got to be some kind of mistake."

About to leave her suite and go back downstairs,

Carson stopped abruptly. Justice skidded to a stop next to him.

"My brother's dead. He wrote Demi's name in his own blood on the asphalt right above his head. Her necklace was found at the crime scene, and there's a witness who said he saw Demi running away from the area some fifteen minutes before Bo's body was found in the parking lot. From what I can see, the only mistake here was made by Demi," he informed Serena curtly, doing his best to hold his anger in check.

Part of the anger he was experiencing was because of the crime itself and part of it was due to the fact that having seen Serena holding her baby like that when he'd first entered had stirred up painful memories for him, memories he wanted to leave buried.

Serena shook her head, refusing to buy into the scenario that Demi had killed her ex-boyfriend in some sort of a fit of misguided jealousy. That was not the Demi she had come to know.

"Look," she began, trying to talk some sense into the detective, "I admit that it looks bad right now—"

Carson barely managed to keep a dismissive oath from escaping his lips.

Serena didn't seem to notice as she forged on. "There's no way that the Demi Colton I know is a killer. Yes, she has a temper, but she wouldn't kill anyone, *especially* not her ex-boyfriend."

Carson looked at her sharply. What wasn't she telling him?

"Why?" he questioned.

Did Demi's cousin know something that he didn't know, or was she just being protective of the other woman? Was it simply a matter of solidarity between women, or whatever it was called, or was there something more to Serena's certainty, because she did look pretty certain?

Serena began to say something else, then stopped herself at the last moment, saying only, "Because she just wouldn't, that's all."

Carson looked at the chief's sister closely. She knew something. Something she wasn't telling him, he thought. His gut was telling him that he was right. But he couldn't exactly browbeat her into admitting what she was trying to hide.

He was just going to have to keep an eye on the chief's sister, he decided.

Just then, the baby began to fuss.

"Shh." Serena soothed her daughter. She started rocking the child, doing her best to lull Lora back to sleep.

But Lora wouldn't settle down. The fussing became louder.

Glancing up, Serena was going to excuse herself when she saw the strange look on the detective's face. In her estimation he looked to be in some sort of pain or distress. Sympathy instantly stirred within her. She hated seeing pain of any kind.

She had to be losing her mind, feeling sympathy for a man who seemed so bent on arresting her cousin. It was obvious that he had already convicted Demi without a trial and looked more than willing to drag Demi to jail.

However, despite all this, for some strange reason, she was moved by the underlying distress she saw in his eyes.

"Is something wrong, Detective Gage?" She waited for him to respond, but he didn't seem to hear her despite their close proximity. "Detective Gage?" she said more loudly.

Suddenly realizing that she was talking to him, Carson looked at the chief's sister. She seemed to be waiting for him to respond to something she'd obviously said.

"What?" he all but snapped.

The man was in no danger of winning a congeniality award, Serena thought. "I asked you if something was wrong."

Damn it, Carson upbraided himself, he was going to have to work on his poker face. "You mean other than the obvious?"

Serena mentally threw up her hands. This was hopeless. Why did she even care if something was bothering this boorish man who had come stomping into her house, disrupting everyone without displaying so much as an iota of remorse that he was doing it. Never mind that her brother had led this invasion into her parents' home, she felt better blaming the detective for this than blaming Finn.

"Never mind," she told Carson, changing topics. "I have to see to my baby, if it's all right with you," she said, a mild touch of sarcasm breaking through.

Rather than say anything in response, Carson just waved her back to her quarters.

Serena's voice was fairly dripping with ice as she said, "Thank you."

With that she turned on her bare heel to walk back into her suite.

"Let's go, Justice," Carson said to the dog, steering the animal toward the stairs.

Keeping a tight hold on the dog's leash, Carson walked out of the house quickly, a man doing his best to outrun memories he found far too painful to coexist with.

Once outside, he saw the other members of the K-9 team. Not wanting to be faced with unnecessary questions, he forced himself to relax just a little.

"Anything?" Carson asked the man closest to him, Jim Kline.

Jim, paired with a jet-black German shepherd whimsically named Snow, shook his head. "If that woman's anywhere on the property, she's crawled down into a gopher hole and pulled the hole down after her," the man answered him.

Finn came over to join them. Carson noticed that the chief looked as disappointed as he felt.

"Okay, men, everybody back to the station. We're calling it a night and getting a fresh start in the morning." The chief glanced over in his direction. "You, too, Gage," he ordered, obviously expecting an argument from Carson.

And he got it. "I'm not tired, Chief," Carson protested, ready to keep going.

"Good for you," Finn said sarcastically. "Maybe when you get a chance, you can tell the rest of us what kind of vitamins you're on. But for now, I'm still the chief, and I still call the shots. We're going back to the station, end of discussion," Finn repeated, this time more forcefully. He left absolutely no room for even so much as a sliver of an argument.

Resigned, Carson crossed over to his vehicle and opened the rear door to let Justice in. Shutting the door again, he opened the driver's side and got into the car himself.

He felt all wound up. Talking to Serena Colton while she was wearing that frilly, flimsy nightgown beneath a robe that wouldn't stay closed hadn't exactly helped his state of mind, either.

Carson shut the image out. It only got in the way of his thoughts. And despite being dragged through the wringer physically and emotionally, he sincerely doubted he was going to get any sleep tonight.

Biting off an oath, Carson started up his car and headed toward the police station.

Serena could tell that the rest of her family was still up. From the sound of the raised, angry voices wafting up the stairs, they were going on about this sudden, unexpected turn of events and how furious her father and mother were that Finn hadn't seen his way to leaving them out of this investigation strictly on the strength of the fact that they were his family.

Instead, Finn had actually treated them like he would anyone else, rousing them out of their beds just because he felt it was his duty to go over the entire grounds, looking for a woman her parents felt had no business being on the family ranch in the first place.

Serena let them go on venting, having absolutely no desire to get involved by sticking up for Finn. Her parents were going to carry on like this no matter what she said.

Besides, right now her main duty was to her daughter. The ongoing commotion had eventually agitated Lora, and she wanted to get the baby to fall back to sleep.

The corners of her mouth curved in an ironic smile as she looked down at the infant in her arms. Funny how a little being who hadn't even existed a short three months ago had so quickly become the very center of her universe. The very center of her heart.

Since the very first moment Lora had drawn breath, Serena felt obliged to protect the baby and care for her, doing everything in her power to make the world around Lora as safe and inviting for the infant as was humanly possible.

These last few months, her focus had been strictly and entirely on Lora. She had long since divorced her mind from any and all thoughts that even remotely had anything to do with Lora's conception or the man who had so cavalierly—and unwittingly—fathered her.

It had all been one huge mistake.

She had met Mark, whose last name she never learned, at a horse auction. The atmosphere at the auction had been fast paced and extremely charged thanks to all the large amounts of money that were changing hands.

Representing the Double C Ranch and caught up in the excitement, Serena had broken all her own rules that day—and that night. She had allowed the devastatingly handsome, charming stranger bidding next to her to wine and dine her and somewhere amid the champagne-filled evening, they had wound up going back to her sinfully overpriced hotel room where they had made extremely passionate love. Exhausted from the activity and the alcohol, she had fallen asleep after that.

She had woken up suddenly in the middle of the night. When she did, Serena found herself alone, a broken condom on the floor bearing testimony to her drastically out-of-character misstep. Managing to pull herself together and taking stock of the situation, she discovered that the money in her wallet as well as her credit cards were gone, along with her lover.

Canceling the cards immediately, she still wasn't fast enough to get ahead of the damage. Her one-night stand had cost her several thousand dollars, racked up in the space of what she found out was an hour. The man worked fast.

It was a very bitter pill for her to swallow, but she felt that there was an upside to it. She'd learned a valuable lesson from that one night and swore never to put herself in that sort of stupid situation again. Never to blindly trust *anyone* again.

Moreover, she made herself a promise that she was through with men and that she was going to devote herself strictly to raising horses, something she was good at and understood.

That was what she planned.

Life, however, she discovered, had other plans for her. Her first and only one-night stand had yielded a completely unplanned by-product.

She'd got pregnant.

That had thrown her entire world out of kilter. It took Serena a while to gather her courage together to break the news to her parents. That turned out to be one of the worst experiences of her life. They reacted exactly as she had feared that they would. Her father had railed at her, absolutely furious that she had got herself in this sort of "situation," while her mother, an incredible snob from the day she was born, carried on about the shame she had brought on the family.

Joanelle accused her of being no better than her trashy relatives who hailed from the two lesser branches of the family. The only ones in the family who were there for her and gave her their support were her brothers, Finn and Anders.

She also received support from a very unlikely quarter. Her cousin Demi Colton. She and Demi had never been really friendly, given the branches of the family they came from. But Demi had done her a favor involving one of the ranch hands about a year ago. That had earned her cousin a soft spot in Serena's heart.

And then, when she found herself pregnant, with her parents pushing for her to "eliminate" her "shame," it was Demi, surprisingly enough, who had come out on her side. Demi told her that she should do whatever *she* felt she should as long as that decision ultimately meant that she was being true to herself.

At that point, Serena did some very deep soul-searching. Ultimately, she had decided to have her baby. Seeing that her mind was made up, her brothers gave her their full support. However, it was Demi she found herself turning toward and talking with when times got rough.

She wasn't ordinarily the type who needed constant bolstering and reinforcement, but having Demi to talk to, however sporadically, wound up making a world of difference to her. Serena truly believed that it was what had kept her sane during the low points of this new experience she found herself going through.

Because Demi had been good to her when she didn't need to be, Serena wasn't about to turn her back on her cousin just because a tall, good-looking detective wanted to play judge, jury and executioner when it came to her cousin. Demi had obviously fled the area without ever coming to her, but if she had, if Demi had come to her and asked for money or a place to hide, she would have never hesitated in either case.

She believed that Demi was entitled to a fair shake. Most of all, she believed in Demi.

"I wish you would have come to me," she whispered into the darkness. "I wish you would have let me help you. You shouldn't be alone like this. Not now. Especially with the police department after you."

Serena sighed, feeling helpless and desperately wanting to do something to negate that.

Lora began making a noise, her little lips suddenly moving against her shoulder. She was clearly hunting for something.

Three months "on the job" as a mother had taught Serena exactly what her daughter was after.

"You want to eat, don't you?" she said.

Walking over to the rocking chair that Anders had made for her with his own hands, she sat down. Holding Lora against her with one arm, she shrugged out of the top of her nightclothes and pressed the infant to her breast. Lora began feeding instantly.

"Last time, little one," Serena promised, stroking the infant's silky hair. "I'm starting you on a bottle first thing tomorrow morning. Mama's got to get back to doing her job, sweetheart. Nobody's going to do it for her," she told the little person in her arms.

Rocking slowly, Serena smiled to herself. She was looking forward to tomorrow, to getting back to feeling productive. But for now, she savored this very possibly last intimate moment of bonding with her infant daughter.

Chapter 5

As he'd predicted, Carson didn't get very much sleep that night. His brain was too wired, too consumed with reviewing all the details surrounding his brother's murder. There was more than a little bit of guilt involved, as well. He hadn't wanted to go to Bo's bachelor party to begin with, but he still couldn't shake the feeling that if he had only got to it a little earlier, he might have been there in time to prevent his brother's murder from ever happening.

Carson finally wound up dozing off somewhere between two thirty and three in the morning. At least he assumed he'd dozed off because the next thing he knew, he felt hot air on his face. The sensation blended in with a fragment of a dream he was having, something to do with walking through the desert, trying to make his way home with the hot sun beating down on him. Except that he'd lost his way and didn't know just where home actually was.

Waking up with a start, he found Justice looming right over him. The hot wind turned out to be the dog's hot breath. Justice's face was just inches away from his.

Scrambling up into a sitting position, Carson dragged a hand through the unruly thatch of dark hair that was falling into his eyes.

"What is it, boy?" he asked groggily. "Did you solve the crime and couldn't wait to let me know?" Blinking, he looked at the clock on his nightstand. It was a little past six in the morning. How had that happened? "Or are you hungry, and you're trying to wake me up to get you breakfast?"

In response, the four-footed black-and-tan active member of the K-9 police department nudged him with his nose.

"I guessed it, huh?" Carson asked, swinging his legs off his rumpled double bed.

Except for the fact that he had pulled off his boots last night, he was still dressed in the same clothes he'd had on yesterday. He really hadn't thought he was going to be able to fall asleep at all so in his estimation there had been no point in changing out of them and getting ready for bed.

Carson didn't remember collapsing, facedown,

on his bed. He supposed the nonstop pace of the last two days, ever since he'd come across Bo's body in The Pour House parking lot had finally caught up with him.

He blinked several times to get the sleep out of his eyes and focus as he made his way through the condo into his utilitarian kitchen.

"I know what you're thinking," Carson said to the furry shadow behind him. "This whole place could fit into a corner of Serena Colton's suite."

Now, why had that even come up in his haze-filled mind, he asked himself.

Just then another piece of his fragmented dream came back to him. He realized that he'd been trying to cross that desert in order to get back home to Serena.

Home to Serena?

Where the hell had that come from?

He hardly knew the woman. What was his subconscious trying to tell him? It wasn't as if he was in the habit of dreaming about women. When he came right down to it, he hardly ever dreamed at all.

He came to the conclusion that something had to be bothering him about his less than successful interview with Serena last night. At the moment, he just couldn't put his finger on what.

Forget about it for now, he ordered himself. He had something more immediate demanding his attention—and it weighed a little over eighty pounds.

"Okay, Justice. What'll it be? Filet mignon? Lobster? Dog food?" Carson asked, holding the pantry doors open and peering inside at the items on the shelves. "Dog food, it is," he agreed, mentally answering for the dog beside him.

As he took out a large can, Justice came to attention. The canine was watching closely where the can's contents would wind up.

"Don't worry, I'm not going to poach your breakfast," Carson told the dog. "I'm not that hungry."

To be honest, he wasn't hungry at all. But given his present state, he desperately needed a cup of coffee. His brain felt as if it had been wrapped up in cotton and he needed that jolt that his first cup of coffee in the morning brought in order to launch him into his day.

Emptying the dog food into Justice's oversize dish, Carson stepped out of the dog's way as his K-9 partner immediately began to inhale his food. Carson tossed the empty can into the garbage pail in the cabinet beneath his sink and turned his attention to the coffee maker.

He bit off a few choice words. He'd forgotten to program the coffee maker to have coffee waiting for him this morning. Moving over to the refrigerator, he took out the half-empty can of ground coffee and proceeded to make his usual cup of coffee. The end product, thick and rich, was always something that could have easily doubled for the material that was used to repave asphalt. It was just the way he liked it.

Time seemed to move at an incredibly lethargic pace as Carson waited for the coffee to brew and the coffee maker to give off the three high-pitched beeps, signaling that the job was done.

The timer barely finished sounding off before he poured the incredibly thick, sludge-like liquid into his mug. Holding the mug with two hands like a child who had just learned how to drink out of a cup for the first time, Carson quickly consumed the product of his efforts. He drank nonstop until he had managed to drain the mug of its very last drop.

Putting the mug down, Carson sighed as he sat back in his chair. He could almost feel the coffee working its way through his veins, waking up every single blood vessel it passed through with a start.

The fuzziness was definitely gone.

Getting up to his feet, he looked in Justice's direction. The German shepherd had inhaled every last bit of what he'd put into the dog's dish. Carson credited the dog with having the same frame of mind that he did. Justice had needed something to jump-start his day.

"Okay, give me five minutes to shower and change so we can hit the road and get started," he told his furry partner.

As if concurring with what Carson had just said, Justice barked.

Once.

True to his word, Carson was in and out of the shower in less time than it took to think about it. Going to his closet, he found Justice lying on the bedroom floor, waiting for him.

"Don't start nagging me," he told the dog. "I'm almost ready." When the dog barked at him a couple of times in response, Carson said, "Yeah, yeah, I know. I didn't shave." As if in acknowledgement, he ran his hand over what was now beyond a dark five-o'clock shadow. It could have doubled as the inside of an abyss at midnight. "I'll do it tomorrow. There's nobody I'm trying to impress anyway," he added, pulling on a pair of jeans, followed by his boots.

He paired the jeans with a black pullover then put on his go-to navy sports jacket. As a detective, he was supposed to make an effort to dress in more subdued, businesslike attire. This was his effort, he thought drolly.

Adjusting his weapon in its holster, he said, "Okay, Justice, let's roll."

He stopped by the precinct first to see if any headway had been made in the investigation into his brother's murder. Specifically, if there had been any sightings of Demi Colton overnight.

There hadn't been.

When he walked into the squad room, he found that Finn was in the process of handing out the names of people he wanted interviewed in connection with Bo's murder. Names from the list he had compiled for the chief, Carson thought.

"Just in time," Finn said when he saw Carson coming in. "I was beginning to think that maybe you'd decided to take a couple of days off like I suggested."

The chief knew him better than that, Carson thought. "Not until we catch Demi."

When he saw the chief shifting, as if he was uncomfortable, it made him wonder what was up.

"Yeah, well, on the outside chance that it turns out Demi *didn't* kill Bo, we do need to look into other possibilities. Like whether there might be anyone else out there with a grudge against your brother strong enough to want to kill him."

The way he saw it, even thought he had compiled the list for Finn, shifting attention away from Demi would be a waste of time and manpower.

"Bo didn't write anyone else's name in his own blood," Carson pointed out in a steely voice. "He wrote Demi's."

Finn threw another theory out there. "Maybe there was something else he was trying to tell us other than the name of his killer."

Carson frowned. Finn was stonewalling. Everyone knew that things between the Colton and Gage families weren't exactly warm and toasty. There was a feud between the two families that went back a long ways, and it flared up often.

Was that why Finn seemed so intent on running down so-called "other" leads rather than going after a member of his own extended family? Finn was a good police chief, but his behavior seemed very suspicious to Carson.

"I know what you're thinking," Finn said in response to the look he saw descending over Carson's face. "You think I'm trying to protect Demi. I'm not. I'm the police chief of this county. I don't put family above the law. Hell, you were there. I roused my own family out of bed to conduct a search for Demi.

"But I'm not about to bend over backward and behave like someone's puppet just to prove to everyone that I won't let my sense of family get in the way of my doing my job. However, just because half the force is out for blood, doesn't mean I'm going to put blinders on and pretend there might *not* be anyone else out there who stood to gain something from your brother's death."

"Like what?" Carson wanted to know.

"Well, we won't know unless we look into it, will we?" Finn answered. "Now, aside from all those girl-friends your brother was always accumulating before he got engaged to Hayley, he was married once before, wasn't he?"

Carson nodded. "Yeah, to Darby Gage," he told

the chief, adding, "They've been divorced for over two years."

"Which one of them asked for the divorce?" Finn wanted to know.

He didn't have to try to remember in order to answer. "Darby did."

Finn was all ears. "Why?"

A half, rather mirthless smile curved Carson's mouth. Just because he wanted to find Bo's killer didn't mean that he had approved of his brother's fast-and-loose lifestyle.

"Seems that Darby didn't care for the fact that Bo couldn't stop seeing other women even though they were married." He knew how that had to sound to Finn. "I'm not making any excuses for Bo," Carson told the chief. "He was an alley cat. Always had been. And personally, in the end, I think that Darby was glad to be rid of him."

"Maybe she decided she wanted to be *really* rid of him," Finn countered. "In any case, I want you to go talk to the ex-wife. Find out if she has an alibi for the time your brother was murdered."

He should have seen that coming. "Okay, will do," Carson told him. "You heard the man, Justice," he said to the dog. "Let's go."

Since her divorce from Bo Gage two years ago, Darby Gage had been forced to stitch together a number of part-time jobs just to make ends meet.

Carson found her at the diner where she worked the morning shift as a waitress.

It might have been his imagination, but his ex-sister-in-law seemed to tense up when she saw him coming into the diner.

Putting on a cheerful face, Darby walked up to him with a menu and said, "Take a seat, Detective Gage. We've still got a few empty tables to choose from."

Carson picked a table that was off to one side. Parking Justice there, he sat down.

"What can I get you?" Darby asked.

He could see that the cheerfulness was forced. It probably unnerved her to see him here, he guessed. "Answers," he told his ex-sister-in-law.

Her blue eyes swept over him. In his estimation, she looked nervous. She gave up all pretense of cheerfulness. "Is this about Bo?"

His eyes never left her face. His gut told him that she didn't have anything to do with Bo's murder, but he was here so he might as well do his job.

"Yes."

Darby sighed as she shook her head. "I don't know what I can tell you."

"Let me be the judge of that," Carson told her.

He'd found that saying something like that took the reins away from the person he was interviewing and put them back into his hands.

Carson kept one eye on Justice, watching for any

sort of a telltale reaction on the dog's part. All the German shepherds on the K-9 force were initially bred and then trained by Bo or one of the trainers employed at Red Ridge K-9 Training Center. That was actually where his brother had met Hayley, who was one of the trainers.

Bo had made his living breeding the dogs for the police department as well as for other clients. Darby had been part of that business until the divorce and even now, one of her part-time jobs was cleaning the kennels at the training center.

In Carson's experience, German shepherds were exceedingly sensitive when it came to certain character traits and if Darby had somehow been involved in Bo's murder, maybe the dog would pick up on that.

But Justice's response to his former trainer's ex seemed favorable. So much so that when Darby absently stroked the top of the dog's head, Justice wagged his tail.

Taking that into account, Carson still pushed on. "Where were you around 6:30 p.m. the night Bo was killed?" he asked Darby. Then, realizing the waitress might play dumb about the date, he started to add, "That was on—"

"I know when Bo was killed," Darby said, cutting him off. "I was just leaving the kennels after cleaning up at the training center."

Technically, he already knew that because he had got her schedule by calling the places where she worked. But he wanted to hear what she had to say. "Anyone see you?"

"Other than the dogs?" she asked.

He couldn't tell by Darby's expression if she was being sarcastic or just weary. Given that Bo had put her through the wringer and was the reason why she had to hold down all these various jobs just to keep a roof over her head, for now he let the remark slide.

"Yes, other than the dogs."

She thought for a moment. "I think one of the handlers, Jessop, was still there. He might have seen me. To be honest, I didn't think I'd need an alibi so I didn't make a point of having someone see me leave." And then she suddenly remembered. "There's a time card I punched out. That should be proof enough for you."

He knew that there were ways to manipulate a time card. But since, in his opinion, Darby wasn't the type who could even hurt a fly, he nodded and said, "Yes, it should." Getting up from the table, he dug into his pocket and took out five dollars. He put it down on the table. "Thanks for your time, Darby. I'll get back to you if I have any other questions."

Darby picked up the five dollar bill and held it up for him to take back. "You can't leave a big tip, you didn't buy anything," she pointed out.

Carson made no attempt to take the money from her. "I took up your time," Carson answered.

With that he and Justice left the diner.

Chapter 6

Bo hadn't done right by Darby.

That was the thought that was preying on Carson's mind as he drove away from the diner.

They might have been brothers, but he was aware of all of Bo's shortcomings. His older brother had always been the typical playboy: self-centered and careless with anyone else's feelings. He was making good money with his German shepherd–breeding service and could have seen to it that Darby had got a better settlement in the divorce—at least enough so that she wasn't forced to take on so many part-time, menial jobs in order to keep a roof over her head.

But Bo's lawyer had been a good deal sharper than the lawyer Darby had been able to afford to represent her, so Bo had wound up keeping almost everything. He got the house, the business and most of the bank accounts, while Darby had clearly got the very short end of the stick.

In his opinion, the ultimate humiliation was when Bo had tossed her that crumb by letting her earn extra money cleaning out the kennels at his breeding operation.

If his brother hadn't written *Demi C* on the pavement with his blood, Carson might have looked a little more closely at Darby as a possible suspect in Bo's murder. He certainly couldn't have blamed her for being bitter about the treatment she'd received at Bo's hands both before and after the divorce.

But Darby hadn't seemed bitter to him, just closed off. And decidedly weary.

She probably wasn't getting enough sleep, given the various conflicting schedules of the jobs she held down, Carson thought.

"What do you think, Justice?" Carson asked the dog riding in the passenger seat beside him. "You think Darby might have got fed up and decided to teach Bo a lesson for treating her so shabbily?"

Justice barked in response to hearing his name and Carson laughed.

"That's what I thought. You like her, don't you, boy? Back to Demi, then," Carson agreed.

About to drive back to the station, Carson abruptly changed his mind as well as his direction.

He was heading back to the Double C Ranch.

Something had been bothering him about Serena Colton's testimony. *Why* was she so convinced that Demi hadn't killed his brother despite what could be considered a deathbed testimony? Why was she so certain that her cousin wasn't capable of killing someone even though everyone knew the bounty hunter had a bad temper.

He'd once seen Demi take down a man at The Pour House who was twice her size and obviously stronger than she was. Thin and wiry, the woman was nonetheless a virtual powerhouse. Ever since that day, he'd regarded Demi as being rather lethal.

Given that and her unpredictable temper, he'd never thought it was a good idea for his brother to have taken up with her. Demi Colton wasn't the type of woman to put up with being treated the way Bo obviously treated women he was no longer interested in seeing exclusively.

Carson couldn't shake the feeling that there was something that Serena had held back last night when he'd questioned her.

He had no idea if that "something" was significant or inconsequential, but he knew it was going to keep eating away at him until he found out exactly what it was that Serena wasn't telling him. He might as well get this out of the way before he followed up on some of Bo's business dealings and talked to the women he'd romanced and discarded.

* * *

When he arrived at the Double C mansion, Carson debated leaving Justice in his car when he went in. After all, it was January and if he left the windows partially opened, the dog would be all right. However, he regarded Justice as his partner and under normal circumstances, he wouldn't have left his partner just sitting in the car, twiddling his thumbs while he went in to reinterview someone connected to a case.

"You're on your best behavior, boy," he instructed, taking the leash as Justice jumped down out of the passenger seat.

Alma, the housekeeper who opened the front door when he rang the bell, looked far from happy to see him. The older woman cast a wary eye in Justice's direction.

"I'm sorry, Detective. Mr. and Mrs. Colton are not in," she informed him formally.

"That's all right," Carson replied politely. "I'm not here to see them. I'm here to talk to Ms. Colton."

The housekeeper raised her chin as she asked defensively, "Which Ms. Colton?"

The woman knew damn well which one, he thought. She just wanted to make things difficult for him. She was being protective of the people she worked for.

"The older one. Serena," he specified.

The housekeeper frowned. "I'm afraid that she's not here, either."

Just as the woman was about to forcibly close the door on him, Serena's voice was heard calling to her from upstairs. "Alma, I'm going to need you to watch Lora for me for a few hours while I'm working with the horses."

Carson's eyes met the housekeeper's. "Looks like she came back. Lucky me," he commented.

"Yes," the older woman responded icily. "Quite lucky. I will go upstairs and tell Miss Serena that you want to see her."

"That's all right," Carson said, moving past the housekeeper and entering the foyer. "Don't trouble yourself. I can go tell her myself. I know my way."

And with that, he and Justice headed toward the winding staircase.

Carson took the stairs two at a time with Justice keeping pace right behind him.

About to go back into her suite as she waited for the housekeeper to come upstairs, Serena was more than a little surprised to see the detective make his way up to the landing in the housekeeper's place.

Now what? Serena thought impatiently.

"Did you forget something, Detective?" she asked, doing her best to sound polite and not as irritated as she felt.

"No," he answered, reaching the landing, "but you did." He signaled for Justice to sit and the K-9 did.

Her brow furrowed a little as she tried to make sense of what he'd just said. "Excuse me?"

"When we talked last night, I got the feeling that there was something you were holding back, something you weren't saying," he told her. "The more I thought about it, the more certain I was that I was right. I figured I needed to get back to you to find out just what that was." He looked at her expectantly.

Alma had just managed to make her way upstairs. The woman was struggling not to pant. "I'm sorry, Miss Serena. He refused to leave."

"Apparently he's very stubborn," Serena said, looking coldly at the invading detective. She drew herself up, moving away from the bedroom doorway. "Alma, if you don't mind looking after Lora, I'll see if I can't put the detective's mind at rest once and for all, so he can be on his way and we can all go on with our lives."

He waited until the housekeeper picked up the baby from her crib and left with Lora before saying anything to Serena.

"Have I done something to offend you, Ms. Colton?" he asked, referring to her rather abrupt tone.

He had gall, she'd give him that. "You want that alphabetically, chronologically or in order of magnitude?" she asked the detective.

"Tell you what, I'll let you pick," Carson said magnanimously.

He didn't think she was going to say anything, did he, she thought. Well, he was in for a surprise.

Serena launched into him. "You come storm trooping into my house at an ungodly hour—"

"You were up," Carson reminded her.

"That's beside the point," Serena retorted. "I was feeding Lora. But that still didn't give you the right to burst in here—"

"The chief knocked," Carson corrected her. He could see she was getting really frustrated. The fire in her eyes was really rather compelling to watch. "And he is your brother as well as the police chief."

Exasperated, Serena switched to another tactic. "You not only accused a relative of mine of an awful crime but already convicted her in your mind, refusing to even entertain the very real possibility that she wasn't the one responsible for killing your brother."

"I might have 'convicted' her a little too readily," he allowed, "but you absolved her just as quickly despite evidence to the contrary."

"That wasn't actual evidence, it was circumstantial evidence," she insisted.

She was beginning to get to him, not to mention that she was obscuring the real reason why he had returned to the Double C Ranch. "I didn't come here to argue with you."

Serena gave him a knowing look. "You could have fooled me," she retorted.

"I'm not here to do that either," he informed her

curtly, just in case she was going to go off on that tangent. "All I want to know is what you're holding back, Ms. Colton."

She could feel herself losing her temper. "I'm not holding anything back," she protested a little too vehemently.

Carson had no intention of dropping this until he had his answer. "Last night, when you told me that you hadn't seen Demi since the day before—"

"I hadn't," Serena reaffirmed in case he was going to go in that direction.

Ignoring her, he pushed on to get to his point. "You were convinced that cousin of yours wasn't capable of murder."

"She's not," Serena insisted. She was prepared to say that as many times as it took to convince the detective—because she believed with all her heart that it was true.

He wished she'd stop interrupting and let him get to the heart of his case. He glared at her and continued talking.

"When I asked you why you were so certain that she hadn't killed Bo Gage, you looked as if you were going to say something, but then you didn't. You just repeated what you'd already said. What is it that you actually *wanted* to say?"

"You're imagining things," Serena told him dismissively.

Carson's eyes met hers. Immovable, he held his ground.

"No, I'm not," he told her. "Now, one more time. What is it that you were going to say?" He saw the stubborn look that came over her face. She was digging in, he thought. He tried another tactic. "Convince me, Ms. Colton. *Why* couldn't Demi kill my brother?"

Serena shook her head. "I don't—"

"Why?" Carson repeated, more forcefully this time. He gave no sign of relenting or backing off until she gave him an answer.

Serena glared at him, but inside, she was beginning to relent.

It wasn't as if, if she remained silent, all of this would eventually just go away. It wouldn't. There was a very viable piece of evidence of Bo's connection with Demi that wasn't about to be erased. It was only going to grow more prominent with time.

She of all people knew that.

Taking a breath, Serena finally gave Carson what he was after, albeit reluctantly. "Because she wouldn't kill the father of her baby."

"Baby?" Carson repeated, completely stunned. He was definitely *not* expecting something like this. Maybe he'd misunderstood. *"What* baby?"

Was he really being this dense, or did he just want her to spell it out for him, Serena wondered, feeling her anger mounting.

"Demi's baby."

He thought of the woman he had seen not that long ago. Demi Colton had no children. Carson shook his head. "Demi doesn't have a baby."

"Not yet," Serena agreed, feeling as if she had just betrayed the other woman, "but she's pregnant."

He continued to stare at Serena. When he saw her, Demi had been as thin as one of those swizzle sticks they used in bars a class above The Pour House. Was the chief's sister jerking him around, trying to win sympathy for her cousin?

Or was she telling him the truth?

"Demi's pregnant?" he finally repeated.

Serena nodded grimly. "Yes."

He felt like someone trying to find his way through a foggy swamp. "And it's Bo's baby?"

"Yes!" she cried, feeling like a game show host who'd painstakingly led a contestant to the right answer after a number of wrong turns.

Although Bo had been a womanizer, he had never actually bragged about his conquests or talked about them in any sort of detailed manner. To his recollection, Bo had never said anything about getting Demi—or any other woman—pregnant. He would have definitely remembered something like that.

"Did my brother know she was pregnant?" he asked Serena.

"She didn't want to tell him." She saw the quizzical look on Carson's face. "Your brother was going to be marrying another woman. Demi wasn't about to say anything about the baby until after she actually gave birth. She felt that saying something now, right before his wedding, when she wasn't even showing yet would make her look desperate and pathetic in his eyes. Like she was just trying to keep him for herself. Demi had way too much pride for that."

All this sounded somewhat far-fetched to him. "You're sure about this?"

Serena didn't hesitate with her answer. "Very."

She was obviously missing what was right in front of her, Carson thought. "Seems to me that your friend had a very good reason to kill my brother. It's called revenge and it's right up there as one of the top two reasons people kill people," he told her.

Didn't he get it? "You're talking in general, I'm being specific." Serena tried again. "Demi wouldn't kill the father of her baby no matter how much she couldn't stand Bo."

Carson moved his head from side to side as if he was trying to clear it. "You realize that you just proved my point with those last few words you said, right?"

"No," she cried. "I proved mine. Demi wouldn't want her baby to someday hate her for killing its father. She wanted her baby to eventually come to know Bo—and make up its own mind about what a low-life your brother was," she concluded with feeling.

Carson laughed shortly again as he shook his

head. "You know," he told her, "that almost makes sense—in a weird sort of way."

"The point is," Serena said, "even though she had a temper, Demi was practical. She wouldn't have killed him—she would have waited until the baby was born and then she would have confronted Bo and made sure that your brother lived up to his responsibilities toward the child." She paused, pressing her lips together. It took effort to keep the bitterness out of her voice. "Men can't just have their fun, sowing their seed and disappearing. Not when there's another life involved."

He thought of the baby he saw her with last night. He was aware of Serena's circumstances. "Is that what you told her?"

But Serena shook her head. She wouldn't presume to give Demi advice. "Nobody tells Demi anything. She marches to her own drummer." Serena paused for a moment, her eyes meeting his. "This is just between the two of us."

He thought of Demi. "Seems like there's more people involved than that."

She blew out an exasperated breath. He knew what she meant. "Demi told me this in confidence the last time I saw her. I don't want this getting out, do you understand? I only told you because I wanted you to understand why Demi wouldn't have killed your brother."

He was far from convinced. "If she didn't kill

him, why was his last act before dying to write her name in his own blood?"

"I don't know," she exclaimed. "You're the detective. *You* figure it out. But she didn't kill him," Serena insisted again. "I'd bet my share of the ranch on that."

She looked intense as she said that, and he had to admit that it did rather impress him. "You're that certain?" he questioned.

"I'm that certain," Serena confirmed.

He lifted one shoulder in a half shrug. "I'll keep that in mind. And I'll be getting back to you," he told her just before he walked away.

She didn't win, Serena thought. She hadn't convinced the detective that Demi had nothing to do with Bo's murder. But she could see that she'd created doubt in Carson's mind, which meant that she didn't lose, either. And for now, that was good enough.

Chapter 7

Out for a ride to clear her head a few days later, Serena abruptly reined her horse in.

She stared at the horizon, trying to make out the two riders in the distance, also on horseback.

Ever since Bo Gage's murder, everyone in the area was spooked and on high alert, taking note of anything remotely unusual or out of the ordinary.

Anyone who had business with her father or mother came up the main road to the house, driving a vehicle, not on the back of a horse.

Because she no longer felt as safe these days as she used to, Serena had taken to bringing her rifle with her when she went out for a ride on the range.

She felt that it was better to be safe than sorry and she was quite proficient with a gun.

Her hand went to her rifle's hilt now as she watched the two riders. There was something uncomfortably familiar about them even though she couldn't make out their faces at this distance.

And then she saw Anders coming from the opposite direction. Her brother was riding toward the two men. Even so far away, Serena could tell from his body language that the Double C foreman wasn't happy.

Rather than hang back, she kicked her mare's flanks, urging Nighthawk to head over in Anders's direction. She didn't know why, but something in her gut told her that her brother might need a little support.

And then, as she came closer, she realized why. The two riders she had observed, who were now engaged in some sort of a conversation, were Noel and Evan Larson.

She felt an icy chill shimmy up and down her spine.

Twins, the Larsons were businessmen with extensive real estate holdings who used both their good looks and highly developed charm to get people to trust them. Word had it from Finn and some of her other law enforcement relatives that the Larsons were dangerous and building a criminal empire involving drugs, guns, high-stakes theft and money laundering.

But to Serena, Noel and Evan Larson would always be the creepy duo who had duped her in high school. Back then, she had briefly dated Evan—up until the time Noel had decided to switch places with his twin. Posing as Evan, he'd tried to pressure her into going further with him than she was willing to go. Upset, Serena summarily dumped Evan only to be told by him that it was his twin who had tried to get her into bed.

Stunned, Serena was furious that he had so cavalierly passed her off to his twin without her consent and Evan had reciprocated by being angry with her because she hadn't been able to tell the difference between him and his twin immediately. He wound up reviling her and calling her a number of names, including a dumb bitch. It was the last time they ever exchanged any words.

From that time on, Serena steered clear of both the twins, wanting nothing to do with either of them because of the deception and because of the demeaning way they had acted toward her.

In a nutshell, the Larsons scared her. They had scared her then and they scared her now, she realized as she rode up toward her brother. Even so, she felt that Anders needed backup.

She reached her brother just as Evan and Noel rode away.

Just as well, Serena thought. The very thought of being anywhere near the Larsons or having to talk to either one of them, left a really horrible taste in her mouth.

The only thing worse was allowing the duo to roam free on the Double C Ranch. She wanted them gone from the family property.

"What did they want?" she asked Anders the moment she reached her brother.

Anders frowned, intently watching the twins as the duo rode away. "Exactly what I asked them—after I told those two that they were trespassing on private property."

"And what was their answer?" Serena had no idea what to expect when it came to those two.

"Noel, at least that was who he said he was," Anders said, "told me they didn't 'realize' that they were trespassing. According to Noel, they were just out here 'admiring the gorgeous land' and they were thinking of buying a ranch themselves. They wanted to know if there were any ranches for sale in the area and asked a bunch of general questions about ranching. Seemed innocent enough, I suppose."

She didn't believe a word of it. There was something underhanded going on, she just didn't know what it was yet.

"They're not," Serena assured her brother with feeling. "Everything the Larsons do or say has some kind of hidden agenda, some kind of underhanded motive. A hundred and fifty years ago those two would have been snake oil salesmen—or made a living as gun runners to the Native population." She felt her stomach turning every time she thought of the twin brothers. "I wouldn't trust either one of them any farther than I could throw them," she told Anders. "From where I was, it looked like those two were riding around, casing the Double C Ranch."

Anders laughed shortly. "They know better than that."

"No, they don't," Serena maintained. "If you ask me, I think we should be on our guard." But waiting for something to happen would put the ranch's hands on edge, she thought. Something more specific was needed. "I think that we should also call Finn so his people will be on alert."

Anders shrugged. She knew he didn't care for the implication. He didn't like the idea of having to go running to his older brother. "I can take care of the ranch."

She was quick to correct the misunderstanding and set his mind at ease. "Nobody's saying that you can't take care of the ranch, Anders. But these guys *are* dangerous," Serena reminded him. "I get a sick feeling in the pit of my stomach just knowing that they're out there, poking around."

Anders sighed. "Okay, if it makes you feel any better, call Finn and tell him the Larsons were out here, looking like they were getting the lay of the land." He paused, his gaze on his sister. "I don't like the Larson twins any more than you do, Serena, but until they do something wrong that can be proved in a court of law, I don't think there's all that much Finn and his people can do about it."

One step at a time, Serena thought. "We can leave that up to Finn. At least we can get him started by giving him the information. Meanwhile," Serena said, as she leaned over in her saddle, patting the hilt of her rifle, "I'm keeping my rifle loaded—just in case."

Turning her mare around, Serena headed back to the stables. She left Nighthawk with one of the stable hands. It wasn't something she would normally do—she liked looking after and caring for her own horse, and that included unsaddling the mare and grooming her—but right now, she felt this sense of urgency nagging at her. She wanted to call Finn and tell him about finding the Larsons on the family ranch.

The call to the station proved frustrating. The person manning the front desk told her that Finn was out on a call. Before she knew it, she was being switched to someone else.

And then a deep voice was in her ear, saying, "Gage. What can I do for you?"

There were a number of Gages working in the police station. The odds of getting Carson were small. And yet, she just *knew* it was him.

Hoping against hope that she was wrong, she asked, "Carson?"

"Yes," the rumbling voice said gruffly.

Oh great, just the person I wanted to have talk down to me, she thought, annoyed. But she had a feeling that it was Carson or no one and she disliked having the Larson twins casing her ranch more than she disliked talking to the K-9 detective, so she decided to remain on the line.

"Detective Gage," she said, addressing him formally, "this is Serena Colton."

The detective's voice was just as cold as hers was. "Hello, Miss Colton. Did you think of something else you forgot to tell me?"

She almost hung up on him then. His tone of voice annoyed her. He sounded judgmental. But then maybe she was reading something into it, Serena told herself, struggling to remain fair. She decided to give him another chance.

"No," she told Carson, "I didn't forget anything. I just thought you might be interested in knowing that the Larson brothers were just out here, riding around the Double C. I swear they were taking measure of the ranch like a tailor measuring someone for a suit."

Mention of the Larsons had Carson immediately sitting up, alert.

"The Larsons," he repeated, digesting what she'd just said. "Anyone in your family have any reason to have dealings with those two?"

"No one in my family deals with vermin," Serena informed him coldly.

"Just checking," he told her. "I meant no offense," he added, taking her tone of voice into account.

And then she suddenly remembered something that had slipped her mind until just now.

"For the record, you might want to look into the dealings that your brother had with them," she told Carson. "Demi mentioned something about that to me one of the last times I saw her," Serena added.

"My brother? Dorian?" he asked.

Dorian, younger than he was by six years, was a bounty hunter, and this last year, Dorian had been Demi's chief competitor.

"No," Serena answered. She paused for a moment for effect before telling him, "Bo."

"What?" He was certain that he had to have heard her wrong.

Serena gave him all the information she had. "Demi told me that Bo sold the Larsons two of his German shepherds and that the Larsons paid one of the trainers at the K-9 center a lot of money on the down low to cross-train the dogs to attack. They were also trained to protect and detect."

"To detect what?" Carson wanted to know. He wasn't exactly happy about this piece of information. Bo had never said anything about selling two of his dogs to the Larsons.

What had Bo been thinking, doing business with the likes of the Larsons? He had to have known that they were under investigation. The twins' unsavory dealings weren't exactly a secret.

"Sorry," Serena answered. "I have no idea. That's something you're going to have to ask the Larsons."

He fully intended to, Carson thought. It was funny how the investigation into his brother's murder was making him come full circle, back to the investigation he'd been focused on prior to Bo's murder.

Were those two would-be crime kingpins somehow responsible for Bo's death? This case was getting more and more complicated.

"Thanks for bringing this to my attention," he told Serena, feeling that he owed her something, especially after the way he'd talked down to her.

It wasn't his attention she'd been after, Serena thought. "To be honest, I was trying to reach Finn to tell him about this," she said, not wanting any credit she didn't have coming to her.

The woman certainly made it difficult to give her a compliment, Carson thought. "Yeah, well, thanks anyway," he said just before he hung up the landline.

The Larson brothers, Carson thought, getting up from his desk. Maybe he was going to get to nail these bastards in this lifetime after all.

Dozing next to Carson's desk, Justice was instantly alert the second Carson had pushed back his chair. The German shepherd scrambled to his feet, ready to go wherever his two-footed partner went.

"I don't want you taking a bite out of either one of these slime-buckets," Carson warned as he secured the dog's leash onto his collar. "Not until *after* we have the goods on them. We got a deal, Justice?"

The German shepherd barked in response and Carson nodded his head as if they had just struck a bargain. "Deal," he echoed.

Noel and Evan Larson had a suite of impressive, swanky offices located downtown. Initially, the office had housed a real estate business. The story was that their business "grew," necessitating more space until their so-called "holdings" caused them to take over the rest of the building.

Decorated to create envy in the eye of the beholder, Carson found that the suite of offices looked to be pretentious. He himself had always favored clean, simple lines. In his home and in his partner, he thought, glancing over at Justice.

Walking into the Larsons' offices, he didn't bother waiting for the administrative assistant sitting at the front desk to announce him. Instead, he walked right past her into the inner suite and announced himself.

One step behind him, the administrative assistant looked at her bosses in obvious distress. "I'm sorry, sirs. He got away from me."

"That's all right, Bailey Jean," Noel said. "We'll

take it from here." He waved the woman back to the front desk.

Carson held up his ID for the two brothers to view. "Detective Gage," he told the duo, although he knew that they were well aware of who he was. "I'd like to have a word with you if I could."

He was sure the look on his face told the two men that this wasn't a request but a flat-out order. Knowing that they liked playing the game, he wasn't expecting any resistance from either one.

"Sure thing, Detective," Evan said, standing next to his twin. "You mind leaving that mutt outside? Like in your car?" he stressed. It was obvious that he felt uncomfortable around the German shepherd.

Carson was not about to leave the dog anywhere but at his side. Having the animal there evened the odds in his opinion.

"This is Justice. My partner," he told the duo. "Justice goes where I go."

"Rather simplistic, don't you think, Detective?" Noel asked with a smirk.

Identical in every way when it came to their appearance, Noel had always been the one everyone regarded as the ringleader, and he had taken the lead now, as was his habit.

"No, I don't," Carson answered flatly. He made it clear that no matter what their unspoken criminal connections were, he was not intimidated. "Can we get on with this, gentlemen?"

"We'll answer any question you have, Detective," Noel said in a friendly, easygoing manner. He glanced in his brother's direction. In contrast to Noel, Evan appeared to be as stiff as a board. "Sit, Evan," Noel told his twin. "You're making the detective's dog nervous."

Evan hadn't taken his eyes off Justice since the dog had walked into the office. Carson saw that there was a thin line of perspiration all along the quiet twin's upper lip.

"The dog's making *me* nervous," Evan retorted.

"Don't mind Evan," Noel told Carson. "My brother doesn't get along well with dogs. Or, on occasion, people," he added as a snide aside. "Now, what is it that we can do for you, Detective?"

For now, Carson just wanted a couple of questions answered. "Did you buy two German shepherds from my brother?" Carson asked.

"Such a shame what happened to Bo," Noel said as if talking about the weather. "But to answer your question, as a matter of fact, we did."

"Why?"

Noel smiled at him. "I really don't see how that's any business of yours, Detective."

"This is a murder investigation," Carson informed him in an unemotional voice. "*Everything's* my business."

"All right," Noel replied in an accommodating tone. "We keep a large amount of cash in our safe for instant sales. We need the dogs to guard the place, keep people from trying to break in and help themselves to it. The dogs, Hans and Fisher," he said, making the two sound more like favored employees rather than guard dogs, "were trained specifically to guard the safe." Noel's grin widened. "I can give you a little demonstration if you'd like."

He had no desire to watch a demonstration, not with Justice at his side. If the other dogs showed any sign of aggression, too much could go wrong.

"No, for now your explanation is good enough for me," he told Noel. Although he couldn't help wondering why the dogs had been purchased, given Evan's obvious fear of German shepherds. Something wasn't adding up.

"Great. Anything else?" Noel asked, making it sound as if he had all the time in the world to spare for the detective.

"Yes." He waited a moment before continuing. "Serena Colton said she saw you riding around on her property earlier. Mind telling me why?"

"Don't mind at all," Noel said. "We're thinking of buying a ranch for ourselves and just wanted to take a look at one of the more successful ranches in the area." Noel flashed two rows of perfect teeth at him.

"And that's it?"

"That's it," Noel told him, "Except I think that we must have spooked her. Didn't mean to, of course. Anything else?" he asked.

"Not right now," Carson answered. Holding

firmly on to Justice's leash, he nodded at the two brothers and took his leave.

"Well, if you think of anything, you know where to find us," Noel called after him cheerfully.

I sure as hell do, Carson thought, walking out.

Chapter 8

As he drove back to the police station, Carson went over the interview he had just conducted several times in his mind just in case he'd missed something.

Without a doubt, Noel and Evan Larson had to be the friendliest, seemingly accommodating cold-blooded criminals he'd ever had the misfortune of dealing with—and he didn't believe a single word that had come out of either one of their mouths.

There was something about the so-called charming duo, something he couldn't put his finger on just yet, but if the Larsons swore on a stack of bibles that something was true, he was more than willing to go out of his way to find the evidence that proved that it was false, because as sure as night followed day, it was.

He didn't think the two were capable of telling the truth if their very lives depended on it.

"I suppose that feeling that way doesn't exactly make me impartial, does it, Justice?" Carson asked, addressing the question to the German shepherd riding beside him. "Maybe the problem is that there're too many people willing to give those two a free pass. Too many people trying to get on their good side because they think that ingratiating themselves to the Larsons might get them to be part of their cushy world."

The real problem in this matter, Carson decided, was that he had no idea if what the Larsons were involved in had anything to do with Bo's death at all or if the two were mutually exclusive of one another. What he did know was that he wanted to find Bo's killer *and* he wanted to put the Larson brothers behind bars.

But that very possibly could be two very separate things.

Focus, he ordered himself. *Focus.*

He needed to find Bo's killer and then he could get back to the business of putting the Larsons behind bars, where they belonged.

One step at a time.

Finding Bo's killer brought him back to trying to find Demi. The woman wasn't exactly a shrinking violet in any sense of the term and she just couldn't have disappeared into thin air.

Someone had to have seen her, talked with her, *something*.

Determined to locate the bounty hunter and confront her with the additional evidence they'd found to see how she explained her way out of that, Carson decided to go back to the beginning and question some of the people Demi had interacted with. That would help him piece together her timeline for the day that Bo was murdered.

He hadn't managed to even get his seat warm at the station before one of the other K-9 cops held their landline receiver up in the air, calling out to get his attention.

"Hey, Gage, someone's asking to talk to you. Says it's about that missing redheaded bounty hunter," Joe Walker called out.

He'd already got a few crank calls, as well as a couple from people just looking for information about the investigation. These days, every third person with access to a computer fancied themselves a journalist.

He made no effort to pick up the phone. "Who is it?" Carson wanted to know.

"They won't say," Walker said. "Just want to talk to you. Line three," he prompted, wiggling the receiver.

With a sigh, Carson picked up his receiver and punched Line Three. "Gage," he announced.

"Carson Gage?" the raspy voice on the other end asked.

It was someone trying to disguise their voice and doing a very obvious job of it, Carson thought impatiently. He didn't have time for this. "Yes. Who am I talking to?"

"My name doesn't matter," the voice on the other end said. Carson was about to hang up when he heard the voice say, "All you need to know is that I work at the Double C Ranch and I just saw Demi Colton running from one of the barns. The one where the studio apartments are kept. You know, the ones the ranch hands live in."

He was a born skeptic. Still, he stayed on the line. "You just saw her?" Caron questioned.

"Less than fifteen minutes ago," the voice told him. Then, as if reading his mind, the caller said, "Look, you can believe me or not, but I saw what I saw and I heard you were looking for that Colton woman so I'm calling it in. Do what you want with it."

"What did you say your name was again?" Carson asked, trying to get the caller to slip up.

"I didn't."

The line went dead.

He dropped the receiver into its cradle. The call could have very well just been a hoax, someone trying to get him to chase his tail for the sheer perverse fun of it.

But on the other hand, Carson felt that he couldn't afford to ignore it, either. He needed to check out this latest so-called "tip."

"I'm going back to the Double C Ranch," Carson told the detective sitting closest to him just in case the chief came looking for him.

Immersed in a report he was wading through on his desk, Emilio Sanchez raised an inquisitive eyebrow. "Got something?"

"I sure as hell hope so," was all Carson was willing to share at the moment as he walked out of the squad room. Justice quickly followed him out.

Serena was just coming out of the stables, talking to one of the horse trainers who worked for her when she saw Carson driving up. Her first thought was that the detective was coming back because he had something to tell her about the Larsons.

"I'll talk to you later, Juan," she said to the trainer. With her eyes riveted on Carson's approaching vehicle, she hurried toward it.

She saw that, despite the cold weather, the window on his side was partially down. "I didn't expect you to be back so soon," Serena told him as she walked up to the driver's side.

"That makes two of us," Carson answered. He turned off the ignition.

Was he waiting for her to pry the information out of him? "So? What did you find out?" Serena asked impatiently.

The woman was standing right up against his door, inadvertently preventing him from opening it. Carson indicated the door with his eyes, waiting.

Annoyance creasing her forehead, Serena stepped back, allowing him to open the door and get out. Justice was right behind him and came bounding out of the driver's side.

If she thought he was here to fill her in on how his meeting with the Larsons went, she was in for a big surprise, Carson thought.

"I found out that you weren't being entirely truthful with me," he said, thinking of the call he'd taken about Demi's sighting. The call that was responsible for his being here.

Her eyes narrowed to brown slits as she glared at Carson. "What are you talking about? What did those lying snakes tell you?"

What was she talking about? "Come again?"

She bit back the urge to tell him to keep up. "The Larson brothers. What delusional story did they try to sell you?"

"The Larsons?" he echoed. Why would his saying that she hadn't been entirely truthful make her think of the Larsons? Was there a reason she'd pointed him in their direction?

Was the detective deliberately playing dumb? She

was beginning to think that the German shepherd was the smart one of the pair.

"Yes, the Larsons," she said evenly. "Didn't you come back to tell me how your meeting with them went?"

Well, she obviously thought a lot of herself, Carson thought, irritated. "No. I'm here because someone from the Double C just called the police station to say that they saw Demi, not fifteen minutes ago, running from one of the studio apartments you have for the ranch hands." He pinned her with a very cold look. "You lied to me, Ms. Colton."

Serena's temper flared. "I *didn't* lie to you and seeing as how you keep insulting my integrity, why don't we just drop the polite 'Ms. Colton' act, shall we?" she snapped.

Maintaining a respectful air came naturally to him, but given the situation, it was apparently lost on this woman.

"Fine by me, *Serena*." He deliberately enunciated her name.

"Well, none of this is 'fine by me,'" Serena retorted. "And doesn't it strike you as odd that someone who has a perfectly reliable vehicle the way, I'm sure you know, that Demi does is always being spotted 'running' around?" She blew out a breath trying to tamp down her temper. "This is all getting very tiresome, Carson," she said, calling him by his first name and saying it through clenched teeth. "Please leave."

He had no intention of doing anything of the sort. "Sorry, I can't do that. Not until I've searched the barns and surrounding area for Demi."

Serena fisted her hands at her waist, ready to go toe-to-toe with him. "And if I tell you that you can't?" she challenged.

Carson took a folded piece of paper out of his pocket, opened it and held it up for her to look at. "This warrant says I can."

Fuming, Serena unceremoniously took the warrant from him and scanned it.

"Meet with your approval?" he asked when she folded the paper and handed it back to him.

"No," Serena snapped. None of this met with her approval. "But it is a warrant," she conceded. "So I guess I can't stop you. But you're wasting your time," she informed him. "Demi's still not here. Whoever called you is sending you on a wild-goose chase. So—"

Serena stopped talking suddenly, her head whipping around to look over her shoulder toward something she thought she heard.

Justice was straining at his leash. Obviously whatever it was, the dog had heard it, too, so this wasn't just an act on Serena's part, he thought.

"What?" he asked her in a hushed voice.

But she didn't answer him. Instead Serena hurried around the side of what had initially been one of the barns on the original ranch, before the ranch had been renovated and expanded.

He read Serena's body language. Something definitely had the horse breeder going, he thought as he and Justice followed her.

He was fairly certain that she was not attempting to lead them to corner Demi, but there was no arguing that Serena was after someone.

Someone she apparently was keenly interested in confronting.

Carson caught her by the arm before she got away from him. When she tried to pull free, he just tightened his hold. Serena glared at him.

"Who are you trying to corral?" he wanted to know.

"My sister," she hissed, annoyed that he was intervening and getting in her way.

Serena tried to pull free again with the same results. The only way this ape was going to let go of her was if she answered his question. So, unwillingly, she did.

"I think the Larsons are trying to get their hooks into Valeria." The second he released her, she made her way around the barn and looked into the first window she could. "She's impressionable and flighty and," she continued, moving to the next window, "with your brother!"

Rapping her knuckles against the window to get

their attention, she didn't stop until the two people on the bed finally separated and looked her way.

The two had been so completely wrapped around one another that had it not been for the different colors of their clothing, it would have been hard to distinguish where all their separate limbs began and ended.

Trying the door, Serena found it unlocked and stormed in. Carson followed behind her just as Justice got past him and got in between the two younger people.

"Vincent?" Carson cried. The last person he expected to find in this compromising position with a Colton was his youngest brother.

Startled at being discovered as well as suddenly having a German shepherd getting in between them and wagging his tail in a display of friendly recognition, Valeria and Vincent instantly pulled apart and were up on their feet.

The two looked somewhat disheveled, not to mention disoriented and embarrassed. At least Vincent was. The nineteen-year-old mechanic had got a job working part-time on the Double C, fixing not just some of the cars but also other, larger mechanical devices on the ranch.

He was not, Carson thought, supposed to be giving the boss's daughter the same sort of close scrutiny he gave the vehicles he repaired.

Vincent gulped and finally found his tongue. "Carson, what are you doing here?"

"Thinking about spraying water on the two of you," Carson answered, frowning.

Incensed, Valeria immediately spoke up, turning her anger on her sister. "Hey, you have no right to be spying on us. We're both over eighteen and we can do whatever we want," she cried.

Serena didn't see it that way. "Are you out of your mind?" Serena demanded. "You know the way Dad feels about Vincent's father, how he feels about the whole Gage family," she emphasized. "If he catches the two of you going at it like two rabbits in heat, he'll string Vincent up without a second thought."

Valeria raised her chin, ready to protect this precious romance she was involved in. "He'd have to go through me to do it!" she declared defiantly, her eyes blazing.

"Don't think for a minute that he won't," Serena retorted. "Nothing is more important to that man than the ideas of family honor—and Dad puts that 'honor' above all of us."

Valeria became angrier if that was possible. "I don't care what's important to *him*," she insisted. "Vincent is important to me," she said, reaching for his hand.

The youngest of the Gage clan closed his hand around hers.

"And you don't have to worry and carry on about

honor," Valeria continued. "Vincent and I are getting married on Christmas Eve." She shared a smile with him before turning back toward her sister and Vincent's big brother. "That happens to be Vincent's birthday and it's mine, too," she told them. "That makes the date doubly special. We'll both be turning twenty that day," she added as if that fact somehow added weight to what they were planning.

Ignoring the man next to her, Serena made a valiant attempt to talk some sense into her sister. "Valeria, you're both too young to make such a life-altering decision at this stage."

"For once," Carson interjected, "I agree with Serena."

Valeria tossed her head and looked at her sister, totally ignoring the detective. This was between her sister and her. "Seems to me that a woman with a baby and no husband shouldn't be lecturing us on what we should or shouldn't do," she said dismissively.

Carson saw the flash of hurt in Serena's eyes. No one was more surprised than he was when he felt something protective stir within him.

"Tossing insults at your sister," he told Valeria coldly, "doesn't change the fact that what you are contemplating doing is foolhardy, and it's opening the two of you up to a real flood of anger—coming at you from both families."

"But, Carson, it's a really stupid feud," Vincent protested.

"I'm not arguing that," Carson granted. "It's beyond stupid. Half the members of both families can't even remember how the whole damn thing got started or what it's even about. Hell, I'm not even sure. Near as I can tell, it was something about land issues that had our grandfathers at each other's throats, or so the story goes according to our father," he said, nodding at Vincent. "But it doesn't matter how it got started. What matters is that it's still going on and if you two go through with what you're planning, that damn feud is probably going to escalate. So, if I were you two," Carson said, looking from one to the other, "I'd hold off getting married for a while."

"Well, you're not us," Vincent told his brother, putting a protective arm around Valeria as if to signify that it was the two of them against the world if that's what it took for them to get married.

Valeria looked at Carson. "And just how long is 'a while'?" she demanded hotly. She had her hand on her hip, the very picture of a woman who was not about to change her mind no matter what.

"As long as it takes to get our families to come around," Serena answered. She knew that was vague, but there was no way to put a timetable on getting the two families to reconcile.

Valeria shook her head. The answer was unacceptable.

"Sorry, can't wait that long. I'll be an old lady by the time that happens. You want them to change their minds?" Valeria laid down a challenge. "You see if you can do it before Christmas Eve," she told her sister. "But one way or another, Vincent and I are getting married."

Taking Vincent's hand again, she laced her fingers through his and said, "Let's get out of here, Vincent. It's way too stuffy for me."

"Yeah," Vincent agreed. The youngest Gage brother only had eyes for Valeria and gave every indication that he would follow her to the ends of the earth if need be. "Me, too."

Chapter 9

Feeling incensed as she watched her sister and Vincent walk away, most likely to find another place where they could be alone, Serena swung around and directed her anger at the K-9 detective who was still standing next to her.

Her eyes were blazing as she demanded, "Are you just going to let them go like that?"

"Can't arrest them for being in love," Carson told her. He was almost amused by the fiery display he'd just witnessed, but he knew better than to let Serena suspect that. "And no matter what your father or my father think about the other person's family, there are no laws being broken here." He could see that Serena was far from satisfied with his answer. "Just what is it that you want me to do?"

Serena threw her hands up, angry and exasperated. "I don't know," she cried, walking back around to the front of the building. *"Something!"*

"I am doing something," Carson shot back. "I'm trying to find the person who killed my brother," he reminded Serena.

From what she could see, all he was doing was spinning his wheels, poking around on her ranch. "Well, you're not going to find that person here, and you're not going to find Demi here, either," she told him for what felt like the umpteenth time, knowing that no matter what he said, her cousin was still the person he was looking for.

"If you don't mind, I'd like to check that out for myself," Carson told her.

"Yes, I do mind," she retorted angrily. "I mind this constant invasion of our privacy that you've taken upon yourself to commit by repeatedly coming here and—"

As she was railing at him, out of the corner of his eye he saw Justice suddenly becoming alert. Rather than the canine fixing his attention on Serena and the loud dressing-down she was giving him, the German shepherd seemed to be looking over toward another one of the barns that contained more of the hands' living quarters.

At this time of day, the quarters should have been

empty. Even so, he intended to search them on the outside chance that this was where Demi was hiding.

Something had got the highly trained canine's attention. Was it Demi? Had she come here in her desperation only to have one of the hands see her and subsequently put in a call to the station? Was she hiding here somewhere?

"What is it, Justice? What do you—"

He got no further with his question.

The bone-chilling crack of a gun—a rifle by the sound of it—being discharged suddenly shattered the atmosphere. Almost simultaneously, a bullet whizzed by them, so close that he could almost feel it disturb the air.

Instinct took over. Carson threw himself on Serena, covering her with his body as he got her behind what had to be Valeria's car. The one Vincent was supposed to be working on.

Startled, Serena couldn't speak for a moment because the air had been knocked out of her. The next second, she demanded, "What do you think you're doing?"

"Trying to save your life, damn it," Carson snapped.

Justice broke into a run and whizzed by him, heading straight for the barn. The main door was open.

Pulling out his sidearm, Carson ordered Serena, "Stay down," and took off after his K-9 partner.

"The hell I will," Serena retorted.

Scrambling up to her feet, she cursed the fact that

it took her a second to steady herself. And then she quickly followed in their wake.

Reaching the barn, Carson began to move from one uniform room to another. Whoever had fired at them had done so from one of the windows facing the other barn. They were also gone.

Cursing under his breath, he kept his gun drawn as he scanned the area.

Justice was barking in what could only be termed a display of frustration. The dog was expressing himself, Carson thought, for both of them.

When he heard a noise behind him, Carson whirled around, his weapon cocked and ready to fire. He could feel his heart slam against his chest when he realized it was Serena and that he had come within a hair's breadth of shooting her.

"Damn it, woman," he said, resetting the trigger, "I told you to stay put. I could have killed you."

Her eyes met his. There was still fire in hers. "The feeling's mutual," she informed him.

The sudden, unexpected feel of his body pressing against hers like that had brought back all sorts of sensations and emotions, which were running rampant through her. She welcomed none of them. Even so, her body refused to stop throbbing and vibrating and it totally unnerved her.

Despite her agitation and the anger it created, Serena immediately recognized the feeling for what it was. She had been aroused.

Was aroused. And damn it, she didn't want to be. The last time she'd felt that way, nine months later she was giving birth to a baby.

Giving birth and vowing that she was never, *ever* going to allow herself to get into this sort of predicament again. And, until just a few minutes ago, she was completely certain that she never would. She'd been positive that she had sworn off men for the rest of her life, dedicating herself to her daughter and to her job on the Double C.

And now, after a year's hiatus, her body was practically begging her to abandon limbo and feel like a woman again. Begging her to revisit that glorious feeling of having every single inch of her body tingle because she was responding to a man's touch.

Carson stared at her in confusion. What the hell was she talking about? "I was talking about you sneaking up on me like that."

"I didn't sneak," Serena declared defensively, desperately trying to regain control over herself. "This is my family's ranch, and I've got a right to know what's going on."

"Of all the harebrain— You want to know what's going on?" he shouted at her. "Someone just shot at you, Serena. *That's* what's going on. And if I hadn't been there just now, they might have killed you!" he exclaimed. "You're welcome!" he yelled at her when she said nothing in response.

He'd knocked her down and almost given her a

concussion, the big oaf! Serena was the picture of fury as she retorted, "I didn't say thank you."

"I can't help it if you have no manners," Carson shot back. Fed up, he began to storm away.

She wasn't about to stand for him turning his back on her like this. "Now, you just wait a damn minute!" Serena exclaimed, grabbing hold of his shoulder and attempting to pull Carson around to face her.

His emotions were running at a fever pitch and not just because someone had discharged a rifle, narrowly missing them. If he was being honest with himself, something had been stirred up when he had first seen Serena standing at the top of the landing with her baby in her arms. Seeing her had unearthed something, keenly digging into his mind and soul. Reminding him of what he had lost before he had ever been allowed to have it.

It had given him a reason to shut Serena Colton out.

But for some perverse reason, it had also given him a reason to want this woman. Want this woman the way he hadn't wanted any other, not since he'd lost Lisa. All the while, as he had been involved in the search for his brother's killer, this feeling had been messing with his mind.

Messing with it to such a degree that he'd allowed himself to entertain irrational thoughts.

Like pulling Serena into his arms and sealing his mouth to hers so he could still the needs that insisted on multiplying within him. That insisted on taunting him and giving him no peace.

Carson came perilously close to going with that desire. And he would have if a livid Anders Colton hadn't picked that exact moment to all but burst onto the scene.

"What the hell is going on here?" Anders demanded as he came upon his sister and the detective.

For a split second both Serena and Carson shared a single thought. That Anders's question was about what had come very close to happening between them—Serena had felt the pull, too—and not about the gunshot that had resounded loud enough for anyone close by to hear.

Serena drew in a deep breath, trying valiantly to still her pounding heart and get control over her all but runaway pulse.

"What?" she asked.

"The gunshot," Anders shouted. His expression demanded to know if she had gone deaf. "I just heard a gunshot," the foremen cried angrily. "What the hell is going on here?"

By now, some of ranch hands had also come running over as well, as had Valeria and Vincent.

At the sight of the two younger people, surprise and then anger crossed the Double C foreman's face.

"What are you doing with my sister?" he demanded, glaring at Vincent. He forgot all about the gunshot as the thought of the mechanic's questionable behavior came to the foreground.

"Later," Carson told Serena's brother authoritatively. "Right now, you've got bigger problems than Romeo and Juliet over there," he said. "Someone just took a shot at Serena." Serena had to be the target, he thought. Had the shooter been after him, there had been plenty of opportunities to shoot at him prior to now.

"Serena?" Dumbfounded, Anders's attention shifted to her. She looked none the worse for wear. Was the detective lying to him? "Why would anyone shoot at Serena?"

"Why does anyone shoot at someone?" Carson countered, exasperated.

Realizing that Carson was telling him the truth, Anders put his hands on Serena's shoulders as he looked his sister over closely. His voice was filled with concern as he asked, "Are you hurt?"

"Just slightly bruised," she answered. "Detective Gage decided he was bulletproof and took it upon himself to act as my human shield."

Anders flushed, torn between being grateful and his natural feelings of resentment when it came to anyone who belonged to the Gage family.

Feeling that he should offer the detective an apology, he began, "Look, if I just came off sounding like an idiot—"

"Save it," Carson said, waving away what sounded

as if it was shaping up to be a very awkward apology. "The first order of business until I can find this shooter is to pack up your family and get them off the ranch and someplace safe."

Anders was in total agreement with the detective. "I'll have my parents and sisters move into the hotel in town until this blows over."

"Wouldn't be a bad idea for you to go, too," Carson told him.

But here they had a parting of the ways when it came to agreement. Everyone on the ranch couldn't just leave. The ranch had to continue being productive.

"I'm the ranch foreman," Anders told him. "I'm responsible for the staff on the Double C. I'm not about to leave them, especially not when there's some crazy shooter loose."

Carson sighed. "Look, I can't make you go—" he began.

"No, you can't," Anders agreed, interrupting the detective.

"And that goes for me, too," Serena informed him, speaking up.

Carson whirled around to face her. This was getting out of hand. "You were the one who was just shot at," he reminded her.

"How do you know?" she challenged, surprising him. "Maybe whoever it was that was shooting just now was aiming at you."

That was ridiculous. She was grasping at straws, pulling thin arguments out of the air. "If that's the case, they would have had plenty of opportunity to shoot at me. They didn't have to wait until I came here to the ranch. You were the target," he insisted.

Be that as it may, she was not about to have Carson tell her what to do. "If that's the case, I'm a big girl, and I can decide whether I stay or go." She raised her chin, sticking it out as a way of asserting herself. "And I've decided to stay."

Stubborn woman! All he could do was block any of her senseless moves.

"I can't let you do that."

Who the hell did this man think he was? "You have nothing to say about it," she informed Carson. "Besides, whoever just shot at us," she said, deliberately underscoring the word *us*, "can and *will* come after us, no matter where we are. There's no point in me running," she argued. "The ranch has a couple of safe rooms inside the mansion. As a last resort, if it comes down to that, I can hide in one of them," she said, her tone clearly declaring that it was the end of the debate as far as she was concerned.

Caught completely off guard, Carson looked at the foreman. This was the first time he'd heard that there were safe rooms within the sprawling mansion.

"Is this true?" he asked Anders. "The mansion has safe rooms in it?"

"Of course it's true," Serena retorted, speaking

up because she was annoyed that the detective had asked her brother instead of her. "There's no reason for me to lie about that."

"No," Carson agreed. "There isn't." He processed this new piece of information, then turned toward Anders. "I want to see those safe rooms."

"Why?" Serena wanted to know, once again interrupting. "You want to inspect them to see if they live up to your high standards?" she mocked.

She felt as if Carson was determined to block her at every turn. She certainly didn't like him questioning her every move the way he did.

Maybe, if she hadn't reacted to him the way she had when he'd thrown himself over her, she wouldn't feel anywhere nearly as combative as she did. She didn't know, but now was not the time for her to suddenly start questioning and doubting herself.

"No," Carson answered Serena. "I want to see if Demi's in either one of them. If you ask me, it sounds like a really logical place for her to be holed up," he told Serena.

"She doesn't know a thing about them," Serena informed him, annoyed that she had essentially been forced to share this secret with the likes of him. "Nobody does. Only family members do. That means," she told him, clenching her teeth, "that Demi's not *there*. Give it up, Detective."

"You won't mind if I satisfy my curiosity, do you?" he asked sarcastically.

"As a matter of fact, I do," she informed him coldly. "And I'm not taking you to them."

"If you have nothing to hide, there's no reason not to take me to those safe rooms," he said, prepared to go toe-to-toe with her—or have a judge sort it out after she spent a night in lockup.

"The reason is I don't want to," Serena informed him stubbornly.

"Not good enough," he said, taking out the warrant again and holding it up to her.

"That doesn't say you can search the safe rooms," she retorted.

"It says," he answered, emphasizing each word, "I can search the immediate premises—so unless the safe rooms are hovering somewhere above the ranch," his voice dripped with sarcasm, "they're considered to be part of the premises."

Valeria uttered a frustrated, guttural sound as she lost her patience. "Oh, take him to go see them, Serena. We're not going to get rid of him or his dog otherwise," she insisted.

"You're getting rid of him because you're going to be staying at the hotel with Mom and Dad," Serena reminded her sister.

Valeria drew herself up to her full height. "I am *not* going," she protested between clenched teeth.

"You're going, little sister, even if you have to be dragged there kicking and screaming," Anders informed her.

Angry, fuming and utterly frustrated, Valeria looked in Vincent's direction as her brother pulled her after him to the mansion. "I cannot *wait* to get married," she cried plaintively.

"Well, you're *not* married, and right now you're my responsibility," Anders informed her, maintaining a tight grip around her wrist as he continued on his way to the mansion.

Chapter 10

As he watched Valeria being dragged back to the mansion, Vincent turned toward Carson. He looked clearly concerned.

"Do you think she's really in any danger?" he asked his older brother.

Carson gave him his honest opinion without sugar-coating it. "I think all the Coltons here are in danger," he answered. "Which is why," he continued, looking in Serena's direction, "you and your baby should go with your parents and Valeria to stay at the hotel in Red Ridge."

Serena made a disparaging, dismissive noise. "Nice touch, Carson, having your baby brother play straight man for you like that, but I'm still not leaving the Double C."

Carson knew he was getting nowhere, but he still felt that he had to try.

"You're being unreasonable," he told Serena, struggling with his temper. "That shooter missed you last time. He—or she—might not the next time."

"There's not going to be a next time," Serena countered with a huff. "Because you are going to catch him—"

"Or her," Carson interjected pointedly.

She knew what he was doing. He was making it seem as if Demi had been the one who'd pulled the trigger. But that was absolutely ridiculous. There was no reason for the bounty hunter to have tried to shoot her. They had actually become friends, at least to some degree. With that in mind, Serena deliberately ignored the detective's interjection and went on talking.

"—like the county's paying you to do."

Carson shook his head, exasperated. The woman was being brave and damn foolhardy at the same time. "You never did have a lick of sense."

Serena flashed a wide smile at him. "Must be nice for you to be able to count on some things never changing," she told Carson sweetly.

He had a feeling that Serena could go on like this until the proverbial cows came home. But he didn't have time for that.

"I hope your brother's having more luck with your parents than I'm having with you," Carson told her as he headed straight for the mansion.

When he walked into the foyer, he was just in time to hear Serena's mother making her displeasure loudly known to one and all. Somehow, though he hadn't walked into the house until just now, Joanelle Colton was holding him *and* his family accountable for this newest inconvenient series of events in her life.

"You," Joanelle cried, sidestepping her daughter as if she didn't exist and making her way directly over to the detective. She stopped short abruptly, pulling back as if she wanted no part of her clothing to touch either Carson or his K-9 partner. "Just exactly *what* is the meaning of all this?" she demanded, furious. "Anders says we have to leave the ranch. Are you the one behind this proposed exodus?"

Aware that there were four pairs of Colton eyes fixed on him, Carson didn't rise to the bait.

Carson removed his hat before he spoke to Serena's mother. "I did suggest it, yes, ma'am. And it's for your own safety," he told her politely.

"Since when is a Gage worried about a Colton's safety?" Judson demanded, coming to his wife's side, his deep, booming voice all but echoing through the ground floor.

"Since I swore an oath to protect all the citizens of Red Ridge, Mr. Colton," Carson replied calmly.

He was determined that neither of the older

Coltons were going to rattle him. If worse came to worst, he could always turn the matter over to Finn and have *him* deal with his family.

Though she had her own issues with Carson, Serena knew that he was only trying to protect her family. She also knew firsthand how overbearing both her parents could get. Memories of their reactions when she was forced to come to them and tell them she was having a baby were very fresh in her mind. Neither parent had been easy to deal with or sympathetic, thinking only how this baby would ultimately reflect on them.

Angry bears were easier to reason with, she thought. Possibly also friendlier. Which was why, just for now, she threw her lot in with Carson.

"Someone shot at me, Dad," she said emphatically. "Detective Gage is just trying to get you to stay somewhere safe until he can catch whoever it is that's out there, using us for target practice."

By the look on the patriarch's face, this was the first he was hearing of this. Incensed, Judson turned on Anders.

"Is this true?" he demanded.

"Someone did take a shot in Serena's direction when she was out by one of the barns where the hands have their quarters." Anders relayed the incident as best he could, given he hadn't been there to see it for himself. He had arrived after the fact, only drawn by the sound of gunfire.

Joanelle gasped, her hand flying to her chest. Carson expected the woman to express concern about her daughter's welfare, or at least ask Serena if she was all right. However, Joanelle appeared horrified that this sort of thing had happened on her ranch—to her.

"I knew it! I knew something like this would happen when you allowed that dreadful girl to invade our home. She had no business setting foot on my ranch!" Joanelle cried. "That branch of the family is just poor trash, tainting everything they come in contact with and you can't expect anything better from them. How *could* you, Serena?"

Her mother's histrionics never ceased to amaze her. "This isn't Demi's fault, Mother," Serena insisted, annoyed.

"Huh! Well, it'll take more than you saying that to convince me," Joanelle declared, wrapping her arms around herself and in essence sealing herself off. "What sort of a woman makes her living by being a bounty hunter for heaven's sake?"

Serena was exceedingly tired of her mother's judgmental, condescending attitude. "A resourceful one would be my guess," Serena countered.

Frosty blue eyes glared at Serena. "That's not what *I* call it," Joanelle fired back.

Serena was aware of the expression on Carson's face. He looked as if he felt sorry for her. Her back went up. She wasn't about to put on a show for the detective's entertainment.

"Shouldn't you be packing for the hotel, Mother?" she pointed out.

Joanelle scowled, obviously insulted by the suggestion. "That's what I have the maid for," she answered haughtily.

Wanting her mother to leave the foyer, Serena rephrased the question. "Then shouldn't you be supervising Marion as she packs for you?"

Unable to argue with that, Joanelle regally turned on her heel and made her way up the spiral staircase. "Come, Valeria!"

There was no room for argument or resistance in her voice.

Uttering an unintelligible, guttural cry, a furious Valeria stomped up the stairs behind her mother.

Judson looked at Serena. "I'd expect Anders to stay and run the ranch, but you should come with us," he told her in a voice that was only mildly less authoritative than his wife's.

"The household staff is staying," Serena began but her father cut in before she could finish.

"Don't worry." He looked at his son. "Anders will make sure that they don't take anything in our absence," Judson told her.

Serena instantly took offense for the staff. She liked the hardworking people, and they were definitely a lot nicer and kinder than her parents were.

How like her father to think that the staff was only interested in stealing from him.

"I'm sure they won't," she immediately replied. "Because they're honest, not because someone is watching them. However, I have work to do with the horses. Anders can't see to that as well as to everything else. Don't worry, Dad, I'll be fine, but you need to take Mother and Valeria out of here," she insisted in case her father was having second thoughts about going to the hotel.

Although she felt she could handle any danger to herself, she did want her family to be safe. "Mother's high-strung. If she stays here, she'll see a gun aimed at her behind every post and tree and make your life a living hell, you know that," she stressed.

The expression on her father's face told Serena that Judson Colton was well aware of what his wife was capable of.

As the elder Colton appeared to be mulling over the situation, Carson spoke up. "I'll stay on the ranch to make sure nothing happens to your daughter or your granddaughter, sir," he volunteered.

Unable to bring himself to actually express his thanks to a Gage, Judson merely nodded curtly.

"I have to pack," he said, more to himself than to the detective or his daughter. With that, he went upstairs.

The second her father left the immediate area,

Serena swung around to confront Carson. "You'll do no such thing!"

She caught him off guard. "What is it that I won't do?" he wanted to know.

"Stay here. I don't need you playing bodyguard," she informed him.

Unfazed by her rejection, Carson told her, "Just think of it as your tax dollars at work."

This wasn't funny. "I don't want—"

He'd held his tongue long enough. Serena would try an angel's patience, and he was far from an angel. "What you want, or need, is of no concern to me, Serena," he informed her. "Someone took a shot at you. I aim to find out who it was and to keep it from happening again," Carson told her fiercely. "Now, if you don't mind, I need to see those safe rooms you mentioned earlier."

Serena blew out an angry breath. She'd just assumed that he'd forgotten about the rooms. "I thought we were past that."

"No," he answered, "we're not." Just like Justice when he was hot on a scent, Carson was not about to get distracted. "And the only way we're ever getting 'past that' is if I can find Demi and question her about how her necklace wound up under the tire of that car that was near my brother's body."

Feeling as if she was the only one in Demi's corner, Serena tried to come up with some sort of an explanation for the evidence.

"Maybe someone's trying to frame her." The moment she said it out loud, it sounded right to her. "Did you ever think of that?" Serena challenged.

"No, gosh, I never did. What an unusual thought," Carson said sarcastically. And then he changed his tone, becoming serious as he told her, "Of course I thought of that, but until I can talk to Demi again and get some facts straightened out, I'm not going to waste time investigating that theory. Not when everything else clearly points to her killing my brother. Am I making myself clear?" he all but growled at her.

Serena's eyes narrowed, shooting daggers at him as she struggled to hold on to her temper. "As transparent as glass."

"Good," he retorted with finality. "Now, then, just where are those safe rooms that you said were in your house?"

She was sorely tempted to tell him to go look for the safe rooms himself, but she didn't want to give Carson an excuse to go wandering around the mansion, possibly tearing things up on his own. Although she found that being around him really unsettled her, especially after Carson had thrown his body over her like that, Serena thought it best if she just showed him the two safe rooms herself.

"They're this way," she said, sweeping past Carson.

Her attention was riveted to the top of the stairs. The less she looked at him, Serena felt, the better. Carson was too damn good-looking and she knew all about good-looking men. They were as shallow as a puddle and only interested in their own self-satisfaction.

Been there, done that, she thought as she went up the stairs.

Finding himself unaccountably more amused than irritated, Carson walked behind her. He maintained a light grip on Justice's leash as he led the canine up with him.

Bringing the detective and his four-footed partner to the second floor, Serena made her way into her suite.

When she entered, she saw that the housekeeper was there, changing Lora. The woman appeared surprised to see her—and even more surprised to see the detective and Justice.

"Are you back, Miss Serena?" the woman asked, one hand on Lora to keep the baby from kicking. Lora's diaper was only half-on.

"Just passing through, Alma," Serena answered. "Detective Gage wants to take a look at something," she explained vaguely.

Carson scanned the area. He'd already been to her suite the other night. There'd been no sign of Demi at the time, except for that discarded sweater.

"Where's the room?" he wanted to know. She had just brought him over to her walk-in closet, but that certainly didn't qualify as a safe room, he thought. Was she trying to pull something on him?

"Right here," Serena answered.

Reaching in, she pressed a button just inside the closet entrance. As she did so, the back wall with all her neatly arranged shoes parted and moved aside, exposing another door. There was a keypad on the wall right next to it.

Serena positioned herself in front of the keypad so that he wasn't able to see which of the keys she pressed. When she finished, the door opened, exposing a room that was nothing short of huge. Carson judged that it took up the entire length of the floor.

In it was a king-size bed, a state-of-the-art kitchenette and all sorts of things that would make having to take refuge here anything but a hardship.

Carson looked around slowly, taking it all in. It was impressive. "My first place was one-third this size," he commented.

Serena didn't doubt it. "My father tends to go overboard," she answered. "And he thought that if it came to us having to actually use a safe room, we might all have to stay in here."

Carson nodded. "It certainly is big enough. Go for it, Justice," he told the dog as he released the animal. "Seek!"

But rather than take off, the German shepherd moved around the huge area slowly. Nothing had caught his attention.

The safe room was actually more than just a single room. There were a couple of smaller "rooms" attached to it. Justice went from one end of the space to another, but unlike when he had uncovered her sweater, he found no trace of Demi.

In the end, the dog came trotting back to him.

"Satisfied?" Serena asked the detective.

Instead of answering her questions, he said, "You said safe *rooms*."

Serena sighed. "So I did."

Resigned, she turned around and led the way out of that safe room and then her suite. She wordlessly proceeded to lead Carson to another wing of the mansion.

"How do you not get lost here?" Carson asked her as they went to the wing that faced the rear of the property.

"I use bread crumbs," she answered drolly, then immediately regretted it.

The sound of his laughter was way too sexy.

This safe room, like the other, turned out to be a room within a room. This one was hidden behind a floor-to-ceiling bookcase that housed a wealth of books as well as expensive knickknacks and memorabilia.

"It's here," she told him, entering another code on the keypad beside *that* door.

In Carson's estimation, the second room looked like a carbon copy of the first one, containing the same supplies, the same well-furnished distractions.

She stood off to one side, silently telling him he was free to search this room the way he had the other.

She felt that the sooner this was out of the way, the sooner Carson would leave and she could stop feeling as if she was having trouble breathing.

"Okay, Justice," Carson said, removing the canine's leash for a second time. "Go for it. Seek!"

Again the German shepherd moved about the large room and its connecting rooms as if there was a heavy dose of glue deposited in his veins.

Nothing seemed to pique the canine's interest, but the dog dutifully went around the entire area, sniffing, nudging items and in general taking a very close account of the room. Again there was no sign that Justice detected Demi anywhere within the very large area.

Finished scouting around the second safe room, Justice returned to Carson's side.

He looked up at his partner's face, waiting for further instructions, or the command that allowed him to lie down on the door and rest.

"Are these the only two safe rooms?" Carson asked her.

She laughed drily. "My father believes in overkill, but even he has his limits, so yes, these are the only two safe rooms in the mansion." She looked at Carson pointedly, expecting him to finally take his leave and go away. "Are you satisfied now?"

"Not by a long shot."

Chapter 11

Serena stared at the detective. He'd asked to see the safe rooms and she'd shown him the safe rooms—why wasn't the man leaving?

"What is that supposed to mean?" she wanted to know.

"It means," Carson said patiently, "I'm still looking for Demi."

"Even your dog doesn't think she's here," Serena pointed out. She petted Justice's head despite the canine's partner annoying the hell out of her. "You're welcome to continue turning over rocks on the property and looking for Demi, but I guarantee that no matter how long you spend here, you're going to have the same results," she told him, straightening up. "You're beating a dead horse, Detective. And where I'm from, that's offensive in too many ways to count."

"It's not my intention to offend you," Carson said as they left that wing.

"Good." She gave it another shot, hoping that this time could induce him to leave. "Then go back to the police station or home or wherever it is you go after you clock out."

"Funny thing about police work," he told Serena. "You really don't get to 'clock out.' It's a twenty-four-hour-a-day, seven-days-a-week calling." His eyes met hers. "I can't go 'home.'"

She made her way to her wing of the mansion. "Sure you can. All you have to do is just get in that car of yours and drive away."

Maybe she forgot the exchange he'd had with her father when Judson had tried to get Serena to go with her family to the hotel. "I told your father that I'd look after you and your daughter."

Did he actually believe that was a compelling argument? "I'm sure he didn't take it to heart. You're a Gage. Not believing a word you say comes naturally to him."

"And living up to my word comes naturally to me," he countered. Maybe the idea of having him stay here made her uncomfortable. He could understand that. He didn't want to make her uncomfortable. "Don't worry, Justice and I will just sack out in one of the empty rooms upstairs. We won't get in your way."

Her eyes met his pointedly. He had got in her way from the first minute he'd stormed into the house that night, waving a warrant.

"Too late," she said.

Blowing out a breath, she tried to tell herself that he wasn't trying to annoy her. That he was just doing his job as a member of the police department. But if he had to be here, she didn't want him underfoot.

"There's food in the refrigerator in the kitchen. Why don't you go help yourself? I've got work in the stable," she said. Maybe keeping him informed of her work schedule would buy her a little good grace and some leeway.

When Carson followed her down the stairs with Justice, she didn't think anything of it. But when the two continued walking behind her as she headed for the front door, Serena stopped dead.

Pointing behind him, she said, "The kitchen's in the other direction."

"I know where the kitchen is," he answered matter-of-factly.

"So why aren't you headed there?" she wanted to know. "It might sound unusual to you, but that's where we keep the refrigerator."

"I'm not interested in the refrigerator," he told her in a no-nonsense voice. "I'm interested in keeping you alive."

Serena rolled her eyes. "Now you're just being melodramatic," she insisted.

And she was in denial, he thought. "You felt that bullet whiz by just like I did. That's not being melodramatic. That's just using the common sense that the good Lord gave each of us. Now, do yourself a favor and stop arguing with me."

"I don't need you hovering over me. I'll be fine," Serena insisted, pushing past him.

Not about to be shrugged off, Carson followed her outside.

Serena took exactly five steps then swung around to face him. How did she get through to this man? "Look, Detective, you're beginning to really annoy me."

"I'm not trying to do that, Ms. Colton," he said, reverting back to addressing her formally. "But someone killed my brother and now someone's taken a shot at you." His voice became deadly serious. "I don't intend to have you added to the body count on my watch."

Serena gave up. Trying to reason with the man was just a frustrating waste of time and she had things she wanted to do before nightfall, which came early this time of year. Besides, she thought, there was a small chance that he was right. She could take care of herself, but there was Lora's safety to think of. Better safe than sorry, she decided.

"Suit yourself," Serena told him as she continued on her way to the stables.

"I intend to," Carson murmured under his breath. Sparing a quick glance at Justice as they followed in Serena's wake, Carson said, "She's a regular spitfire, isn't she, boy?"

The dog made no sound, but Carson still took it as tacit agreement on the canine's part.

Carson had learned how to take in his surroundings and be vigilant without calling any attention to himself or what he was doing—and without missing a thing.

As daylight began to wane, he took note of Anders watching him in the distance, saw the handful of ranch hands the Double C foreman had working with him to reinforce a length of fence just beyond the corral. And all the while, he continued to look for something out of the ordinary, for that one thing that didn't mesh with everything else.

"Don't your eyes get tired, staring like that?" Serena finally asked him after she'd taken in the horse she'd been working with and brought out another from the stable.

Carson slid his gaze down the length of her, taking in every curve, every soft nuance her body had to offer. "Depends," he answered.

The man was as communicative as a rock, Serena thought, waiting for him to say something more.

When Carson didn't, she finally asked impatiently, "Depends on *what*?"

There was just possibly the smallest hint of a smile on his lips when he answered, "On what I'm staring at."

Serena knew he meant her but there was no way she could say anything about that without sounding full of herself or, at the very least, without borrowing trouble. All she could do was say something as enigmatic as what he'd just said.

"Careful your eyes don't get tread worn."

She saw the corners of his mouth curve just a tiny bit more as he answered, "I'll do my best."

Serena continued to feel like she was under a microscope, even when she looked up to see that Carson was scanning the horizon and not looking at her. Somehow, she thought, he was managing to do both.

Serena did her best to concentrate on the stallion she was working with and not on the man who had somehow done the impossible—he made her feel warm despite the cold temperature.

An hour later, exhausted, Serena decided to wrap it up and call it a day. The sun had gone down and it was really cold now. It was time to go in. Anders and his men had already gone to their quarters.

Bringing the stallion back into the stable, she brushed the horse down, the way she had the others and then walked out. Before she headed toward the mansion, she made sure to lock up the stable. In her present state of mind, the last thing she needed was for something to spook the horses and cause them to get out of the stable. She had no desire to spend hours tracking them down and rounding them up.

"You do this all the time?" Carson asked, picking up his pace as he and Justice fell into step beside her.

For just a moment, she'd forgotten he was there. It took all she had not to react as if the sound of his deep voice had startled her.

"Yes, when I'm not taking care of my daughter or going to horse auctions," she answered.

"You look like you're really good at it," Carson observed.

The detective was actually complimenting her, she realized. Serena hadn't expected that.

"I am," she answered. She wasn't boasting, she was just stating what she knew to be true.

"Must be nice to do something you're good at," Carson commented.

"It is." She'd enjoyed working with horses for as far back as she could remember. His comment piqued her curiosity about the man, who refused to go away. "How about you? Do you like what you do?"

His answer was vague, leaving it up to her to interpret. "I like keeping order," Carson replied.

Was that his way of avoiding telling her the truth? She decided to prod him a little. "I thought you like ordering people around."

Carson actually seemed to consider her question for a moment before giving her an answer. "That's part of it sometimes."

They'd reached the house and she, for one, was grateful. The walk from the stables to the mansion wasn't technically long enough to warm her. However it turned out to be long enough to make her aware of just how warm talking to him actually made her.

Opening the front door, the first thing that hit Serena was how quiet it all was. Her parents and sister made more noise than she'd realized. Shaking herself free of that thought, Serena proceeded to shrug out of her sheepskin jacket.

Hanging the jacket up in the hall closet, she turned toward Carson and asked, "Are you hungry now?"

Hunger had never governed his eating habits. He'd learned how to deal with perilous conditions and how to ignore a rumbling stomach. Ignoring it became a habit.

"I don't get hungry," he told her. "I eat to keep going."

"You sound like you have a lot in common with my horses," she commented. Feedings were carried out at regimented intervals.

The term "magnificent animal" suddenly flashed across her mind out of nowhere, catching her completely off guard and stunning her. The moment she thought of it, Serena realized that it just seemed to fit.

She found herself staring at Carson almost against her will.

"If you're trying to insult me, you haven't," he told her.

"I'm not insulting you," she said crisply. "But maybe I shouldn't have compared you to a horse. I find horses to be very noble animals."

He surprised her by laughing, but it wasn't at her. Her comment just seemed to tickle him.

"They are," he agreed. "And if you're interested, I don't fancy myself as being noble, just hardworking." He paused for a long moment, just looking at her. "Sometimes I just have to work harder than other times."

She struggled not to shiver. There was just something about the way he looked at her that caused her self-confidence to disintegrate into little tiny flakes that blew away in the wind.

"Why don't you go into the kitchen and have Sally whip up something for you?" she told him, referring to the cook. "I'm just going to go upstairs for a minute and check on Lora."

Carson never hesitated. He just started to walk upstairs with her. "I'll go with you."

Serena sighed. "You really are determined to be my shadow, aren't you?"

The detective said neither yes nor no. Instead, he told her, "Just doing whatever it takes to make sure that you and your daughter are safe."

Serena surrendered. She didn't even bother trying to argue with that.

* * *

The housekeeper was on her feet the moment Serena walked into her suite. The woman placed her finger to her lips, warning them not to raise their voices.

Crossing over to Serena, the housekeeper told her, "She just now fell asleep."

Serena lowered her voice to a whisper. "Did she give you any trouble?"

Alma shook her head, beaming. "No, she was a little darling. But she doesn't really sleep all that much for a three-month-old," she observed. "I was trying to keep her up so she'd sleep through the night for you, but just when I didn't want her to, she dozed off."

"Don't worry about it, Alma. I'm not planning on getting much sleep tonight anyway," Serena told the housekeeper.

Alma's eyes darted toward the man standing behind Serena. Understanding suddenly blossomed on the woman's round face. "Oh."

At that instant, it suddenly dawned on Serena what the housekeeper had to be thinking. She was about to protest and set the woman straight. But then she caught herself. She knew that if she protested, that would only convince the housekeeper that she was right in thinking there was something going on between her and the detective.

So, hard as it was, Serena pressed her lips together and kept silent about the misunderstanding.

Instead, she told the housekeeper, "I'm going to go downstairs and get some dinner. After I finish, I'll be back for the night. You'll be free to go on with your evening after that."

Stealing another long look at the detective, Alma said, "Take your time, Miss Serena. I don't mind staying here with your daughter. She's a little angel. Reminds me of my own when they were little."

As she and the detective walked out of the suite, Serena was positive the housekeeper was watching every step they took. The woman, she knew, was a great fan of romances, both on the screen and within the pages of a book. She had no doubt that Alma was probably fabricating a story about her and the brooding detective at this very moment.

The less said, the better, Serena decided.

Sally, the cook who was currently in her parents' employ—they had gone through an even dozen in as many years—was just cleaning up the kitchen when she and Carson walked in.

Immediately coming to attention when she saw them, Sally, a pleasant-faced woman in her early fifties, asked her, "What can I prepare for you and your guest, Miss Serena?"

"He's not my guest. He's a police detective, part of the K-9 division," Serena added before Sally could ask about the dog. She didn't want the cook to think that she was willingly entertaining Carson.

"What can I prepare for you and the police detective?" Sally asked, amending her initial question.

But Serena shook her head. "That's all right, Sally. You can take the rest of the evening off. I'll make something for myself. For us," she corrected, remembering to include the silent shadow beside her. Given what he'd said earlier, Carson probably ate nails or something of that nature.

Sally looked at her hesitantly. "Are you sure, Miss Serena?"

"My parents and sister have gone to stay in a hotel in town," she said by way of an answer, indicating that this was going to be an informal meal. "I'm sure."

"There are some leftovers on the two top shelves," the woman began, still not leaving.

"I'm good at scrounging, Sally. Go. You deserve some time off," Serena said, smiling as she waved the woman out.

Sally's smile was as wide as her face. "Thank you, miss!" she cried before she hurried off.

Turning back to the refrigerator, Serena found that the detective was already there.

"Can I help you find anything?" she asked him a little stiffly. It was a large kitchen, but somehow, it felt smaller to her because of his presence.

"No," Carson answered simply. Then, because she continued to stand there next to the refrigerator, he told her, "I'm good at scrounging, too."

Giving him space, Serena looked down at Justice. The dog was never more than a few paces away from his partner. "I don't have any dog food."

Carson didn't seem fazed. "That's okay. He adjusts. Same as me."

She wasn't sure exactly what that comment meant when it came to Carson, but she had an uneasy feeling that maybe this was the detective's way of putting her on some sort of notice.

As if she wasn't tense enough already.

Chapter 12

After watching Carson stand there, looking into the refrigerator without taking anything out, it was obvious to Serena that the detective either couldn't make up his mind, or he really didn't feel right about helping himself to something from the giant, industrial-size refrigerator.

Serena decided to take matters into her own hands. "Sit down, Gage," she said, elbowing Carson out of the way.

"Excuse me?" Carson made no move to do what she'd just very crisply ordered him to do, at least not until he knew what she was up to.

Okay, maybe she'd been a little too abrupt, Serena silently conceded. She decided to word her request a little better. "Well, you've taken it upon yourself to be my and my daughter's bodyguard so the least I can do is get you something to eat."

He didn't want her to feel she needed to wait on him. "I'm perfectly capable of getting something to eat for myself."

Serena rolled her eyes as she suppressed a sigh. "Does *everything* have to be an argument with you?" she asked. "Just sit!" she ordered.

Justice dropped down where he was standing, his big brown eyes trained on Serena. She laughed. "At least one of you doesn't have trouble following instructions."

"Hey," Carson pretended to protest. The protest was directed toward the German shepherd. "You're only supposed to listen to me, remember?" he told the canine.

"Too bad your dog can't teach you a few tricks," Serena quipped. Because the refrigerator was rather full and she had no idea what Carson would prefer eating, she asked, "Do you want a sandwich or a full meal?"

Carson had always leaned toward expediency. "A sandwich'll do fine."

There were sandwiches, and then there were *sandwiches*. "Okay, what do you want in your sandwich?"

Wide, muscular shoulders rose and fell in a dismissive, disinterested shrug. "Whatever you've got that's handy. I'm easy."

"Ha! Not hardly," Serena observed. His eyes met hers as if to contest her statement. However, Serena was not about to back down. "You, Detective Carson Gage, might be many things, but easy isn't one of them."

"And just what are some of those 'many things'?" Carson wanted to know, his eyes pinning her in place. He was ready for another argument.

There it was again, Serena thought. That flash of heat when he looked at her a certain way.

Stubbornly, Serena shut out her reaction, telling herself that she was smarter than that. There was no reason in the world for her to react like that to this rough-around-the-edges man or regard him as anything beyond a necessary evil.

Finished putting slices of freshly baked hickory-smoked ham on the extra thick bread that Sally baked for the family every other morning, she topped the sandwich off with slices of baby Swiss cheese. Serena put the whole thing on a plate with some lettuce and tomato slices on the side and pushed the plate over to him on the table.

"I see you finally sat down," she commented as she took out a bottle of ketchup and jars of mayonnaise and mustard. Serena paused over the last item. "Spicy or mild?"

Carson's mouth curved as he looked at her. "I like spicy."

There was that flash again, Serena thought in exasperation. She was just going to have to stop making eye contact with the man. But if she did that, he'd probably think she was avoiding him for some reason that she'd wind up finding insulting when he voiced it.

She took the jar of spicy mustard out of the refrigerator and placed it next to the other condiments. "Spicy, it is."

Eyes as dark as storm clouds on the horizon took measure of her as he reached for the mustard. He nodded toward the mayonnaise and the ketchup. "I don't need the others," he told her.

There was absolutely no reason for her heart to have sped up, Serena told herself. For pity's sake, it was just a conversation about some stupid mustard, nothing else. But she could feel her neck growing warmer, her palms getting damp and her knees felt as if they were getting ready to dissolve any minute now.

It was just the tension of recent events that were getting to her, Serena silently argued. A panic attack after the fact. Once everything got back to normal, so would she.

Carson took a bite of the large sandwich that now also included lettuce as well as a healthy slice of tomato.

"The ham's good," he pronounced.

Serena smiled. "I'll tell Sally you said so. She doesn't get any positive feedback from my family.

My mother usually berates her over things that she found lacking, things that poor Sally usually has no control over. Mother demands perfection—as well as mind reading—which would explain why we've been through a dozen cooks in the last twelve years," Serena commented, placing several slices of ham on a plate and then putting the plate in front of Justice.

The plate was cleaned before Carson had finished half his sandwich.

Done, Justice looked up at her, clearly waiting for more. When she made no attempt to move toward the refrigerator to give him more ham, Justice nudged her with his nose as if he was trying to get her to go back to "the magic box" that contained the meat.

"Justice, sit," Carson ordered sternly.

The canine instantly obeyed, looking rather dejected about it in Serena's opinion. Feeling sorry for the canine, Serena pulled a slice of ham out of the sandwich she had just fixed for herself.

She was about to give it to Justice when she heard Carson gruffly tell her, "Don't."

Startled, she looked in Carson's direction. Her eyes narrowed. "Are you ordering me around?"

Rather than answer her question, Carson felt it would be wiser to explain why he'd stopped her.

"Like the rest of the K-9s, Justice was painstakingly trained. If I give him a command and you do something that negates what I'm trying to convey to him, he's getting mixed signals that are bound to confuse him. There are times when my life depends on his reaction, and I'd rather that Justice wasn't confused."

Serena frowned. "I really doubt that he's going to have to defend you from being assaulted by a slice of ham," she told him sarcastically.

"The point I'm trying to get across is that disobedience just breeds more of the same," Carson informed her matter-of-factly. "And as I said, all the dogs that are part of the K-9 unit were very specifically trained."

"I know," she said, trying not to sound impatient, "by your brother."

But Carson shook his head. "Bo just raised the dogs," he told her. "He did some early work with them, but then the K-9 Training Center selected professional dog trainers for their program. Professional trainers like Hayley," he said, thinking of the woman Bo had been engaged to, "who worked with the dogs to train them for a number of diverse fields within the K-9 department. My brother definitely wasn't disciplined enough in his private life to train a goldfish, much less a German shepherd.

"Hell, Bo couldn't even discipline himself. Part of me," he admitted seriously, "is rather surprised that a jealous boyfriend didn't take him out long ago. Bo was always playing fast and loose, seeing one girl behind another one's back, jumping out of bedroom windows to avoid being on the wrong end of a jealous boyfriend's or enraged husband's gun."

Serena suddenly felt her opinion validated. "So you do have other people to investigate instead of just Demi," she cried.

"Yes and no," Carson said. "Bo actually settled down once he took up with Hayley," Carson said. Of course, he added silently, that had been for only the last three months, but it was a new pattern. "He didn't cheat on her, so jealous husbands and boyfriends were no longer prominently in the picture." He couldn't help thinking of what a terrible waste it all was. "I thought that maybe he finally grew up."

"Grew up?" Serena repeated, surprised. She thought about how Lora's father disappeared on her, taking her money and her credit cards with him. She'd been abandoned, humiliated *and* robbed, a veritable trifecta. "I thought that most men felt that this was the kind of lifestyle they aspired to—juggling women, enjoying them, then disappearing once it got too serious."

"I wouldn't know," Carson told her. "I never took a survey."

She decided the detective wasn't going to squirm out of giving her a straight answer. "How about you?" she pressed. "Did you look up to Bo? Did you want to be like him?"

Carson looked at her as if she had lost her mind. "Why the hell would I want to be like Bo? I'm already looking over my shoulder to make sure that there aren't any bad guys trying to take me out as it is. I wouldn't want to add disgruntled husbands and angry ex-girlfriends to that number."

He almost sounded as if he meant it. Serena caught herself wanting to believe him, but her experience with Lora's father had tainted her.

"So then you're monogamous?" she asked.

"What I am," Carson told her with a finality that said he wanted to be done with this conversation, "is focused on my job. That takes up all of my time. Right, Justice?" he asked, looking at the dog.

Justice barked, then looked at Serena. The German shepherd began to drool, clearly eyeing the remainder of her sandwich.

Serena, in turn, looked at Carson. "Here," she said, pushing her plate and what was left of her sandwich toward him. "You give it to Justice. I wouldn't want to interfere with the connection you two have."

"Justice," Carson said sternly. The dog immediately became alert, looking at Carson and waiting for his next command. "At ease."

With that, the canine relaxed, almost flopping down on the floor.

"Okay, now you can give that to him," he told Serena, nodding at what was left of her sandwich.

She could only stare at him, stunned. "'At ease'? You're kidding."

"No," he answered. "Training is training. Trust

me, this is for everyone's own good. Justice has to know who to listen to. If I tell him 'at ease,' he knows it's okay with me if he goes with his instincts."

"All that with 'at ease'?" she said, marveled but somewhat skeptical nonetheless.

"There's a little more to it than that," Carson admitted. Now, however, wasn't the time to get into it. It was getting late. "But yeah."

She shook her head, then held out her sandwich to Justice. The dog quickly consumed every last bite, carefully eating it out of her hand.

His teeth never once even came close to nipping her skin.

When the sandwich was gone, Serena brushed off her hands against one another, still marveling at how gentle Justice had been.

"You're right," she told Carson. "Your dog is very well trained."

"He's not my dog," Carson corrected her. "He's my partner. Best partner I ever had," he said, affectionately petting the animal and ruffling Justice's black-and-tan fur. "He doesn't mouth off, doesn't give me any grief and always has my back."

"Sounds like a match made in heaven," Serena commented.

"It pretty much is," Carson agreed.

He got up and carried his empty plate to the sink. She expected the detective to leave his plate there and was surprised to see him wash the plate and place it in the rack to dry.

Turning around to see that she was watching him, Carson made an assumption as to what she was probably thinking.

"I wasn't raised in a barn," he told her.

"I didn't think you were," she assured him quickly. "It's just that nobody does that around here," she explained. "I mean, I do sometimes, but Anders doesn't take his meals here and my parents and sister just assume that's what the housekeeper is for. In their opinion, it's all just part of 'keeping the house.'"

She'd managed to arouse his curiosity again. "What makes you so different from them?" he asked.

She hadn't given it much thought. It was just something that had always been that way. Since he asked, Serena thought for a moment before answering.

"I think for myself. And I like working with the horses." She thought of the way Joanelle turned her nose up at things. "My mother wouldn't be caught dead near the corral unless the rest of the ranch was on fire. Maybe not even then," she amended with a whimsical smile.

Serena realized that the detective had grown quiet and was just studying her. She'd said too much, she admonished herself.

Clearing her throat, she picked up her own plate

and glass and made her way over to the sink, where she washed them.

"I'd better be getting back up to Lora," she told him, paving the way for her retreat. "She's probably waking up about now. Poor Alma's practically put in a full day taking care of her. It might not look it, but taking care of a baby is exhausting. Alma doesn't complain, but I know she'd welcome having the rest of the evening to herself. With the rest of the family gone, there won't be any sudden 'emergencies' cropping up."

When Carson began to follow her out of the kitchen, she was quick to try to divert him.

"You don't have to come up right away. There's a big-screen TV in the entertainment room if you want to watch anything." She gestured toward the large room as she passed it on her way to the staircase.

"I'm not here to watch TV," he told her. "I'm here to watch you."

"I didn't think you meant that literally," she protested. At the very most, she'd thought he'd just be somewhere on the premises, not really with her. Not for the night.

Carson could almost read her mind. "I don't intend to hover over you, if that's what you're afraid of, Serena. But I do intend to be close by."

Serena made her way up the stairs, then paused and turned around. She was two steps above Carson. Just enough to bring them eye to eye, literally rather than figuratively.

"Define 'close by.'"

"A room near your suite," he answered. "Or I can just bed down in front of your door if need be."

What she needed, Serena thought, attempting to reconcile herself to this turn of events, was to get her life back.

She blew out a breath. "You really intend to go through with this."

"I said I would and I always live up to my word."

"Why couldn't you be a liar like every other man?" she murmured under her breath as she turned around and started to go up the stairs again.

He couldn't make out what she'd said, only that Serena had said something. "What?"

Serena merely sighed and continued walking up the stairs. There was no point in repeating what she'd said. "Never mind."

Chapter 13

The housekeeper was on her feet the moment that Serena walked into the suite.

Serena could see by the look on Alma's face that the woman seemed very interested in the fact that Carson still hadn't left the Double C.

Not only hadn't the detective left it, but he gave no indication that he was going anywhere this evening.

Normally, Serena prided herself as being a private person who didn't go out of her way to justify her actions. What people thought about her was their own business and she was not in the habit of making any excuses. But she liked Alma. The woman had been exceptionally helpful and kind to her, especially when she'd been pregnant with Lora.

Right now, she could see that Alma was dying to ask questions, but her mother had been very specific when it came to what her "place" was as a house-keeper for Judson Colton and his family. Conse-quently, the woman would explode before asking anything concerning why the detective was still here.

"Justice and I are going to take a look around the second floor," the detective told Serena, walking out of her room. "We're going to make sure that there's nobody up here, present company excepted."

Serena waited until Carson was out of earshot. "Alma," she began. "I'm going to need you to bring some bedding into the spare bedroom that's next to my suite. Detective Gage is spending the night," she added, watching the housekeeper.

Alma's expression remained impassive. She nod-ded dutifully. "Very good, Miss Serena."

"No, it isn't," Serena corrected, knowing exactly what was going through the other woman's head. "But it is what it is and we're just going to have to deal with it for the night." That didn't come out right, Serena thought. She tried again. "It's the detective's intention to stand guard over us to make sure that Lora and I stay safe."

This time she saw Alma smile, sanctioning what the detective was doing. "Very good, Miss Serena."

"Then you approve?" Serena asked, trying to find out just what the woman thought of the whole setup. As for herself, she hadn't reconciled herself to the idea of having Carson hovering around like a brooding guardian angel.

"It's not my place to approve or disapprove, Miss Serena. I'm only supposed to follow orders," Alma replied quietly.

"But you must have an opinion," Serena pressed.

"I am not being paid to have an opinion, Miss Serena. Only to make things as comfortable as possible for you and your family." When Serena gave her a look that clearly said she wanted the woman to give voice to something a little more personal than that, Alma gave every indication that her lips were sealed.

And then the housekeeper leaned in a little closer to the young woman, who, unlike her parents and younger sister, always treated her with kindness and respect.

Lowering her voice, Alma said, "It's a good thing to have someone so capable and good-looking watching over you."

Serena bit back a laugh despite herself. Obviously Carson's looks had won the housekeeper over. "I didn't know you noticed things like that, Alma."

"I'm not dead, miss," the woman replied just as Carson and his four-footed partner returned to the suite.

Carson looked from the housekeeper to Serena. Judging from the housekeeper's expression and the sudden onset of silence as he walked in, he guessed that something was up. "Did I miss something?" he asked after the other woman left the room.

Serena looked at him with wide-eyed innocence. "I thought you never missed anything," she told him. "Isn't that why you're here?"

She was clearly baiting him. He deliberately ignored it. Instead, he merely gave her his report. "Justice and I swept through your floor. Everything looks to be in order."

She couldn't explain why, but Carson's solemn expression just made her want to laugh. "Nobody's hiding in the closet?"

His eyes went flat. "This isn't a joke, Serena," he said gruffly. "Someone took a shot at you today."

She was not about to allow herself to be paralyzed by fear. "I'm really not worried about someone who can't hit the broadside of a barn," Serena told him.

He didn't like the fact that she was taking all this so lightly. Didn't she realize the very real danger she could be in?

"Maybe they can and they're just toying with you first," Carson pointed out. "Are you willing to bet your daughter's life that you're right?" he demanded, struggling to keep his voice down so as not to wake up the sleeping baby.

Serena frowned, glancing over her shoulder toward the crib. "You really do know how to get to a person, don't you?"

Carson definitely didn't see it that way. "If I did," he

told Serena, "you and your daughter would be in town by now, staying in the hotel with the rest of your family."

This wasn't going anywhere, and she was not about to just stand here, listening to him go over what he viewed as her shortcomings.

"My housekeeper put fresh linens in the guest room for you," she told the detective. "It's this way." Crossing to the doorway of her bedroom, she found Carson blocking her exit. She could see that he wasn't about to go anywhere. She glared at the man. "I can't walk through you," she said pointedly.

He had no desire to be down the hall from her. If something went wrong, seconds would count. "That's okay. Justice and I'll just bunk down outside your door. It's closer that way," he emphasized.

Enough was enough. "Aren't you carrying this whole thing a little too far?" she asked, irritated. "If this person is dumb enough to show up here, we're dealing with someone with an ax to grind, not a professional cat burglar who's light on their feet."

And then Serena decided to attempt to use another tactic.

"Alma made the bed up for you," she reminded him. "If you don't use it, the woman's feelings will be hurt and heaven knows my family's done enough of a number on her. To be honest, I have no idea why Alma puts up with it and stays."

Carson laughed shortly and shook his head at her

in wonder. "And that's supposed to get me to use the guest room?"

"No," she corrected, "common sense is supposed to do that. Besides, you're probably the type who sleeps with one eye and both ears open, so if anyone does try to break in and shoot me, you'll hear them before they get off a shot."

Carson knew she was mocking him. But he also knew that he wasn't about to get anywhere arguing with her. Justice was with him; he was confident that the German shepherd would alert him if anyone who didn't belong on the premises entered the house.

So, because it was getting late, and in the interest of peace, Carson gave in. "Okay, you win. If you need me, I'll be in the guest room."

Serena looked at him in surprise. She'd expected him to put up more of a fight than this. Was he up to something?

"You're being reasonable?" she asked, looking at him uncertainly.

The expression on her face was worth the capitulation. "It's been known to happen."

She decided it was best to call it a night before Carson decided to change his mind and resurrect the argument.

"Good, then if you don't mind, I'm going to try to get some sleep while my daughter's still napping." She gestured to the open door down the hall. "That's your room. I'll see you in the morning, Detective."

"Yes," he assured her, standing there a moment longer and looking at her, "you will."

Why did such a simple sentence cause her to suddenly feel hot ripples going up and down her skin? He wasn't saying anything out of the ordinary. The detective was agreeing with her, for pity's sake.

So why did she feel as if he'd just set up some sort of a secret rendezvous between them?

He hadn't done anything of the sort, Serena silently insisted, firmly closing her bedroom door behind her. All he'd said was that he'd see her in the morning, which right now seemed like an inevitable fact of life. But by no means was he making some sort of an earthshaking revelation.

Was he?

She was getting punchy, Serena told herself with a sigh. Punchy. That was why she wasn't thinking straight and coming up with all these strange thoughts and reactions.

She supposed that, in all honesty, the missed shot really had unnerved her.

What if it *had* been someone out to shoot her?

But why? Why would anyone want to shoot *her*? She just didn't understand. No one had come out and threatened her and she certainly wasn't a threat to anyone. It all had to be some kind of a gross misunderstanding, and the sooner it was cleared up, the sooner she would be able to get back to her old life.

Her relatively uneventful, humdrum life, she

thought as she sat pulling a hairbrush through her hair, something she had done religiously ever since she'd been old enough to hold her own hairbrush.

Feeling exceptionally tired all of a sudden, Serena gave up brushing her hair and laid the brush aside.

She slipped into the nursery, checking on her daughter. The crib had just been moved there from her own room yesterday. Lingering, she watched Lora sleep for a minute or two, then crossed back to her bedroom. Mechanically turning off the lamp, Serena crawled into bed, bone weary beyond words.

She was asleep within less than five minutes.

It was the dream that woke her. A dream that a tall slender person had slipped into her room and was now running off with her daughter.

A scream rose in her throat, but try as she might, Serena just couldn't make herself release it, couldn't scream to alert Carson so that he could come and rescue her daughter.

Oh, why hadn't she allowed him to spend the night on the floor right outside her suite the way he'd wanted to? The kidnapper would have never got in to steal her baby if Carson had been standing guard right by her door.

Frightened, she tried to scream again, but nothing came out. It was as if her throat had been sealed shut.

Just like her eyes. They were shut, too, she realized. Shut and practically glued together.

Was that it? Were they glued shut?

Why couldn't she open her eyes? She needed to be able to see the person who had broken into her suite. The person who had just made off with her baby.

How could she give Carson a description of the fiend when she couldn't see him?

A hot wave of desperation washed over Serena as she tried to scream again. To make some kind of a noise, any kind of a noise, in order to scare away the intruder.

No sounds came.

She felt absolutely powerless.

Carson wasn't in the habit of falling asleep while on duty. It had never happened to him before. He prided himself on being able to get by with next to no sleep for several days on end.

But he'd been going nonstop for more than a few days now and though he really hated to admit it, hated what it ultimately said about his stamina, it had finally caught up to him.

Carson didn't remember his eyes shutting. But they must have because the next thing he knew, they were flying open, pried open by a sound.

A sound that had seeped into his consciousness.

The sound of Justice's nails along the marble floor as he suddenly scrambled up, completely alert.

Carson was still groggy and half-asleep, but he knew that his K-9 partner had been awakened by something.

Or someone.

Suddenly as alert as his dog, Carson immediately scanned the darkened room, searching for movement, for some minute indication that something was out of place.

Everything was just the way it had been when he'd settled back on the bed.

But he knew he'd heard something.

And from the way Justice had gained his feet, so had the German shepherd.

Opening the door ever so carefully, Carson slipped out into the hall. Nothing was moving, nothing was out of place.

Maybe he'd been dreaming after all.

But glancing at Justice told him that it wasn't a dream. Something was definitely up.

Exercising the same stealth movements, Carson opened the door leading into Serena's suite. He knew he ran the risk of having her think he was taking advantage of the situation, but that really didn't matter in this case. His gut was telling him to push on.

Something was up.

Moving in almost painfully slow motion, Carson opened Serena's door. With his fingertips against the highly polished door, he eased it back until he was able to look into the room.

It was cold, unusually cold.

The door between the bedroom and the nursery was open.

A movement in the nursery caught his eye.

As his vision acclimated to the darkness, Carson
saw a tall slender figure dressed completely in black
leaning over the baby's crib.

Reaching in.

Carson had his gun in his hand, but he couldn't risk
taking a shot. The dark figure was too close to Lora.

"Freeze!" he ordered in a loud, menacing voice.

Startled, the figure bolted toward the open balcony doors on the other side of Serena's bedroom.

Serena had jackknifed upright in bed and
screamed when she realized that someone was in
her room. Instinctively, she knew that her daughter's
life was in danger.

She hadn't been dreaming; this was very real!

Justice and then Carson whizzed by her bed, running toward the balcony. There was a new moon out
so there was nothing to illuminate her room and help
her see what was happening.

She sensed rather than saw that someone was in
her suite. It was possibly more than just one person.

Serena quickly turned on the lamp next to her
bed. Light flooded the room at the same time that
she reached into the nightstand drawer. She pulled
out the handgun she always kept there.

Carson and Justice had reached the balcony, but
they were too late to stop the fleeing potential kidnapper. All Carson saw was a dark figure who had
managed to get down to the ground unhurt and was
now sprinting away from the mansion.

The darkness quickly swallowed the would-be kidnapper up.

"Damn it," Carson cursed under his breath. His weapon was still drawn, but he wasn't about to shoot at what he couldn't really see.

Turning back toward the suite, he went in and was about to close the door—by now the suite was absolutely freezing—when he saw Serena. She was pointing a handgun at him.

"Whoa, whoa, whoa," he cautioned, raising one hand while the other still held his weapon. "Put that thing down. I'm one of the good guys, remember?"

But Serena kept her weapon trained on him. She wasn't about to lower it until he answered some questions to her satisfaction. She was breathing hard and her heart was racing like crazy.

It took her a second to catch her breath. "What just happened?" she wanted to know.

Turning his back on her, Carson secured the balcony doors and then turned around to face her. "As near as I can figure it, Justice and I just stopped someone from kidnapping your baby."

Serena's arms sagged. The handgun she was holding suddenly felt as if it weighed a ton.

With concentrated effort, she put it back in the open drawer. All she could do was stare at the detective, dumbfounded.

Her throat almost closed up as she cried, "Kidnapping?"

Chapter 14

"That's what I said," Carson confirmed quietly with just the slightest nod of his head as he looked at her. "Kidnapping."

If anything, the idea of someone shooting at her ultimately made Serena angry. She could deal with that, find a way to fight back and defend herself. It was in her nature to fight back.

But the thought of someone kidnapping her child, that was an entirely different matter. That was scary.

She could feel a cold chill not only running up and down her spine, but gripping her heart and squeezing it so hard that she could barely breathe.

She moved over to the crib in the nursery. Somehow, Lora had slept through all the commotion. Serena felt a very real desire to stand here forever and just watch her daughter sleep. The scene was such a contrast to what *could* have happened.

"Who would want to kidnap Lora?" Serena wanted to know, her voice quavering as she tried to come to terms with the frightening thought.

Carson shrugged. He moved a little closer to Serena but still managed to maintain a safe distance. He didn't want her to feel that he was crowding her. He just wanted her to realize that he was there for her. For her daughter and her.

"Maybe Demi was looking for some leverage to use to get the police off her back."

"Demi again," Serena cried, stunned. She moved away from the crib, taking their conversation to the threshold between her bedroom and the nursery. "You think that Demi Colton is behind this, too," she said incredulously, then demanded, "Are you kidding me?"

Carson's expression was deadly serious. "That shadowy figure could have easily matched a description of Demi's body type."

At another time, she might have been rendered speechless, but this was about her daughter as well and she needed Carson to find whoever was behind this threat—and it *wasn't* Demi.

"Good Lord, by the time you're done, Demi Colton is going to be behind every crime committed in the county, maybe even in this part of the state." Did he see how ludicrous what he'd just said sounded? "Demi's smart, I'll give you that. But she isn't some kind of criminal mastermind," Serena cried.

"What is this obsession you have with her?" she wanted to know. And then, as if hearing the exasperation in her own voice, Serena took a breath and backed off. "Look, I'm sorry. You saved my baby, and I am very grateful to you. I didn't mean to go off on you like that." She dragged her hand through her hair. "I guess I'm just on edge. But I think I got a better look at whoever was in my room than you did—"

Carson was immediately alert. "You saw the kidnapper's face?"

She only wished she had. "No, the kidnapper had on a ski mask. But whoever it was that ran by was too tall to be Demi."

Carson wasn't so sure. "Demi's about five foot nine, five foot ten and slim. The kidnapper was under six feet and on the thin side."

But Serena just shook her head. "No, it's not her," she said with conviction. "She doesn't need to steal *my* baby."

There was something in Serena's voice that he couldn't quite put his finger on. Maybe she was just being overly protective of the other woman.

Carson pressed on. "Maybe she wants to hold your daughter for ransom. She knows you'll pay whatever she asks and a big payoff will go a long way in setting her up in a new life somewhere else." And then he stopped, thinking. If the kidnapper had tried once, maybe Demi, or whoever it was, would try again. "Maybe you should reconsider staying at the hotel with your family until this blows over."

But that was definitely the wrong thing to say to her. "No. I'm not going to let whoever's doing this run me off my own land," Serena said fiercely.

There was bravery—and then there was such a thing as being *too* brave without considering the consequences. "Even if it means putting your daughter in danger?" Carson wanted to know.

"I have you to protect her, don't I?" Serena responded. She could feel anger bubbling up inside of her. "And just what kind of a mother would I be, teaching my daughter that it's all right to run at the first sign of trouble?"

Serena had leaped out of her bed when he and Justice had raced into the room. Confronted with the possibility of her daughter being stolen, she hadn't thought to put on a robe.

She still hadn't, and now he found himself wishing that she would. It wasn't his place to say anything. The nightgown she was wearing wasn't exactly transparent, but it did cause his imagination to wreak havoc.

Carson forced himself to focus on what had almost just happened and not on the tantalizing way her breasts rose and fell.

"Your daughter is three months old. I don't think she'll know the difference if you dig in or leave," he told her sternly.

Serena's eyes flashed. Did he think that she was going to hide behind the fact that her daughter was an infant? "Maybe she won't," she agreed. "But I'll know."

There were several choice words he wanted to say to her about taking risks and being foolhardy, words that were hovering on the tip of his tongue. With steely resolve, Carson managed to refrain from uttering any of them.

Instead, he merely grunted in response to the sentiment she'd expressed. He was learning that arguing with the woman was just an exercise in futility.

"Justice and I are going to have another look around the place, make sure your night caller didn't get it into his head to double back and try again." He crossed to the balcony, checking to make sure that the doors leading out were still locked. "When I leave, I want you to lock your doors. Don't open them to anyone."

"Except for you," she amended, certain he had omitted that part of the instruction.

"You don't have to concern yourself with me," he told her. He nodded toward her bed. "Just try to get some sleep before morning."

Right. Sleep. Easy for you to say, Serena thought

as she closed her bedroom doors behind Carson and then locked them.

She went to the balcony doors and checked them even though she had seen Carson lock them earlier and just check them before he left.

She crossed back into the nursery. It amazed her again that Lora had not only slept through the kidnapping threat but had slept through the raised voices, as well. As for her, she knew that there was no way she was going to get back to sleep, not in her present frame of mind. Every sound that she would hear—or *thought* she heard—was going to be magnified to twice its volume, if not more.

Resigned, Serena didn't even bother lying down. Instead, she decided just to sit and keep vigil in the oversize rocker-recliner that Anders had got her as a gift when Lora was born.

Wanting to be fully prepared for whatever might happen, Serena took her handgun out of the night-stand drawer and put it on the small table next to the rocker-recliner.

Sitting down, she proceeded to wait for the intruder to return or for dawn to break, whatever would happen first.

Serena was still in the recliner when daybreak finally came. It seemed like an eternity later to her and she felt somewhat stiff after spending what was left of the night in an upright sitting position.

But she'd had no intention of being caught off guard again if the intruder returned. An aching body was more than a fair trade-off to knowing her daughter was safe.

As it was, the only "intruder" she had to deal with was Lora, who woke up twice in the last few hours, once because she was wet, once because she was hungry. Taking care of both needs as they arose, Serena returned her daughter to her crib and each time Lora obligingly went back to sleep.

Feeling achy and stiff, Serena really wanted to take a shower, but she wanted to make sure that nothing else had gone down during the past night. She'd half expected Carson to check in on her. When he hadn't, she just assumed that he and his German shepherd had gone back to the guest room.

However the more time that passed, the more uneasy she became. So finally, pausing only to throw on some clothes, Serena opened her bedroom door, ready to go and knock on the guest room door in order to wake Carson up.

She didn't have to.

Carson was right there, sitting cross-legged on the floor in front of her door. The second she opened the door, the detective was up on his feet—and Justice was right there beside him.

Startled, she was quick to silence the gasp that rose to her lips. She did her best to look unfazed about finding him even though the exact opposite was true. Bending down to pet Justice—the canine appeared to have taken a liking to her—she was able to effectively mask her surprise.

"I thought you were going to spend the night in the guest room," she said, straightening up.

"Never said that," Carson reminded her. He was relieved that she'd got dressed before coming out, although there was a part of him that had to admit he'd liked the previous view.

"You spent the whole night on the floor outside my bedroom?" Serena questioned. Who did that when there was a comfortable bed only yards away?

"There wasn't a whole night left after the kidnapper ran off," he corrected.

Serena sighed. Her surprised observation wasn't meant to be the opening line for a debate.

"Isn't *anything* a simple yes or no with you?" she asked, frustrated that there wasn't such a thing as a simple conversation when it came to this man.

"No," he answered honestly.

The maddening impossibility of the whole situation suddenly hit her and Serena started to laugh.

Her laughter was infectious and after a minute, Carson's laughter blended with hers. The laughter continued for more than a couple of minutes and managed to purge some of the ongoing tension that was shimmering between them.

It also managed to draw the housekeeper, who was already up and dressed, to Serena's suite.

The woman made a quick assessment of her own about the state of affairs. Alma looked from Serena to the detective, then smiled. "Apparently, from the sound of it, the night went well."

Serena decided to wait to tell the woman about the aborted kidnapping after she had a chance to get some coffee into her system.

So all she said in response now was, "Well, we're still here."

Alma nodded, looking pleased. "Yes, so I see. There's a pot of fresh coffee downstairs," she told Serena.

"Music to my ears, Alma," Serena responded.

Obviously thinking that the two were about to go downstairs to the kitchen, the housekeeper offered, "If you give me a moment, I'll get Sally up to make you breakfast."

But Serena waved away the suggestion. "No, don't bother. Let Sally sleep in for once. I can handle breakfast for the detective and myself," Serena told the housekeeper.

"Are you sure, Miss Serena?" Alma asked.

"I'm sure," she told the housekeeper. "As long as you watch Lora for me."

"Consider it done," Alma answered with pleased enthusiasm.

"Should I be worried?" Carson asked Serena as they went downstairs.

Reaching the landing, Serena went on to the

kitchen. The house seemed almost eerily quiet to her. She was accustomed to hearing her mother's voice raised in displeasure, ordering someone around.

"Only if you get me angry when I have a frying pan in my hand," Serena replied. "But if you're referring to my cooking, I haven't poisoned anyone yet."

It was hard for him to believe that a pampered Colton was serious about making breakfast. "I didn't know you cooked."

"Lots of things about me you don't know," she answered. Opening one of the refrigerator doors, she took out four eggs. "I don't like being waited on," she went on, "so I learned how to cook."

Putting the eggs on the counter, she paused as she reached for some bread. And then it occurred to her that she had just assumed what he wanted for breakfast without asking.

Turning toward Carson now, she remedied the situation. "I didn't ask you. Eggs and toast okay, or do you want something else? I can make pancakes or waffles, or—"

"Eggs and toast will be fine," he answered before she could go through an entire litany of all the different things that came under the heading of breakfast.

"Eggs and toast, it is," Serena agreed. "How do you want your eggs?"

He'd already told her last night that he was generally indifferent to food. "Any way but raw."

Serena laughed in response.

He wasn't aware that he'd said anything amusing. "What's so funny?"

She shook her head. She supposed that the man just didn't see it. "Anyone who didn't know you would say you were easy."

So far, he still didn't see what was so amusing to Serena. "I *am* easy."

She put four slices into the toaster, adjusting the lever for medium.

"You keep telling yourself that, Carson."

"I *am* easy," Carson stressed. "I have few requirements." Serena handed him a cup of black coffee. He accepted it automatically. "One of which is that I don't like being lied to."

She stopped pouring coffee into her mug and turned to look at him. Was he deliberately being enigmatic, or was he just fishing for a response from her? "Are you saying I did?"

Carson raised one eyebrow, his gaze pinning hers. "Did you?"

Serena never flinched or looked away. Instead, she raised her chin defiantly and told him, "No."

Carson decided to believe her—unless she gave him reason not to. "Then we should keep it that way," he told her.

"No problem here." She took a long sip of her coffee, then turned her attention to preparing the rest of the breakfast. "By the way, does that go both ways?"

"Are you asking me if I lied to you?" Carson wanted to know.

Two could play at this vague game of his. "I am."

His voice was dead serious as he answered her. "I didn't."

Maybe she was just being naively foolish, but she believed him. Or maybe she just wanted to feel that there was someone on her side. "Looks like everything's just coming up roses between us then," she responded. And then she saw him grin. "What?"

"That strange, ungodly sound that you're hearing are dead Coltons and Gages, collectively rolling over in their graves," he said.

Buttering the slices of toast that had just popped up, she laughed. "They would, wouldn't they? You know, I kind of like that idea, doing something to cause past generations of Coltons and Gages to roll over in their graves.

"I always thought the idea of a family feud was the stupidest waste of time imaginable," she continued. "That sort of thing belongs to the Hatfields and the McCoys, not to people who live in the twenty-first century," Serena said as she scrambled the four eggs together in a large frying pan. Looking at the pan, she grinned. "My mother would be horrified if she saw me making a Gage breakfast in our kitchen. Hell, she'd be horrified if she saw me making breakfast, period, but especially for a Gage," she told him.

"I said you didn't have to," he reminded her.

Detective or not, the man could be very dense, Serena thought. "You're missing the point," she told him.

"I guess I am," he was willing to admit. "Educate me. What is the point?"

She lowered the temperature under the frying pan. "That two intelligent families feuding over something that happened between two people decades ago is stupid and anyone with half a brain should definitely not allow themselves to be pulled into this feud."

"Do I qualify as someone with half a brain?" he wanted to know, amused by her description.

Still scrambling the eggs, Serena looked at him. "At least half," she deadpanned.

"Thanks."

"Don't mention it," she managed to say before the grin won out, curving her mouth. "Get a couple of plates from the cupboard, will you?"

There was no shortage of cupboards and cabinets in the large kitchen. He could be opening and closing doors for several minutes.

"You want to point me in the right direction?" he asked.

Responding, Serena moved the frying pan off the active burner. "Typical male," she commented with amusement. Hands on his shoulders, she literally pointed Carson toward the cupboard that held the everyday dishes. "That one," she told him.

He knew it was his imagination, but he could swear that he felt the warmth from her hands coming through his shirt, seeping into his shoulders. The warmth found its way into his system, spreading out through all of him.

He hadn't been with a woman since Lisa had died, and for some reason, he was acutely aware of that lack right at this moment. Aware of the fact that it had been eating away at him, bit by bit, from the first time he had laid eyes on her.

"Are you all right?" Serena asked when he made no move toward the cupboard.

"Yeah." Carson forced himself to shake off the feeling that was taking hold of him and got the plates she'd requested. He placed them on the counter. "Just wondering why anyone would need this many cabinets, that's all."

"That's an easy one to answer," she told him, dividing the eggs between the two plates. The mansion belonged to her mother when her father had married her and Joanelle was responsible for every part of its decor. "For show."

Chapter 15

"For show?" Carson repeated as Serena took her seat at the table.

He thought he understood what she was saying, but he wanted to make sure he wasn't assuming too much, so he waited for a little clarification.

And Serena had no problem giving it. "It is my mother's life ambition to make every other living person be in total awe and envy of her—and she won't rest until that happens." As far as she was concerned, her mother's attitude was deplorable, but she wasn't about to say it out loud.

Joanelle Colton's shallowness was nothing new as far as Carson was concerned. He shrugged, paying far more attention to his bracing cup of coffee than to the conversation.

After taking a long sip, he quipped, "I guess everyone should have a goal in life."

"Well, the baby and I definitely put a crimp in her goal," she commented more to herself than to Carson as she quickly consumed her breakfast. She had a full day ahead of her and she needed to get to it.

Carson, however, seemed to have other ideas. Serena was about to get up when he asked her another question.

"Earlier, you said that Demi didn't need to kidnap your daughter. What did you mean by that?" The way she had phrased it—as well as her tone of voice—had been preying on his mind.

That had been a slip on her part, Serena thought. She shouldn't have said anything.

She shrugged now, trying to dismiss the whole thing. "Oh, you know. The usual."

"No," he answered, not about to let the matter go so easily. "I don't know. Enlighten me." As he looked at her across the table, Carson once again had the distinct feeling that there was something she wasn't telling him. "Serena, if you're holding something back, I need to know. What is it you're not telling me?" he pressed. "You used the word *need* before. Was that just you talking a mile a minute, trying to find a way to make me stop looking at Demi as a suspect, or was there something more to this? I know that she took a lot of cash with her, but that doesn't mean she has enough to fund being on the run."

When Serena made no answer, it just reinforced the idea that he was on to something. "*Why* did you say she didn't *need* to kidnap your baby? Oh wait—you mean because she's pregnant herself."

He was crowding her and Serena lost her temper. "Exactly. She's going to have one of her own," she snapped. "That's all I meant. The idea of her kidnapping Lora for ransom is ludicrous and never would have occurred to me."

Serena stared up at the kitchen's vaulted ceiling, searching for strength.

"As I already asked, please don't say anything to anyone," she implored, looking into his eyes, trying to make contact with his soul—if he had one. "Demi didn't want anyone else to know. She only told me because she thought that I'd understand since I'd just gone through the same thing myself."

Carson looked at her, debating whether or not he was buying this. He hadn't told Finn, despite the pregnancy speaking to motive, no matter what Serena had said in opposition about how Demi wouldn't kill her child's father. Maybe because he wasn't sure yet if Demi was really pregnant at all. For reasons of her own, Serena might have made up the pregnancy to get him to feel sorry for Demi or go easier on her cousin.

For the moment, he decided to go along with

Serena's story. "And she was sure that Bo was the father?"

Serena nodded. "Yes."

He waited, but Serena didn't say anything further. Instead, she reached over and gathered his empty plate, then stacked it on top of hers.

Carson put his hand over hers, stopping her from getting up with the plates.

"You said he didn't know about the baby."

"Right. Demi didn't want to tell him yet. He was marrying someone else. She didn't want to look as if she was trying to get him to call off the wedding and marry her instead. She didn't *want* him to marry her. Demi told me she had finally come to her senses and realized that Bo was loathsome—no offense."

"None taken." Serena wasn't giving voice to anything that hadn't crossed his mind about his brother more than once.

Serena went on to tell the detective, "Demi told me that she wouldn't marry Bo if he was dipped in gold and covered with diamonds."

He wondered if Demi had laid it on a little thick to cover her tracks. "Pretty harsh words for the father of her baby," Carson observed.

"Demi had caught him cheating on her more than once and, don't forget, they'd broken up," Serena reminded him. "Bo being the baby's father was just an unforeseen accident."

He saw the pregnancy in a slightly different light. "Certainly gives her motive to kill Bo."

He was back to that again? Serena rolled her eyes in exasperation. "Only if she'd wanted something from him, which she *didn't*. All Demi wanted before Bo went and got himself killed was just to have her baby and make a life for the two of them."

"Well, the simplest thing for Demi to do would be just to—"

Serena knew what he was going to say. He was going to say that Demi should do what her mother had told her to do when she had to tell her parents that she was pregnant. She cut Carson short before he was able to finish his sentence.

"No, that's not the 'simplest thing' for some women," she informed Carson, annoyed that he'd even think to suggest it. "For some women, that would be the worst course of action to take. Besides," she passionately maintained, "it's a baby, not a mistake."

Taking a breath, she forced herself to calm down. "But all that aside, you can see why she wouldn't want to kidnap my baby. She's already got one on the way to worry about."

"Yes, but a sizable ransom would go a long way to helping her raise that baby," Carson reminded her again.

"Except for one thing," Serena countered.

"What's that?"

"I already offered to *give* Demi money to see her through this, and she turned me down," she told the detective. "She wouldn't just turn around and then kidnap my baby."

He really did want to believe this scenario she'd just told him. "All right, let's just say that for now, you've convinced me—"

"Let's," Serena agreed, a semblance of a relieved smile curving her mouth.

There were other avenues to explore regarding the foiled kidnapping. For now, he went that route. "Do you have any enemies who would want to get back at you by kidnapping Lora?"

"I'm sorry to disappoint you but I don't have any enemies, period," she told him. "At least," she qualified, "none that I'm aware of."

Given her personality, he tended to believe that was true. He tried something else. "How about the baby's father?"

The smile vanished and her face sobered, darkening like a sky just before a winter storm rolled in. "What about him?"

"Would he kidnap Lora?" he asked. "You know, because he wants full custody of her?" He was familiar with cases like that and they left a bad taste in his mouth, but that didn't change the fact that they existed. "If you give me his name and where I can find him, I'll go question him, see if we can rule him out."

"I'll give you his name," she willingly agreed, "At least the one he gave me, but it's an alias," she told him. "And I have no idea where you can find him. Besides, even if you *could* find him, you'd be wasting your time asking him if he tried to kidnap Lora."

"And why is that?" Before she answered him, Carson read between the lines. "You're telling me he doesn't want to be a father?"

Serena's laugh was totally without a drop of humor. "I don't know what he wants to be, other than a full-time thief." She took the dishes over to the sink and began rinsing them.

Carson came up behind her. "You know you're going to have to give me more details than that," he told her.

She didn't look at Carson at first. She just braced her hands against the sink, desperately trying to center herself. "You're not going to be satisfied until you make me wind up spilling my insides to you, are you?"

His tone softened just a little. "I have no interest in your private life, Serena, but there's more at stake here than just your pride," he told her.

Serena closed her eyes for a moment, trying to separate herself from the words she was about to say. And then she turned around to tell Carson what he was waiting to hear.

"I was out of town at one of the region's bigger horse auctions. We were both bidding on the same horses. When I outbid him, he asked if he could buy me a beer to celebrate. A number of beers and whiskeys later, we were in my room, discussing the finer points of a horse's flanks," she said wryly.

"The next morning, I woke up to find that he was gone, along with all the cash in my wallet and my credit cards." She tried her best to keep the edge of bitterness out of her voice, but some of it came through. "I thought that was the worst of it—until three months later when I found that I was pregnant. And, like I said, the name he gave me was an alias so there was no way I could get in touch with him and tell him that he was about to become a father. He probably still doesn't know—and that's fine with me."

Offering comfort had never been something he was good at. Right now, Carson found himself wishing that it was. "I'm sorry."

She raised her eyes to his. "For asking?"

"No," he said honestly, "for what you went through."

That caused her to instantly rally—and grow slightly defensive. "Don't be. Lora's the most important person in my life and if I hadn't gone through all that, she wouldn't be here. She's my silver lining."

He took his cue from that. "I'm sure she is. And I'm going to keep you both safe." He said it matter-of-factly, but it was a promise, one that he intended to stand by.

"Thank you for that," she told him, her voice growing a little raspy. "If I ever lost her, I don't know what I'd do or how I'd ever recover from that."

The very thought of that happening caused tears to form in her eyes. Serena was immediately embarrassed about being so vulnerable in front of someone, especially in front of the detective.

"Sorry, you don't need to have me carrying on like a hysterical female. Go about doing whatever you're supposed to be doing," she told him, turning away so Carson wouldn't see the tears that she couldn't seem to stop from falling.

He stood there for a moment, watching her shoulders as they moved ever so slightly. He knew she was crying, and he hated that he had inadvertently caused that. He was torn between pretending he didn't notice and trying, ineptly, to comfort her.

But he was afraid that if he took her into his arms, strictly to comfort her, something of an entirely different nature might result.

However, he couldn't bring himself to just callously walk out, either. So he plucked a napkin from the napkin holder on the table and handed it to her.

"Thought you might need this," he murmured as he and Justice left the room.

Carson and his canine partner made the rounds on the ranch, covering the perimeter outside the mansion first. Urging Justice over to where the would-be kidnapper had jumped from Serena's balcony, he had the canine carefully survey the entire area, looking for a scent that would lead the dog to find whoever had made the inept attempt.

Justice suddenly became alert, finding a scent and eagerly following it for approximately a quarter of a mile where the scent, from the K-9's reaction, began to fade. Right next to a set of tire tracks.

Carson cursed under his breath, frustrated. Whoever the kidnapper was, he'd apparently made his escape via some sort of vehicle. Most likely a Jeep from the looks of them, he guessed.

The Jeep had driven onto a gravel road several yards away and that was where both the tire tracks and the scent abruptly ended.

Justice moved around in circles, looking as frustrated as he felt, Carson thought.

"You did your best, Justice," he told the dog. "But if the guy's stupid enough to come back, we'll be ready for him and he can kiss his sorry butt goodbye."

It occurred to Carson as he continued covering the grounds, looking for another lead or clue, that he was no longer referring to the person who had invaded Serena's home as "she."

"How about that?" he muttered to himself.

He supposed that Serena had finally won him over. Despite the necklace and the name written beside his brother's body, he was beginning to consider that Demi Colton was not behind any of this. Maybe Serena was right.

Maybe someone *was* trying to frame her.

With Demi out of the running—for now, he qualified—that brought him back to square one and a world full of possible suspects.

Carson dug in.

He spent the rest of the day questioning ranch hands to see if any of them had heard or seen anything last night that could help him identify who the potential kidnapper was.

As he'd expected, none of the hands had anything in the way of positive information to offer. The one thing he came away with was that they all sounded as if they were eager to help. They all seemed to like Serena.

"Hell, she doesn't treat us like we're dirt under her fingernails, like her mama does," one of the hands, Jake Rowan, confided when he was out of Anders's earshot.

"She's fine with working right alongside of us," Ramon Del Campo, another hand, told Carson. "You need anything to help find whoever took that shot at her, you let us know."

Carson nodded. For the most part, he'd found that when civilian volunteers got involved, things became more dangerous, not less. But wanting to foster this display of goodwill, he made a point of thanking each of the ranch hands before moving on.

During the course of the day, while conducting the interviews, Carson also checked in a number of times on Serena. She was working with the horses in the stable and the corral under the watchful eyes of several ranch hands at any one time. It put his mind somewhat at ease about her welfare.

Carson also stopped at the house to make sure that Lora was safe. Alma seemed capable enough, but the housekeeper, although quite sturdy, wouldn't be a match for anyone who chose to overpower her. Carson directed a couple of the ranch hands to keep watch outside the house, both front and back. They had instructions to fire off a round to get his attention in case someone they didn't know tried to get into the house.

Dusk was just setting in and he was bone tired as he walked into the mansion. Serena was in the living room, sitting on the sofa with Lora on her lap.

"So how are you?" Carson asked, crossing over to her.

"Tired. Why?" Serena asked warily. It was obvious that she thought he was about to spring something on her.

Carson shrugged, thinking that maybe he shouldn't have said anything. But he had had enough of isolating himself the way he'd been doing these last few years. A man shouldn't have to live like that, he silently argued.

He forced himself to continue. "It's just that when I left this morning, you seemed kind of upset. I just want you to know that I wasn't trying to pry."

He definitely wasn't the kind to pry, Serena thought. If anything, he was the kind to encourage building up barricades. Barricades kept him safe from making any personal contact.

"I know that," she said.

Carson forced himself to go on. "I just wanted to rule out the possibility of Lora's father kidnapping her, either for the ransom or because he just wanted custody of the baby."

"I know that, too," she replied quietly. She didn't want to talk about what amounted to a one-night stand. "Could we change the subject?"

He wasn't finished yet. "In a minute."

Annoyed, she asked, "What else do you want to ask me?"

"Right now, nothing," he answered. "I just felt that since I burrowed into your life, making you uncomfortable, I should tell you something about mine so we're on equal footing."

She didn't quite understand where this was going, but she felt she had to tell him that, "I have no desire to make you feel uncomfortable."

"Yeah, well, then, maybe I feel that I owe this to

you," he said. This was hard for him, but he felt he needed to share this with someone and if anyone would understand what he'd gone through, it would be Serena. "Just listen, okay?"

"Okay," she agreed, hoping he wasn't about to tell her something that she was going to regret hearing. "Talk."

Chapter 16

Carson thought of sitting down before he spoke, then decided that he would rather be on his feet when he told Serena what he had been keeping to himself for such a long time.

For some inexplicable reason, standing made him feel less vulnerable and more in control of a situation.

The silence began to deepen.

It is now or never, he told himself.

"I was in a relationship—" he began slowly.

"'Was' or 'are'?" Serena wanted to know.

Despite the fact that she was having feelings for him, it occurred to her that she had no idea about Carson's actual personal life, knew nothing about him at all outside of the fact that he worked for her brother. If Carson had someone in his life, she needed to know now, before anything went any further.

Before her feelings went any deeper.

She'd been blindsided by a good-looking man before and she didn't intend for that to ever happen to her again. Carson might be here at the mansion for the sole purpose of keeping her and Lora safe, which was quite admirable of him, but that still didn't mean that the man wasn't out to further his own personal agenda.

"Was," Carson told her, stressing the word. "Her name was Lisa," he added, knowing that Serena, like most women, would want to know that. "We were starting to get really serious when she told me that she was pregnant."

Haunted by her own memories, Serena's back automatically went up. "Let me guess, you dropped her like a hot potato."

"No," Carson replied, then further surprised her by saying, "I asked her to marry me, but she wouldn't. Said she needed time so that she could work some things out."

"And?" Serena asked, fully expecting Carson to tell her that he then had his own second thoughts and used the time to make his getaway.

"She took a *really* long time thinking," he continued stoically, "and while she was doing all this thinking, the baby decided to come early. Lisa went into premature labor." There was a great deal of emotion brimming in his voice as he told her, even though he was doing his best to keep that emotion at bay. "I didn't find out until after the fact."

Serena grew very quiet, waiting for him to finish his story. At this point, she no longer knew what to think or where this was going. All she knew was that he sounded extremely sad.

Carson avoided looking at her. "I got to the hospital just before Lisa died," he said quietly.

"I'm so sorry." Moved, Serena reached over and covered his hand with hers in an effort to offer comfort. "And the baby?"

"It was a girl." His eyes met hers. "She died the next day."

Serena felt her heart twisting in her chest. For a moment, she couldn't even breathe. "Carson—"

He shrugged away her pity and whatever condolences she was trying to convey.

"These things happen," he told her gruffly. "I didn't tell you this to get your pity. Since you felt I was digging into your life, I wanted to tell you something about mine so that you didn't feel like you were the only one who was exposed." He nodded toward the baby. "I think you'd better get her up to her room," he told her. "She's asleep."

"In a moment," Serena answered.

She rose to her feet and placed Lora in the cradle by the sofa, then walked over to Carson. She had sworn to herself that she had absolutely no time for any meaningless dalliances with men. As far as she was concerned, her life was full just the way it was, with her daughter and her work. Good-looking men were nothing but trouble.

But there was something in Carson Gage's eyes that not only moved her, it spoke to her.

As he was telling her about his unsuccessful relationship and the newborn who had died, even though he'd tried to turn away, she'd seen indescribable pain in his eyes. That was something that couldn't be faked.

She found herself pushing aside her own situation, her own barriers, and wanting to comfort him. At least that was what she told herself.

Before she could think it through, she'd moved closer to Carson and in the next heartbeat, she found herself raising her face up to his and kissing him.

Everything became blurry.

She wasn't even sure if Carson met her halfway or if he had just stood very, very still and allowed her to make the final move.

All she knew was one moment her heart was reaching out to him, the next her mouth was sealed to his.

But while she might have started the kiss, Carson certainly completed it.

His arms went around her, drawing her even closer to him as the kiss deepened to the point that she felt as if she was falling headlong down into a wide, bottomless abyss.

She caught herself clinging to him, trying to keep the room from spinning so fast that she lost her balance. So fast that she lost all perspective.

Carson was the one who ended the kiss, drawing back from her.

She looked at him in dazed surprise.

His pulse was racing faster than the car he'd once taken for a joyride years ago. Part of him, the part that belonged to the reckless teen he'd once been, wanted to take her right here and make love to her. Wanted her so badly, he physically ached.

But he wasn't that reckless teenager anymore, he was a police detective with responsibilities. That meant that he couldn't allow his desires, no matter how strong they were, to dictate his behavior.

Taking hold of Serena's shoulders, he looked into her eyes. "You don't want to do this," he told her.

Serena's heart was hammering so hard, she found that she could hardly breathe. With slow, measured words, she told Carson, "I'm only going to say this once. I'm going to go upstairs to put the baby to bed. After that, I'm going to my room. If you want me, you know where to find me."

She wasn't sure exactly how she managed to walk over to the cradle. It almost felt like she was having an out-of-body experience. She could see herself doing it. Her legs felt so wobbly, she was certain she'd collapse on the floor before she got to the baby.

But she didn't collapse. She made it to the baby's cradle.

Digging deep for strength, Serena picked Lora up in her arms.

With the sleeping baby cradled in her arms and operating on what amounted to automatic pilot, she went to the staircase and slowly made her way up the stairs. All the while, Serena kept praying for two things: that the baby would go on sleeping and that Carson would come upstairs.

Reaching the nursery, she went in and very gently placed her daughter down in the crib. She stood there for a moment, watching Lora sleep. Then, leaving the door between the two rooms opened just a crack, she tiptoed out again and went into her own bedroom.

Her hands were actually shaking as she shed her clothes and then slipped on a nightgown. It was her favorite nightgown, a soft, light blue garment that looked and felt as if it had been spun out of gossamer angel wings.

She looked down at the nightgown. *That's it, Serena. Play hard to get. You're going to wind up with gooseflesh, waiting for a man who isn't going to show up.*

Her heart stopped the very moment she heard the light rap on her door. The roof of her mouth felt so dry, she could barely get the two words out.

"Come in."

The next moment, the door slowly opened and then Carson slipped into the room. He closed the door behind him but made no move to come closer.

Instead, he remained where he was, as if second thoughts had immobilized him.

But he wasn't having second thoughts. He was looking at Serena. His gaze washed slowly over her. She looked like a vision.

Serena was standing next to her bed. The light she'd left on shone right through her nightgown, leaving very little to the imagination.

His imagination took flight anyway.

Carson had no idea how he didn't wind up swallowing his own tongue.

"It's cold tonight. You're going to wind up freezing to death," he told her in a voice that was so low, it was hardly audible.

"Not if I find a way to keep warm," Serena answered him.

Was he going to turn away? Had she made a terrible mistake? She refused to allow her mind to go there.

Her eyes never left Carson's face, waiting for him to make a move. Praying it was the right one.

And then, because he could resist her for only so long, because he needed what Serena was offering him, needed it not just physically but emotionally as well, he cut the distance between them and swept her up in his arms.

This was wrong and he knew it, but he just couldn't help himself. "I should have my head examined," he whispered.

"Later," she said just before she brought her mouth up to his.

His last ounce of resistance disappeared, evaporating in the heat that had just flared up between them as her body pressed up against his.

Any last efforts he might have put forth to talk her out of what they were about to do vanished, burned away to a crisp as one kiss mushroomed into another.

And another.

It was hard for him to say which of them was more eager for this to happen. Up until now, he'd thought of himself as a tower of restraint. But faced with her eager mouth trailing along his face, his neck, his throat, restraint shattered into more pieces than he could ever possibly count.

When Lisa had died, followed by the death of their daughter, Carson had felt like a man who had been literally gutted. He became merely a shell of a man who was just going through the motions of pretending to still be alive. He walked, he talked, he got things done, but he simply didn't feel.

Not a single thing.

But now, tonight, with Serena in his arms like

this, he felt as if he had suddenly been brought back from the dead.

And it felt incredibly wonderful to realize that he was alive.

Carson couldn't remember stripping off his clothes. There was a vague awareness that Serena had helped, but he couldn't say that for sure. All he knew was that the clothes had been in his way and he'd got free of them as quickly as possible.

The diaphanous web that Serena'd had on was discarded as well, becoming a shimmering, barely blue heap on the floor next to his clothes.

Then there was nothing left between them except for unresolved passion.

Pulling her against him, Carson exulted in the intoxicating feel of Serena's bare skin heating against his.

His hands traveled along the length of her body, caressing, stroking, glorying in the softness that had him all but drunk with desire.

He made love to her a hundred different ways, his lips trailing along the curves and swells of her supple form, lingering over her breasts, her hips, working his way slowly down to the very core of her.

When she suddenly gasped and reared, grabbing hold of the comforter beneath her and all but shredding it, Carson lingered longer. He used his tongue, his lips and his very breath to bring her up and over into a climax that had her biting her lip to keep from crying out his name and waking up the baby.

When he moved up along her body again, Serena was all but numb for a moment.

And then, as if suddenly infused by a bolt of sheer energy crafted out of her ecstasy, Serena reversed their positions, straddling him. Working magic she hadn't known that, until this very moment, she was capable of.

With carefully calculated movements, she teased his body until she managed to bring him close to the brink of fulfillment.

Carson caught her hand, stilling it. Then, with his eyes on hers, he switched their positions again until he was over her.

His eyes holding her prisoner, he parted her legs and entered.

But where she expected an overpowering thrust, Carson delivered a gentle, determined one instead. The thrusts became magnified and increased with every movement thereafter until they were both moving so fast, she found herself as breathless as he was.

They raced up the steep incline together, silently focused on mutual satisfaction.

She clung tightly to him and then it happened. The final plunge that sent them into a star-filled euphoria that exploded, then embraced them as the stars showered down around them.

Her heart was pounding so incredibly hard, Serena didn't think she was going to be able to ever catch her breath again, to ever have her heart slow down to a decent rate.

It didn't matter. At that moment, it didn't matter. If this was the way she was going to exit the world, so be it.

And then, slowly, the world came back into focus. The room took on form and dimensions, and just like that, she was back in her bed again.

Back in her bed but not alone.

Serena knew she should say something, but she didn't want to.

Not yet.

Right now, all she wanted to do was lie there and feel the heat of his body mingling with hers, feel his heart hammering as hard as hers.

Listen to the sound of his ragged breathing as it echoed hers.

Later there would be time for all the other things. For words and for the inevitable regrets that were bound to follow in their wake.

But right now, at this very moment, she wanted to pretend that she lived in a perfect world and that every glorious thing that had happened just now would continue to happen.

Given enough time.

As his euphoria slowly dissolved, he realized that Serena was being extremely quiet. Had he hurt her?

Had she gone into some kind of shock over what had just happened between them?

Or was that fear that had immobilized both her tongue and her body this way?

Carson wanted to reassure her. To say something to make her feel better about what had just transpired between them—something that he thought was wonderful—but for the life of him, he didn't know how.

So for now, he chose to take the easy out.

He remained silent, just listening to her breathe.

And wishing that there was a way to make this moment last if not forever, then at least for a long, long time.

Chapter 17

She was alone.

Serena could sense it even before she opened her eyes to verify if that the sinking feeling in the pit of her stomach was true.

Carson had gone.

After a night of what she felt was the most incredible lovemaking she had ever experienced, Carson had slipped out of her bed while she was asleep, disappearing from her room without a word.

Exactly the way that the man who had fathered Lora had done.

Disappointment raked long, sharp fingernails across Serena's soul, scarring her. Making her want to throw things.

Making her want to cry.

She rubbed the heel of her hand against her eyes, wiping away tears before they had a chance to fall. How could she have been so stupid, so wrong about someone? Yet here she was, alone in bed, so there was no other conclusion left for her to draw except that Carson was just like every other male on the face of the earth: self-centered.

He had seen his opportunity and he'd taken it without a single qualm.

Serves you right for being such a blind idiot, Serena upbraided herself. *Now, just stop feeling sorry for yourself and get over it!* she silently ordered. *You've got a baby depending on you, that's the only thing that matters here.*

The second she thought of her daughter, Serena realized that Lora had been unusually quiet during the night. Was there something wrong? Or had the housekeeper got up early and gone to the nursery to look after the baby?

She's a better mother than I am, Serena thought, feeling ashamed of herself. She should have been thinking about Lora, not about her own long-suppressed needs and desires.

What was wrong with her? she silently demanded, annoyed with herself.

Kicking aside her covers, Serena suddenly realized that she still had nothing on. Swearing softly, she grabbed a robe in lieu of a nightgown and quickly made her way to the nursery.

Softly opening the door so as not to wake her daughter on the outside chance that Lora actually *was* asleep, Serena looked into the room.

And stopped dead.

Carson was sitting in the rocking chair with Lora in his arms, quietly rocking her. Not only that, but he was feeding the baby a bottle. He'd obviously found one of the formula bottles that were kept in the miniature refrigerator for just these sort of midnight feedings. She'd put them there so that there'd be no need to go all the way down to the kitchen while she was half-asleep. A bottle warmer stood on the counter and she could see that it had been pressed into use, as well.

Justice lay on the floor right in front of Carson's feet. The German shepherd had raised his head the moment she walked in, alerting Carson to her presence.

When he looked at her over his shoulder, Serena asked, "What are you doing?"

It absolutely stunned her at how very right this incredibly domestic scene seemed.

"Lora was hungry. I didn't want her to wake you up, so I got a bottle to feed her," Carson answered simply.

If he knew Lora was hungry, she must have been

crying. Guilt took a bite out of her. She should have been up at the first whimper.

"How did I not hear her crying?" she asked, puzzled.

"I think probably because you were pretty exhausted at the time," Carson told her, his voice low, soothing.

She knew he didn't mean it this way, but she felt patronized. "And you weren't?" she challenged.

Was Carson saying that even though he'd worn her out, he was still full of energy and ready to go? In either case it seemed that of the two of them, he made a better mother than she did.

"I'm used to sleeping with one eye and one ear open, remember?" he reminded her. "I heard Lora stirring and making noises, so I figured it was just a matter of time before she'd start crying. I thought you might appreciate sleeping in for a change. My guess is that you haven't had a decent night's sleep in a while now."

He talked as if he knew what new mothers went through. Pretty insightful for a man who had never been married, she thought.

"I haven't," she admitted, staring at him as if he had just suddenly acquired a halo.

This, to her, was almost better than the night they had just spent together. That had been wondrous, but this spoke of a type of kindness that she knew wasn't all that common. It touched her heart in ways that their lovemaking hadn't.

Serena roused herself before she melted completely. "I'd better change her," she said, moving closer to take Lora from him.

He rose but not to turn the baby over to her. Lora had fallen asleep midfeeding, and he wanted to place her in her crib.

"Already taken care of," he said.

He was telling her that he had actually changed Lora's diaper. She stared at Carson again, stunned speechless.

Finding her tongue, she said, "I don't believe you."

"The old diaper's in the covered pail," he told her, nodding to the container next to the changing table. "You can check if you want to."

Serena was almost tempted to do just that. Pressing her lips together, she could only shake her head in wonder. "How did you—"

He grinned. "It's not exactly rocket science, and despite what you might think, I'm not an idiot. Disposable diapers, wipes, lotion, a secured place to do the changing and voilà," Carson rattled off in a low whisper. "No big mystery."

He placed the sleeping baby back into her crib and quietly withdrew from the nursery.

Leaving the door open just a crack as he entered Serena's suite, he turned toward her. "When

I was with Lora just now, I had a chance to do some thinking."

He was about to tell her what had occurred to him while he'd been rocking and feeding Lora, but he never got the chance. Because the moment he'd turned toward her, Serena threw her arms around him and sealed her mouth to his in an expression of utter gratitude.

Whatever he was going to say was lost for the next hour as they once again became reacquainted with just how very in sync they were with one another.

Lovemaking begot lovemaking.

Finally, tottering on the edge of exhaustion, they lay next to one another, wrapped in the last fragments of soul-comforting euphoria. Carson drew her a little closer to him.

He was in total awe of how she seemed to be able to unlock all these feelings within him, feelings that had him wanting to protect her and her baby, not just as a member of the police department, but as a man. A man who hadn't realized just how very lonely and alone he'd been until last night.

So, with one arm tightly around her, he stroked Serena's hair, content to remain that way for as long as humanly possible.

That was exactly the moment that Serena chose to raise her head from his chest and look up into his eyes. "You said something about you thinking of something while you were feeding Lora. What was it?"

It took him a moment to recreate that moment. Making love with Serena had a way of clouding his brain and making everything else vanish.

And then he remembered. "A while back you mentioned something about seeing the Larson brothers riding around on your ranch."

She recalled the incident perfectly, as well as the cold shiver that had gone down her spine. "They were. They told Anders that they were thinking about getting their own place and just wanted to take a look around ours."

"Did you believe them?" He thought he knew the answer to that, given her tone of voice, but he just wanted to be sure.

"No," she retorted with feeling. Rising above the last of the intoxicating feeling that making love with Carson had created, she was now focused on telling him about how she'd felt seeing the Larsons skulking around her ranch. "I couldn't shake the feeling that they were somehow casing the Double C Ranch. You know, getting the lay of the land, things like that."

Carson filled in what she wasn't saying. "So a kidnapper would know what he was up against and which way he needed to go to make a quick getaway once he had the baby."

The very thought filled her with horror. Serena was fully alert now and sitting up. She put into words what he hadn't said yet. "Do you think one of them tried to kidnap Lora?"

He'd already discarded that idea—in part. "Probably too risky for one of them to make the actual attempt. They don't like putting themselves on the line like that. But that doesn't mean they wouldn't send someone else to do it."

He saw Serena's eyes widen and he wished he didn't have to be the one to tell her this. But he knew she wasn't the type who wanted to be kept in the dark. Serena was better off being made aware of all the possibilities.

"Your father's a powerful man around here, Serena, not to mention wealthy. Kidnapping Judson Colton's grandchild would mean a fast payoff for the Larsons." He could see that he'd struck a nerve and he was quick to reassure her. "Don't worry, I'm not going to let anything happen to you or to Lora."

She wanted him to focus on Lora, not her. "I can take care of myself, Carson," she told him. "But you can't be everywhere, and Lora's just a baby."

"How do you feel about protective custody?" he wanted to know. "I can have one of the K-9 officers take her to an undisclosed location and watch over her."

"And Alma," Serena added. "I want Alma to go with Lora."

"You would be the more logical choice to go with Lora," Carson pointed out.

"I know," she admitted, but she just couldn't indulge herself that way. She had responsibilities here, as well. Responsibilities to the ranch. "But Anders can't watch over everything on the ranch on his own. Besides, I can't just abandon the horses. As much as I hate to think about this, there's no telling just how long it'll take you to find this would-be kidnapper," she said. And then she added hopefully, "Maybe you scared him off and he's long gone by now."

He shook his head. "We can't count on that. I'll call Finn and tell him that you've agreed to protective custody—for Lora," he added quickly when he saw the protest rise to her lips. "He'll have one of the detectives come out to the ranch and pick up Lora and your housekeeper," he said. "Meanwhile, I suggest you go tell Alma that she's in for a change of scenery for the time being."

Serena was already up and slipping her robe back on. She quickly crossed back to the nursery in order to get together some things for Lora to use for her protective custody stay.

"Alma loves the baby," she told Carson just as she was about to leave the room. "She'll go anywhere if it means keeping Lora safe."

When he made no answer, she turned around to look at Carson, but he had already left her suite.

"Man moves like smoke," she murmured, shaking her head.

She focused on packing a suitcase for Lora.

* * *

Carson admitted to himself that he was operating purely on a hunch. The other day he'd searched only some of the ranch hands' studio apartments, the ones that had been opened to him. But there were other living quarters that he hadn't looked into. At the time, he had been strictly searching for some sign of Demi.

But now, since he believed that perhaps the Larson brothers were somehow involved in this unsavory business, he needed to look through all the ranch hands' quarters, looking for anything that might connect the brothers to the botched kidnapping attempt and/or the equally unsuccessful attempt on Serena's life.

He was keenly aware of the fact that he had a myriad of questions and so far, no answers, but he had nothing to lose by pushing ahead with this search.

Because the ranch hands were working on the ranch that belonged to Judson Colton, they had no right to an expectation of privacy. They had all signed contracts to that effect when they came to work on the Double C; the thinking being that if any of the ranch hands decided to take it into their heads to steal something—anything at all—from the ranch, a search of their living quarters would be conducted at any time to find it.

So, after telling Anders what he was about to do and with Justice beside him, Carson went from studio apartment to studio apartment, meticulously searching through everything. It was a case of "I'll know it when I see it" since he had no idea just what he was looking for. He just knew that he needed *something* that would help him connect one of the ranch hands to the Larsons.

For the most part, the search wound up being an uneventful parade of one small messy studio apartment after another. They all looked depressingly alike to him, yielding nothing.

He was close to giving up when Justice suddenly came to life in the next to last studio apartment they entered. The canine barked several times and began trying to dig his way under the ranch hand's bed.

Carson got down on his belly and, snaking his way under the bed, he found nothing but dust bunnies for his trouble.

"Nothing here, boy," he said, getting back up again and dusting off his knees.

But Justice kept barking.

"Really wish you could talk, Justice," Carson said. "It would make my life a lot easier."

On a hunch, since Justice continued barking at the bed, Carson lifted the mattress up off the box springs. There were a number of large sealed plastic packets tucked between the two pieces that made up the twin bed.

"Well, what do you know? Sorry I doubted you,

boy," he said, gathering up all the packets from their so-called hiding place.

"Hey, what do you think you're doing?" Pete Murphy, a tall, skinny cowboy demanded as he came into the studio apartment behind Carson. "That's my stuff!"

By now there were seven large packets on the floor and Justice was circling the lot, growing more and more agitated.

Carson squatted down to examine one of the packets more closely. "Are you dealing drugs, Pete?" he asked the cowboy.

"Am I— What? Dealing drugs?" he repeated, his voice cracking in the middle. "No, those are mine. For me," he emphasized.

Carson held up the packet he'd been examining. "Are you trying to tell me that you take these for 'recreational' purposes?"

"Yeah, right. Recreational purposes, that's it. Now, give them back!" he demanded, trying to take possession of the packets that were closest to him.

Rising, Carson looked into the ranch hand's eyes, pinning him in place. "You're selling these for the Larsons, aren't you? How much are they cutting you in for?"

"I don't know what you're talking about," the cowboy denied. "They're not cutting me in for anything."

Which meant that the brothers probably had something on the cowboy that they were holding over his head, Carson thought. "You tried to kidnap Serena Colton's baby, didn't you?"

"Kidnap the baby?" Murphy stuttered, growing visibly frightened. "No, I wouldn't do something like that!"

Carson continued to press, "You certainly match the description of the kidnapper who broke into Serena Colton's suite, trying to steal her baby."

Murphy was sweating now. "You're out of your mind! Okay, maybe I do a little business on the side for the Larsons, but it's strictly the drugs—working out here is hard, damn it, and a man can't be faulted for wanting to take the edge off once in a while. But kidnapping? Hell, no way!"

The cowboy suddenly turned and ran, leaving behind the drugs and everything else in his quarters.

For a split second, Carson debated giving chase, but the cowboy was moving pretty fast. Carson decided that it wasn't worth working up a sweat. Instead, he looked down at Justice. The canine was so well trained, he refrained from running after the cowboy until told to do so.

Carson gave his partner the go-ahead.

"Justice, fetch!" was all he had to say. It was the key phrase he used to train the K-9 to stop someone from fleeing the scene.

Murphy got approximately ten feet beyond his studio apartment before the German shepherd caught hold of his boot and brought him down. Justice pinned the cowboy to the ground with the force of his weight.

"Justice, off!" Carson ordered as he calmly walked up to the fallen cowboy. Murphy began to scramble up to his feet, most likely intending to run again. "I wouldn't do that if I were you," Carson advised quietly.

Murphy froze, fearfully eyeing Justice. To anyone watching, it appeared that the German shepherd was eyeing him in return.

Carson took out his handcuffs.

Chapter 18

"Then it's over," Serena said, breathing a sigh of relief.

It felt as if a huge weight had been taken off her shoulders. Carson had sought her out in the stables after he had returned from town, specifically from the police station where he had taken Pete Murphy. The cowboy had been placed under arrest for possession of cocaine with the intent to sell.

Serena was overjoyed when Carson told her about the arrest. "This means that I can bring Lora back to the ranch."

It had only been less than a day since she'd handed her daughter over to the police detective who had taken the baby into protective custody, but it felt as if it had been weeks.

Carson frowned. He hated doing this to Serena, but in all good conscience, he had to. Lora couldn't be allowed to be brought home yet.

"Not so fast," he warned.

She was ready to have Carson take her to wherever her daughter was being held. Her heart sank when he just stood there.

"Why not?" she wanted to know. "You got the guy, right?"

"I'm not so sure about that."

"But those drugs you found in his room tie Murphy to the Larsons," Serena cried. "They're drug dealers. He's working for them."

Carson shook his head. He'd spent two hours interrogating the cowboy, but he'd got nowhere and it frustrated him.

"Murphy claims that he's not working for anyone, that he just bought those drugs from a dealer to sell on his own. He swears he's not working for the Larsons and that he doesn't know anything about a kidnapping."

"But he's lying, right?" Serena cried desperately. "You told me that the Larsons' thugs are afraid of testifying against them. This could just be another example of that."

He felt for her. He knew exactly what she was going through, but that still didn't change anything. "They are, and I've got no doubt that Murphy is selling drugs for the two brothers. I also wouldn't put it past the Larsons to try to steal a wealthy family's baby just to ransom it back to them—"

Serena didn't let him finish. "So I can't bring Lora home yet."

"Not until I get some proof of that," he continued, determined to get his point across even though it really aggravated him to be the bearer of bad news. "I can't charge Murphy with kidnapping, and as much as I would like to, I can't charge the Larsons with conspiracy to kidnap or anything of the kind."

Disappointment spread out all through Serena. She felt as if she was caught up in a nightmare. She wanted to keep Lora safe, but she missed her daughter more than she thought possible.

"So you're telling me that it's *not* over," she concluded, exasperated beyond words.

"Not yet. But soon," he added quickly. "I promise, soon. Until then, Lora's safe and I'm going to keep you safe, as well. And to make sure nothing happens to you, I'm going to have Detective Saunders stay with you," he told her, mentioning another member of the K-9 team. "I'm leaving Justice here with you, too."

Serena had an uneasy feeling he was telling her that he wasn't going to be around. She looked at him suspiciously. "Why? Where are you going?"

"I just got a call from Bo's lawyer, Jonathan Witherspoon," Carson answered. "He told me that he's going to be reading Bo's will to his heirs this afternoon, and I feel I need to be there."

"Out of respect, or because you think he left you something?" Serena wanted to know.

He laughed shortly. He'd long since lost all respect for Bo, and he knew without being told that he wasn't in his brother's will. He had a different reason for attending the reading.

"Neither," he answered. "I want to see who else turns up at the reading and if there are any 'surprises' in the will. Maybe that'll give me some kind of a lead as to who might have actually killed my brother."

She looked at Carson, taking solace where she could find it. "So you don't think it's Demi anymore," she assumed.

He knew how much that meant to Serena and if he was being perfectly honest with himself, he was beginning to have suspicions that someone actually *had* tried to frame Serena's cousin.

"Let's just say I'm more open to other possibilities," he answered.

Serena nodded. She didn't care how he phrased it just as long as he stopped obsessing that Demi was the one who had killed his brother. "Good. What time's the reading of the will?"

"Two o'clock." Carson looked at her, his curiosity aroused. "Why?"

She was already stripping her leather gloves off. "Give me half an hour, and I'll get ready," she said, already halfway out of the stable.

Carson still didn't understand. "Why?" he asked again.

"Because I'm going with you," she answered Carson simply.

Maybe she'd misunderstood him. "There's no need for you to go—" he began.

Carson had been the one to discover his brother's body and since then, she knew that Carson had gone through a lot, even though he kept it all bottled up. She didn't want Carson sitting through the reading of the will by himself. Who knew what emotions he'd wind up dealing with? She wanted to be there for him, to let him know, even silently, that he wasn't alone.

However, she knew that if she began to explain any of this, he would just balk at her reasons. Most likely he'd just tell her to stay here.

Knowing that the detective appreciated minimalism, she merely told him, "Yes, there is," and hoped he'd leave it at that.

Carson was about to argue with her, to insist that there was no reason for him to drag her to the reading. He wouldn't be going himself if Bo had died in his sleep at some ripe old age. There'd be no reason to go then. It was Bo's murder that was forcing him to attend this reading like some undercover voyeur.

Given that, he reconsidered and grudgingly admitted that he needed to have her with him. So he sighed and echoed, "Half an hour," as if putting her on notice that he would wait half an hour and no more. He wanted her to believe that if she took longer, he'd just leave without her—even though he knew he'd wind up waiting for her anyway.

As it turned out, he didn't have to wait.

"Five minutes to spare," Serena told him proudly, sliding into the passenger seat of his car. She looked in the rear of the vehicle and saw that Justice was already in the car. They had *both* been waiting for her to come out. "Is he going to the reading, as well?" she asked. The question was asked only partially tongue in cheek.

"I'm on duty," he told her. "I don't go anywhere without Justice."

Leaning back, she put her hand out for the dog to sniff, then petted his head. "Does the lawyer know you're bringing a 'friend'?"

"I don't think Witherspoon'll mind my bringing you," Carson said, starting up his vehicle.

He didn't fool her, she thought. He knew perfectly well that she was referring to the K-9. But she said it anyway.

"I was referring to Justice. This is a will reading. Mr. Witherspoon might not be prepared to have a German shepherd 'attend' the reading."

"Justice goes wherever I go," he told her matter-of-factly. "We're a team."

"I know that," she said, petting the dog again, "but

some people might not be comfortable having a big German shepherd so close to them."

Carson met her observation with a shrug. "Well, that's their problem, not mine," he told her. "Besides, if they don't have anything to hide, everything'll be all right."

Serena settled back into her seat. "This should be interesting," she said, bracing herself for what the next hour or so held.

Jonathan Witherspoon looked as if he had been born wearing a three-piece suit with a matching shirt and tie. The two or three times that Carson had crossed paths with the lawyer, he got the impression that the word *casual* had no meaning for the tall, angular man who looked at the world through thick, rimless glasses. Sporting prematurely gray hair since he had turned thirty-five, the lawyer was only now approaching the age where his gray hair finally suited him, even though it had begun to thin considerably.

When Carson arrived with Serena for the reading of the will, the folding chairs that Witherspoon had his administrative assistant set up in his office were almost all taken. There were only a few remaining empty seats.

Carson guided Serena in first and took a chair on the aisle so that he could easily hold on to Justice. Specifically, he wanted to see if Justice would react to anyone at the reading. He'd always felt, right from the beginning, that Justice seemed to be able to actually *sense* evil. Carson took himself to task for not having brought the dog with him to the bachelor party, despite being off duty. He might have been able to find the killer right then and there and there would be no need for this elaborate game of hide-and-seek.

Witherspoon drew his shallow cheeks in even more than he usually did when he saw the dog sitting beside Carson. The lawyer looked none too pleased about the four-footed attendee, but apparently knew better than to say anything to Carson. He only scowled.

Looking around, Carson noted that Bo's ex-wife, Darby, was seated all the way in the back. Hayley, Bo's fiancée was front and center, just as he had expected her to be. As he watched, she turned around twice to shoot dirty looks at Darby.

This, he thought, was really shaping up to be a very interesting afternoon.

Leaning in closer to Serena, he whispered, "You sure you want to be here?"

"You're here, so I'm here," she told him. "Besides," she added, keeping her voice low, "this makes me realize why I like working with horses so much more than working with people."

Carson suppressed a laugh.

The next moment, Witherspoon cleared his throat

rather loudly, indicating that they should all stop talking and pay attention to what he was about to say.

"All right, it looks like we're all here," the lanky lawyer said. He sat down behind his desk as he looked around at the various people who had gathered here in hopes of getting at least a piece of the considerable amount of money that Bo had accrued or, if not that, then a part of his breeding business. "Let's get started, shall we?"

In a monotonous, droning voice that seemed incredibly suited to the lawyer's face and demeanor, Witherspoon read the will in its entirety, stating every single detail that the law required in order for the will to be deemed a binding legal document.

When the lawyer came to the part that everyone had been waiting for—the distribution of Bo's possessions—the reading went far more quickly than anyone had actually anticipated.

"And I leave the entirety of my dog breeding business, as well as my ranch, both located at—" Witherspoon paused to read the address that everyone was well acquainted with, unintentionally stretching out the drama.

Almost everyone in the room had leaned forward. No one wanted to miss a single syllable of this part.

"—to my ex-wife, Darby Gage. I hope that this will make up for some of the things that I put you through, Darby."

"No!" Hayley screamed, all but going into shock.

She jumped to her feet, knocking over the folding chair she'd been sitting in and discarding any and all pretense of grief. "There's got to be some kind of a mistake," she cried glaring accusingly at Witherspoon.

Witherspoon maintained his composure. It was obvious to Serena that the lawyer had to have been the target of angry heirs before Hayley's vitriolic display.

"I assure you that there's no mistake. I was there when Bo signed this." Holding up the last page of the document he'd been reading from, he displayed a seal. "It's been notarized."

"I don't care if it was signed by all the saints in heaven and half of Congress. That piece of paper's a fake! Bo would never have done something like this to me! He wouldn't have given that little scheming witch everything!"

Practically choking on her fury, Hayley gave every indication that she was going to lunge at Darby. Her hands went up and her freshly lacquered nails were outstretched, ready to rake over the ex-wife's face. Carson was immediately on his feet and got between his brother's fiancée and his ex-wife.

Justice growled at the woman, ready to take Hayley down on command. Serena had got to her feet as well, waiting to help Carson if he needed it. Since she was a woman, she felt she could restrain Hayley in ways that Carson couldn't.

But he caught Hayley's hands before she could do any damage.

"Settle down, Hayley," he ordered sternly.

"Settle down?" she shrieked, trying to pull free. "Didn't you just hear what Witherspoon just read? Everything's hers! That miserable liar didn't leave me *anything*!"

The more Hayley struggled, the tighter his grip on her hands grew. "You can get a lawyer and contest the will if you feel this strongly about it," he told her, his voice unnervingly calm.

"I'm not getting a damn lawyer," she spit, then retorted, "There are other ways to resolve this injustice!"

Carson immediately cut her short. "Don't say anything you're going to regret," he warned.

"What I regret is wasting my time with that backstabbing, worthless brother of yours," Hayley cried.

Still watching her carefully, Carson released the woman.

Swinging around, Hayley glared at Witherspoon. "You haven't heard the last of this!" she declared.

With that, she stormed out of the lawyer's office, pausing only long enough to spit on the floor right in front of Darby.

For her part, Darby didn't react. She appeared to be absolutely stunned.

The people sitting near her, many of whom had either been bequeathed a nominal sum of money or had learned that they would be receiving nothing at all, murmured among themselves. They filed out of the lawyer's office one by one, many in a state of disbelief.

In the end, only Carson, Serena and Darby were left with Witherspoon.

"Are you all right?" Carson asked his ex-sister-in-law.

He couldn't quite read the expression on Darby's face. It was a cross between what he took to be utter shock and something like subdued joy. He had the feeling that Darby wasn't quite sure exactly where she was right now.

"Fine," she finally managed to reply. And then, as if coming to, she turned to look at Witherspoon. "Did you just say that Bo left *everything* to me?" she asked in total disbelief.

"Why don't you come over here closer to my desk so I don't have to shout?" the lawyer told her, not that he appeared to be capable of shouting.

Rising from the last row, Darby made her way forward, moving in slow motion like someone who wasn't sure if they were awake or caught up in some sort of a dream.

Still looking dazed, she sat down in the single chair that Witherspoon had facing his desk.

The lawyer raised his tufted gray eyebrows and looked over expectantly toward Carson and the woman who was beside him. "I'm going to have to ask the two of you to leave now. I have several details to discuss with Ms. Gage."

Carson nodded. Bo had managed to drop a bombshell, even in death.

Chapter 19

"Well, certainly didn't see that one coming," Carson commented to Serena.

He was driving them away from Witherspoon's office. For all intents and purposes, Justice appeared to have fallen asleep in the back seat the moment they'd taken off.

"Then Bo and his ex-wife weren't on friendly terms?" Serena asked.

She was totally in the dark about Carson's older brother in general beyond the fact that Bo Gage owned a breeding business and supplied the K-9 unit with German shepherds.

"Bo wasn't the type to worry about being on good terms with any of his exes, including his ex-wife,"

Carson told her. "I think it's fair to say that he was always only looking out for himself." As far as brothers went, he and Bo were as different as night and day. "Once Bo got what he wanted, he moved on. When he decided that Darby was cramping his style, he shed her like a snake sheds its skin, without so much as a backward glance. When the marriage ended, he only tossed a couple of crumbs her way and by crumbs, I mean literal *crumbs*. Bo gave her a part-time job cleaning kennels at the breeding business they *both* had once owned."

Serena viewed that as pretty callous, but she did always like to think the best of people. "Maybe it was like Bo said in his will. He felt guilty about the way he'd treated her and this was his way of making it up to Darby."

"Maybe," Carson answered, but he was highly skeptical. Bo wasn't nearly that noble. There had to be some other reason for what he had done.

Serena glanced at him. Carson didn't sound convinced. "You think the will was a forgery?"

Carson thought of the lawyer. "No, the will's real all right. Witherspoon's so conscientious, he would have known if there'd been a substitution or switch. No, I'm thinking something else."

He'd mounted his cell phone on the dashboard when he'd got into the car and he now pressed a button that connected him to his boss's cell. When he heard the deep voice answer, Carson started talking.

"Chief, it's Gage. I think we just might have ourselves another suspect in my brother's murder," Carson told Serena's brother.

"Make this quick, Gage. I'm in the middle of something right now," Finn prompted. "And this better be something more than just an off-the-wall theory."

There was noise on the other end of the line and Carson couldn't quite make it out, but he knew better than to ask. The chief would tell him what was going on if Finn wanted him to know.

"I was just at the reading of Bo's will," he told Finn.

"And?"

He knew he had to cut to the chase, but he felt certain that this would give the chief pause. "You're never going guess who my brother left his ranch and dog breeding business to."

"Well, it's not you because you would have led with giving me your notice," Finn said impatiently. "And I take it that it's not his fiancée because that was what everyone was expecting. Okay, I'll bite. Who did Bo leave his ranch and business to?"

"Darby Gage, his ex-wife."

For a moment, there was nothing but silence on the other end, as if Finn was trying to make heads or tails out of what he'd just been told.

"You're putting me on," he finally cried. From the sound of his voice, Carson surmised that the chief was as stunned as everyone else at the reading had been. "Seriously?"

"Seriously," Carson confirmed. "You realize what this means, don't you?"

"Yeah, I realize," Finn answered with a heavy sigh. "You're right. We just got ourselves another suspect." He had a question for Carson. "You think your ex-sister-in-law knew she was getting everything?"

Carson told the chief what he'd observed upon coming into the office. "I don't think she even knew she was in the will. From what I gathered, she was only there because Witherspoon told her to be there."

"Well, what do you know," Finn murmured more to himself than to Carson. "This certainly expands our playing field, doesn't it?"

"That's what I was thinking," Carson replied, glad he and Finn were on the same page.

Listening in on Carson's part of the conversation, Serena couldn't hold her tongue any longer.

Raising her voice so that her brother could hear, she said, "Maybe Darby found out about the will and she decided to kill Bo to get her hands on the business—and to pay him back for the way he'd treated her. To cover her tracks, she could have framed Demi for the murder out of spite. You know, as gruesome as it sounds, dipping Bo's finger in his own blood and guiding it to write Demi's name. That way you'd find the blood under his fingernail."

Carson nodded in agreement. That sounded about right to him. "Did you hear that?" he asked, addressing Finn on the cell.

"Is that my sister?" Finn wanted to know. There was a note of confusion in his voice.

"Yeah, she's right here in the car," Carson answered. Knowing Finn wanted more detail, he added, "She insisted on coming to the reading of the will with me."

He heard Finn laugh shortly.

"That's pretty good. Maybe she should be working at the police department instead of with the horses," Finn said.

"No, thank you," Serena said, speaking up. "Horses don't have agendas."

"You want me to bring Darby in for questioning?" Carson asked him.

"No, she's your ex-sister-in-law. You're too close to this," Finn answered. "Let's keep this all above reproach. I'll have Galloway bring her in."

"While you're at it, maybe you should have another go at the 'eyewitness,'" Carson suggested. "It's entirely possible that someone looking to frame Demi paid Paulie Gains off to say that he saw Demi fleeing from the area just before Bo's murder."

"For that matter, if we're considering possibilities, Darby could have put on a red wig and pretended to be Demi as she ran from the crime scene," Serena chimed in.

"Yeah, maybe," Finn agreed. "Anything else happen at the reading, Gage?"

"Yeah, I think you might want to consider putting Darby into protective custody. Bo's fiancée looked like she could have killed Darby with her bare hands once she heard that Darby was inheriting practically everything. Unless you've got any objections, I think I'm going to go and have a word with Hayley, see if she had any clue that this was coming. She looked surprised, but you never know."

"Sure. Go talk to her and get back to me on that," Finn told him.

"Right." As he was about to end the call, a thought occurred to Carson. "Oh, any word on Demi?" he asked.

"There've been a few so-called Demi-sightings in the area, but nothing that panned out. The rest of the team's still out there, looking for her. But now that you've told me about the will, I'm thinking we're going to be changing the focus of our search. At least for the time being. Get back to me if you find out anything," Finn told him again, then terminated the call.

"So we're going to see Hayley?" Serena asked as soon as she heard her brother end the call.

"*I'm* going to see Hayley," Carson corrected. "*After* I take you back to the Double C."

But Serena had other ideas. Now that she'd finally got out, she wanted to help Carson. The sooner all this was resolved, the sooner she could get her daughter back and life could return to normal.

"I think I should come with you," she told him, sounding a lot more confident than he'd anticipated. "Hayley looked like she wanted to kill someone. She won't kill you if there's a witness."

"Or she could kill the witness, too," he pointed out, momentarily indulging in some black humor.

"There's safety in numbers," Serena reminded him. "Besides, I'm not as fragile as I look."

A smile curved his mouth. He thought of the other night. Delicate, yes, but definitely not fragile. Still, out loud he told her, "Good to know."

She got the feeling that he wasn't talking about anything that had to do with Hayley.

They found Bo's former fiancée at home. As they approached her house, they heard the sound of breaking glass and crockery and Hayley yelling at the top of her lungs.

Carson decided to leave Justice in the car for everyone's safety. He didn't want to get the dog unnecessarily agitated. There might be unforeseen consequences of that.

He cracked the windows before turning his attention to the screamfest in Hayley's house.

Still apparently grappling with the huge disappointment she'd just experienced, Hayley Patton was calling Bo every name in the book. And with each name, she hurled another breakable object against the wall.

Carson hesitated and looked at Serena. "Maybe you should stay outside," he told her.

"The hell I will," she countered. "She can't hit both of us at once."

"That's not exactly a consolation," Carson informed her.

The incensed, newly spurned dog trainer's door was unlocked. Carson pushed it open slowly in order not to attract Hayley's attention. He still just narrowly avoided getting hit by a brightly painted vase that smashed into smithereens after a fatal encounter with the wall just beside the door frame.

"Hey!" Carson cried sternly, pushing Serena behind him so she wouldn't get hurt with any flying debris.

Caught up in her rampage, Hayley swung around to face him and glared. "What the hell do you two want?" she demanded angrily, looking as if she was going to hurl the next object at them.

Since Carson was Bo's brother and possibly a target for Hayley's rage, Serena was quick to take the lead and answer the woman's question. "We just came by to see if you're all right."

"All right?" Hayley echoed incredulously. "Of course I'm not all right! I'm the laughingstock of Red Ridge. That no-good, womanizing jackass made me look like a fool in front of everyone I know."

Angry tears came to her eyes. "We were supposed to get married, damn it! Everything was supposed to be mine, not hers! Mine! How could he just give it away to her like that? Like I didn't matter?" Hayley shrieked.

Serena tried to sound as understanding and sympathetic as possible when she asked, "Did Bo ever do or say anything to make you think that he was going to leave it all to Darby?"

Hayley looked at her as if she was crazy. "You think I would have stayed with him if he so much as *hinted* that he was going to do that?" she demanded. "Looks and charm wear pretty thin pretty fast, even Bo's," she told them. "I was in it for the long haul because I thought I'd be taken care of."

Her face darkened as another wave of fury took hold. "Well, he took care of me all right, that dirty, rotten son of a bitch," she cried, picking up another glass and throwing it against the wall.

Carson and Serena moved out of the way as shattered glass flew everywhere.

Carson stayed a few minutes longer, asking Hayley several more questions in between her tirade and the ongoing cavalcade of objects being hurled against the wall and meeting their untimely demise.

It became very clear that as far as knowing that Bo was about to leave the breeding business and his ranch to another woman, Hayley hadn't had a clue.

* * *

When Carson told her he had to make one more stop before they went back to her ranch, Serena thought he wanted to talk to another possible suspect. Either that or he wanted to talk to her brother about Hayley's meltdown in person.

She didn't know what to think when Carson stopped his car in front of a toy store.

"What are we doing here?" she asked as she followed him inside.

The only thing that occurred to her was that he wanted to buy her daughter a toy, but she sincerely doubted that. At three months of age, Lora's favorite playthings were still her fingers and toes. The baby could spend hours just moving them in front of her face, fascinated by the sight.

The answer he gave her caught her off guard. "I want to buy a doll."

Lora was too young for a doll at this point. "Excuse me?"

"I'm buying a doll," he repeated. Caught up in his plan, Carson realized that there was no way Serena could know what he had in mind, so he explained. "I'm looking for one of those lifelike dolls. You know, the ones that look like a real baby." And then he qualified what he meant. "I'm sure this store doesn't carry one of those really specialized ones that I saw advertised in a catalog, the ones that look and feel like a real baby. Some of them even move when you touch them," he said, recalling the description. "I just want one that's about the size of a three-month-old and lifelike enough to fool a kidnapper."

She felt as if her throat was closing up again. There was only one reason he would be doing this. "You think he's coming back, don't you?"

He hated bringing fear back into her life, but she had to understand that there was still a very real danger of her daughter being kidnapped.

"I'm counting on it," he told her. "Because we're going to set a trap for him so that he stops being a threat to you and Lora." He looked at her and saw that she had grown a little pale. He stopped looking up and down the aisles and put his hands on her shoulders, in essence creating a "safe space" for her. "It's the only way, Serena."

"I know," she answered in a hoarse voice.

Pulling herself together, she joined the search for the perfect doll to use as a decoy. Carson was right. Until the would-be kidnapper was caught, she would continue to live in fear for her daughter—and that really wasn't living at all.

"I didn't realize that they could look *this* lifelike," Carson said. They were back in her room at the Double C and he was looking at the doll that had taken them close to an hour to find and cost a great deal more than he'd expected. "Too bad we couldn't have just rented the damn thing," he commented.

He thought of the receipt in his wallet. "These dolls are expensive."

"That's because a lot goes into making one of them. Touch its face," Serena urged.

"Once was enough, thanks." He'd already done that in the store. That was how he'd decided which doll to pick. When he'd picked up the doll from its display, he found that the doll's actual weight felt as if he had a real baby in his arms. It was damn eerie, he thought.

She couldn't tell if it was the doll's lifelike quality or its expensive price tag that made him more uncomfortable.

"Once this is over, maybe you can take the doll back to the store and get them to refund your money," she suggested.

He glanced at the doll again. "I've got a better idea."

She had no idea where he was going with this. "Oh?"

"Yeah, once this is over, I'll give you the doll for Lora. When she gets bigger, she can pretend it's her baby sister, or whatever it is that little girls pretend when they're playing with baby dolls."

She was both touched and impressed. "That's very generous of you," Serena told him.

Carson shrugged. Praise of any sort always left him feeling uncomfortable, like finding out he'd put on two different boots.

"Beats the hassle of trying to get my money back from a salesclerk," he told her.

He was just making excuses. "You're not fooling me, Detective Carson Gage. You might have everyone else thinking that you're this big, hulking tough guy with a heart of steel, but I know better."

For the time being, the doll and its purpose was forgotten. "Oh, do you, now?"

"Yes, I do. Underneath that scowl of yours is a heart made out of pure marshmallow."

"Marshmallow?" he echoed, amused. "Well, that doesn't sound very manly now, does it?"

"Oh, you're plenty manly," she assured him. "But you're also kindhearted and generous, and that's even more important than being manly."

He found himself getting all caught up in this woman that fate had brought into his life. "That all depends if you're staring down the barrel of a gun— or looking into the deep brown eyes of a woman with the kind of wicked mouth you've spent your whole life dreaming about."

She could feel that excitement generating in her veins, the excitement that he could create just by touching her face.

"Oh? And do I have the kind of wicked mouth you've spent your whole life dreaming about?" she asked him, lacing her arms around the back of his neck.

Carson pulled her to him, fitting her body against his. "What do you think?"

His grin was so sexy, she could hardly stand it. "I think you should stop talking and show me."

"I thought you'd never ask," he said, and the next moment, he did.

Chapter 20

Lying there in the dark beside Serena, Carson was beginning to think that the kidnapper had lost his nerve and wasn't going to make a second attempt to abduct the baby.

Two nights had gone by since the first attempt. It was the third night and still nothing.

Carson had to admit that it was getting harder and harder for him to stay awake, allowing himself to take only ten-minute catnaps every few hours as he waited for the kidnapper to make a reappearance.

Maybe it had been strictly a one-shot deal, he thought. Maybe—

Despite the darkness in the bedroom, he saw Justice suddenly sit up. The canine's entire body looked to be rigid and alert. In addition, Justice's ears were moving so that they were directed toward something he heard coming from Lora's nursery.

Tense now, Carson did his best to noiselessly slip out of bed, but Serena still woke up.

Her eyes were wide as she looked in his direction. "Did you hear something?" she asked in what amounted to a stage whisper.

Carson nodded. "Stay here," he mouthed. There was no mistaking that it was an order.

But Serena slipped out on her side anyway. "You might need help," she told him, her voice so low it was all but inaudible.

"Damn," Carson muttered under his breath, but with no less feeling than if the word had been shouted. He didn't have time to argue with her. This could all go south in the blink of an eye and his window to capture the kidnapper was small.

Aware that there was no way he could get Serena to remain in her room, he waved for her to stay behind him, then made his way into the nursery, his weapon drawn and ready in his hand.

Moving just ahead of his partner, Justice saw the intruder first.

The thin, shadowy figure dressed in black had found a way into the nursery. Carson had wanted to make the nursery accessible but not so accessible that the kidnapper smelled a trap.

The intruder was just leaning over the crib and

about to scoop up what he believed to be the baby. At that moment Justice flew across the nursery, grabbing the kidnapper's arm.

Startled, there was a guttural screech from the man, whether out of pain or surprise was unclear.

Somehow managing to pull free from the canine, the kidnapper tried to barrel out of the room. Moving deftly, Carson was quick to block the man's exit. In doing so, he managed to pull off the intruder's ski mask, exposing his face.

"Mark!"

The cry of recognition came from behind him.

Surprised, Carson looked over his shoulder at Serena. It was just enough to throw his timing off, causing Carson to lose the upper hand. The kidnapper immediately took advantage of the opportunity, grabbing Serena's arm and pulling her against him like a human shield. Out of nowhere, a handgun materialized. The unmasked kidnapper held the muzzle against her temple.

Afraid that the canine would jostle the kidnapper and possibly cause the gun to go off, Carson caught hold of Justice's collar, pulling him back to keep the canine still.

"If you don't want her pretty brains splattered all over the room, you'll put your gun down, cop," the man holding Serena hostage snarled.

"Take it easy," Carson told the intruder, speaking in a tranquil, sedate tone and doing his best to harness both his anger and his fear. He shifted his eyes toward Serena. Wanting to keep her calm, he told her, "It's going to be all right."

"Only if you put your gun down and keep holding on to that dog of yours," the man Serena had called Mark snapped. "Now!"

Still holding on to Justice's collar with one hand, Carson raised the weapon in his other hand, pointing the muzzle toward the ceiling.

"I'm putting it down. Don't do anything you'll wind up regretting," he warned the intruder.

"Same goes for you," the man growled. He cocked the trigger.

"I'm putting it down," Carson repeated more urgently, making an elaborate show of laying the handgun down on the floor beside his foot.

The second that Carson's gun was on the floor, the intruder shoved Serena into him. With a startled cry, she stumbled against Carson and Justice.

Carson caught her before she could land on the floor. "You okay?"

She nodded. "I'm fine. Go, get him," she cried urgently.

Carson ran after the man, but as fast as he was, the foiled kidnapper turned out to be faster. The man fairly flew down the stairs and out the back way. Carson kept going until he reached the nearby creek that ran through the property.

That was where Justice lost the would-be kid-napper's scent.

Carson kept searching the area for another twenty minutes, hoping that Justice would pick up the scent again. But after twenty minutes, he was finally forced to give up.

"It's okay, Justice," he said, calling the dog off. "You did your best. We'll get him next time. Let's go back, boy."

When he returned to mansion and went up to Serena's suite, Carson found that she had got dressed. It was still the middle of the night, but it was obvious that she'd given up all hope of going back to sleep.

The second he entered the room, she ran up to Carson. "Did he get away?" she asked.

Despite the fact that she'd asked that, Serena was nursing the outside hope that he'd caught the man and that he was sitting handcuffed in Carson's car, waiting to be transported to jail.

But one look at Carson's face told her that wasn't the case. Mark had indeed got away from him. The nightmare was to continue.

"Yeah," Carson answered darkly. "He ran through the creek and Justice lost his scent."

"You'll get him, Carson," she said with such conviction, it was obvious that she firmly believed that there was no other way for this scenario to play out.

Carson sat down on her bed. Serena dropped down beside him, her courage flagging.

"Who is he, Serena?" Carson asked. "You called him by his name."

"I called him by *a* name," she corrected. She wasn't sure just what to expect or how Carson would handle being told about her connection to the man. "The one he told me when we met."

Carson shook his head. "Still doesn't answer my question. Who is he—to you?" he specified.

"Someone I thought I'd never see again," she told him.

Serena paused, pressing her lips together. It took her a moment to gather her courage together. What she and Carson had was all still very brand-new and fragile. She didn't want to jeopardize it by throwing this other man into the mix.

But she had no choice.

She took a deep breath and told him, "He's Lora's father."

"Oh."

It was one thing to know that Serena had lost her head one night and got involved in what amounted to a one-night stand. It was another to actually meet the other person who had been involved in that evening.

It took Carson a moment to come to grips with the situation, to deal with what he was feeling—a strong flare-up of jealousy. With effort, he tamped it down and forced himself to put it all into proper perspective.

He blew out a long breath. "Well, it's obvious that he's not looking for a happy reunion between himself and his daughter."

Serena felt relieved and threatened at the same time. Relieved because Carson was taking her side in this. She knew that there were men who would have taken the situation and turned it into an opportunity to revile her for foolishly getting intimately involved with a stranger. The fact that Carson didn't, that he didn't lash out at her or upbraid her, making this all her fault, made her feel incredibly relieved and grateful.

"I know it's no excuse," Serena began, "but I'd had too much to drink and—"

"Stop," Carson said sternly. When she did, looking at him quizzically, wondering if she was wrong about him after all, Carson told her, "You don't owe me an explanation, Serena. Whatever happened between you and that man is in the past. What matters is now. We have to move forward from here—and we've got to get that bastard. Do you have any idea where he lives? Is he local or from out of state?"

"Not a clue," she admitted, embarrassed at her helplessness in this matter.

There were other ways to find things out, Carson thought. "I'll get in contact with the county's forensics team, and they can at least dust your suite for any fingerprints that don't belong. Maybe we'll get lucky and Lora's father is in the system."

Serena nodded. Although she was doing her best to get herself under control, she could feel the tears forming. That just made things worse. She didn't want to cry in front of Carson. Crying was something a helpless female would do, and she refused to see herself as helpless.

But despite her resolve, she couldn't find a way to just blink back her tears.

She could feel her eyes welling up so she turned her head away from him. She cleared her throat and said, "Um, maybe I should go down and make breakfast for us."

Rather than let her leave the room, Carson circled around until he was in front of her, blocking her way out. Taking her face in his hand, he tilted it toward him. Looking at her, his suspicions were confirmed. He wasn't about to ask her if she was crying until he knew for certain.

However now that he saw for himself that she was, he wasn't about to fall into that old cliché and tell her not to cry. He just silently took her into his arms and held her.

"We'll get this SOB and find out what his game is. I promise," he told her.

She pressed her lips together, burying her face against Carson's shoulder.

"I'm not going to cry," she told him, her voice breaking.

"Nobody asked you to," he answered matter-of-factly, trying to lighten the moment for her.

"I just want my life back," she told him.

"I know, and you'll get it back," he said, stroking her hair, wishing there was some way he could really reassure her.

Her sigh created a warmth that penetrated right through his shoulder, causing his stomach to tighten. He was prepared to go on holding her for as long as she needed him to.

But the shrill sound of the landline ringing shattered the moment.

He felt Serena instantly stiffen against him, as if the phone call couldn't be anything positive despite the fact that there could be a whole host of reasons why someone might be calling.

He looked over toward the phone on the white antique desk. "You want me to get that?" he offered.

"No, it's my house," she told him, grateful for his offer but refusing to hide behind it. She wasn't going to allow what was happening to diminish her in any way. She'd always been strong and she intended to remain that way. "I should be the one answering my own phone."

Moving away from the shelter of Carson's arms, she crossed over to the antique desk and picked the telephone receiver. "Double C Ranch."

"I know the name of the freaking ranch," the voice on the other end snarled.

It was him, the kidnapper. She would have recognized the man's voice anywhere. Serena instantly made eye contact with Carson, urging him over.

He was at her side immediately, gesturing for her to tilt the receiver so that he could hear what the caller was saying.

Holding the receiver with both hands, she asked, "What do you want?"

Instead of answering her question, Mark said, "I'm calling to find out what you want."

Still looking at Carson, she shook her head, mystified. "I don't understand."

"All right, I'll spell it out for you," Mark said, irritated. "I'm guessing that you want me to disappear and never bother you and that cute little girl, our daughter, again."

Serena cringed. She wanted to shout at the man and tell him that he had no claim to Lora. That Lora *wasn't* his little girl and never would be, that it took more than a genetic donation to make a father.

But she knew she had to remain calm. If she didn't, then Mark would get the upper hand. So she took a deep breath, and as Carson silently urged her on, she told Mark, "Yes, I do." Taking a shaky breath as she desperately tried to steady her nerves, she asked, "How do I make that happen?"

"Easy." His voice sounded almost slimy, she

thought. "All you have to do is bring me a million dollars."

She hadn't been expecting for him to demand that much. "A million dollars?" she repeated, stunned.

As if sensing her reaction, Mark went on the defensive immediately. "Hey, that's not too much for your peace of mind—and your brat. Not to someone like you. Hell, that's practically like petty cash for your family. A million dollars and I'll go away."

She clutched at that phrase. "For good?" she asked.

"Yeah, sure. For good," he told her. "That sound good?"

"Yes." It also sounded like a lie, she thought. "I don't have that kind of cash readily accessible. I need time to gather it together."

"How much time?" he asked angrily.

Her mind scrambled as she tried to come up with a reasonable answer. "At least a couple of days."

"Too much time," he snapped. "You've got nine hours."

"I can't get that much money in nine hours," she cried, thinking of the logistics that were involved.

"*Find* a way," he retorted. "Unless you want to deal with the consequences."

Her eyes met Carson's. He nodded, mouthing instructions and encouraging her to tell Mark that she'd meet him with the money.

Serena let out a shaky breath. "All right. Where and when?"

"Atta girl, now you're playing the game. I want you to meet me in front of that fancy restaurant in town. The one that just opened up. The Barbecue Barn. Be there at three o'clock. Just you and our daughter," he instructed with a mocking laugh. "Bring the million in unmarked bills in a backpack, the kind that schoolkids use. And make sure you come alone. I see anyone else there, if I see anything out of the ordinary, I promise I'll make you very, very sorry—and our kid'll be playing a harp. Understand, princess?"

He was making her skin crawl, as well as making fear skewer her heart. "I understand. If I get you that money, I don't ever want to see you near my daughter or me again," she said with feeling.

"Why, Serena, after everything we've meant to one another? I'm hurt," Mark said sarcastically. And then his voice became deadly serious. "You bring that money, then yeah, you'll never see me again and you and that cop you got guarding your body can go on playing house to your hearts' content.

"Remember, tomorrow, three o'clock. Unmarked bills in a backpack. You can put the backpack in the kid's stroller so nobody'll get suspicious," he added. "You got that?"

"I've got it." Sensing he was about to hang up, she said, "Wait a minute. How do I know you'll keep your word and disappear after you get your money?"

She heard him laugh on the other end. The sound caused another cold chill to slither up and down her spine.

"Well, honey, you're just going to have to trust me on that," he told her.

"Trust you," Serena repeated. What she wanted to do was rip his heart out and feed it to him, but she forced herself to sound docile.

"Yeah, trust me," he said.

Carson was silently telling her to stay calm. But Lord, she was finding it hard to stay civil. "Okay. I'll hold you to that."

He laughed again, the sound slicing through her this time. "You do that, honey. You just do that."

Chapter 21

Serena didn't remember hanging up the phone. She didn't remember crossing to her bed. She *was* aware of her legs giving out from beneath her so that she wound up collapsing onto it.

The next moment, she felt Carson's arm encircling her shoulders. "By this time tomorrow, it'll all be over," he promised.

His words echoed in her head. In the meantime, she thought, she had all this terrible blackmail to deal with. Had to see that disgusting excuse for a human being again for the handoff.

She just wanted this to be over with. "Maybe I should just pay him off," she told Carson.

He looked at her in surprise. "What are you saying? No, don't even think about doing that," Carson told her sternly. He realized that this was her fear talking, but paying this bastard off was not the way to go, she had to know that.

Serena felt as if she was in between the proverbial rock and hard place. "But if paying him off means getting rid of him—" she began.

He stopped her right there. "But that's just it, Serena. You won't. You won't get rid of him. He'll keep coming back, always asking for more money. Blackmailers never stop blackmailing, Serena. They just keep getting greedier." Carson took hold of her shoulders, looking into her eyes and trying to cut through her fear. He had to get her to understand. "You're going to the bank and taking out just enough to fill the top portion of that backpack he wants you to bring. The rest of it will be filled with cut-up newspapers."

"He also said to bring Lora," she reminded Carson.

"You'll be bringing her stand-in instead," he told Serena, nodding toward the crib in the other room where he'd put the decoy doll. "Don't worry," he said, "I'm going to be with you every step of the way."

Much as she wanted him there, she felt she couldn't risk it. "You heard that bastard. He said if he saw anyone with me—"

"He won't," Carson cut in. "Don't worry. I'm very good at my job," he assured her without any bravado. "And after today, he's never going to bother you again." Very gently, he raised her chin so that her eyes met his. "You believe me, don't you?"

"I believe you," Serena answered, although her voice sounded a little hoarse.

"It'd be better with a little more enthusiasm," Carson said, "but I'll accept that."

He kissed her on the forehead in an attempt to comfort her. His lips migrated down to her cheek, then to her other cheek. Before she knew it, the small act of comfort mushroomed into something much more than that.

For the next hour, Serena found solace in his arms as well as sanctuary from some very real fears that existed just beyond the boundaries of her suite.

"That is one hell of a stroller," Carson commented as he helped her load it into her car later that afternoon.

Because they really weren't sure, despite the fact that the blackmailer said he would meet her in front of the restaurant, exactly where Mark might be hidden, Carson didn't want to take a chance on the blackmailer seeing them come into Red Ridge together. So he was driving his own car to town while Serena was going to Red Ridge in hers.

"How much did you say it cost?" he asked her, still looking at the stroller.

Serena flushed, knowing that the pink stroller was

exceedingly ostentatious. It had been a gift from her mother. Joanelle Colton always needed to make a big show out of everything, even something as simple as a stroller. Ordinarily Serena wouldn't have accepted it, except that after what her mother had put her through, she felt the woman did owe her something. The stroller was her mother's way of apologizing. Throwing money at something had always been preferable for her mother than admitting to a mistake.

She'd seen the price tag. There was no doubt in her mind that her mother had left it there on purpose. "A thousand dollars."

Carson let out a low whistle. "For something Lora's going to outgrow in a year? Does your mother always throw money around like that?"

"Always," Serena answered without hesitation, then added as she shook her head, "She thinks it puts people in awe of her."

Carson held his tongue, thinking it best not to say what he thought of that. Instead, he handed the decoy, dressed in Lora's clothes, to Serena.

"Don't forget to put this in the car seat and buckle it up. You don't want this Mark creep to suspect something's wrong," Carson cautioned.

Taking the doll, Serena had to marvel about it again. "This is just *too* lifelike," she told Carson. Not to mention that it felt a little eerie, handling the doll and pretending it was her daughter.

Carson went to the heart of the matter. "Just as long as that doll does the trick and fools Mark, that's all that counts."

She had her doubts about that. "Anyone stopping to look at 'my daughter' will see that it's not Lora—or a real baby."

He had a solution for that. "Then just pull that little cotton blanket down over 'her.' Tell people she's coming down with a cold, and you don't want to take a chance on it getting worse because people are touching her and breathing on her."

Serena got in behind the wheel. "Shouldn't I have left her at home if she's coming down with something?" she asked.

Carson shook his head. "You're overthinking this thing. Just tell them what I said and people will be sympathetic—and they'll leave 'Lora' alone." Standing next to the open driver's-side window, he bent down and put his hand on hers. "Okay, remember to do what we rehearsed. You go to the bank, make that withdrawal, then put the money into the backpack and tuck the backpack into that carry section at the back of the stroller."

Serena was doing her best not to allow her nerves to get the better of her. There was a great deal riding on this. She wasn't worried about getting hurt, she was afraid that Mark would get away again.

She ran her tongue along her very dry lips. "And where will you be again?"

"Out of sight," he told her. "My team and I will be watching you. The second that guy turns up and grabs the money, it'll be all over for him." Carson squeezed her hand. "Trust me."

"I do," she told him. And she did. With her life *and* her daughter's.

Just to reassure her, Carson added, "I won't let him hurt you."

She could see the concern in his eyes. He was worried that *she* was worried. It touched her heart. "I know that."

Even so, Serena was still nervous as she drove from the ranch.

Serena parked away from the bank. She wanted to be able to walk slowly back to her car once she had made her withdrawal from the bank. She reasoned that the longer the walk, the more opportunity Mark would have to steal the backpack from her. What she *didn't* want was to be close enough to her car to have Mark push his way into it, stealing both the backpack *and* her.

The thought galvanized her and made her more determined than ever that the only place Mark was going after today was prison.

"This is rather a large amount of money you're withdrawing, Ms. Colton. Is everything all right?" Edward Abernathy, the bank manager asked.

When she'd initially handed the teller the with-drawal slip, taking the sizable amount from her savings account, the teller had mumbled something about needing to get approval for such a large sum and then went to get the bank manager.

The portly man had greeted her with a profusion of banal small talk ranging from the weather to the state of her family's health. Then he looked at the withdrawal slip as if he hadn't already seen it when the teller had brought it to him.

The bank manager eyed her now, waiting for her answer to his question.

"Everything's fine, Mr. Abernathy," Serena told him with a broad, easy smile. "It's just that I'm deal-ing with a seller who insists on being paid in cash. I think he's paranoid about having checks bounce on him. It's happened before," she added for good measure.

"That must be some horse you're acquiring," Ab-ernathy marveled. After a beat, he signed his ap-proval for the transaction.

"Oh, it is," Serena assured the man, wishing he would hurry up. It was a quarter to three and she felt that she was cutting it very close. "It's a beautiful palomino. I have to act quickly. There are two other buyers who are interested in the stallion."

"I quite understand," Abernathy said sympathet-ically. "I'll be back in a moment. Wait right here, please," he told her just before he went into the vault.

He returned a few minutes later.

"Well, there you go," Abernathy said, counting out a number of banded stacks of hundred-dollar bills before tucking all of them neatly into a sack for her. "I see you brought your daughter in with you. Never too young to start them on a sound financial footing. We could open an account for your little darling today if you're interested," the bank manager told her.

"Some other time, Mr. Abernathy," Serena said, then reminded him, "I have that appointment with the seller to keep."

"Of course, of course," the manager answered, watching her tuck the sack into her backpack. He angled his head, as if trying to get a look beneath the screen cover draped across the front of the stroller. "That certainly is one well-behaved baby you have there. I don't believe I heard a single peep out of her this whole time."

"She's a heavy sleeper," Serena replied.

Abernathy chuckled. "Both of mine were screamers. Or so my wife said. I had to work of course, so I missed all that."

"You were lucky," Serena told him, knowing the man was expecting some sort of a comment.

Turning away from the bank manager, she quickly began to make her way to the bank's double doors, anxious to leave the bank before Abernathy could ask any more questions or, worse, ask if he could sneak in one peek at her "baby."

Serena could feel her heart hammering hard as she approached the exit doors.

The bank guard moved toward them at the same time, then obligingly held one of the doors open for her. He tipped the brim of his cap. "Nice seeing you again, Ms. Colton."

"You, too, Eli," she murmured, forcing a smile to her lips.

She had less than five minutes to make it to the rendezvous point.

Focused on getting back to her car in order to make it to the restaurant in time, Serena didn't see him until it was too late. One second, she was walking quickly, pushing the stroller in front of her; the next, she felt a jolt coming from the left and going through her whole body.

It sent her flying to the ground.

Mark had darted out of the alley next to the bank and lunged at her, catching her completely off balance.

Rather than grab the backpack, he grabbed the whole stroller and made a mad dash for the parking lot that was across the street. Obviously intent on upping his game, he was running to his truck with both the money and what he presumed was the baby. The latter was to be his collateral, assuring him of a safe escape.

But he never reached the truck. Instead, he howled in pain as Justice came out of nowhere and caught his arm, dragging him down to the ground.

The second the canine caught him, Mark let go of the stroller. It hurtled toward the street and would have been smashed by an oncoming truck if Finn hadn't managed to grab it just before it went careening off curb.

Several of the K-9 team closed ranks around Mark, although the latter wasn't really necessary. The moment Mark had lunged out of the alley and grabbed the stroller, Carson had transformed from an elderly man dozing on a bench to a K-9 detective and sprinted over toward the blackmailer. Justice had brought the man down, but Carson had been less than half a second behind the German shepherd.

Grabbing Mark by the back of his collar, he shoved him in Finn's direction. "Here's the guy who wanted to steal your niece. I'll be in to do the paperwork as soon as I make sure that your sister is all right and bring her home," Carson told the chief.

"You're making a mistake," Mark cried, appealing to Finn. "The stroller was about to go into the street and I was just trying to catch it before the baby had a terrible accident."

Carson snorted. "You're the one making the mistake if you think any of us are actually buying that lame story," he told the blackmailer.

The next moment, he turned away, not giving the

brazen blackmailer another thought. Right now, all his thoughts were centered on Serena. He swiftly checked her out, his eyes sweeping over every inch of her. She'd got back up to her feet, but Carson wanted to see for himself that she was unharmed.

"Are you all right?" he asked her anxiously.

She didn't bother answering that. Instead, she had an important question of her own. "Is Mark going to be going to jail?"

"Yes. For a long, long time if your brother and I have anything to say about it," Carson answered.

"Then I'm fine," she said, answering his question as she breathed a huge sigh of relief. Turning toward Carson, she looked up at him and very plaintively asked, "Can I please go get my daughter now?"

He grinned. "I'll take you there myself," Carson said.

She remembered what he'd just told her brother. "But what about the paperwork you said you were going to write up?"

"It's not going anywhere," he assured Serena. He glanced over toward the blackmailer. One of the officers was pushing the man's head down and getting him into the back of a squad car. "And neither is Mark." Giving her his full attention, Carson asked, "You ready for that reunion now?" he wanted to know.

"Oh, so ready."

He grinned, expecting nothing less. "Then let's go

see that little girl of yours." Carson let out a piercing whistle. "Justice, come!"

The German shepherd was instantly at his side, ready to follow him wherever he went.

As it turned out, Lora wasn't sequestered all that far away.

Will Taggert, the detective—and father of three—who Finn had entrusted with the baby's safety, had taken her as well as the Colton housekeeper to stay at his family's small ranch.

The second they walked into the room where she and the baby were staying, Alma made no secret of the fact that she was overjoyed to see Serena *and* Carson.

"Did you catch that hateful scoundrel?" the housekeeper asked, excitement and hope clearly written all over her face.

Carson smiled at the woman and nodded his head. "We did. He won't be threatening anyone anymore," he told Alma.

"Oh, thank you!" Alma cried.

Carson murmured something in response, however his attention was focused on Serena. When they had entered the bedroom where Alma and Lora were staying, Serena had instantly rushed over to the cradle and scooped her daughter up in her arms.

"Oh, I have missed you," she told her daughter, pressing the baby against her breast. Serena took in a deep breath. "You smell so good," she said with enthusiasm.

"You're lucky you didn't get here ten minutes earlier, Miss," Alma said with a laugh. "You might not have said that then."

Serena raised her eyes to look at the housekeeper. "Oh, yes I would have. I missed everything about Lora, even changing her diapers." Turning toward Carson, she said, "I don't know how to thank you."

He smiled in response. He had a few ideas on that subject, but nothing he could say right now, not in front of the housekeeper or in front of Taggert, who had just walked into the room. So instead, he said, "Just all part of the job. Right, Justice?" he asked, looking down at the German shepherd.

As if knowing that he was being asked a question, the canine barked in response.

Carson looked over at the housekeeper. "How long will it take you get pack up and get ready to leave?" he asked.

"Is five minutes too long?" she asked.

Carson laughed. "You can have half an hour if you'd like."

"No, Miss Lora and I are all ready," Alma assured him. "No offense," she said to Taggert, "But I never bothered unpacking when we got here."

"None taken," Taggert assured the woman with a laugh.

"Well, if you're all ready," Carson began.

"Then let's go home," Serena said, concluding his sentence.

Carson grinned as he took the suitcase that Alma had produced out of the closet from the woman. His heart swelled as he joined Serena and her daughter.

"Let's go home," he echoed.

Epilogue

Order, to some extent, had been restored.

Serena's daughter as well as the family house-keeper were back at the Double C, as they should be. The rest of Serena's family—her parents and younger sister, Valeria—would be coming back in the morning, Finn had told his sister. Returning on such short notice was "inconvenient" for the older Coltons according to Joanelle. Carson imagined that packing up alone, even though someone else would undoubtedly be given that task, would take some time.

Carson had to admit that he wasn't exactly overly thrilled anticipating Judson and Joanelle's return to the ranch. They had both made no secret of the fact that they looked down on him, as well as down at his family, but in the grand scheme of things, he viewed that as just a minor problem.

Besides, he still had tonight with Serena and tonight, if all went according to his plan, was all he needed.

"You're thinking about your brother, aren't you?" Serena asked, putting her own interpretation to the pensive expression on Carson's face.

It was evening and they were back in her suite at the ranch. For now, Lora was dozing in the other room in her crib.

"No, actually I'm thinking about finding his killer," Carson said. Now that the threat to Serena was over, finding Bo's killer had become his main focus again. "And finding Demi Colton."

She immediately focused on his phrasing. "So now those are finally two separate concerns—aren't they?" she asked hopefully.

Carson smiled. The woman's loyalty was incredible. "If you're asking me if I still think that Demi killed my brother, no, I don't. We're following up on other leads and looking at other suspects." He tucked his arm around her as they lay on her bed. "But that doesn't change the fact that Demi is still out there somewhere, missing—*and* pregnant with my brother's baby. I need to find her," he said seriously, "and bring her in—for her own safety."

Sitting up, Serena shifted so she could look down at him. "Really?" she asked.

"Really," he replied with sincerity. "She shouldn't be alone at a time like this."

Would wonders never cease? "Who *are* you and what have you done with Carson Gage?" she asked playfully.

"I'm right here," he answered, slowly running his hand along the swell of her curves and relishing every sensation that contact created within him. "You're responsible for this, you know, for changing me and making me see things I'd never noticed before."

He watched the warm smile blossom in her eyes before spreading to her lips. That, too, gave him an immense amount of pleasure.

"Then I guess I did a good thing," Serena said.

He laughed, toying with the ends of her hair. "That all depends on whether or not you like the new me."

Crossing her arms on his chest, she leaned her chin against them as she gazed into his eyes. "Oh, I like him. I like the 'new you' a great deal," Serena told him and she pressed a kiss to his lips to show Carson just how much.

"Good, because that makes this a lot easier."

And just like that, Serena could feel herself starting to grow uneasy. Things had been going too well. They'd caught Mark and she'd been reunited with her daughter. That meant that she was due for something to go wrong.

Trying not to sound as nervous as she felt, Serena asked, "Makes what a lot easier?"

Carson took a deep breath. He'd never found himself lacking courage before, but this was an area he'd never ventured into until now. The whole idea of marriage and family was all new to him and there was a part of him that worried it might all be one-sided.

He backtracked. "On second thought, maybe it doesn't."

"Doesn't what?" Serena wanted to know. "What are you talking about—or *not* talking about?"

Because he was accustomed to always having an escape route for himself, he edged his way into what he was about to say slowly.

"I know that your parents don't much care for anyone who's part of the Gage family—"

"I am not my parents' daughter," she was quick to assure him. "And I don't think the way they do. Now, will you *please* tell me what you're trying to say before *my* daughter wakes up and I have to tend to her—instead of you?" she urged.

As if on cue, Lora began to cry.

"Too late." Serena sighed. She tossed off the covers and began to get out of bed. "I'd better go get her."

Carson caught her by the wrist, holding Serena in place.

"She only gets louder," she told Carson.

He wasn't thinking about the baby right now. "Will you marry me?"

The four words stopped her cold. Did she just imagine that? "What did you say?"

This wasn't the way he wanted to propose. "I didn't want to blurt it out that way, but I was afraid I'd lose my nerve if you—"

She shook her head. She didn't want an explanation. She wanted the words. "Again, please," she requested.

"You want me to ask you again?" he asked, not quite sure this was what she was telling him.

Serena bobbed her head emphatically up and down. "Yes, please."

"I know that your parents don't much care for—"

"Not that part," she told him. "The *good* part."

And then he knew what she was asking him to say. "Will you marry me?"

"Yes!" she cried, throwing her arms around his neck. Then, in case there was *any* lingering doubt, she repeated, "Yes!" And then her eyes suddenly widened. "Listen."

She'd lost him again. He cocked his head, doing as she'd asked. "What am I listening for?"

Her grin all but split her face. "Lora stopped crying. You really do have a magic touch," she told him with unabashed approval.

"Then let me give you a real demonstration of that," he said, bringing his mouth down to hers.

"Yes, please," she said one more time before she lost herself in the wondrous world that only Carson could create for her.

For them.

* * * * *

BATTLE TESTED

JANIE CROUCH

This book is dedicated to my aunt Donna.
You are a blessing to me and so many others.
Thank you for all the times you brushed my
hair (because goodness knows I didn't do it) and
loved me like a second mother. And for teaching
me that romance books are the best books.

Chapter One

Rosalyn Mellinger had reached her breaking point.

She was exhausted, frightened and about to run out of money.

Sitting in a diner in Pensacola, Florida, one she'd chosen because she could see both the front customer door and the rear employee entrance from her corner booth, she huddled around the third cup of coffee she'd had with her meager meal, stretching out her stay here as long as possible.

Although sitting with her back to the wall didn't help when she had no idea what the person who stalked her looked like. She tensed every time the tiny bell chimed signaling someone new had come through the door, like it had just now.

The couple in their mid-eighties, entering and shuffling slowly to a table, were definitely not the Watcher.

But she knew he was around. She knew because she would get a note later tonight—or an email or a text or a phone call—that would say something about her meal here. About what she'd eaten or the name of her waitress or how she'd used sweetener in her coffee rather than sugar.

Some sort of frightening detail that let her know the Watcher had been nearby. Just like he had been for the last five months. She scanned faces of other patrons to see who might be studying her but couldn't find anyone who looked like they were paying her any attention.

It always seemed to be that way. But still the Watcher would know details as if he had been sitting here at the booth with Rosalyn. And would mention the details in a message to her, usually a note slid under her door in the middle of the night.

Rosalyn clutched her coffee cup, trying to get her breathing under control.

Or maybe the Watcher wouldn't say anything about the diner at all. Maybe he wouldn't contact her for days. That happened sometimes too. Rosalyn never knew what to expect and it kept her on the precipice of hysteria.

All she knew for certain was the constant acid of fear burning in her gut.

Her waitress, Jessie, who couldn't have been more than eighteen or nineteen years old, wiped the table next to Rosalyn's, then came to stand by her booth. The kid looked decidedly uncomfortable.

"I'm sorry, ma'am, but my manager said I would have to ask you to leave if you're not going to order anything else. The dinner crowd is coming in."

The burn in Rosalyn's belly grew at the thought of leaving the diner, although she didn't know why. She was no safer from the Watcher in here than she was somewhere else.

He'd found her again last night. Rosalyn had been in Pensacola for four days, staying at a different run-down hotel each night. Three nights had passed with no message, no notes, and she'd let just the slightest bit of hope enter her heart that she had lost the Watcher permanently.

Heaven knew she had driven around enough times to get rid of anyone who followed. Hours' worth of circles and sudden turns around town to lose any tails. Then she had parked at a hotel before sneaking across strip malls and a small park to *another* hotel about a mile away just in case there was some sort of tracker on her car. It seemed to have worked for three nights.

Rosalyn thought maybe she had figured it out. That the Watcher had been tracking her car and that's how he always found her. She would gladly leave the car rotting in the wrong hotel parking lot if it meant she could get away from the man who stalked her.

But then last night a note had been slipped under the hotel door as she slept.

When she saw the envelope lying so deceptively innocently on the floor of her hotel by the door as she woke up this morning, she promptly vomited into the trash can by the bed.

She finally found the strength to get up and open the unsealed envelope and read the note. Handwritten, like them all.

Sorry I haven't been around for a few days. I know you must have missed me. I missed you.

She almost vomited again, but there was nothing left in her stomach.

She took the note and put it in the cardboard box

where she kept all the other notes. Then she meticulously put the box back inside her large duffel bag. From her smaller tote bag, the one she always kept with her, she took out her notebook. With shaky hands she logged the date and time she found the note, and its contents.

She'd taken her bags and gone back to her car—a tracker there obviously wasn't the problem—and driven toward the beach and ended up at this diner. She needed to get on the move again. But she didn't know how—her savings from when she'd had a decent-paying job as an accountant were gone. And she didn't know where she would go even if she had had money.

The Watcher found her no matter where she went.

Sometimes she was convinced he was in her head since he seemed to know everything she did and thought. But that would mean she was crazy.

An idea that was becoming more and more acceptable.

Rosalyn rubbed her eyes. Exhaustion weighed every muscle in her body.

"Ma'am?"

None of this was her waitress's fault. She turned to the girl, who seemed so much younger even though she was probably only five or six years less than Rosalyn's twenty-four. "Of course. I'm sorry, Jessie. Just let me pay my bill and get my stuff together."

Jessie shuffled her feet. "No need to pay anything. I already took care of that for you. Pay it forward and all that."

Rosalyn wanted to argue. Jessie had been working hard the three hours Rosalyn had been in the booth.

The girl was probably saving up for college and needed the money.

But the truth was, Rosalyn was down to her last twenty dollars. Not having to pay six dollars for her meal would help a lot.

Being able to live a normal life and return to a regular job would help a lot more, but Jessie's gesture was still touching.

"Thank you," Rosalyn whispered to the girl. "I truly appreciate it."

"I can probably hold my manager off for another thirty minutes if that will help you. I'm sorry I can't do more."

"No. I'll be fine. Thanks."

The girl nodded and walked away.

Rosalyn wondered if she would read about her conversation with Jessie later tonight in the note the Watcher left her. Or even worse, if Jessie would end up dead. That had happened three months ago with the detective in Shreveport, Louisiana, when she'd passed through. Rosalyn had taken a chance and told him what was happening and found, to her surprise, that he believed her. Detective Johnson was the one who suggested she keep all the notes and take photos of any texts and try to record any phone messages. He was the one who got her the notebook and told her to write down everything that happened.

The relief to find someone who believed her, who didn't think she was just out for attention like her family had, was overwhelming. Finally the feeling of not being utterly alone.

Unfortunately, Detective Johnson—a healthy fifty-year-old man—suddenly died of a heart attack two days after meeting with Rosalyn. He was found in his bed. Natural causes, the newspaper said. Rosalyn was heartbroken that she'd so unfortunately lost the one person who had listened and believed her.

Until she received an anonymous email the next day with a link to a drug called succinylcholine. A drug that in a large enough dose caused heart attacks but was virtually untraceable in a victim's system.

Detective Johnson's death had been no accident.

Neither had the mechanic's—a man named Shawn who had been super nice and repaired Rosalyn's car at a deeply discounted rate a month ago in Memphis. She mentioned to him that she was on the run. Didn't want to say more than that, but he asked. Shawn's sister had an ex who had turned violent and terrorized her. Shawn recognized some of the same symptoms in Rosalyn. He pressed and Rosalyn gave him some details. Not all of them, but enough. He invited her to his mother's house for dinner, explaining the importance of not going through something like this alone.

Rosalyn, almost desperate for a friend, agreed. When she came back to the shop that night, she found the place surrounded by cops.

Shawn had been a victim of a "random act of violence" as he was closing up his garage. He was dead.

She still had the newspaper clipping that had been slipped under her door the next morning.

Rosalyn rubbed her stomach against the burn. She hadn't spoken to a single person about the Watcher since that day. She'd just kept on the run, trying to stay ahead of him.

He'd found her again. Pensacola was the sixth town she'd moved to in five months. He always found her. She wasn't sure how.

Exhaustion flooded her as she grabbed her tote bag and walked toward the door. Jessie gave her a small wave from behind the servers' station and Rosalyn smiled as best she could. She was almost to the entrance when she stopped and turned around, walking back to Jessie.

The girl looked concerned. For Rosalyn or *because* of her, Rosalyn couldn't tell. Rosalyn took six dollars out of her bag.

"Here." She handed the money to Jessie. "Paying for my meal was very kind and I'm sure it will get you karma points. But I know you're working hard, so I'll pay for my own meal."

"Are you sure?"

No, she wasn't sure. All she knew was that she couldn't take a chance that something would happen to this pretty young woman because she'd spotted Rosalyn six dollars' worth of salad and chicken.

"Yes." She pressed the money into Jessie's hand. "Thanks again, though."

Rosalyn turned and walked out the door feeling more lonely than she had in…ever.

She couldn't do this anymore.

What good was it to run if the Watcher was just going to find her again? What good did it do to talk to people if any ties she made were just going to get them hurt?

And at what point would the Watcher stop toying with her and just finish her off? Rosalyn had no doubt

her death was his endgame. He always knew when
or how.

Maybe she should just save him the trouble and do
it herself. At least then she would have some measure
of control.

She looked down the block toward the beach. She
would go sit there. Think things through. Try to figure out a plan.

Even if that plan meant taking her own life. That
had to be better than allowing innocent people to die
because of her. Or living in constant fear with no end
in sight.

She began walking toward the beach. She would
sit on the sand, watch the sunset. Because damn it, if
this was going to be her last day on earth—either by
her own hand or the Watcher's—she wanted to feel the
sun on her face one last time.

Beyond that, she had no idea what to do.

Chapter Two

Steve Drackett, director of the Omega Sector Critical Response Division, was doing nothing. He couldn't remember the last time that had happened.

And even more so, he was doing nothing in a tiki-themed bar on the Florida Panhandle. In *flip-flops*.

He was damn certain that had *never* happened.

It was his first real vacation in ten years. After his wife died twelve years ago, there hadn't been much point in them. Then he'd become director of the Critical Response Division of Omega—an elite law enforcement agency made up of the best agents the country had to offer—and there hadn't been time.

But here he was on the Florida Panhandle, two days into a weeklong vacation for which his team had pitched in and gotten for him. Celebrating his twenty years of being in law enforcement.

And to provide him with a little R & R after he was almost blown up last month by a psychopath intent on burning everything and everyone around her.

Either way, he'd take it. Home in Colorado Springs could still be pretty cold, even in May. Pensacola was already edging toward hot. Thus the flip-flops.

Steve sat at the far end of the bar, back to the wall, where he had a nice view of both the baseball game on TV and the sunset over the ocean, along with an early-evening thundershower that was coming in, through the windows at the front of the bar. It also gave him direct line of sight of the entrance, probably not necessary here but an occupational hazard nonetheless.

The cold beer in his hands and an order of wings next to him on the bar had Steve just about remembering how to unwind. Nothing here demanded his attention. The bar was beginning to fill up but everyone seemed relaxed for the most part. The hum of voices, laughter, glasses clinking was enjoyable.

As someone whose job on most days was literally saving the world, the tiki bar was a nice change.

Then the woman walked through the door.

He glanced at her—as did just about every pair of male eyes in the bar—when she rushed in trying to get out of the sudden Florida storm. Another couple entered right behind her for the same reason, but Steve paid them little attention.

She was small. Maybe five-four to his six-one. Wavy black hair that fell well past her shoulders. Slender to the point of being too skinny. Mid-twenties.

Gorgeous.

Steve forced his eyes away, although his body stayed attuned to her.

She didn't belong here—he had already summed that up in just a few moments. Not here in a tiki bar where the patrons were either on vacation or trying to just relax on a Sunday evening.

She wasn't wearing some flirty skirt or shorts and

tank top or any of the modes of dress that bespoke enjoying herself on a Florida beach in mid-May. Not that there was anything wrong with how she was dressed: khaki pants and a blue button-down shirt. No flip-flops for this black-haired beauty, or any other type of sandals. Instead she wore athletic shoes. Plain. White.

Her bag was also too large for a casual outing or catching a couple of beers for an hour or two. And clutched too tightly to her.

This woman looked ready to run. From what or to what, Steve had no idea.

Steve had been out of active agent duty for the last ten years. His job now was behind a desk on most days. A big desk, an important one. But a desk nonetheless. He didn't need to be an agent in the field to know the most important thing about the woman who'd just walked into the bar: she was trouble.

Since trouble was the very thing he was trying to get away from here in flip-flop Florida, Steve turned back to his beer and wings. Back to the game.

But as he finished his food, he found his eyes floating back to her.

She was obviously over twenty-one, so it was legal for her to be here. If she wanted to take off in a hurry—with her oversize tote-type bag—as long as she wasn't doing anything illegal, it was her own business.

She didn't want to buy a drink—he noticed that first. But as the storm lingered, then grew worse, she obviously knew she'd have to or else go back out in it. She ordered a soda.

She sat with her back to the wall.

She tried not to draw attention to herself in any way.

She was scared.

Steve finished one beer and started another. He flexed his flip-flop-enclosed toes.

Not his monkeys. Not his circus.

This woman was not his problem, but he still couldn't stop glancing her way every once in a while. She barely moved. Unfortunately, Steve wasn't the only one whose attention she had caught. Just about every guy in the place was aware of her presence.

At first men waited and watched. Was she meeting someone? A husband? Boyfriend? When it became obvious she wasn't, they slowly began circling. Maybe not literally but definitely in their minds.

Then some began circling literally.

A couple of local boys who had been here since before Steve arrived—and had been tossing beers back the whole time—worked their nerve up to go sit next to the woman. She didn't give much indication that she was interested, but that didn't deter them.

Since the baseball game was over, someone turned on the jukebox and a few couples were dancing to some Jimmy Buffett song. One of the guys stood and asked the woman to dance but she shook her head no. He reached down and grabbed her hands and tried to pull her to a standing position, obviously thinking she was playing hard to get.

Steve could read her tension from all the way across the bar, but the guys talking to her obviously couldn't.

He should leave now. He knew he should just walk away. The boys weren't going to get too out of hand. As soon as the woman put them down hard, they would leave her alone.

She was trouble. He knew it. He should go.

He sighed as he put money on the bar for his meal and began to walk toward the woman and the two men who were now both trying to get her to dance. He hadn't become the director of one of the most elite law enforcement groups in the country by walking away from trouble.

He stepped close to the first local guy, deliberately invading his space. The way the guy was invading the woman's.

"Excuse me, fellas. The lady doesn't want to dance."

"How do you know?" The other guy snickered. "Are you her dad?"

The woman's eyes—a beautiful shade of blue that stood out in sharp juxtaposition against her dark hair—flew to Steve's. She winced in apology at the crack about his age.

Steve was probably fifteen years older than the woman. Not quite old enough to be her father, but probably too old to be anything else to her.

"No, not her father. Just someone old enough and sober enough to realize when a woman is uncomfortable."

"She's not—" The guy stopped and really looked at the woman then—the way she was clutching her bag, discomfiture clear on her face.

"The lady doesn't want to dance," Steve said again.

The local guy and his buddy released the woman, murmuring apologies. Steve stepped back relieved he wasn't going to have to make some show of strength. He could've. Could've had both men unconscious on the ground before they were even aware what sort of trouble they were facing. But the guys hadn't meant any harm.

Steve nodded at the woman as the locals walked away. He didn't step any closer or try to talk to her. His flirting skills were rusty at best and this lady obviously wasn't here to scope out men. Steve turned to make his way back to his seat only to find someone had already taken his place.

Looked like it was time to go.

That was fine. It wasn't like Steve had any grand plans for his evening here in the tiki bar. He began walking toward the door.

"Thank you."

He heard her soft voice as the black-haired beauty's hand touched his arm. Steve stopped and turned toward her.

He smiled. It felt a little unpracticed. "I don't think they meant any harm, but it was no problem."

"There was a time I would've let them both have it, but I just don't seem to have it in me lately." She looked a little surprised that she was even talking to him.

She was skittish, scared. She'd been that way since the moment she'd walked in. It made him want to wrap an arm around her, pull her close and tell her to take a breath. He'd protect her from whatever demons she was trying to fight.

It surprised him a little that he felt that way. His entire life had been spent helping people, first as an FBI agent, then as he was recruited into Omega Sector. But usually he was more at a distance, less personal.

He already felt personal with this woman and he didn't even know her name.

"I'm sure you could've handled them. I just was doing my fatherly duty."

She snorted and humor lit her blue eyes. "Father, my ass. You're what? Thirty-nine? Forty?"

"Forty-one."

"Oh. Well, he should've said *grandfather*, then."

Her smile was breathtaking. Steve couldn't stop himself from taking a step toward her. "I'm Steve Drackett."

She shook his outstretched hand. He knew the thought that a flash of heat hit them both as their skin touched was both melodramatic and sentimental. Steve was neither of those things.

But he still felt the heat.

"I'm Rosalyn."

No last name. He didn't press. It was just another sign she was trouble, but Steve somehow couldn't bring himself to care.

"Can an old man buy you a drink or something?"

She studied him hard as they finally released hands. They were halfway between the bar and the door. He honestly wasn't sure which way she'd choose. To stay with him or to leave.

She ended up choosing both.

"May I ask you something?" She slid her tote more fully onto her shoulder. She had to step a little closer so they could hear each other over the noise in the bar. He found himself thankful for the chaos around them.

"Sure."

"Are you some sort of psycho? A killer or deranged stalker or both?"

She asked the question so seriously Steve couldn't

help but laugh. "Nope. Scout's honor." He held up his
hand in what he was sure was an incorrect Scout sa-
lute. "I'm an upstanding member of society. Although
you know if I was a crazy killer, I probably wouldn't
answer that question honestly."

She shrugged, her eyes back to being haunted. "I
know. I guess I just wanted you to tell me so I could
see if I would believe you."

"Do you?"

She smiled so sadly it damn near broke his heart.
"I think so. Or maybe I just don't care anymore. And
to answer your question, yes, you can buy me a drink.
But let's get out of here."

Chapter Three

Rosalyn knew her actions bordered on reckless. Even if she hadn't known she had a deranged stalker following her every move, leaving a bar with a man she'd just met would still have been pretty stupid.

He'd laughed—in a kind way, but still obviously thinking she was joking—when she'd asked if he was a killer or crazy. But like he'd said, no true villain would give her an honest answer about that.

Actually, she believed the Watcher would. If she ever met him face-to-face and asked him outright if he was her stalker, she believed he might actually tell her.

Steve Drackett wasn't the Watcher. He might be an ordinary garden-variety psycho, but he wasn't the psycho she was desperately attempting to escape right now.

And in that case, she was willing to take her chances with him.

She looked up at him as he led her to the door. He had joked about being a grandpa but that couldn't have been further from the truth. His brown hair might be graying just the slightest bit at the temples, but that was the only sign whatsoever that he wasn't a man fifteen years younger. His green eyes seemed kind, at least to her, but the rest of his face was hard and unforgiving. Stark cheekbones, strong chin. Definitely not a pretty face but very much a handsome one.

His body was well honed—the black T-shirt Steve wore left no doubt he was in excellent physical shape. His khaki shorts were quite appropriate for a bar in Florida on a May evening, but she doubted it was what he normally wore. She was positive the flip-flops weren't.

"If you're not a psychopath, what do you do, Steve?" she asked as they walked out the door. Humid air from the coast blasted them. The storm had moved out to sea, but dampness still hovered everywhere, a sure sign another storm would be coming.

"Present occupation is beach bum. I'm here on vacation from Colorado."

They walked down the steps. "Mountains. Nice. I've never been there. Are you a bum there, too?"

He hesitated slightly before he smiled. "Worse. Management."

He didn't want to tell her what he did for a living. Okay, fair enough. She hadn't told him her last name.

Of course, she was doing it for his own safety.

"Are you from around here?" Steve asked. "Do you have a bar you'd suggest?"

She didn't want to go to a bar. Not somewhere the Watcher could hear them, see them.

"How about a six-pack and walk on the beach?"

He smiled down at her. "That might break some open-beverage-container laws, but I'm willing to risk it."

Rosalyn didn't know exactly what she'd been expecting when she'd left the bar with Steve, but the next few hours were not it.

They bought their beers and sat alone, where no one—not even the Watcher—could possibly hear them.

And they talked. About everything and nothing.

He told her about his wife—his high school sweetheart—who had died in a car accident twelve years ago. About places he'd traveled. Even a little bit about his job, that he was a manager in some sort of division office and how he sometimes felt more like he was babysitting than anything else.

Rosalyn was vague without being dishonest. She told him she had a mother and sister but wasn't close to either—an understatement. She told him a little about her college years and her job as an accountant. When he made a joke about the size of her bag, she told him she never went anywhere without it. Told him she was taking some time off, traveling around a little bit, trying to "find herself."

She somehow managed not to laugh hysterically as she said it.

Steve was a good listener, a friendly talker. He never made a move on her or made her feel uncomfortable. He seemed to be both completely at ease but at the same time completely surprised at their continued, comfortable conversation.

He obviously didn't spend a lot of time picking up strangers at a bar.

At some point deep in the night—it had to have been nearly four o'clock but Rosalyn wasn't sure—it began to rain again, gently, but enough that they couldn't stay here on the beach any longer.

It looked like her reprieve was over. She needed to make her way back to her car. Maybe she'd catch a couple hours of sleep in it—the thought of being out in the open like that made her skin crawl, but what choice did she have? She was out of money. A hotel, even a cheap one, was no longer an option.

She stood and Steve got up beside her, helping her. She smiled at him. "Thanks for hanging with me. It was nice to have a peaceful night."

"Been a long time since you had one?"

She was tempted to tell him about the Watcher. To share while they had complete privacy. But knew she couldn't. Some middle-management guy from some business in Colorado couldn't remedy this situation.

"Seems like it," she said instead.

"Anything I can help with?"

She looked up at him. He was a nice guy. A nice, hot, utterly delectable guy. For the hundredth time that evening she wished she had met Steve under different circumstances.

"I'm fine. But thank you for asking." She smiled, trying to make it as authentic as possible. Trying not to think about the darkness that hovered all around them that she would have to face alone in just a few minutes.

As if the weather could hear her thoughts, it started raining a little harder.

He touched her gently near her elbow. "I need to tell you something I probably should've mentioned earlier but couldn't figure out how to do it without coming across like a jerk."

She braced herself for bad news. "Okay."

"My beach bungalow is about two hundred yards

that way." He pointed up the beach. "It's a ridiculous room. Some sort of romance package. My colleagues at work chipped in and got it for me."

She didn't know what she'd expected him to say, but that wasn't it. "Oh."

"You're welcome to come in. Get out of the rain. No expectations or anything like that." He shrugged, the awkwardness on his tense face adorable. He obviously didn't want her to feel pressured. "The peaceful night doesn't have to end right now."

Rosalyn looked out at the darkness again. She knew what waited for her there. Fear. Isolation. Panic.

Steve reached up and tucked a damp strand of her hair behind her ear. He didn't say anything. Didn't try to talk her into it or put pressure on her in any way. Just stood silently, letting her know he was there if she wanted to go with him but he was fine if she didn't.

The lack of pressure, more than anything, helped her make the decision.

"Okay, just for tonight."

She couldn't take a chance and let the Watcher find her again. Find Steve.

He smiled and took her hand. They began to run through the sand toward his room. Like he'd said, it wasn't far.

The oceanside bungalow was nice inside: sort of what one would expect for the romance package on the beach. A king-size bed with a teal bedspread and canopy roof. A couch and chair over in the reading-nook section.

And a huge heart-shaped Jacuzzi tub in the far corner. Rosalyn looked over at Steve, who grinned sheepishly.

"You failed to mention the giant heart-shaped Jacuzzi in the middle of your room."

Steve laughed. "I wasn't sure if it would work in my favor or against me."

"Are you sure you weren't supposed to be on your honeymoon here or something?"

Steve laughed again, crossing to the bathroom to grab them both a towel to dry off from the rain. Rosalyn set her tote bag down on the chair in the sitting area.

"Honestly, I just booked a normal room in the hotel section. When I got here, I found out I had gotten an upgrade—thanks to my colleagues chipping in. I'm sure they scoped out pictures and knew exactly what they were getting for me. Including the huge roll of condoms." He rolled his eyes, gesturing to the sparkling box on the nightstand. Rosalyn couldn't help but laugh.

"It's nice that they like you so much."

Steve shrugged. "They like to get rid of me for a week, that's for sure. And a not-so-subtle hint to come back more relaxed."

She had no doubt Steve was well respected, a good man. Guilt over the danger she was putting him in washed over her.

"Hey, what's going on?" He saw her face and walked over so he was standing in front of her. He put his thumb under her chin when she wouldn't look at him. "Do you regret coming here? Feel uncomfortable? If so, I can give you a ride wherever you need to go."

She didn't regret coming. She wanted to stay. Wanted more than just the safe haven Steve was offering.

She wanted him.

He looked so big standing in front of her. So able to take care of himself. Not someone who could be taken by surprise by someone else.

But she knew the Watcher didn't play fair. He'd taught her that.

"No, I'm not uncomfortable with you. The opposite, in fact. I just—" She stopped, not knowing what to say. She couldn't explain. Couldn't take the chance.

"What?" he asked gently.

"It's not good for you to be here with me, Steve. I'm afraid I'll only bring heartache for you." Or worse.

"Are you married?" he asked.

"No." She shook her head. "Never have been."

He took a step closer. She could smell his damp skin, the saltiness of the sea air and something that was distinctly male. She breathed in deeply.

"Are you running from the law?"

"No," she whispered as he moved closer again, his body now so close to hers she could feel the heat. She leaned closer, unable to stop herself.

"Then I don't think there's any reason at all for you to leave this room if you don't want to."

His lips closed the inches between them and she couldn't think of any response even if there'd been a good one anyway. Instead she just gave herself over to the kiss.

If she was going to lose everything, she was going to have this one night with this gorgeous, strong man first. Tomorrow be damned.

The heat all but consumed them both. Her arms reached up to wrap around his shoulders, then his neck. She clutched at his hair, too impassioned to be gentle.

Steve didn't mind at all. His arms circled her waist, then reached lower to cup her hips and pull her up and into him.

Both of them gasped.

He took possession of her mouth. There was no other word for it. *Possession.* His tongue stroked against hers and fire licked at them both. Her fingers linked behind his neck to capture him. Not that he seemed interested in being anywhere but pressed up against her.

"Rosalyn." Her name was reverent on his lips.

She began walking forward, causing him to move backward toward the bed. His arms were still wrapped around her hips making sure they were fully pressed together. When his knees finally hit the bed and he fell backward, he lifted her—as if she weighed nothing at all—and pulled her on top of him.

"Are you sure this is what you want?" he murmured. "It's still okay if you just want to be here. Nothing has to happen."

He would say that while she was lying flat on top of him? They weren't undressed yet, but Rosalyn had no doubt they would be soon. In her experience most guys would call her a tease—or much worse—if she decided to call a halt to everything at this point.

"You would stop now if I asked you to?"

He threaded his hands in her hair and pulled her back so he could see her more clearly.

"Of course. Is that what you want?"

"No. Just most guys would give a woman a hard time if she decided to change her mind now."

"Honey, a real man accepts that a woman can change

her mind at any time and respects the word *no* if he hears it."

Was it possible to fall a little bit in love with someone you'd known for only a few hours?

Rosalyn sat up, her legs straddling Steve's hips. She unbuttoned her shirt and slowly peeled it over her shoulders. "Well, thanks for asking, but I have no desire to stop." She pulled her sneakers and socks off and threw them over the side of the bed.

Steve crossed his arms under his head and just watched her. "Thank goodness. I would've stopped, but I sure as hell didn't want to."

She gasped as he sat up suddenly, forcing them even closer together. He spun and scooted them farther on the bed before dropping her down so he was now on top. She helped him discard his shirt, then pulled him back down to her.

His lips met hers again. No, she wasn't interested in stopping. She was already coming apart inside. She held on to Steve and let his lovemaking chase away the demons that weren't far outside the door.

THEY DIDN'T LEAVE the bungalow the entire next day, which was fine with Rosalyn. Who needed the beach? Especially on a cloudy, dreary day. Instead they made use of the bed and the couch and very good use of the heart-shaped hot tub. Steve ordered room service for every meal.

Steve's colleagues might have meant the room as a joke—and heaven knew it wasn't tasteful in its decorating—but Rosalyn loved every bit of it.

It was her own hideaway. The Watcher obviously

didn't know she was here. And as long as she stayed inside, there was no way he would find her.

She wondered if she could talk Steve into staying in the room forever. She looked over at him sleeping in the bed next to her right now, so late at night. His sexy face relaxed in sleep. It hadn't always been that way. She'd seen his face tensed in passion or smiling as he talked to her and told her a story from his past. She'd also seen the concern when she caught him studying her when he thought she wasn't paying attention.

He was worried about her.

If he knew about the Watcher, he'd be less concerned about her well-being and more concerned with his own. Might even ask her to leave right away.

Every person she'd told about the Watcher who believed her had wound up dead. She wouldn't take that chance with Steve. She'd just live in this little bungalow of fantasy until it didn't exist anymore. Then she would go.

But she knew she'd be leaving a little part of her heart behind when she did. She rolled onto her side so she could study him more fully. She reached out and stroked his hair by his ear, drawing her fingers down his cheek. He turned his face toward her, seeking her touch even in his sleep.

She should sleep now too. It had been a pleasurable but exhausting day and now it was late. Who knew what tomorrow would bring.

Her eyes were drifting closed when she heard the sound.

It didn't wake Steve. Why would it? It was just the barest whisper of a noise. If her body and mind hadn't already been programmed to listen for it—to fear it above all else—Rosalyn wouldn't have heard it either.

The sound of an envelope being slid under the door.

Her heart stopped and her breathing became ragged. The acid that burned in her stomach—blessedly missing for the last day—returned with a force that caused Rosalyn to ball up on the bed.

She bit her fist, tears streaming down her face. She didn't want to awaken Steve. If she did, she'd never be able to keep this a secret from him.

The Watcher had found her again.

Rosalyn lay on the bed for what seemed like forever trying to get herself under control. She finally managed to crawl off, dropping silently to the floor, and stumbled over to where the envelope lay.

With shaking hands she picked it up and pulled out the paper from inside.

If you like Steve so much, I guess I'll need to meet him soon.

She swallowed the sob in her throat. No. She couldn't allow the Watcher to come after Steve. The thought galvanized her into action.

Within minutes she had silently dressed and grabbed her bag. Steve had rolled over toward her side of the bed, as if he was seeking her missing form, but Rosalyn refused to let herself think about it. If she did, she would never make it out.

And she had to concentrate on where she was going to go. The time with Steve had given her the strength not to give up her battle against the Watcher. To keep fighting. But it hadn't given her a course of action with which to do that. She didn't have any money and she had no plan.

She spotted Steve's wallet on the dresser. He'd used it each time he'd paid for the food that had been delivered. Food he wouldn't even consider letting her help pay for—good, considering how broke she was.

Shame beat down on Rosalyn as she opened his wallet and took out the cash. One hundred and eighty-three dollars.

She didn't know how far it would get her, but at least it would get her away from here. Get the Watcher away from Steve.

She looked down at his naked back, his hips and legs tangled in the sheets. He'd never know how much he'd meant to her. What he'd given her in a time she'd needed so much.

He'd just remember her as a one-and-a-half-night stand and the woman who stole his cash. She'd become a cocktail story for him. A joking warning to his friends.

The tears leaked out of her eyes. This time she didn't even try to stop them.

Thinking about her would be distasteful for Steve.

But at least he would be alive.

Chapter Four

Six months later

"Would it be okay for us to see Steve now or should we make an appointment?" Brandon Han, Omega's top profiler, asked one of Steve's assistants in the outer office.

"Yeah, maybe we should make an appointment. For around eighteen months from now." That was Liam Goetz, leader of the hostage rescue team. "When hopefully Steve is in a better mood."

Cynthia, the assistant who kept his entire office running, laughed. "I think it's safe now."

Steve winced. Obviously nobody realized the door to his office was cracked and he could hear everything they were saying.

"Should we remove our weapons?" Liam asked.

"Why? Are you afraid you might shoot him?" Cynthia's gentle laughter didn't make Steve feel better.

"Are you kidding? I'm afraid he might take them and shoot *us*."

The topic moved on to more neutral ground: Liam's

twins and Tallinn, the little girl he and his wife had adopted. Liam had pictures. Steve stopped listening.

Liam's jokes didn't bother him—Liam was always making jokes—but Brandon's initial question did. These men were an important part of the Critical Response Division's inner team. Steve's team. Moreover, they were his friends. They didn't need an appointment to see him.

But evidently they thought so given Steve's behavior over the last few months.

Rosalyn.

He ran a hand over his eyes, then turned his chair so he was facing the Rocky Mountains out the window.

When he'd awakened as the sun began to rise in Pensacola and found her gone, he'd at first thought she'd decided to walk on the beach or run out to get donuts or something. Heaven knew they hadn't left the room in a day and a half. Maybe she'd needed some air.

Then he realized all her stuff, including that giant catchall bag she carried, was gone.

Going against his nature, Steve still gave her the benefit of the doubt. She was scared of something, he knew. He'd hoped to convince her to tell him what it was, to let him help.

Every time he'd considered broaching the subject—telling her he worked in law enforcement and could help her with whatever had her so afraid—they'd ended up making love instead.

Not that Steve had minded that. The only time he didn't see shadows floating in Rosalyn's eyes was when they were filled with passion. He had hoped to convince her to stay the rest of the week with him and during that time get her to tell him what was really going on with her. To share whatever burdens she carried. And the secrets she was obviously keeping.

Starting with her last name.

But it soon became obvious Rosalyn wasn't out to grab coffee or go for a jog. Steve had known that from the beginning, although he hadn't wanted to face it. Someone who looked over her shoulder as much as Rosalyn, who'd been so willing to stay inside the bungalow even when there was a gorgeous beach right outside, wouldn't be going out for a casual walk.

Checking his wallet confirmed it. She'd taken every bit of his cash.

She'd played him.

Even now, six months later, the thought sat heavily in his gut. The time they'd spent together hadn't meant anything to Rosalyn. He was just a means to an end.

Steve had packed up his stuff that afternoon and returned to Colorado Springs. He'd been in a bad mood ever since. Obviously something everyone was aware of, from the conversation that had just occurred outside his door.

The thing was, he would've given Rosalyn the money—more if she'd needed it—if she had let him know what was going on. Would've done it without her having sex with him or waiting until he was asleep to steal it.

But she hadn't. She'd found him to be an easy mark and taken off.

Steve stood and walked over to the plastic evidence bag on his windowsill and picked it up. It held a glass inside. One from the bungalow that he knew contained Rosalyn's fingerprints.

Steve had brought it back with him like it was some damn souvenir or something.

"Hey, boss."

Steve put the bag back down quickly. "Brandon, hi."

"Liam is showing Cynthia pictures of the twins."

Steve rolled his eyes. "Who would've thought the great womanizer would become such a family man."

Brandon joined Steve at the window. "Just takes the right woman."

Brandon had found the right woman a couple of months ago—Omega behavioral analyst Andrea Gordon—and Steve couldn't argue the change it had brought about in the man. The peace it had brought both Brandon and Andrea.

"You brought that home from Florida, right?" Brandon asked, pointing to the evidence bag. "Prints, I'm assuming. But you've never run them."

Steve shrugged. Brandon was a certified genius and a profiler. Not much got past him.

"I'm assuming something happened with a woman down there. If I had to guess, I would say a one-night stand."

Sometimes Han was spooky good at his job. Steve shrugged again. "It was Florida. And you guys did pitch in to get me the romance package."

"Then I'm assuming she took off suddenly, probably while you were unaware."

"Why do you say that?" Steve crossed back over to his desk chair.

Brandon leaned a shoulder against the wall. "You

sure you want me to go into this? I didn't come here to profile you, Steve."

"No, please. Continue." Brandon was rarely wrong and Steve needed to hear what the man thought of his behavior.

"Okay, you met a woman. You were extremely interested in her. I would assume the relationship became intimate, but you didn't and still don't know much about her."

All right so far. Steve gestured for Brandon to continue.

"Something happened. Something not good. The fact that you have an evidence bag with a glass with her prints suggests that you want to know more about her. Who she is. But the fact that you haven't run them suggests that she hurt you personally in some way rather than actually committing a crime against you, in which case you would try to find and arrest her. She hurt your pride."

Actually, Rosalyn had done both, committed a crime and hurt his pride.

"And you're mad at yourself."

Steve's eyes narrowed. "Why do you say that?"

"You keep that bag in the center of the windowsill. You look out that window at least a dozen times a day. Every time you do, you're reminded of the woman who got the best of you. Who got past your guard, then hurt you. You want to remind yourself never to be weak like that again."

Steve leaned back in his chair. "I'm glad you're on our side, Han."

Brandon walked over to Steve's desk. "It's okay to

want to check on her, Steve. To see if she's okay. To be concerned about her even after she did whatever she did."

Now he was getting further off course. "You getting that from an evidence bag too?"

"No. I can tell that from knowing you for so many years. Nobody just gets the drop on you. You let this woman close to you for a reason—more than just a physical one. No matter how it all ended, you're still a little concerned about her."

A picture of Rosalyn's haunted blue eyes jumped into Steve's mind but he pushed it away. Rosalyn was a consummate actress. She'd faked passion with him, then stolen his money. She was lucky he wasn't running her prints—he was sure she'd end up in the system somewhere—and having her arrested.

He told himself it was because stealing less than $200 wasn't worth the taxpayers' money needed to have her arrested and put in jail for a few months.

It had nothing to do with being concerned for her.

"Well, most of your profile of me and this situation is correct, except for the last part. I don't have any concern about her." Steve smiled, but it was stiff, as if it had been so long the muscles seemed to have forgotten how. "Just want the reminder not to be a jackass again."

"Oh man, are we profiling Steve?" Liam asked from the doorway. "I missed all the good stuff."

Liam would probably make the worst profiler ever. The man didn't care how people thought, just wanted to understand the best way to bring down bad guys.

"Don't worry, Liam, I'll try to control myself and not use your own weapon against you."

Liam at least had the good grace to look sheepish. "Sorry about that, boss. I know I—"

"Don't worry about it." Steve cut him off. "I know I haven't been the easiest person to be around for the last few months."

"Are you kidding me? I have a wife trying to nurse newborn twins. She hasn't gotten a decent night's sleep since they were born. You are not the grumpiest person I know."

Steve snickered. "Glad to hear I at least beat out an exhausted new mother."

"Yeah, well, I keep my weapons away from her too." Liam grinned.

The two men took a seat. It was good to feel something besides anger. Listening to Brandon's profile had helped Steve realize it was time to let it all go.

Yeah, he'd been a fool and had gotten played. But now it was time to move on.

Steve left late that night and was back in the office early the next morning, as per his usual habits. Like always, Cynthia was in the office before Steve got there.

"Morning, Steve." She handed him a stack of papers as he came in. "I've got your overnight Washington, DC, briefings, your weekly Omega Division Directors' update and your Pensacola police briefings."

Steve took the papers from her. "Thanks."

As he got to the door to his office, he turned back. It was time. Past time.

"You can stop the Pensacola PD briefings. I don't need those anymore."

He didn't even know why he had started them in

the first place. Well, actually, he did. He figured Rosalyn would probably be arrested at some point. If she was a small-time crook preying on traveling salesmen, she would probably get arrested eventually.

What he really didn't know was what the hell he planned to do if her name came across his desk in an arrest report. Press charges himself? Or go get her released and keep her with him and make sure she never did anything that stupid again?

He shook his head, irritated with himself for his thoughts. He walked over to the evidence bag with the glass. He picked it up and carried it to the trash can by his desk. He hesitated just the briefest of moments before tossing it in.

It was time.

Steve set the division updates—the weekly reports that allowed all the directors to know what was happening in the different sectors of Omega—in one pile. He grabbed the Pensacola police reports and prepared to throw them in the trash.

A picture from that group caught his attention and brought him up short. A Jane Doe the Pensacola police hadn't been able to identify.

It was Rosalyn. She looked like she was sleeping peacefully.

But the picture was from the county morgue.

Rosalyn was dead.

Chapter Five

Steve caught the first flight he could get to Pensacola. Sadness and guilt weighed on him the entire time.

The prints on the glass in his office—immediately fished out of the trash—were being run right now. If Rosalyn was in any law enforcement system, Steve would have the full results by the time he met with the Pensacola police.

Damn it, he should have run them earlier. Should've gotten her information and gone after Rosalyn himself. Okay, maybe she might have had to do a short stint in prison for theft, but at least she would be alive.

Steve had known something was wrong, known Rosalyn was in serious trouble, but he hadn't been able to look past his wounded pride to see she got the help she needed.

And now it was too late.

He got the information about the prints via email as he was getting off the plane in Pensacola.

Rosalyn Mellinger.

Twenty-four years old from Mobile, Alabama.

Her prints actually weren't in any of the law enforcement databases; that's why the Pensacola PD hadn't been able to identify her. Cynthia had been able to identify Rosalyn from something to do with her juvenile record. She couldn't access the full record but had been able to link the print from the glass to the record.

Steve drove straight to the police department, which also housed the coroner's office. It was midafternoon but Steve was determined to identify Rosalyn's body today. Somehow he couldn't stand the thought of her sitting another night unidentified in the morgue.

The Pensacola county sheriff and the coroner were both waiting for Steve when he walked in.

"Agent Drackett." The sheriff, a portly man in his fifties, extended his hand for shaking. "Is agent the right title? I'm Sheriff Harvey Palmer."

"Just call me Steve." He shook the man's hand.

"This is Dwayne Prase, our county coroner." Steve shook his hand too.

They began walking down the hallway to the morgue.

"We really appreciate you coming all the way from Colorado," Sheriff Palmer said. "I have to be honest—I didn't expect your call."

"I don't know the victim in any official capacity. I met her when I was on vacation here six months ago. We spent a few days together. I recognized her immediately when the Jane Doe picture came across my desk."

"I see." The sheriff nodded and thankfully didn't ask why Steve would be getting police reports from Pensacola. "No one here has missed her at all. No missing-persons report or anyone asking about her. Her prints didn't show up in any of our computers."

Steve nodded. If he hadn't had access to the Omega

databases, he wouldn't have known anything about Rosalyn either.

"She was definitely murdered?"

Palmer nodded. "Yes, strangled. In her car in a parking lot."

"She'd been dead for hours before anyone found her," the coroner chimed in. "And has been here unidentified for nearly thirty-six hours."

Steve brought his fingers up to the bridge of his nose. There was so much he wished he'd done differently.

They reached the cold chamber of the morgue, where the body was being kept to reduce decomposition. Steve entered with the two men and saw the body was already on the table ready to be identified.

Prase pulled the sheet slowly off the body's face.

Steve hadn't realized how much he'd been praying there had been some type of mistake, that it wasn't really Rosalyn, but looking at her now, he couldn't deny it.

"That's her. That's Rosalyn Mellinger."

STEVE SPENT THE next couple of hours with Sheriff Palmer, filling out some paperwork. He'd asked the sheriff if his men would mind if Steve stuck around for a couple of days and helped in any way he could with the investigation. Thankfully, Palmer hadn't felt threatened by the offer and readily agreed.

He'd called back into Omega and let them know he'd be out for a few days. One thing about having a team as good as his: they could continue to function without him when necessary.

Steve planned to find Rosalyn's killer. It was the least he could do.

But not tonight. Tonight he was going to go back to the tiki bar where he'd met her and have a drink in her memory.

Steve decided to stay at the same hotel he'd used before. Not the romance package, but still a nice place. It was only a few blocks from the station. He checked in and unloaded his overnight bag. He took off his suit and changed into jeans and a T-shirt. No shorts and flip-flops this time.

He decided to walk to the tiki bar from his room even though it was through sand. He stopped for a minute as he reached the area where he and Rosalyn had sat and talked for so long that first night, partially because he wanted to take a moment to remember that place.

But also because Steve could feel eyes on him.

Someone was watching him.

As inconspicuously as he could manage, Steve turned. He didn't see anything to his left. He knelt down into the sand as if he'd found some great shell and spun to the right. No one there either.

Maybe this feeling was just a result of stress. God knew today had been stressful enough.

He stood back up and began walking to the bar.

It was a Wednesday now, not a Sunday like when he'd been here before. The TVs had some basketball games on, and the place wasn't nearly as full.

No Jimmy Buffett playing on the jukebox, no storm driving in beautiful women from outside.

Steve didn't plan to be here long so didn't get his

seat at the end of the bar. Instead just sat at the first seat he came to and ordered a beer.

He was only a few sips into it when he felt eyes on him again. Steve quietly paid the bartender in case he had to leave in a hurry but then sat back and eased himself casually around in the barstool.

No one seemed to be paying him much mind, but he'd been in law enforcement too long to ignore a gut feeling twice in one hour.

Somebody was following him. Probably had been since he left the police station.

Maybe it was the killer trying to see who had identified his victim. Or maybe hoping to make another victim out of Steve.

Steve felt adrenaline pump through him. Bring it on. There was nothing he'd like better than a physical altercation with Rosalyn's killer before arresting him. They would have to send the perp to the hospital before taking him to a holding cell.

Steve took a sip of his beer and allowed his vision to become slightly unfocused so he could better see everything happening in the room at once. After just a few moments he caught what he was looking for.

Someone out on the deck in a hooded jacket watching him through the window. The figure ducked as soon as Steve glanced his way.

Steve moved immediately but had to go out the side door to make it to the deck, losing valuable moments. The guy had already headed down the outer stairs and was moving quickly toward the closest set of hotels. Picking out his black jacket and hood was difficult in the darkening sky.

But Steve had no plan to let him get away.

Steve looked forward to the hotel buildings where the man obviously planned to go—his car was probably parked there. Then he ran down the back stairs, jumping down the last few. He began running up the path to the hotel also, but on a different path so the guy wouldn't look back and think Steve was following him and move faster.

Steve was going to come around the other side of the building and cut him off.

It was a risky plan, dependent on the perp not changing course, but Steve didn't dwell on it. He put all his effort into getting around the other side of the building before the person got there.

Racing through sand wasn't easy but Steve knew he was gaining ground. From the corner of his eye Steve could see the perp was slowing down. Probably because he didn't see Steve behind him. Or maybe he was trying to blend in with some other tourists now that he was closer to the hotel.

Steve didn't slow down as sand gave way to a sidewalk, then to the asphalt surrounding the hotel. Glancing over, he saw the hooded figure slip down a slim walkway between two buildings. This was his chance.

Steve forced another burst of speed out of his body. He had to make it around the corner and to the walkway before the guy got through and made it into the parking lot. Steve wouldn't have much chance of finding him then.

Steve barreled around the corner ready to make a flying tackle if necessary, but the guy wasn't there. He immediately scanned the parking lot but saw only one group of teenage girls getting into their car and two parents removing kids from car seats in another.

No hooded man. Damn it.

Steve squinted in the fading light. He could be hiding behind a vehicle. Or had made it around the corner and run the other way.

Something caught his attention away from the parking lot. About halfway down the corridor he'd been expecting the perp to run through, a head stuck out, looking the other way. It was the guy, looking for Steve but looking the wrong way.

Steve flattened himself against the wall and began making his way toward the man. He pulled out his weapon, although he kept it low and pointed to the ground. He didn't want to cause any panic for vacationers who might alert the suspect that Steve was coming up behind him.

Quickly but silently, Steve approached the hooded figure, who still watched the other way.

"I'm armed law enforcement," Steve said as he made his last few steps and pointed his Glock directly at the man. "Very slowly put your hands behind your head."

Steve saw the guy stiffen and stepped closer in case he tried to run again or fight. He was small, but Steve had seen plenty of small people who could do a lot of damage. Hell, he'd helped train some of the best himself.

Steve didn't have cuffs with him, so he'd have to call Sheriff Palmer to come make the arrest.

"Just stay right there," he said as he pulled his phone out of his pocket.

The guy began to turn around.

"Hey, did you hear me?" Steve poked him in the back with his weapon. "Just stay right where you are."

"Steve." The voice was soft. Almost a whisper, but it sent a bolt of electricity through him.

Steve did something he hadn't done in twenty years of law enforcement: lowered his weapon in shock.

This wasn't a man at all. It was a woman.

"Rosalyn?"

She reached up and lowered the hood of her Windbreaker as she turned completely around.

It was her. Beautiful black hair, gorgeous blue eyes. Even the splattering of freckles over her nose. Rosalyn was alive.

Which was impossible because he'd just ID'd her dead body a few hours ago. Steve didn't care. By whatever miracle she was here—and he would get her to explain it all, no doubt—he would take it.

He holstered his weapon and pulled her into his arms. Then yanked her back immediately, looking closer at the rest of her body.

Rosalyn was here. She was alive.

And unless he was very, very wrong, she was definitely pregnant.

Chapter Six

Steve stared down at her belly for a long time. He finally looked up at her face again.

There were so many questions in his eyes she hardly knew how to start answering them all.

His hand gently touched her stomach, so that's where she started.

"Yes, I'm pregnant. Six months."

It wasn't terribly difficult math, so she let him work out for himself that the baby was his. She didn't want to say it outright, because she wasn't sure if he would even believe her. They hadn't parted on the greatest of terms, after all.

He studied her for a long time without saying anything. Rosalyn just stood there. She was as surprised to see him as he was to see her.

"I just identified your dead body," he finally said.

Okay, maybe not *quite* as surprised.

"My twin sister," she whispered. "Lindsey Rose. I didn't know she was dead until today. I was coming into the police department when I saw you leaving."

She'd been skeptical about going to the police station anyway, knowing the Watcher would probably be waiting for her there. When she saw Steve exit the building, she'd been totally thrown.

What was he doing there?

Steve was the last person Rosalyn expected to see. His presence had to have something to do with Lindsey's death. Why else would he be here from Colorado?

"Have you been following me from the police station?"

"Yes."

Steve's eyes narrowed. "Why? To tell me about the baby? Why did you run when I saw you at the bar?"

He fired off the questions faster than she could answer them. Not that she knew how to answer them anyway.

She hadn't expected to see Steve. She'd been about to cross the street into the police station, knowing her sister was dead and the Watcher had found her again.

She was six months pregnant, alone, frightened and grieving. She'd pushed back the terror, so her only thought had been identifying her sister so Lindsey could have a proper burial.

Then Steve had walked out the door. He'd looked so strong. So capable of handling anything life threw at him.

Rosalyn had gotten in her car and followed him without even meaning to. When she saw he was going to the same hotel and then the same bar where they'd met, she'd felt a little hope inside.

Maybe he didn't hate her.

Maybe she could tell him about the baby.

Maybe she could tell him about the Watcher and everything that had happened.

She needed help.

But when his eyes had flown to her at the bar, obviously suspecting trouble, she'd panicked. She'd run—well, run as fast as her body would let her—to get away.

But she hadn't gotten away. He'd caught her and said—

He was law enforcement?

"You're a *cop*?"

He took a step closer, obviously trying to use his size to intimidate her. "You didn't answer my questions."

She couldn't get into the entire story now. They were too out in the open. "I will answer your questions, but not out here. You told me you were in management before."

Steve shrugged. "I never said what sort of management I was in. And I want answers to my questions before I arrest you."

"Arrest me for what?"

"How about the theft of nearly $200 six months ago?"

Rosalyn's face heated. "I'm sorry about that. I didn't have any other choice. I was desperate. My whole time with you I was pretty desperate."

That wasn't the right word, or at least she should've phrased it differently, she realized when he stiffened and stepped back. She hadn't meant that she'd spent time with him because she was desperate, but he'd obviously taken it that way.

"I guess your little souvenir from our time together—" he gestured at her belly "—wasn't what you wanted, then. Is the baby even mine?"

"Yes." She took a step toward him without even meaning to. "I know you probably don't believe me, but you're the only man I've been with for a long time." The only man she'd allowed herself to trust in a long time.

"Yeah, well, once the kid is born, there are paternity tests that are probably in our best interests to complete."

Rosalyn knew she shouldn't be hurt given what had happened between them but she couldn't help it. "Of course. I don't expect you to just believe me."

Now that the Watcher had found her again, she needed Steve's help whether he believed her or not. She had more than just herself to look out for. Steve didn't know the entire situation but at least she knew she could trust him.

Steve ran a hand through his hair. "Look, I'm not trying to be an ass. You've caught me off guard on multiple levels here. But I need some answers."

"Okay. I have a room at a hotel a few miles from here. Let's go there."

ROSALYN WAS ALIVE.

Rosalyn was alive *and* pregnant. Steve could hardly get his head around the first part, much less the second.

She was sitting right in front of him in a pretty scary run-down hotel room they'd driven to in her car, eating a packet of crackers. He was sitting in the desk chair that he'd pulled over and placed right in front of the bed just watching her. Like her eating crackers was the most interesting thing he'd ever seen.

Did she need more food than that? Was she taking care of herself? Had she been seeing a doctor throughout her pregnancy to make sure everything was okay?

Was the baby honestly his? They had used protection. But he knew accidents still happened.

He wanted to believe her when she'd said yes. She'd taken off her jacket and he could more clearly see the outline of her stomach under the T-shirt she wore. There was very definitely a baby bump. Not one that had her waddling or anything like that, but very definitely pregnant. Someone as petite as Rosalyn couldn't hide it.

He wanted to ask her all sorts of questions about her pregnancy but had so many other questions to ask that those got pushed to the back burner.

Steve sorted through important information for a living, made decisions on where Omega's Critical Response team would go and what they would do, based on his reading of a situation. Knowing what questions to ask to get the information he needed was his *job*. And lives depended on his ability to do it well.

But damned if he knew where to start with Rosalyn.

The dead body seemed the most reasonable place.

"So the woman I identified in the morgue—"

"Like I said, my identical twin, Lindsey Rose Mellinger. My mom—in a fit of soberness—thought it was quite clever."

Rosalyn and Lindsey Rose. "The reversal of each other. Well, almost."

She nodded. "Yeah. And it ended up being true in just about everything. We were twins, but we were complete opposites. Very different from each other except for how we looked."

"When was the last time you saw your sister alive?"

Tears came to Rosalyn's eyes, but she brushed them away. "At least a year and a half ago. We've never been close but grew even further apart as adults. Lindsey was in and out of drug rehab all the time. She still lived in Mobile."

"And that's where you're from?" Steve already knew the answer to that but wondered if she would lie.

"Yes, but I haven't lived there for nearly a year."

Steve wondered where she'd been for the past six months, but he'd get to that.

"Do you know anything about your sister's death?"

She shook her head. "No, but she was murdered, wasn't she?"

"What makes you say that?"

This time the tears overflowed before Rosalyn could wipe them away. "Lindsey was in Pensacola because I asked her to meet me. We were supposed to meet at a restaurant a few blocks from here two days ago, but she never showed up."

She gave him the name and address of a local café. Lindsey's body had been found inside her car very close to that area.

"Lindsey's pretty flighty," Rosalyn continued. "I thought she'd just gotten the day or time wrong. Or that she was high again. I didn't know she was dead until a waiter showed me a tiny section of the local paper that stated the police were looking for information about a deceased Jane Doe who looked exactly like me."

Rosalyn stood up and grabbed a tissue from the box

on the small desk. "I was coming by this afternoon to identify the body when I saw you."

"You said she did drugs a lot, so what makes you think she was murdered? Don't you think it's more likely something happened with her drug abuse?"

"Normally, yes." She sat back down. "But I suspect foul play because she was meeting me."

"I don't understand."

Rosalyn's blue eyes bore into him. "You saw her body, right?"

Steve nodded.

"I'll answer your questions, I promise. But first please tell me, was she murdered?"

Steve couldn't see any good in lying to her. "Yes, I'm sorry. She was strangled in her car."

Rosalyn began to cry quietly, holding her face in her hands. Steve moved to sit next to her. No matter what had happened between the two of them, he would never deny comfort to someone who had lost a family member.

"I had hoped you would tell me something different. That it was related to drugs," she finally said.

"I don't understand why you don't think it would've been." In Steve's experience, when regular people heard a family member had died, they did not assume it was murder. And if Lindsey had been involved in illegal drugs, Steve didn't know why Rosalyn didn't assume the murder wasn't centered around that.

Because Rosalyn knew something. Something she wasn't telling him.

"Rosalyn." He tilted a finger under her chin so she

was looking directly at him. "Tell me. Whatever is going on, I need you to tell me."

She tried to look away, but he wouldn't let her.

"I can't." Another tear slid silently down her cheek. "I can't risk you too."

Steve stared at the tiny woman—tiny, *pregnant* woman—determined to protect him. Why would she care about him if he was just someone she had scammed and robbed? Either way, he was getting to the bottom of all this.

"I can take care of myself, Rosalyn. Just tell me what's going on."

At first he didn't think she was going to answer, but finally she did.

"For the past year someone has been stalking me."

Steve sat up straighter. "Stalking you how?"

"Mostly he leaves notes. Ones he slides under my door while I'm sleeping at night." She shuddered. "Although on occasion he has emailed, texted or called me."

He'd been in law enforcement long enough to take stalkers very seriously. Especially ones who were close enough to leave notes under doors. That meant they were close and probably deadly. "What types of messages?"

"Never anything threatening. Not even 'We'll be together forever' stuff. Usually just little comments about something that has happened in my day."

Odd for a stalker, making it about her rather than about him. Stalkers were usually caught up in their own fantasy world and tried to make their victims a part of that.

"And you reported it?"

"Yes. I told my family first about a year ago. They just accused me of wanting attention. I decided to move across town, just to get rid of the weirdo, hoping that would stop it all."

"But it didn't?"

"The first night I moved into my new apartment, someone slid a note under my door."

Steve frowned. The guy had been following her closely. "Did you go to the local police?"

"Yes, I talked to them in Mobile, but I had thrown a lot of the letters away, so they didn't believe it was anyone wishing to do me harm."

It was easy to be frustrated with the Mobile police for doing nothing to help Rosalyn, but the truth was, funds were always limited in local departments. If the notes weren't threatening Rosalyn in any way, it would be easy to not give them or her much attention.

She stood up and began walking back and forth.

"It got so bad that after about a month I chose to just leave town. I had a pretty big savings account, so I quit my job and decided to go somewhere different. Anywhere different. I didn't have a moving truck, didn't grab a bunch of suitcases—I just got in my car one morning and left."

She stopped walking for a minute.

"I ended up in Dallas. Thought it would be a cool town to vacation in while I was losing my annoying little follower. Thought I had done it too, until the second night. Another note under my door mentioning the crème brûlée I had eaten at dinner."

She wasn't looking at him, but he could hear the fear in her voice.

"I left just minutes later. Drove all around to make sure no one was following me. Ended up in Shreveport. I went straight to the police station."

It wasn't the best of plans, since nothing had happened in their jurisdiction, but Steve didn't tell Rosalyn that. She would've been better off going to the Dallas police.

But a note that mentioned a dessert probably wouldn't have been taken seriously there either.

"Nobody wanted to listen to me, but this one detective, Johnson, offered to meet me after he got off his shift. I told him everything, and he helped me. Or he tried."

"What did he do?"

She began rubbing her hands on her legs, a nervous gesture he didn't think she was aware of.

"I showed him what notes I had kept. He told me to keep them all, and any I got from now on, in a box. And he gave me a notebook and showed me how to keep track of everything that the Watcher did."

He reached over and grabbed her hands so she would stop the rubbing. "The Watcher?"

"Yeah, that's what I call him. I've kept everything since Detective Johnson showed me what to do."

"And did he do anything with it? Did it go any further?"

"Unfortunately, he died of a heart attack the next day."

Steve's head snapped up. "Was he old?"

"Maybe fifty. And in pretty good shape."

"That's a damn unfortunate coincidence." And probably a devastating blow for Rosalyn, to have found someone who wanted to help, then died.

"I thought so too until I got an anonymous email the next day about a drug that caused heart attacks."

"What?"

"The Watcher killed Detective Johnson. He's killed everyone I've told about him. I'm afraid you'll be next."

Chapter Seven

Steve didn't believe her.

He wasn't overt in his disbelief, didn't mock her or anything like that. But she could tell he didn't think the Watcher was actually a credible threat. He thought Detective Johnson, a fifty-year-old policeman, had died of a heart attack.

It certainly happened all the time. Police work was stressful.

Her sister was also dead, but she'd been a drug addict. That happened all the time too.

She didn't tell him about Shawn, the mechanic, who'd also died after she'd told him about the Watcher. Because she could already tell Steve thought she was exaggerating.

She'd recognized the placating look. The attempt to figure out how to convince her of reason without offending her. He didn't want to add to her stress, but he also didn't think there was anything sinister to her story.

Not to mention he was still pretty shocked about her reappearance and pregnancy. So she should probably cut him a little slack.

She hadn't planned to drag him into this. Because whether he wanted to believe her or not, she knew it was true: the Watcher would try to kill him next.

Rosalyn wanted to run, to try to keep Steve safe. But she couldn't anymore. She had to face the fact that soon it wouldn't just be her. She'd have the baby. She couldn't go back on the run with a child in tow.

She'd had six months of relative peace. Although she'd lived in fear every single night of the Watcher contacting her, he hadn't. Rosalyn didn't know why. She'd thought he'd given up, decided to leave her alone.

She'd made a huge error, she realized now, contacting her sister. It had not only cost Lindsey her life, but put Rosalyn back on the Watcher's radar.

She knew she wouldn't escape him again. Not without help.

Steve turned to her. "Look, let's just sleep on everything tonight. We can discuss this more in the morning."

She nodded. Maybe if she showed him the notes, he'd take her more seriously. Plus, she knew the questioning was nowhere near done on either side.

He was a cop and had deliberately withheld that information from her. She wasn't mad, but it changed some things. Maybe he could help protect her from the Watcher.

Of course, Detective Johnson had been in law enforcement too, and the Watcher had killed him. But that had been before she had realized how far the Watcher would go. Until Johnson's death Rosalyn had assumed only she would be his victim. She knew better now.

When they met tomorrow, she would have to make sure Steve understood the danger he was in.

"Okay, what time do you want to meet tomorrow?"

Steve looked at her like she'd lost her mind. "I'm not leaving you here. You're coming with me."

She hadn't been expecting that. "Why?"

"Multiple reasons. One, I don't trust that you're not going to be gone again in the morning."

Rosalyn felt her face heat but didn't say anything.

"Two, by your very own account you have a stalker and possibly a murderer after you. I'm not sure what all the facts are in this case, but I intend to find out. You can believe I won't be leaving you alone as I do it, especially not if you're carrying my child."

Rosalyn felt relief wash through her. Steve might not believe her completely but at least he was willing to look into it. And help protect her and the baby.

"Now, I will stay in this fleabag motel if you really insist on remaining here. But I would prefer we go to my hotel." He glanced around in distaste, then looked straight at her. "Either way, you can plan on spending tonight—every night until we figure out this stalker situation and the baby is born—with me."

He obviously didn't necessarily believe the baby was his, but at least he was willing to try to keep Rosalyn safe until he knew for sure. She wasn't sure whether to be thankful or offended.

But to stay here when he had a nicer place would just be foolish.

"Okay. Just let me get my stuff."

He took her duffel bag and walked her to her car. He took the key from her and put her bag in the trunk.

"Have you been going from town to town for the last six months?"

Rosalyn bit her lip. Telling him the truth, that the Watcher hadn't contacted her since she'd last been in Pensacola, wasn't going to help him believe her about how dangerous her stalker was.

She didn't know why the Watcher hadn't contacted her while she'd been hidden at the Ammonses' home in Georgia, had lived in constant fear that he would, but she'd been thankful for the reprieve.

"Let me go pay for the room. You stay here," he said.

"No, I'll pay. I can afford it."

One of his eyebrows raised. "I don't even want to know how you got the money."

"I didn't steal it, all right? That was a one-time thing and only because I was desperate."

He still didn't look like he believed it.

"You stay here with the car and I'll go pay." She gave him the evilest glare she could.

Which only made him smile. "Fine, you pay. I'll be here."

The motel office was at the other end of the parking lot, close to the main street. Rosalyn was aware she was marching off in a huff and had neither the size nor stature to pull that off with any authority, especially when she looked like she'd swallowed half a basketball. She knew Steve was probably laughing at her, but she didn't care.

At least if he was laughing at her, he wasn't threatening to arrest her. Not that she really thought he planned to.

She went inside and paid her bill, a little mad that

they still charged her for two nights even though she'd stayed only one. Regardless, she wasn't going to let Steve pay. At least the extra cost didn't cause her the panic it once would have, since she now had some money saved up from being able to work the last six months. She signed the paperwork, paid her bill and walked back out the door toward her car.

"I'll pay you back all that money, you know," she called out, moving directly toward him.

He walked toward her. "It's not necessary to pay me back. You can—"

Rosalyn heard the roar of an engine and turned. A car, headlights off, was screeching toward her, swerving back and forth.

"Hey, look out!" someone yelled from a second-floor walkway.

Rosalyn couldn't figure out which way to move to get out of the car's oncoming path. All she knew was that it was going to hit her.

She was still frozen in place, certain of her own demise, when a huge force hit her from the side.

Steve.

He pulled her to his chest and continued their momentum out of the car's direct path, somehow managing to spin them so he took the weight of the fall.

Both of them covered her belly with their arms.

They were on the ground for only a split second before Steve jumped back up to his feet. He pulled his gun from the holster and pointed it at the car.

But the driver put the car in Reverse and began speeding at Steve. The vehicle hit him and knocked him backward.

"Steve!" Rosalyn screamed from where she lay on the ground.

He sat up and got one shot off, but when the car sped toward him again, he had to stop and roll to the side out of the way. He began firing again.

Rosalyn scooted herself back, unsure what the car would do. But thankfully, it sped off.

Steve ran over to her and placed his hands over hers on her stomach. "Are you okay? I'm sorry I hit you so hard."

Her heart was still racing but she didn't think she was injured. "Better you than the car. I'm fine. And I'm pretty sure the baby is okay. You took the brunt of the fall."

The manager ran out of the office. "Oh my gosh, are you guys all right? I just called 911. That guy had to have been drunk."

Two other people ran out from the building. "We saw the whole thing. Did anybody get the license plate?"

They all began to talk over each other.

Rosalyn tuned them out and started to stand up, but Steve's hands kept her gently on the ground. "Just stay there, okay? There's an ambulance coming. Let's just be safe and wait."

She nodded. Her heart still beat erratically but otherwise she didn't feel too bad. But Steve was right—better to let them check her out, just in case.

"Damn drunk driver. You guys are lucky to be alive," the manager said. "I mean, the way he reversed like that? Couldn't figure out which way was forward."

Rosalyn looked over at Steve. His eyes said the same thing as hers. That had been no drunk driver.

"Are you okay?" she asked him. "You're the one who got hit by the car."

He let out a small groan as he sat down on the asphalt beside her. "Yeah, nothing broken, I'm pretty sure."

Activity buzzed around them, but Rosalyn and Steve just sat in silence. His hand was never far from her stomach. Soon the ambulance and police showed up. Rosalyn was assisted onto the stretcher and put inside the ambulance while Steve talked to the cops.

She didn't know exactly what he said to them, but within minutes the ambulance was on its way and Steve was riding beside her. He left her side only when they arrived at the hospital, to talk to some member of the staff.

Again, Rosalyn couldn't hear but twenty minutes later she was being seen by the hospital's chief OB-GYN physician even though it was nearly ten o'clock at night. Dr. Puglisi had her hooked up to an ultrasound machine as soon as she heard what happened.

"There," Dr. Puglisi said, pointing to the monitor. "Good, strong heartbeat. Baby is absolutely fine."

Tears poured down Rosalyn's cheeks as she grabbed Steve's hand beside her. "Thank God."

"A woman's body is pretty amazing at protecting the fetus growing inside it. It generally takes more than a fall to cause real problems." Dr. Puglisi moved the ultrasound wand. "Do you know the gender of the baby?"

Rosalyn shook her head. "Not yet. It was scheduled for my next appointment."

"Would you like to know?"

Rosalyn looked over at Steve but he just shrugged. "That's completely up to you."

She tried not to show the hurt she felt by his nonchalance but knew she couldn't blame Steve. It was too soon.

Rosalyn turned back to the doctor. "Yes, I'd like to know, if you can tell."

The doctor smiled. "Congratulations—your strong resilient baby is a boy."

Chapter Eight

He was going to have a son.

Dr. Puglisi had run a number of tests on Rosalyn, just to double-check that everything was okay. That she was healthy, the baby was healthy and nothing was going to creep up on them unawares.

Some of the tests she did were to establish the gestational age of the child.

Every indication was that the fetus was twenty-five weeks developed. That would mean he was conceived six months ago.

Steve knew that didn't mean the baby was his. But it was definitely a step closer.

The most important thing right now was that both Rosalyn and the baby were healthy. His flying tackle hadn't hurt either of them in any way.

When he'd seen that car speeding toward Rosalyn his heart had stopped. Only years of training, his body responding almost before his mind did, had him moving forward to get her out of the way.

Drunk driver, his ass.

Steve might possibly have believed it if the guy hadn't backed up to run over him.

Someone had been trying to kill Rosalyn or Steve or both of them. He'd made it look like he was a drunk driver, but after everything Rosalyn had told him, that was one coincidence too many.

Funny thing was, until the attack happened, he hadn't really believed Rosalyn about her Watcher theory. To Steve, her description of the situation broke too many of the typical patterns that would be found in a stalker committed enough to kill people.

He'd spent the last hour in a room the hospital had lent him for privacy, on the phone with Sheriff Harvey Palmer. He explained about Rosalyn and her twin, Lindsey. Explained how Lindsey's prints weren't in the system but Rosalyn's were, although he still didn't know why.

Steve also told Palmer what had happened with the car. A dark two-door Toyota with no plates wasn't going to be particularly helpful, but the sheriff agreed to run the description against other incidents in the area. Maybe they'd get lucky.

Steve finished the call by telling Palmer he'd be taking Rosalyn with him out of Florida.

He was going to take her to Colorado Springs. Back to Omega Critical Response headquarters. If they were fighting some villain intent on hurting Rosalyn and her baby, Steve planned to fight on his own turf.

Once he finished with Sheriff Palmer, he called his office.

"Steve Drackett's office."

"Angela, it's me." Someone was in Steve's office twenty-four hours a day, seven days a week to be able to field calls that might come from as far up as the White House. Angela tended to work the evening shifts.

"Hey, boss. I thought you were taking a couple of personal days."

"I was, but my situation has changed. I'm going to need you to book me two tickets on a flight from Pensacola to Colorado Springs for as early as possible tomorrow. Me and a Rosalyn Mellinger."

"Okay, no problem. I'll text you with the details."

"Anything exciting happening around the office?"

"All in all, a pretty quiet day. If you can believe it."

A *quiet day* might have only meant there were no events threatening national security.

"I'm glad to hear it. I'll be back tomorrow."

"See you then, sir."

A doctor had already looked over Steve's wounds—some road rash and bruises—and declared him free to go. What had happened tonight could've been much worse.

He walked down the hallway and saw Rosalyn joking with one of the nurses. He was struck again by her natural beauty and animation.

It could've been much, much worse.

He'd spent six months angry with her, followed by a day of terrible sadness when he thought she was dead. He'd then been given the precious gift of a second chance when he'd found out she was alive.

Her smile still took his breath away just like it had six months ago.

"You ready to go?" he asked her.

She jumped down from the table. "Yep. Dr. Puglisi said I was done as soon as you were."

"Good. It's getting pretty late. I think we both could use some sleep. We'll go back to my hotel like we'd originally planned."

A uniformed officer had driven Rosalyn's car over from the scene of the accident at Steve's request. He opened the door for her to get in and made his way over to the driver's side.

He eased slowly out of the parking lot and began to drive. He didn't go directly to the hotel, instead took leisurely routes going nowhere near where they would be staying.

After an hour Steve was absolutely positive no one was following them. He'd actually been sure of it for twenty minutes before that, but Rosalyn had fallen asleep and waking her up seemed heartless. She'd had a hell of a day. First Steve pulling a gun on her, then someone trying to kill her. Not to mention dealing with her sister's recent death.

She deserved a nap.

They had so much they needed to talk about. He needed to find out all the details she had about the Watcher. Needed to know where she'd been for the last six months.

Needed to tell her that he was the director of an elite law enforcement agency and was probably more uniquely situated to protect her than anyone else. Even though he'd almost been killed today.

Yes, it was possible it was a drunk driver who had nearly run them over, but Steve would still be on high guard until he knew exactly what it was they were up against.

He drove around a few more minutes before pulling the car up to his hotel on the beach. He got out and looked around for a few minutes, making sure no one had picked them up in the last few minutes. Unlikely but possible.

Nothing. It was completely quiet in the parking lot. The beach was deserted also. All to be expected at nearly midnight on a Wednesday.

Steve walked over and got Rosalyn's duffel bag out of the trunk. She was still clutching her tote bag in her arms, just like she had been when he'd known her six months ago.

He opened her door and nudged her gently on the shoulder. "Hey, Sleeping Beauty, let's get you inside so you can sleep properly."

Her eyes barely opened but she got out of the car. He put an arm around her and led her through the lobby and up the elevator to their room on the seventh floor. He used his key card to get in.

This room was definitely less romantic than the setup six months ago. But from the look in Rosalyn's tired eyes, she didn't care about romance tonight.

"I'm just going to go straight to bed. Is that okay?" She lay down on the bed, on top of the covers, shoes still on. Evidently, having only one bed didn't bother her. She was sound asleep again.

Steve set her duffel bag on the chair and walked over to her. He untied and slipped off her athletic shoes. He then lifted her body with one arm—it shouldn't be that easy; if they hadn't just been reassured by one of the best doctors in the area that Rosalyn was perfectly healthy, Steve would've worried much more about how little she weighed—so he could tuck her under the blankets.

She never even stirred.

Steve shook his head, smiling. She was like a child. He didn't know if that was how she normally slept or if it was a product of exhaustion, pregnancy and stress.

It had been a long day. Steve took a shower, wincing at the sting of the water against his scrapes, and changed into fresh clothes.

Tomorrow he would have Rosalyn in Colorado. He realized she hadn't actually agreed to that yet. He wasn't trying to keep the information a secret, but neither was it up for negotiation. Steve needed to figure out what was going on. The Critical Response Division headquarters was the best place for him to do that.

The body of Rosalyn's sister still needed to be taken care of, but Rosalyn's mother would have to do that. He hoped Rosalyn wouldn't fight him about going to Colorado.

Not because he wouldn't take her if she did. He would still take her. It would just make it much more difficult.

But he'd fight that battle if he came to it. Right now she was sleeping peacefully and he should do the same.

He slid next to her into the king-size bed. His body wanted to grab her and pull her into his arms, but he knew that wasn't wise. Too many unresolved issues between them. Until he knew exactly what was happening, how much he could trust her, he knew he needed to keep his distance.

He looked over at Rosalyn, who had turned onto her

side in an attempt to get more comfortable. She looked innocent, lovely, fragile.

But in his line of work he'd learned how very easy it was for looks to deceive.

He would keep on his side of the bed. It was better for everyone that way.

STEVE WOKE UP and immediately sensed something was wrong.

Rosalyn lay completely snuggled in his arms, draped over him like a blanket. So much for keeping his distance from her.

But that wasn't what was wrong.

He looked over at the window. No light was peeking through, so it was obviously still night. He estimated about four o'clock in the morning.

What had awakened him?

He listened for any sounds that would be foreign. Someone trying to break into the room or yells from farther away.

Nothing.

Then he smelled it. Smoke. Too heavy to be just some cigarette somebody was toking on illegally on a balcony.

He shook Rosalyn. "Wake up, sweetheart."

She just mumbled and tried to move away from the hands disturbing her sleep. Steve shook her again. "Rosalyn, come on, you need to wake up." He pulled her until she was in a sitting position.

"What's going on?" she asked, blinking multiple times. "Is it morning?"

"There's trouble, I'm pretty sure."

He ran over to the door. He could see smoke seeping under the crack. He ran back and grabbed the hotel phone. As soon as someone answered, he barked out, "I'm in room 742. There's a fire in the hallway but the alarm isn't sounding. You need to call the fire department and get some sort of alarm working."

He didn't wait for the person to answer. He grabbed one of Rosalyn's shoes. "Can you put these on or do you need help?"

"I can do it. I'm slow, but I can get them."

He handed her one shoe and put the other on her foot himself. "We're going to have to get out of here. I'm not sure how bad the smoke and fire will be."

She grabbed her tote bag and pulled it over her shoulder. Fine, she could take that, but the rest of the stuff would have to stay.

He stood and led her to the bathroom. "Soak these towels. We'll keep them over our faces to protect us from the fire and smoke as best we can."

She began running water over them as he went to check the door again. The smoke was even heavier under the crack.

He opened the door slightly to see exactly what they were up against. He couldn't see three feet down the hall, the smoke was so thick. There was no way they'd be able to wait for the fire department to get up to their floor.

He shut the door, taking the wet towels from her. "It's bad out there. We're not going to be able to see much of anything. But we need to make it to the stairs."

"I don't know where they are." Panic pinched her face. "Are they near the elevator?"

"No." As a force of habit Steve had memorized the general layout of the hotel when he'd checked in. "They're a little bit farther. Just keep hold of my hand, no matter what."

She nodded, eyes big. He wrapped one of the wet towels around the lower part of her face. "I'm not sure the extent of the fire, but the smoke is thick out there. It's going to be rough. Stay low and breathe through the towel as much as possible."

When he opened the door again, he immediately felt heat to the right. The fire was closer than it had been moments ago.

And blocking their way to the stairs.

"We're going to have to go to the far staircase," he told Rosalyn. "Stay with me no matter what."

She nodded and he pulled the door open farther. Smoke immediately filled their room. Steve bent at the waist to get lower than the worst of the smoke in the hall. He knew bending that way would be difficult for Rosalyn. He was glad she was significantly shorter than he was to start with.

He lost all visibility only a few feet from their hotel room. He had to rely on his instincts and his mind's ability to process spatial data to get them to where they needed to be.

He could feel Rosalyn's small hand in his and knew that if he made a mistake, missed the door to the stairs or turned down the wrong hall, it could mean their deaths.

About halfway to where he estimated the stairs were, the smoke got so thick they had to crawl. Steve's eyes burned, although the wet towel at least protected his throat from the worst of the smoke.

He turned back to Rosalyn. Tears were streaming from her eyes. He knew his looked the same.

"Pull the towel all the way over your face," he yelled back at her. "I'll guide you out."

She didn't argue, just pulled the towel past her nose, over her eyes. It wouldn't help her for long, but it had to be better than nothing.

She was putting her trust in him completely to guide her out. He wouldn't let her down.

He crawled as rapidly as he could—feeling her hand on his ankle as she crawled behind him—until he found what he hoped was the right door. If not, they would be in dire straits. He could feel heat licking behind them.

The sound of glass breaking came from the other end of the hall, probably firefighters, but they wouldn't get the blaze and smoke under control quickly enough to help Rosalyn and Steve.

Steve reached up from his crawl to the door handle and sighed in relief when it opened.

They were at the stairs. Steve dragged Rosalyn inside the much cooler stairwell. People were running down the stairs, some crying, some screaming.

Steve stood and scooped Rosalyn up in his arms. He pulled the towel down from her face to find her looking out at him with those blue eyes.

"I'm okay," she whispered, voice a little husky. "I can walk."

He shook his head. He wasn't going to take a chance on her getting trampled or knocked down the stairs by someone in a panic.

He'd almost lost her twice today. And that was *after* he'd already ID'd her dead body.

He carried her to safety himself.

Chapter Nine

Rosalyn found herself being checked out by Dr. Puglisi for the second time in eight hours. Another ultrasound.

And thank God again both she and the baby were all right.

"I can admit you if you want, especially since it seems like fate wants you here in the hospital." Dr. Puglisi peered over her medical chart at Rosalyn. "But honestly, there's no reason for you to stay."

Rosalyn's eyes and throat hurt, like Steve had told her his did. Neither of them had inhaled enough smoke to do any real damage, thanks to Steve's quick thinking and ability to get them to the stairwell and out of the smoke rapidly.

"You're fortunate, of course," the doctor continued. "Both times tonight. Especially for someone who seems to be a magnet for trouble."

"I don't want to stay at the hospital if I don't have to, and if the baby is safe." Rosalyn put a hand protectively over her stomach.

"That little guy is perfectly fine. As a matter of fact, any day now you're going to be feeling him move more pronouncedly."

"All I've felt is like I have bubbles in my stomach all the time."

Dr. Puglisi smiled at her. "Those bubbles, the fluttery feeling, is your son."

"It is?" Rosalyn looked over at Steve. He was looking as shocked as she felt.

"Trust me." The doctor smiled again, then turned toward the door. "It won't be long until it's less like bubbles and more like karate kicks. Now, please, don't let me see you back here again tonight."

The doctor left and Rosalyn turned to Steve. He'd been by her side on the ride to the hospital—he'd driven them himself this time instead of taking an ambulance—and the entire time she'd waited to see Dr. Puglisi. He'd been pretty quiet that whole time too, pensive. The only time he really talked had been when he'd stepped out into the hallway to discuss something with someone from the sheriff's office. He'd also been back and forth on his phone all night.

"I'm going to take a shower." She slid her legs over the side of the hospital bed. They'd been given a private room with a bathroom; she might as well make use of it. She had a change of clothes in her tote bag.

"Good idea. I'll take one as soon as you're done." He walked beside her to the door, as if he was afraid she might need help.

"I'm okay," she told him. "I didn't get hurt."

He flattened his lips, narrowed his eyes, obviously upset. They'd both almost been killed twice tonight, so his anger was justified.

She wanted to talk to him about the fire. That had to have been just a terrible coincidence, right?

Or had the Watcher been so close he'd followed them or heard them talking about where they would be staying.

Rosalyn couldn't stop the shudder that ripped through her at the thought.

Steve was close enough to see it. "Sure you're okay?"

No, she wasn't sure she was okay. The opposite. And now she had dragged Steve down the rabbit hole with her.

A dark, dangerous rabbit hole where someone was determined to kill everyone who got close to her. And now it looked like maybe the Watcher was trying to kill her too.

She opened her mouth to ask Steve what he thought, what they should do. But he put a finger over her lips before she could get the words out.

"Shower. You'll feel better. You're safe here—we both are. Let's take advantage of that."

Rosalyn nodded. He was right.

"Do you mind if I borrow your cell phone while you're in there?"

"I don't have one. It was one of the first things I got rid of."

"You haven't had one since you've come back to Pensacola?"

She shook her head. "I haven't had one since the Watcher followed me to Dallas and sent me a series of texts. I destroyed it. Thought it might be the way he was following me."

"Smart girl. I was thinking the same thing."

She shrugged. "I didn't want to give him any extra means of being able to communicate with me."

"Okay."

Steve was right—the shower did help her feel better. Or at least washed away the smell of the smoke that had almost taken their lives.

Steve took one after her but didn't have a set of his own clothes to change into. A nurse brought a set of scrubs for him to wear, as well as a T-shirt.

Steve made a hot doctor as well as law enforcement officer.

Which was another thing they needed to talk about. Exactly what he did in law enforcement. Just add that to the list of all the stuff they still needed to talk about.

Less than an hour after changing they walked out of the hospital. Steve hadn't said much to her during that time, but he definitely had a plan.

"Do you want to tell me what exactly the plan is?" she asked as they got back into her car.

"I'm a cop who works in Miami. I've booked us a flight there that leaves in a couple of hours."

Of all the things he might have said, that wasn't what she'd expected. "You told me you were from Colorado."

He looked over at her, eyes narrowed. "I guess neither of us was telling the truth that night."

Rosalyn knew she had stolen from him. She was the one who had left him without a word. But somehow finding out that he had been lying about things he'd told her during their time together hurt her. He'd obviously wanted to make sure she could never track him down.

He winced. "Rosalyn—"

She sat up straighter in the seat. "No, you're right. We were both dishonest. And you don't have to take me with you now. As a matter of fact, that's probably better."

"No, you'll stay with me."

Why did he need her to stay with him now when he had gone out of his way to make sure she wouldn't be able to find him six months ago? She wanted to argue further but he had pulled into the parking lot of a superstore.

"Let's go. I need some clothes and you'll need some other stuff."

"Can't this wait until we get to Miami?" Why would he want to buy clothes here when he'd be back to his own home and stuff in just a couple of hours? His scrubs were unusual, but not overly so.

"No. Let's go." He got out of the car and went around to her side. "Bring your bag, everything."

She left the sweater in the seat and got out.

"No, bring that too."

"But I'm not cold."

He grabbed it out of the seat. "Bring it all anyway. Let's go."

She barely resisted rolling her eyes at his gruff tone. What had happened to the man who had been talking to her so kindly—trying to understand everything about what had been happening to her over the past year—a few hours ago at her run-down hotel room?

This gruff stranger had replaced him. He didn't seem to want to talk to her at all.

Maybe it was the two near-death experiences in one night since hanging around her. She couldn't blame him for that. Whether he was in law enforcement or not, it looked like Rosalyn might be back on her own again soon.

His actions inside the store didn't reassure her. He grabbed a cart, then kept her right next to him as they went through both the women's section, where he told her to grab jeans and a shirt, and men's, where they did the same for him.

He even grabbed underwear for both of them. When she tried to protest that she'd had a spare set in the tote bag, he ignored her and grabbed a set anyway. He pulled her to the dressing room, which was thankfully empty of everyone, including an attendant, since it was nearly six o'clock in the morning.

"Change all your clothes." He turned and walked toward the men's changing room.

Rosalyn had had just about enough of the manhandling.

"Look, I don't know exactly what your problem is, although honestly, I can understand if you're upset because of both the drunk-driver guy and the fire. But let's just talk about it, okay?"

Steve looked at her for a long time, then finally just turned away again. "No, not right now."

She could actually feel her eyes bugging out of her head. "Not right now? What is the matter with you?"

"Just go put on the other clothes."

"Maybe I'm just fine in the clothes I'm in. Have you thought of—"

The air rushed out of her body as he grabbed her by the arms and walked forward—forcing her backward into the dressing room. He went in right along with her and didn't stop until her back was up against the wall and he was pressed all the way up against her.

She would've thought he'd lost his mind if she hadn't been so turned on by the feel of him pressed against her. His mouth was just inches from hers and she couldn't stop staring at it.

But his lips didn't kiss her. Instead he dipped his head right next to her ear.

"You're bugged."

At first all she felt was the delicious heat from his breath on her earlobe. Then his whispered words made their way through her desire-addled brain.

"What—?"

She barely got the words out before his lips were on hers. She realized it was a kiss to stop her from saying anything that would give away the information about the bug, but she still couldn't stop her arms from circling up around his shoulders.

His lips moved back down her jaw until he was at her ear again.

"It's important that we not say anything that gives away that we know. I'll explain more later, but right now, we need to ditch everything."

Rosalyn nodded.

"Ahem, excuse me, mister. Men aren't allowed in the ladies' dressing room." A young store associate peeked his head into the room. "I'm afraid you'll have to change in the men's section."

Steve nodded and looked at Rosalyn on the way out. "Everything. Okay?"

As soon as Steve and the clerk left, Rosalyn closed the door and stripped off all her clothes.

A bug? Like a transmitting device?

She'd thought maybe her car was being tracked but hadn't considered some sort of tracking device on her clothing. But as she thought of it more, she cursed herself for being so obtuse. All those times she had thought the Watcher was in her head, he'd really just been on her clothes.

That even explained why sometimes he waited many days between contacting her but sometimes he communicated with her more than once within a few hours.

Because some clothes were bugged and some weren't.

Most of her clothes had been destroyed last night in the fire, along with her duffel bag. She tore off the rest and put on the new clothes Steve had left her. Everything changed, down to a new pair of socks and athletic shoes, bile caught in her throat the whole time.

She was just coming out of the changing room as an alarm started blaring overhead. Steve was standing, waiting for her. He turned to the clerk.

"What does that alarm mean? Fire?"

The kid shook his head. "No. I don't think so. I haven't worked here very long but I don't remember that one from my training. Tornado, maybe?"

Steve grabbed her hand. "We've got to go."

"I'm ready. All new clothes."

"Your bag has to go too. It could also easily be tracked."

She hated to give up the bag—it had been a part of

every single move she'd made for nearly a year—but didn't argue. Steve had another similar one he'd grabbed.

"I want to keep my notebook—is that okay? It has all entries about the Watcher."

Steve took it and flipped through it. "It looks clean."

She also took out her money and driver's license. Everything else—makeup, pens, knickknacks—got thrown in the trash with the pen.

The siren suddenly cut off. "It must have been a drill," the clerk muttered.

Steve looked at the guy's name tag. "Hey, Paul, you want to make a hundred dollars?"

Paul stood up. "Am I going to get fired for it?"

"No. I just need you to take the tags off all these clothes and pay for them up at a register. Any change left over is yours to keep."

Nobody had to ask Paul twice. He took the money and the tags from their clothes and left.

Steve took Rosalyn's hand and they walked toward the front.

"Should we do something with our old clothes?"

Steve shook his head. "I found two transmitting devices in your clothes. There's no telling how many more there might be. Hopefully, leaving them in the dressing room will throw your stalker off."

"And we're just going to waltz out the front door?"

"Yep."

"Isn't that dangerous?"

"I think the siren was an attempt to get us to do something stupid like run out the back door. Instead we'll just walk out the front like everyone else."

"And get on a flight to Miami."

"Nope. We were never going to Miami. I was just hoping to mislead whoever might be listening to our conversation."

"Oh. So you really are from Colorado?"

"Yep. And that's where we're headed. That's the best place for me to keep you safe."

Chapter Ten

"We're driving to Colorado Springs? Won't that take like three days?"

They were on their way, via rental car, and were already out of Florida.

"A day and a half at most. Barely more than it would have taken to fly, given the stopovers."

When Steve's assistant had sent him the flight list, they'd all looked pretty miserable: late starts, long layovers. When he'd found the transmitting device on Rosalyn's sweater, he'd known he had to get her out of there right away. Waiting ten hours for a flight wasn't an option.

He glanced over at her. "It's the best way, I promise. It got us out of Florida the quickest. Hopefully your stalker thinks we're on our way to Miami."

"That's how he's known where I was." Rosalyn shook her head. "I thought he might have some sort of tracker in my car, so I ditched it a couple of times. But he always found me."

"I don't know how you've kept away from him for the past few months." The thought of Rosalyn—alone and pregnant—trying to stay ahead of a killer sent ice through Steve's veins. It was all he could do to stop from grabbing her hand, which sat in her lap.

Hell, it was all he could do not to pull over the car at the first hotel and make love to her for a few days. Away from all the crazy surrounding her life and the fanatic trying to hurt her.

"Actually, I haven't heard from him since I last saw you in Pensacola. He left a note under your hotel room door and that's why I left."

He looked at her. *"What?"*

She shrugged. "For six months I haven't heard anything from the Watcher."

Steve brought his eyes back to the road. "No, go back. The Watcher left you a note at my hotel six months ago?"

"He slid it under the door that second night."

"Do you remember what it said?" Now Steve could appreciate why she wanted to keep the notes so badly.

"No, I try not to remember, because it would drive me a little crazy. That's why I write them down in my notebook." Rosalyn reached down in her bag and pulled out the notebook she'd begged him to let her keep. She turned to an entry. "It said 'If you like Steve so much, I guess I'll need to meet him soon.'" She closed the notebook and laid it in her lap.

Steve's hands gripped the steering wheel tighter. "When did this note arrive? What time?"

"At around three o'clock in the morning. You were asleep. I heard it slide under the door."

The Watcher had been at his door. For him to have been so close and Steve to have known nothing about it infuriated him. "So you opened it, right? When you saw what it was, why didn't you wake me up?"

He understood why Rosalyn wouldn't run after a stalker, but Steve wouldn't have any qualms whatsoever about doing so.

She stared at him for a long minute. "I thought you were some businessman. I had no idea you were in law enforcement."

"I didn't have to be in law enforcement to help you. Any decent human being would've wanted to help you deal with a maniac who was tracking your every move."

"I had already lost two decent human beings for that very reason! I couldn't go through that again. Couldn't drag you into my own personal hell."

Steve gritted his teeth. Logically he could understand why she hadn't wanted to tell him about the Watcher, but he still wished she had. This could've already been settled by now.

"Two? Someone else tried to help you? What happened?"

"A mechanic in Memphis named Shawn. It was before I knew better. And certainly before I knew he had some sort of bug transmitting everything I said."

"He died?"

Rosalyn nodded. "The night I told him about the Watcher."

"Another heart attack, like the detective?"

"No. The news called it a random act of violence. Some sort of gang retaliation, even though the guy had never been involved with gangs and wasn't even near that part of town." Rosalyn turned toward the window. "So no, I wasn't about to tell you about the Watcher and see you die also."

She'd carried a lot of weight by herself for many months, having to worry about not only herself but other people too. And now a baby. Most people would've buckled under the pressure.

He redirected the conversation. "But you haven't heard anything from the Watcher since that night at the hotel when we were together?"

"Well, once I got back to Pensacola three days ago to meet my sister, I heard from him. Another note under my hotel room door." She shuddered.

"This one was worse than the others?"

"No, it had just been so long since I'd received anything."

"So you mean after the morning you left me six months ago, you hadn't heard from the Watcher until you came back to Pensacola this week?"

That meant something. Steve didn't know exactly what yet, but he knew that the Watcher's absence from Rosalyn's life for six months would be a big clue in solving the case.

"Where did you go when you left me?"

She looked over at him and flushed. "I'm sorry I stole your money. I didn't have any left."

"I would've given it to you if you'd asked."

"That would've involved giving you more information than was good for your health."

"I would've preferred that to waking up with you gone and thinking the worst of you for six months."

Actually, he'd thought worse of himself than her. That he'd been a gullible fool. But he'd thought pretty badly of her too.

That wasn't what was important now. "So you took nearly $200..."

"You have to understand, I was at a pretty low place. Everywhere I'd gone, the Watcher had found me. Admittedly, he hadn't tried to hurt me like he has this week, but it was still wearing me down. A note slipped under my door every night or so, knowing he was that close..."

"I'm sure it was nerve-racking."

"It was nerve-racking the first couple of months. By the time I met you, I was considering just killing myself and saving the Watcher the trouble."

He glanced over at her. "Seriously?"

She nodded. "That night at the bar when we met, I ran in because of the rain. I'd been out watching the sunset, considering if taking my own life would be better than letting the Watcher continue to kill innocent people."

Steve couldn't even bear to think about it. "Rosalyn—"

"Then I met you," she continued. "It didn't change anything really, but—"

She stopped and looked away.

"But what?"

"I connected with someone. With you. It was the first time I hadn't felt alone in so long." She tucked a strand of hair behind her ear. "I wasn't using you for money, Steve. I panicked when I saw the Watcher's note. All I could think of was getting away."

He believed her. She hadn't taken his credit cards or stolen his rental car. If she'd been trying to take him for all she could, she wouldn't have left those behind.

"Okay, so what did you do when you left that morning?"

"I took a bus as far as the money I stole from you would take me. I didn't want to go back to my car—I just wanted to get out of town. That ended up being Ellijay, Georgia."

"Never heard of it."

"I'd be shocked if you had. It's a tiny town north of Atlanta, in the Blue Ridge Mountains. Population just over fifteen hundred."

"What was in Ellijay?"

"Nothing whatsoever. That's just where my money ran out."

She stared out the window for a long time.

"Did Ellijay end up being good or bad?"

"Good. Definitely good. I needed to get some money right away, so I asked the couple who owned the small café in town if I could wash dishes or do any odd jobs just for the day, for cash.

"Mr. and Mrs. Ammons—Jim and Cheryl—said yes. I washed dishes a couple of days and didn't really have anywhere to go."

Steve's teeth gritted but he didn't say anything.

"Cheryl invited me to stay at their house, which was above the café. I slept in their son's room. He had died in the army a long time ago."

"And you had no notes or communication with the Watcher the whole time?"

"Nothing. I thought maybe he'd moved on or I was out of the territory he considered 'his.'" She shrugged. "Or maybe he had followed me but once he saw I was pregnant, I no longer interested him."

Any of those scenarios were possible.

"I definitely didn't tell the Ammonses about him," Rosalyn continued, shifting on the seat to get comfortable. "I didn't want to take a chance with their lives. Plus, Jim was already pretty paranoid since their son died due to a military communication breach or something. Jim and Cheryl live completely off the grid. No cell phone, no television, no computers or internet."

"I'm glad you had someone to help you."

"They're amazing. Gruff and not very talkative, and pretty old-fashioned. When I found out I was pregnant, I was afraid they might turn me out, but they didn't even think about it."

"Why did you leave? If the Watcher had lost track of you, why didn't you just stay in Ellijay?"

From the corner of his eye he could see Rosalyn's hands begin twisting in her lap. "As I was getting further and further along in my pregnancy, I began to think about the future. To worry that the Watcher was playing some sort of game. That maybe he was waiting until the baby was born and then would take me or both of us.

"I like the Ammonses a lot, but they're older, in their seventies. They couldn't take care of a baby. So I decided to call Lindsey. To just meet with her and see what shape her life was in."

She glanced at him, then out the window quickly. Obviously there was more to the story.

"And?"

"And what?"

"And what are you trying to get away with not telling me?"

"Nothing. It's not important."

"Rosalyn, anything having to do with you and the baby is important."

She shrugged. "I had Lindsey meet me in Pensacola because I was going to try to talk the hotel into giving me your info so I could contact you."

"For what, money?" As soon as the words were out of his mouth, Steve wished he could cut off his own tongue.

Rosalyn didn't look at him, just shifted her weight so her back was to him and she was looking completely out the window.

"I'm sorry. I didn't mean that." He wished he could see her face.

"Yes, you did. At least part of you did. The part of you who knows me as someone who lied, stole from you, then showed up pregnant with what may or may not be your baby. The part of you who doesn't want to be taken in again."

"Rosalyn—"

"You know what? I don't even blame you. You're right to be wary. Hopefully that will keep you alive longer."

Steve tried to figure out how to undo the damage his words had done.

She laid her seat back, still facing away from him. "We've got a long drive ahead. If you don't mind, I'm going to rest now so I can take a driving shift later. It'll make it easier on everyone."

He wasn't sure if she meant sleeping now would make it easier or driving later would do so. Clarifying would just make it worse, so he decided to let it go.

He knew she hadn't been coming to find him for money. For physical security, yes, but not money.

He shouldn't have said what he had. Even if he did still mistrust her. She hadn't given him much reason to trust her, truth be told.

Some of that he could alleviate right now. He knew Rosalyn was asleep, so he called his office.

"Cynthia," he said to his assistant by way of greeting. "I need everything you can give me about Rosalyn Mellinger. And anything you can find on Jim and Cheryl Ammons. North Georgia."

"Got it."

"I'll need you to call me back and read it to me. There's been a change of plans. We're driving from Pensacola back to HQ."

"That's quite a trek."

"Couldn't stay in Pensacola any longer. Had two attempts on our lives in under twelve hours." Steve explained about the driver and fire.

"Damn, boss. Do you want me to redirect an Omega plane to you? Or send Liam or one of the guys out to meet you for protection?"

"No, I got rid of how he was tracking us. We should be fine now. We'll stop at a hotel tonight, but I should be in the office by tomorrow afternoon."

"I'll make sure Joe has all the party paraphernalia gone by then."

Steve snickered. Joe Matarazzo was the team's hostage negotiator and was known for his partying. Or had been until his wife, Laura, reined him in a few months ago.

Rosalyn hadn't budged during his entire conversation. Her breathing hadn't changed; there'd been no sudden tension to make him think she was awake. She was exhausted. She'd barely gotten any sleep before the fire had awakened them again.

She was still sound asleep two hours later when Jon Hatton, one of Omega's best profilers and Steve's personal friend, called him back.

"Hey, boss, Cynthia and I have been gathering the info you wanted."

"Anything interesting?"

"Rosalyn Mellinger, twenty-four years old. Daughter of Crystal Mellinger and twin sister to Lindsey Rose. Hey, I see what the mom did there with the names—"

"Yeah, already got that, Jon. Keep going."

"No father listed on the birth certificate. Arrested as a teenager for shoplifting. That's where her prints are from and that sealed juvenile record was a bitch to get opened. But that little run-in with the law must have scared her straight because she's been straight as an arrow as an adult. Went to college, became an accountant. Worked every day until the day she quit. Not even a parking ticket."

Steve glanced over at Rosalyn, still asleep. "Okay."

"Sister has been in and out of juvie rehabs, then adult versions since her mid-teens. No college, barely finished high school. The mom is pretty much a deadbeat also. Alcoholic. Lives on welfare."

Okay, so no family support for Rosalyn. That explained why she'd been on the run by herself for a year.

"In the last few months Rosalyn's name has been mentioned in multiple police reports, all over the

Southeast and Texas. She's been talking to them about a stalker, but nothing has come of any of the investigations. Nobody has been taking her seriously."

"Well, I'm taking her seriously now, Jon. Someone nearly killed us twice in the last day."

"I'll see what I can dig up on the reports."

"Thanks, Jon. And if you can find out all you can about a Detective Johnson in Shreveport—he would've died of a heart attack eight or nine months ago—and a mechanic in Memphis who was killed in a random act of gang violence. Shawn something."

"Okay, these two related?"

"Just look for anything suspicious in either."

"All right, and we're still checking on the Ammonses. All I can find so far is a dead son in the military nearly fifteen years ago. They keep a low profile, whoever they are. I can't even find a bank account."

"That fits with what Rosalyn told me. Let me know if there's anything else."

"Got it. You watch your six, boss. I've already got a hinky feeling about this whole thing."

Steve took Jon's "hinky" feelings very seriously. Not to mention, Steve felt like they were dealing with something pretty major too. He said his goodbyes and disconnected the call.

Rosalyn turned in her sleep toward him, obviously finding it difficult to get comfortable. He had thought about driving all the way through the night and getting to Colorado Springs in one push.

But that wouldn't work. Rosalyn needed a bed where she could get a proper night's rest. Somewhere where no one was trying to run her over or set the building on fire or slipping notes under her door.

Rosalyn had been on her own for way too long. Steve planned to show her she wasn't alone anymore.

Chapter Eleven

She awoke to Steve's voice again, but at least this time he wasn't trying to tell her the building was on fire.

"Let's get you inside. Then you can go back to sleep if you want."

She looked at the handsome man, so strong and able, who had her tucked into his side leading her into the hotel lobby. Oh, she wanted, but sleep wasn't it.

She wanted him. Sometimes he said stupid stuff, but she still wanted him.

He used the key card to enter their room and turned on the light. This was a much nicer room than the ones she'd slept in for the last year when she hadn't been at the Ammonses' house. Generic, sure, but clean, tasteful, new. With a king-size bed in the middle of it.

She walked all the way in, then turned to him. "No hot tub this time."

She almost smiled at the speed with which his eyes flew to hers. Good. She wasn't the only one affected by the heat between them.

"Yeah, a shame." He pulled himself together and turned to close the door behind them. "Sorry we don't have any change of clothes. Once we get to Colorado Springs, I'll make sure you get something right away."

"It's no problem. I'm sure I'll be okay for one more day in these."

Maybe it was the fact that she'd slept most of the day or maybe it was because Steve had found the electronic transmitters and that just explained so damn much, but Rosalyn felt different.

For the first time since this nightmare began nearly a year ago, she was positive there would not be a note under the door tonight.

All those times she thought she was crazy, that the Watcher could hear her thoughts, that he lived inside her head? He'd simply lived inside the fiber of her clothing, able to hear who she'd talked to, where she'd checked in. That's how he'd found her.

All the times Rosalyn had talked to herself, he'd been privy to those conversations. Embarrassing, but at least it all made sense now.

The fact that he had gotten close enough to put transmitters on her clothing was terrifying. Steve had found two. Who knew how many more there might have been in the clothing that had been destroyed by the fire.

But there weren't any transmitters anymore. Rosalyn didn't even mind the ill-fitting supermarket clothes she was wearing now, because it meant nobody could hear her. Nobody but she and Steve knew where they were.

She hadn't realized how much weight she had shouldered for so long until a great deal of it was lifted. It allowed her to focus on other things.

Like how she was in a hotel with a gorgeous man. Six feet of muscle and awareness. Dark hair and green eyes staring at her like he was slightly nervous about what she would do next.

She hadn't had anyone but him hold her in the last year. No one had kissed her or pulled her into any embrace at all except for Steve. No one had touched her.

Sure, Jim and Cheryl Ammons had given her a brush on the shoulder or pat on the back here and there. Physical demonstration of affection wasn't the older couple's way. They weren't heartless, and cared about her for sure, but they just weren't very demonstrative in showing it.

It wasn't like she missed it. Rosalyn had been raised in a house where affectionate touches were few and far between. It was one of the things she'd promised herself her child would never go without. Her son would be hugged and kissed until he squirmed to get away. He would know every day he was loved, not just by words but by gestures.

But watching Steve cross the room, secure the door to make sure they were safe and turn those intense green eyes back on her, Rosalyn was quite sure of the type of touch *she* wanted right now.

And a hug wasn't it.

She wasn't looking for comfort, like she had been six months ago. She wanted the heat she and Steve had felt together.

He slowly took a step toward her. She smiled at his hesitancy. The cop in him must be aware of the predator in the room.

Her.

And he was the prey. Big, strong sexy man probably wasn't used to that.

"Do you want to take a shower first or do you want me to?" he asked.

"What about taking one together?"

"Rosalyn…" His words were a protest, but she saw the tightening of his body. The slight flare in his eyes.

She took a step toward him. "We'll at least save water that way."

"I have a feeling we'd be in there too long to save any water." He tried to step around her so he could get to the other side of the room, but she moved so she was right in front of him.

"So take a shower with me and don't save water."

She could almost see his conscience pour over him. "Rosalyn, it's been a really long couple of days. Traumatic couple of days."

The words were for her benefit, not his. She raised one eyebrow and gave him a little snicker. "And you're tired? Need a little you time? Drink a chai latte or something?"

She saw the smile he fought against. He wanted her—she knew he did. She wasn't going to give up at his first token protest.

"No, I'm talking about you. You've had a rough couple of days, hell, a rough few months. There's no need to jump into anything just because you're relieved or grateful or whatever."

"Generally I don't pay my debts with sex, if that's what you're thinking."

He winced. "No, I didn't mean you were trying to pay me. I just meant—"

She stepped closer to stop him from saying anything further. He was digging himself a hole and she was afraid he was going to piss her off with whatever asinine thing came out of his mouth next.

"Steve, don't overthink it."

"Somebody needs to overthink it. Or at least think at all."

He was protective of her and she appreciated that. But right now she didn't want him to use his strength to protect her. She wanted him to use his strength to help her celebrate how good it felt to be unfettered for the first time in as long as she could remember.

She ran both her hands up his arms. She felt him tense but he didn't pull away. She leaned in closer.

"I'm happy to be alive. I'm happy no one is going to find me and slip a note under the door tonight. I'm happy we're both safe here together."

She slid her arms to his shoulders, then around his neck, pulling his lips down to hers.

The heat was still there. Thank goodness it wasn't just something she'd remembered, something she'd dreamed about. His lips were still as firm and hot and inviting as she'd known they would be.

But he wasn't pulling her to him. His hands were on her waist, but they seemed neutral—neither encouraging nor discouraging.

"Rosalyn…" he groaned against her mouth.

He was going to let her go, she could tell.

"Steve, you got me away from a lunatic. I want to celebrate that."

Those were the wrong words. He stepped back from her. "You don't owe me anything."

Were they really back to that again? "I know. And I appreciate very much that you're not the type of guy who would try to lord that over my head. But that's not the point."

He grabbed her arms and set her back from him. "Look, I've worked around people who have been traumatized by violence. Sometimes it's hard to recognize the symptoms in yourself. I just don't want you to do something you might regret."

Rosalyn smiled. She appreciated his concern, she really did. But this wasn't something she was going to regret—she was positive about that. "Believe me, I'm not going to regret this."

She tried to step forward but he stopped her.

"Well, have you considered that maybe I don't want to do this? That it's something I'll regret?" Frustration flavored his tone.

He didn't want her. The reality hit her like a bucket of ice. She immediately stepped back from him.

What did she expect, really? She'd lied to him, stolen from him, dragged him into a situation that had almost gotten him killed twice. Not to mention shown up pregnant with his baby.

Of course getting involved with her physically wasn't a good idea for him. Yeah, there was heat between them, but he was smart enough to know that wasn't enough to justify getting close to her.

All the perk, all the joy seemed to drain out of her. "You're right—I hadn't thought of that. Smart move on your part."

"Rosalyn..." He took a step toward her.

She immediately jerked back. He couldn't touch her.

Not now. If he did, she might shatter into a million pieces. "I'm going to take a shower."

She turned and all but ran.

STEVE WATCHED ROSALYN nearly run across the room to the bathroom.

Damn it. What the hell was the matter with him? Why would he say that to her?

He was the director of one of the most prestigious law enforcement agencies in the country. He regularly spoke to the congressmen, senators, the president's advisers. Hell, he'd even spoken to two different presidents in his tenure as the director of the Critical Response Division.

He was known for being well-spoken. Known for reading a situation and doing and/or saying whatever was needed. He had a team of dozens of people who looked to him to provide guidance and leadership. To know the words that needed to be said when everything around them was falling apart.

Yet somehow he'd just managed to say the worst possible thing to one small, fragile woman who'd just been reaching out to him for human contact.

And the worst thing about his ridiculous words? None of them were true.

Not want her? That was so far from the truth he could barely wrap his mind around it.

But he was convinced she felt beholden to him. That she wouldn't really want him under normal circumstances that didn't involve life-threatening situations.

Of course, he wanted her pretty desperately, and life-threatening situations were commonplace for him.

His fingers itched to touch her. To run through her hair and along her body. To see the changes pregnancy had made, beyond what he could make out from beneath her clothes.

He wanted her with a passion that went against everything in his calm, collected nature. He couldn't ever remember wanting anyone this much. Not even his wife, Melanie. They'd loved each other, absolutely, but with the low simmer of the knowledge that they would have the rest of their lives together to work through their love.

The rest of their lives together had ended up being only six short years.

The fire that consumed him every time he was around Rosalyn was so different from that it almost couldn't be compared. Being around her caused him to lose his cool. Lose his focus.

Melanie would approve. Deep in the back of his mind, Steve knew his wife would approve of the young woman in the bathroom who had stayed alive under some pretty desperate circumstances. Would approve of the fact that Rosalyn shook him up enough to make him say stupid things.

He heard the shower turn on in the bathroom.

And maybe Rosalyn just wanted him because she wanted him. Not because of anything else but this damn heat between them. An itch that had just barely gotten scratched six months ago and had been driving them both crazy ever since.

Maybe he'd just sent her running despondent into

the bathroom not because he didn't want her—he almost laughed outright at the thought—but because of some ridiculous, completely wrong feeling of over-protection.

He was an idiot.

The bathroom door opened but her head didn't pop out. "You know what, Drackett? You're an idiot."

His legs were moving before his brain had even processed what was going on. He caught the bathroom door just before it shut and pushed it all the way open.

Rosalyn's mouth made a little o.

But the heat burned in her eyes the way he knew it burned in his.

"You know what? I *am* an idiot."

He kissed her.

There was no gentleness in the kiss. No finesse.

But there was plenty of heat and need and passion.

He lifted her up and set her on the bathroom vanity, then grabbed her hips and slid her all the way to the edge until she was flush up against him. They both groaned as her calves hooked around the backs of his thighs. Her fingers linked behind his neck, keeping him against her.

"Rosalyn, I'm sorry—" He began his murmured apology against her mouth, but she stopped him.

"No apologies. No talking. No thinking."

He couldn't hide the effect she had on him, didn't even try to pretend he could control his response. He just let the heat take over.

As he stripped them both out of their clothes and slipped his arms around her hips to carry her with him to the shower—unwilling to separate their bodies for even the few steps it would take for them to walk—he hoped the heat consuming them both wouldn't burn them away.

Leaving nothing but ash in its place.

Chapter Twelve

They got on the road again early, after catching a quick breakfast. By lunch they were only a few hours from Colorado Springs. They stopped at a truck-stop diner just outside Dalhart, Texas, off Highway 87.

Rosalyn felt rested. She shouldn't, since she'd been awake for a big chunk of the night for the best of reasons, but she did.

Steve had seemed fascinated by the changes in her body that had come about from the pregnancy. She was right at the perfect stage: not sick and tired all the time like she'd been in the early days, but not so big that she was waddling around. She knew that would be coming soon.

There were a lot of things unsettled about her future. What was she going to do when she got to Colorado Springs? Get a job and stay there? She had some money she'd saved from working at the diner, but not enough. Especially not when the baby came.

Another thing she and Steve needed to talk about. The list was getting pretty long.

She was concerned about the future but for the first time the thought didn't send her into a near panic.

Maybe it was the knowledge that the Watcher could no longer find her now that the transmitting devices in her clothes were gone. Maybe it was because Steve was here and believed she was in danger.

But she had slept like she hadn't been able to sleep in months. Even when she'd been at the Ammonses' house and it seemed liked the Watcher couldn't find her, she hadn't slept this good.

She was sure having Steve's arms around her helped.

But even if they hadn't made love, if he hadn't held her, she knew just his presence made a huge difference to her psyche. She wasn't alone. And although there was a lot she and Steve still needed to work out, she knew it would happen eventually.

He was looking through her notebook now, the one with all the dates and recordings of the notes or messages the Watcher had given her.

"I wish we hadn't lost all the notes in the fire." She sipped on her iced tea, knowing she shouldn't be drinking caffeine, but surely one cup wouldn't hurt. She savored it as well as her large lunch.

Steve shrugged. "They would've helped for sure, especially with prosecution for stalking. But this notebook gives us a lot of information. My people will be able to see what patterns can be established from this."

"Detective Johnson steered me right by telling me to write everything down. Actually, at the time, I think he just told me that to give me something proactive to do. Make me feel less like a victim, more like an active part in an investigation."

And it had worked. For the first time Rosalyn had

felt hopeful. Right up until Johnson had died two days later.

Steve took her hand. "I already have people looking into his death and the mechanic's. They'll dig through what it looks like on the surface to what's actually underneath, okay?"

Rosalyn nodded. "Thank you."

He handed the notebook back to her. "I'm going to pay and use the restroom. Then we'll hit the road again. We should make it to Colorado Springs by this afternoon."

She smiled. "I'll try not to sleep the entire day away this time."

He stood up. "You can do whatever you need to— don't worry about that. It's been a stressful couple of days. Your body needs rest."

It had been a stressful year. But she just nodded.

She was thankful Steve was looking into Detective Johnson's and Shawn the mechanic's deaths. She still didn't know exactly what Steve did in law enforcement, but evidently he was pretty high up. He hadn't offered any information and she hadn't wanted to ask.

She needed to call the Ammonses before they got back on the road. She needed to let them know she was okay. They didn't have a phone upstairs at their house, due mostly to Jim's paranoia that the government was listening or watching them, but had one at the café.

Rosalyn got change from the waitress and went into the hallway lined with phones, a throwback from before everyone had cell phones and truckers used to have to make calls to their loved ones from pay phones. She dialed the number for the Ammonses' café, then put in the change required to connect the call.

"Main Street Cafe."

"Hi, Cheryl, it's—"

"Oh, Rosalyn, honey! Thank goodness you're okay."

It was the most emotion she'd ever heard out of the stoic Cheryl.

"I'm sorry if you've been worried about me. I should've called earlier."

But a deranged stalker found me again, killed my sister, then tried to kill me twice.

Rosalyn had never told the Ammonses about the Watcher. She suspected they knew she was on the run from someone but had never pressed for details and she'd never given any.

"That's all right. I'm just glad to hear you're safe now. Jim was worried too."

Rosalyn laughed. "I don't think Jim worries about anything but the government encroaching on his boundaries."

"Well, he talked yesterday about putting a phone line in the house so you could call there if you needed anything."

Rosalyn felt tears come to her eyes. For Jim to have considered that, he really did care about her. "Cheryl, I'll just call the café, okay? Tell Jim he doesn't need to do anything so drastic like get a phone in the house."

The words were in jest, but Rosalyn meant it. She knew what it meant for Jim to have even considered it.

"Are you coming back? You know you're welcome anytime. You and the baby."

"Thanks, Cheryl." Emotion choked Rosalyn's voice.

"I've got some things to take care of. But I might be back. I don't know yet."

"Well, we both mean it when we say we want you here. Don't forget that, okay?"

"Yes, ma'am. I'm with the baby's father now and we're trying to get some stuff figured out." Probably not the stuff Cheryl was thinking of, but that didn't matter. "I'll call in a couple of days with an update, okay?"

"You be careful, hon. And remember you've always got a home here if you want it."

"Thanks, Cheryl. Give Jim my love."

"I will. Bye."

Rosalyn put the phone receiver back in its cradle and leaned her head against it. It was nice to know she had someone who cared about her. That she had options. But she wondered if she was opening up the Ammonses to the Watcher's clutches. What if he found her again? If she went back there, would she be leading him to them? She couldn't stand the thought of the older couple falling victim to him.

Maybe she'd done the wrong thing by calling them at all. But surely with the transmitters gone, no harm would come to them.

She looked up to find Steve staring at her, eyes narrowed. She gave him a little wave as he walked over, but all the easy camaraderie they'd had at lunch, the closeness they'd shared last night seemed to be gone.

"I would've let you use my phone if you needed to make a call. You didn't have to pay for it."

"That's okay. I didn't want to bother you. And I didn't want to waste time. I know we're trying to make it to Colorado Springs as quickly as we can."

Rosalyn was still a little overcome with emotion after talking to Cheryl. It must be pregnancy hormones or something. But the thought of Jim agreeing to put a phone in his house just because of her had tears rushing to her eyes again. She turned away so Steve wouldn't see.

"Ready to go?" she asked.

Steve grabbed her arm. "Who were you talking to, Rosalyn?"

The anger behind the words took her aback. "Who do you think I was talking to?"

"I don't know. All I know is I leave you alone for the first time in twenty-four hours and you're making mysterious phone calls."

"I was calling Cheryl and Jim Ammons. The people in Ellijay with whom I had been staying. I wanted to let them know I was all right."

"And you couldn't wait to do that in the car on my phone?"

He was still holding her arm. Rosalyn snatched it away. "I didn't think of that, okay? I've been on my own for a while now and I'm not used to having other people around or their resources."

Steve's eyes narrowed more, so she turned and walked out toward the car. Let him believe whatever he wanted to.

It was going to be a long ride to Colorado Springs.

THE HOURS ON the way to Colorado Springs were tense at best. Rosalyn never told him exactly who she had been contacting, but he didn't believe her when she said it was the Ammonses, the couple in Ellijay who had taken her in. After all, hadn't she already told him the husband didn't trust the government and they lived off the grid?

No computer, no phone. So how exactly had she called them?

Steve didn't want to let it, especially after last night, but true doubt about Rosalyn crept in. He was trained to see evil in innocent actions, to question all possibilities.

He had to face the fact that Rosalyn could be using him right now. That she had initiated contact with him in Pensacola for a particular purpose that had nothing to do with the baby or the Watcher.

To what end, he didn't exactly know. But he had to admit she could be working with some sort of partner to get something from him or maneuver him in some way. Maybe she knew who he really was in Omega. He had access to top secret information on a regular basis. Maybe she was hoping to obtain something through him.

He just couldn't get out of his mind how sad she'd looked when getting off the phone. How guilty.

Like she'd done something distasteful and wished she could take it back.

Why would she feel that way after talking to a couple she'd been close to for half a year? And for that matter, why wouldn't she just have used his phone to contact them? It would've made a lot more sense.

Or was it just like Rosalyn had said? She wasn't used to depending on other people. She hadn't had a cell phone in a while. Maybe she hadn't even considered it. She'd just seen the pay phone—a rarity these days—and decided to make the call while Steve was doing other things.

Certainly not nefarious when thought of that way.

Steve's hands gripped the steering wheel tighter. It wasn't often that he called his own judgments and gut feelings into question.

But when it came to Rosalyn, he had to admit that he was not neutral.

He decided to try to talk to her. They couldn't spend the rest of the five hours in silence.

"I'm going to take you into my office. I have people looking into your situation."

She nodded. "Okay. You still haven't told me exactly what you do or who you work for."

He didn't answer. Was it interesting that she would be pressing for info on that topic now or was he just reading into things that weren't there? He looked over at Rosalyn, her crystal-blue eyes staring at him.

He'd swear she was guileless. But he couldn't take the risk. The Critical Response Division wasn't one of the covert divisions of Omega, but Steve still couldn't take a chance on giving Rosalyn any information if he suspected she was working with someone.

God, what a mess that was going to be if she was. Because what if a paternity test proved the baby was his but Rosalyn was really in cahoots with a criminal?

Complicated was an understatement.

Chapter Thirteen

Great. She was trapped in the car with Broody McScary.

What had happened to the passionate man she'd made love with last night? He been here with her until they'd eaten lunch.

Maybe he had indigestion.

No, it wasn't lunch. It was her phone call. He didn't like that she'd had a conversation he couldn't hear. It didn't take a genius to figure out why.

He didn't trust her.

She didn't know exactly what bad thing he kept expecting her to do. Hell, she didn't think *he* knew what bad thing he expected her to do. But obviously he expected something.

She didn't even really want to talk to him, and avoided doing so by pretending to sleep part of the way. But about an hour outside Colorado Springs, she had to go to the bathroom.

"Can we make one short pit stop?"

"We've got less than an hour. We're almost to Pueblo. Can't you hold it?"

If he'd been annoyed, she would've argued with him. But he didn't look annoyed. He looked distrustful.

"Fine." She would hold it, even if it killed her.

Thirty minutes later she was afraid it really would.

"Look, we're going to have to stop, okay? I know you think I'm planning some sort of nuclear attack or whatever, but my pregnant body is not going to wait to go to the bathroom."

He almost cracked a smile at that. "Fine. I'll get gas while we stop."

He pulled up at the gas pump and Rosalyn ran inside to use the restroom. She felt much better when she came back out. She wondered what she could do to help ease the tension between her and Steve. She had to accept it was his job to be distrustful—he was a cop, after all. She shouldn't be offended if he was butting into her business with questions all the time. Especially if it was because he was trying to keep her safe.

She would be the better person. Maybe buy him a candy bar as a peace offering. Who could resist chocolate? Plus, she was hungry.

Then again, she was always hungry.

She looked out the gas-station convenience-store window at Steve, wondering what he would like. A guy on a motorcycle was moving slowly toward Steve as he pumped the gas. Steve was looking at her. Probably to make sure she wasn't robbing the cash register.

At first she didn't pay any mind to the motorcycle except to wonder why he was coming up directly behind their car rather than to one of the empty pumps. But then she saw the rider pull something out of his jacket. It looked like a small stick.

Then he flicked his wrist and it grew into a much longer club.

He was going to hit Steve with it.

Rosalyn dropped the candy and ran toward the door knowing there was no way she'd make it outside in time to warn Steve or stop the motorcycle guy.

Something in her face alerted him, or maybe just his cop instincts, and he spun and threw up his arm just as the club came at his head.

A soft scream came out of her mouth as she saw the impact. It had to have hurt—had maybe even broken his arm—but at least Steve was still on his feet. A blow that severe to his head would've killed him.

In the corner of her mind the agony of what this meant—the Watcher had found her again—tried to take control, but she wouldn't let it. She couldn't have a breakdown right now. She had to help Steve.

"Call the police!" she yelled at the cashier. "My friend is being attacked."

She didn't wait to see if the cashier did it; she just ran through the doors.

The guy pulled the club back for another swing, but Steve was more prepared this time. The attacker swung from the side rather than in a downward motion and Steve ducked. He brought his uninjured arm up like he planned to use it to punch the guy, but the man was too far away for Steve to be able to reach him. The stick gave him all the advantage.

He brought it down at Steve again, with not as much force, but it still knocked Steve to the ground as it hit his shoulder. He got back up, but the attacker was already bringing his arm around again.

"Hey, leave him alone!" Rosalyn didn't think through the wisdom of being unarmed, smaller and pregnant when facing the attacker, just knew she had to get him away from Steve. The best way to do that would be to bring as much attention to the situation as possible.

The motorcycle man looked at her, but she couldn't see his face through the darkened visor.

"Yeah, you, get away from him. Somebody help us!"

Rosalyn might not be able to do much but she could scream her head off. She also reached for bottles of oil that were stacked by the front door as she ran past them, throwing them as she went. None of them got far enough to hit the attacker, but at least she was making enough of a spectacle of herself to draw even more attention.

Other people were coming out of the store and a car on the road had pulled in to see what was going on. The motorcycle man realized the situation and threw his stick down and sped off. Nobody could do anything to stop him.

Rosalyn ran over to Steve.

"Are you okay?"

He was still cradling the arm he'd used to block the first—and hardest—hit. "Yeah. I'm okay. I don't have much feeling in my arm, but better than if he had hit me in the head."

Rosalyn clenched her teeth to keep them from chattering at the thought. "It would've killed you."

"Probably not. But it definitely would've knocked me unconscious long enough for him to finish the job."

They heard sirens heading toward them.

"I told the clerk to call the cops. I didn't know what else to do."

Steve tilted his head sideways and looked at her. "You had the clerk call the police?"

"Yeah, well, I wasn't sure my oilcan throwing was going to stop the motorcycle guy, so I thought we better get reinforcements here as soon as possible. Is your arm okay? Let me look at it."

She took a step toward him but stopped when he backed up. She tried not to let his actions hurt her feelings. It probably wasn't personal. He was in pain. Trying to figure out what had happened. Cop mode.

It wasn't long before two police cars and an ambulance were pulling up.

"Do you mind waiting by the car?" Steve asked. "It'll be less complicated if I talk to the locals alone at first."

"Yeah, okay." She shrugged. "I'll be over at the car."

A paramedic walked up to them before she went, so Rosalyn waited. She wanted to make sure Steve was okay.

"Ma'am, were you hurt in any way?" the paramedic asked her.

"No. I was in the store, nowhere near the guy with his club."

"Guy on a motorcycle came up, had an expandable baton." Steve began rolling up his sleeve so he could show his injuries to the paramedic.

Rosalyn gasped when she saw his forearm. It was swollen and already turning purple.

The medic took Steve's arm in his hand. "Can you move all your fingers without pain?"

Steve wiggled them. "Nothing sharp. Just an all-over ache."

The medic probed gently around the bruise. "It doesn't seem to be broken, but you should probably get it x-rayed to be sure. You're fortunate. Whoever did this was trying to do you serious harm. It could've shattered your arm."

Steve nodded. "It could've done much worse if he had gotten me on the skull like he was aiming for."

The medic whistled through his teeth. "Yes, for sure. Do you have any other injuries?"

"He got me across the shoulders also, but not with nearly as much force." Steve turned so the medic could see.

"You'll want to get these photographed so it can be used against whoever did this when they catch him," the medic said. "But beyond that, there's no reason for you to come with me. You'll probably be hurting pretty bad for a few days."

"Thanks. I'll take care of it." Steve turned to her. "I'm going to talk to the officer. You stay right at the car, okay?"

Rosalyn nodded and walked over to lean against the trunk. Steve went to talk to the two officers who had shown up, turning so he was facing her. She saw him pull out some sort of badge or ID and show it to the officers.

Now that she was alone and not worried for Steve's immediate well-being, the weight of what had just happened hit her.

The Watcher had found her again.

There was no way this incident could be a coincidence. But how? They had left all the clothes, with the electronic transmitters, in that superstore dressing room. The only thing she'd kept had been her notebook.

And she'd searched every single sheet of paper in it during the car ride. There had been absolutely nothing unusual.

She didn't know how he had found her, only that he had. And Steve had almost paid the price for it right before her eyes.

Maybe she should run. Right now. Maybe if she left and got away from Steve, the Watcher would leave him alone.

She turned and put her elbows against the passenger-side window, cradling her head in her hands. What was she going to do? She was going to have the baby soon. She couldn't keep running forever.

Especially since running didn't seem to matter. The Watcher found her no matter where she went. The only place he hadn't found her was at the Ammonses' house. Or if he had, he'd never made his presence known.

Rosalyn turned and glanced at Steve. He was still talking to the officers, but he was looking at her. One of the men nodded at whatever Steve was saying and looked at Rosalyn too. The other gave something to Steve that he put in his pocket. Steve shook hands with both men again and began walking toward the car.

"You seem pretty upset. Are you okay?" he asked her.

Rosalyn laughed, but there was no humor in the sound. Was she okay? No. She wasn't certain she was ever going to be okay. "No, I'm definitely not okay."

"Why? Because he didn't succeed or because you changed your mind?"

She studied his face more carefully. His green eyes were cold. The angles of his jaw set in anger.

"What?"

"I saw you looking at the guy on the motorcycle. You were looking at both of us right before he hit me."

She shook her head, trying to process exactly what Steve was implying. "Yeah, I noticed him, but I didn't think anything of it."

He took a step closer to her, his height intimidating rather than comforting. "Why were you studying me so intensely from inside the convenience store, then?"

"I was trying to figure out which candy bar to get you." Her words were small. They sounded ridiculous even to her own ears.

"You called someone earlier, someone you didn't want me to know about. Was that him? The Watcher? Are you working together?"

Rosalyn could feel the blood leaving her face. "Wh-what?"

He grabbed her arm with his good hand. "Did you decide you didn't want me dead at the last minute? Did you change your mind? Is that why you made that horrified face in the store and tipped me off?"

"I made the face because I saw he was going to hit you—"

"Which was the plan all along, right? Except you had some sort of change of heart and decided to tip me off. If you hadn't made that face, I have to admit, I'd be dead now."

She couldn't believe what she was hearing. "No. No, I didn't know what he was going to do until he flicked out that stick thing—"

"Really? You expect me to believe he just happened to find us right after you just happened to make a secret call at lunch today? Is that why you had me stop here when we were so close to Colorado Springs?"

"No. Steve, I—"

He took a step back. "You know what? Save it. We'll do official questioning when I get you into the Critical Response office."

"The what?"

He didn't answer. Instead he pulled a set of handcuffs out of his pocket. That's what the officer had handed him. Rosalyn looked over at them. They were watching her and Steve. Evidently he had already told them why he would need the handcuffs.

Almost as if from a distance, she felt a cuff slip around one wrist, then the other.

"Rosalyn Mellinger, you're under arrest."

Chapter Fourteen

She was playing him. Had to have been this entire time. There was no other explanation for it.

Steve could feel the anger coursing through his body. Not just at Rosalyn, although he was plenty pissed at her, but at himself also.

She'd taken him as an easy mark once, six months ago, and obviously had found he was still just as dense even after being fooled by her before.

Even worse? He still wanted to believe her now. That the crushed look on her face was real, that he'd made a mistake in slipping her into handcuffs.

But damned if he'd let himself fall prey to her for a third time.

And the baby… He couldn't even think about that right now.

She had to be playing him. Had to be conspiring with the Watcher. There were no tracking devices anywhere on either of them. He had meticulously searched her clothes, his, her notebook and wallet and found nothing.

He'd watched mile after mile in the rearview mirror to make sure they weren't being followed. There was no way any one vehicle—hell, even two or three taking turns—could've followed without his knowing. Steve had been watching. No one had tailed them.

The only suspicious happening since they'd left Pensacola had been Rosalyn's call to the Ammonses. To a couple she'd previously stated had no phone in their house.

How exactly did you call someone who didn't have a phone?

You didn't.

But you could be calling a partner you were working with. Tip him off about where you were going. She might not have been able to give her partner specifics, but she could get him close enough that he could start tailing without Steve's awareness.

He remembered her head against the telephone cradle at lunch today. The same guilty expression she'd had while standing over at the car while he'd been talking to the local cops.

Like she felt bad for tipping her partner off, then felt bad again that Steve had been hurt.

He should be thankful for her guilty conscience. Without it, he would be dead.

Or maybe—if he was willing to give Rosalyn a slight benefit of the doubt—*maybe* she hadn't known exactly what her partner's plan was. Maybe she hadn't known the plan was to kill Steve outright.

Maybe she was a thief and a con but not a murderer.

The thought made him feel slightly better, which made him even angrier, which made his arm hurt like a bitch. Steve gritted his teeth. He'd have to take some aspirin when he got to Omega HQ, because he wasn't going anywhere else but there.

Not giving Rosalyn any chance to escape. He could've sworn she was about to run while he was talking to the cops. Maybe she'd known he was onto her.

He was surprised she didn't try to plead her case while it was just the two of them in the car. She had to know that once other people were involved—people not so blinded by their obvious gullibility for her like Steve—it would be harder for her to fool them. To fool him.

But she hadn't said anything. Not a single word since he'd put the cuffs on her. Hadn't gotten angry. Hadn't cried. Hadn't reasoned with him.

If he hadn't known better, he would've said she'd just shut down. Even now, she had her arms wrapped protectively around herself, around the baby. She was looking straight ahead, but it didn't seem like she saw anything.

Obviously she hadn't thought he would figure it out. At least not this soon.

There was only one thing Steve knew for absolute certain. He was going to get some answers. Maybe he couldn't trust his own judgment around Rosalyn. Was too close to her.

But he was taking her to Omega's Critical Response Division. He had some of the best profilers and behavioral analysts in the entire world working on his team. He might not be able to get to the truth with Rosalyn.

But they would.

STEVE SAW ROSALYN perk up a little when he pulled into the Omega complex. Obviously she hadn't been expecting him to take her somewhere as sophisticated as his unit.

That's right, sweetheart—you didn't just pick some local yokel to mess with. You're in the big leagues now.

"Not what you were expecting?"

She looked over at him. "I don't know what you think I was expecting, but no, this wasn't it." She turned back to look out the window. Her hands were rubbing at the handcuffs on her wrist.

He wondered if she wished she'd chosen her mark better. Or maybe getting some sort of information about Omega had been her plan all along.

He steeled himself against any softness toward her. He couldn't allow her to get the upper hand again. The cuffs were probably overkill, but it was a necessary reminder—for both of them—that she was a criminal.

When Steve walked in through the front door with Rosalyn, the guards did a double take. They were probably equally as disconcerted to see Steve in a casual shirt and jeans as they were to see him bringing in a prisoner. Neither were commonplace for Steve.

He went through standard procedures to enter the building, ID scan, weapon check-in. He signed in Rosalyn as being in his custody and walked her through the metal detector. She set it off, of course, because of the handcuffs.

The guard looked uncomfortable. "Um, protocol says we scan all prisoners entering the building, Mr. Drackett."

"That's fine." Steve didn't really like it, but damned if he'd give her preferential treatment.

Rosalyn raised her cuffed hands in front of her face so the guard could use the wand to run up the front of her body, then down the back. Nothing else set off the detector.

Steve had to admit he was a little relieved. If she'd had a hidden cell phone or weapon on her, he would've never been able to trust his own judgment again.

The guard allowed them through and he took Rosalyn's arm to the elevator and into the division offices.

As soon as he walked into the large open area that housed most of the desks of the Critical Response Division, Steve knew he had made a mistake. He should not have paraded Rosalyn in like this. He should've let the locals handle her arrest. There were going to be too many people with too many questions about who Rosalyn was and what was going on.

Personal questions.

Steve wanted answers from Rosalyn. But at the same time he did not want his private life being broadcast all over the office.

He looked over at her. Her head was bowed and her hair was framing her face on either side. Between her hunched shoulders, pregnant belly and handcuffs, she made quite the pitiful picture.

Steve wasn't surprised when Andrea Gordon, one of the most naturally gifted behavioral analysts Steve had ever known, approached them, her concerned look focused on Rosalyn.

Hell, even Steve felt sorry for her and she'd almost gotten him killed an hour ago.

"Steve, is there anything I can help with?" Andrea asked him.

"In a minute, Andrea." Steve glanced around until he found the person he wanted. He wasn't surprised to see him leaning against the wall on the other side of the room watching what was going on.

"Waterman!" Steve jerked his head to the side, indicating Derek should come over.

Derek Waterman, head of the Omega SWAT team, was always aware of what was going on around him. He was focused and deadly and an asset to the team for multiple reasons.

But right now Steve wanted Derek because of what he wasn't: friendly. Steve needed Rosalyn escorted down to an interrogation room. Most of the other men on the team would be friendly, try to set Rosalyn at ease. That's not what Steve wanted. He wanted Rosalyn nervous, uncomfortable, unhappy.

That's how he would get answers.

And if a little voice said he was making a huge mistake, well, he'd just squash that. He was done giving her the benefit of the doubt.

"Derek, will you please escort Ms. Mellinger to interview room 2?" It was the starkest of the interrogation rooms, the least comfortable.

Out of the corner of his eye he saw Andrea stiffen. She didn't like how he was treating Rosalyn. But then again, Andrea tended to be tenderhearted toward everyone.

Derek didn't even bat an eye. "No problem, boss." He turned to Rosalyn. "If you could come with me, ma'am." Respectful yet distant. He took her arm and escorted her down the hall.

Steve turned back from them and found at least a dozen of his team watching him.

"All right, people, let's get back to work. I know you have other things to do besides gape at me."

Many of them sat back down at their desks or went back to their normal tasks. Liam Goetz, hostage rescue team captain and resident smart-ass, just walked closer.

"But, boss, how are we supposed to go back to work when we know there's such a big, bad criminal nearby?"

That got a couple of snickers. Steve turned to Liam. "I can fire you, you know."

"If I had a dollar for every time you said that," Liam muttered, but eased back down to his desk.

The good thing about his team was that the members knew each other well enough to know when to leave something alone. He also knew he could trust them to provide him with the information he didn't seem capable of getting himself. Or have the neutrality required to do it.

"Brandon, Andrea, Jon, I need to see you in my office."

He turned and walked out of the main room. He didn't check to see if the people he'd asked for were following. He knew they were. If for curiosity's sake as much as anything else.

He walked through his outer office door. Cynthia and his other assistants stood when they saw him, all with pressing matters that needed his attention, he was sure. He held out a hand.

"For the next few hours, unless there is a national

or international crisis, consider me still unavailable. I don't want to know about it." He saw Brandon and Andrea make eye contact with each other at his words but didn't care. For his own sanity, unless there was some sort of real emergency, he had to get this issue with Rosalyn settled.

"Do you need something for your arm?" Andrea asked. All eyes flew to it. Damn it, he'd been trying not to let anyone know about the throb and what he was sure was going to be stiff and painful tomorrow. He glared at Andrea for bringing it up. He should've known she'd be able to read his nonverbal communication too accurately for him to hide or fake.

"Sorry." She shrugged. "It wasn't that noticeable, but I could tell."

"What happened?" Brandon asked.

"I was on the wrong side of a steel telescopic baton." Steve grimaced. "I'm fine."

"I'll get ice and ibuprofen. It will help with swelling and pain. We'll handle everything, Steve." Cynthia, the assistant who'd been with the team the longest, the one he trusted the most, nodded at him. "You handle your crisis. We'll handle anything else."

Steve opened the door for his inner office and held it for the others. Jon Hatton and Brandon Han were two of the finest profilers—honestly two of the most brilliant, trustworthy men—Steve had ever known. Andrea was much quieter and kept to herself more due to her past, but as a behavioral analyst she couldn't be beat.

"What's going on, Steve?" Jon asked. "I'm assuming that woman you walked in with was the Rosalyn Mellinger you had me looking into."

Steve went over to the window looking out at the Rockies. Normally the view gave him a measure of peace, but not right now. "She is."

"You didn't mention she was having a baby."

"No." Steve shook his head. He really didn't want to get into that yet if he didn't have to. "I didn't."

"You also didn't mention that she was a suspect." He could hear the frustration in Jon's voice. "That would've changed how I was reading the information."

Steve turned and looked at them. "She wasn't a suspect until lunchtime and then about an hour ago."

He explained what had happened with the phone call and the attack at the gas station. He was just finishing as Margaret, another one of his assistants, brought in the pain medication and some ice. Someone had also dug up a sling. That would at least take the pressure off his shoulder and hopefully ease some of the throbbing. He thanked her.

"What did Rosalyn say to your accusations?" Brandon asked as Steve took the medication.

"She denied them, of course."

Andrea walked over and helped him ease his arm into the sling. Immediately the pain eased somewhat.

"And you're not completely sure about your accusations either," she said softly. "You're angry with her, but also protective. And confused most of all."

Steve nodded. "Yes. All of those things." He looked over at the other two men. "I've lost my perspective when it comes to Rosalyn Mellinger."

"Because the baby is yours," Brandon said. Jon nodded, not looking surprised.

Steve shrugged. "She says so."

Andrea touched his arm. "It's okay to believe her. Until you know for sure otherwise, it's okay to believe that what she says about that is true."

"Well, if it is, then it seems an awful lot like she was just part of a plan to kill or at least seriously injure the father of her baby."

He walked around his desk and looked out at the three of them. "I can't be neutral around her. So I need you three to figure out the truth for me. To be my eyes and ears."

Chapter Fifteen

Rosalyn sat in a room that was like something out of a crime-investigation show on television. A table with four chairs around it, none of them comfortable, cement walls all the way around painted a gray color that wasn't very different from their original hue. Fluorescent lights blared down from overhead, unflattering at best, downright painful after a few hours.

And on one wall was a large mirror covering half the surface. Of course, it would be a two-way mirror.

She'd known Steve was in law enforcement, but she'd had no idea he worked at a place like this. That he was evidently the *boss* in a place like this.

She'd told him everything she knew about the Watcher and he'd just made it seem like he was a beat cop or something. He was obviously so much more than that. He hadn't tried to give her any insight or any knowledge about what he thought would be the next steps.

Because he hadn't trusted her. She could almost understand the misunderstanding with the phone and the guy on the motorcycle. But Steve hadn't trusted her from the beginning. Not today, not last night when they were making love, not ever.

She'd started feeling like she was finally not alone, not knowing she was actually more alone than ever.

The guy who had brought her down to this stark room hadn't been mean or rough. He hadn't said much to her at all, beyond reading her the Miranda rights. Rosalyn wondered if she should call a lawyer but didn't know one to call here. Plus, she hadn't done anything wrong.

Besides trust that Steve Drackett was looking out for her best interests.

The big guy—what had Steve called him? Derek?—had escorted her to her seat.

"Stay here," had been all she'd gotten out of him before he'd left, closing the door behind him with a resounding click.

How long ago had that been? Probably twenty minutes. It felt like hours. Rosalyn could feel panic scratching at her subconscious, trying to work its way in. She refused to let it. She hadn't done anything wrong. Surely someone would believe her.

Although she was quite sure it wouldn't be Steve.

And once someone did believe her and she got out of here, where was she going to go? The Watcher had found her again. She wrapped her still-handcuffed arms around her belly, rocking back and forth, fighting panic once again.

What was she going to do?

Rosalyn nearly jumped out of her seat as the door opened. Two men, both of whom had been out in the office when Steve had brought her in, entered.

"Are you okay, Ms. Mellinger?" One, a stunningly handsome Asian man, asked her. He looked genuinely concerned.

"I just…I just…." The words wouldn't come out.

I just realized the enormity of the fact that a killer has found me again and the one person I thought I could trust wants to throw me in jail.

"I was just startled. That's all," she finally finished.

They both came and sat in the chairs on the other side of the table. The other man, very tall and also handsome, had a key in his hands. "Can I take those handcuffs off? I'm sure you'll be more comfortable without them."

Rosalyn brought her wrists up to the table so he could release her. She had to get some measure of control over herself. She could do this.

"Are you sure you fellas will feel safe with me unfettered?" She raised an eyebrow at them. They both had her by nearly a foot and at least fifty pounds apiece. Not to mention her range of motion with her extended belly would make her escape skills almost nonexistent.

Both men glanced at each other and cracked a smile. "We'll be sure to keep our guard up," the tall one said. "I'm Jon Hatton and this is Brandon Han. We're both profilers and behavioral analysts here at the Critical Response Division of Omega Sector."

"I'm not sure I know exactly what Omega Sector is."

Agent Han leaned back in his chair. "We're an interagency task force. People working together with backgrounds in the FBI, DEA, ATF and other relevant agencies. We even have some Interpol and other international agencies as part of our ranks. Helps us cut through red tape."

"We'd like to ask you some questions about what happened at the gas station a couple of hours ago," Hatton said. "Did you know the man on the motorcycle was going to attack Steve?"

"No." She looked at one man and then the other. "I was inside the store when I saw the guy pull up. I thought it was pretty stupid that he was coming right behind our car when there were other pumps open, but I didn't know who he was or that he was going to hurt Steve until I saw him flick out his stick thing."

Agent Han had pulled out a notebook and began writing. "It's called a telescopic baton. A weapon that can be easily transported and then, like you said, be fully expanded with just a flick of the wrist."

She nodded. "Steve was looking at me, so I knew he wasn't paying attention to the guy and was going to get hurt." She remembered knowing she wouldn't get outside in time to warn him. "Fortunately, Steve turned at the last second and blocked the hit with his arm."

"And you had no idea who the man was or that he was going to be there at that time?" Han asked.

"No." Rosalyn could feel the panic pulling at her again.

Hatton tilted his head to the side. "You didn't notify him in any way that you were traveling to Colorado Springs with Steve?"

It was almost like it was a friendly question. That this was all some dinner-party conversation. Rosalyn could feel hysteria building up inside her and fought to keep it tamped down.

"No. I did not contact the man who has been stalking me almost daily for the last year, who has caused me to leave my job, all my friends, and for six months live on the run in sleazy hotels. I did not contact the man who has driven me to the precipice of insanity and thoughts of suicide more than once."

She leaned forward in her chair. "I did not contact the man from whom I, for the first time in a year, had found a measure of peace because I had finally felt like I had gotten away from him for good. I did not bring that man back into my life."

Agent Han leaned forward too. "Then how did he find you and Steve?"

Rosalyn couldn't stop the tears now. "I don't know," she whispered before huddling back into her chair. "He always finds me."

The two men looked at her for a long time. Rosalyn finally just covered her face with her hands.

After a long pause she heard Agent Hatton say, "I think we need to start at the beginning."

STEVE WATCHED IT all from the adjacent room, able to see everything through the two-way mirror and hear everything through the audio that was pumped in. Andrea had wanted to go in with Brandon to help question Rosalyn, but Steve had asked her to stay.

He needed Andrea's opinion. Not only could she read other people's nonverbal communication with remarkable accuracy, she also had a sixth sense about their emotions. She could feel what they were emoting even if it didn't match what the person was saying.

He'd trusted Andrea's abilities when he'd pulled her

out of a pretty horrible situation nearly five years ago; he trusted them even more now.

"Steve, I've got to say, there is nothing Rosalyn has done nonverbally that has given me any indication that she's not telling the truth."

Rosalyn had started back at the beginning like Jon had asked her to do. She'd spent the last hour telling Jon and Brandon about the Watcher and everything that had happened. She was giving much more detail than she had to him.

It made him physically ill to think about what she'd gone through.

Steve rubbed his good hand over his face, his hurt arm still in the sling. He didn't have to have Andrea's talent at reading people to see that Rosalyn was telling the truth.

"I've made a pretty bad mistake."

Andrea looked at him, eyebrow raised.

"When the attacker showed up at the gas station, just a couple of hours after she'd made what I deemed to be a suspicious phone call, I was positive she'd played me again."

"Again?"

Steve realized this all came back to when Rosalyn had left him at the hotel six months ago without a word.

"She fooled me. Snuck out in the middle of the night. Took all my cash."

Andrea studied him. Steve knew he wouldn't like whatever it was she was going to say.

"She hurt you."

"My pride, sure. Personally and professionally. I'm the head of one of the most prestigious law enforcement agencies in the world. If I can't tell when I'm being set up as a mark, maybe I don't deserve to run this place."

Andrea shook her head, the tiniest of smiles on her face. "No, it's a lot more than that. You opened yourself to her and she hurt you."

Steve thought of that time in Pensacola before Rosalyn had fled. He had known she was scared of something, that something was happening in her life. He'd planned to ask her to stay with him the rest of the week. Hell, if being outside made her nervous for whatever reason, they could stay in the bungalow.

He'd planned to keep her there, to make love to her, to talk to her and listen to her until she realized she could trust him. Then they could solve whatever scared her together. Maybe he'd even see if she needed a fresh start in Colorado. She'd mentioned the beautiful mountains.

Steve ran his hand through his hair. He couldn't deny it to himself any longer. He, jaded law enforcement officer who saw the worst of humanity on a daily basis, who hadn't been on more than a handful of dates since his wife died, had fallen in love at first sight. Or at the very least had been willing to try a relationship with Rosalyn, invite her into his life.

But she'd bailed before he had the chance.

So yeah, she had hurt him.

And evidently he still hadn't forgiven her for any of it. Because he'd put cuffs on her, for God's sake, and had her dragged into their least comfortable interrogation room like she was a terrorist or murderer or something.

"Damn it." He ran his hand over his face again. "I'm an idiot. I've got to get her out of there."

Andrea touched him on his arm. "Let Jon and Brandon finish talking to her. It's helping her, Steve. To go through the details. To talk about it with someone else."

Steve watched through the mirror again and saw Andrea was right, as she most always was. Rosalyn was sitting up straight, had unwrapped her arms from the protective stance around herself. Her shoulders weren't hunched. She had more color in her cheeks.

Brandon had asked for Rosalyn's notebook when she'd mentioned it, and it had been brought to them. The three of them were now poring over it.

Obviously Jon and Brandon believed Rosalyn, and were trying to help her make sense of it all. To discover the pattern in the Watcher's actions concerning her.

Exactly what Steve should've been doing rather than worrying about whether she was in on her own terrorizing.

Derek Waterman entered the room. "Some more info for you, boss, about the Ammonses in Georgia. Seems like they don't have a phone in their house, but they do have one at their café, for orders and such."

Of course they did.

"We checked, and there was a record of a call from Dalhart, Texas, made to them this morning at ten o'clock Eastern time. I think that would line up with the call Rosalyn was making."

"Yep, it definitely would. Thanks, Derek."

And just like that, Rosalyn was cleared. Although he'd already cleared her in his mind anyway.

Derek turned toward the mirror. "She looks a lot better than she did when I brought her in there."

"That's because the idiot quota surrounding her has dropped significantly." Steve grimaced.

Derek chuckled. "Hey, only my wife is allowed to call me an idiot."

"Your wife is a certified genius. She's at liberty to call everyone an idiot." Derek's wife, Molly, was the head of the Omega forensic lab. "But in this case, I was referring to myself."

Derek slapped him on the shoulder and Steve winced from the blow he'd taken there but didn't say anything. "We all can be idiots when it comes to the women we care about."

Steve heard a muttered "Amen" out of Andrea.

"Andrea, will you take some food and water in to them? Make sure Rosalyn is okay? I don't want to disrupt their progress by going in there myself."

"Sure. That's a good idea. I'm sure she'll appreciate your thoughtfulness, Steve."

He shook his head. "No, don't say it's from me. Just make sure she has what she needs."

Steve wasn't sure Rosalyn was ever going to want to talk to him again after how he'd treated her. All he could do now was catch the psycho trying to harm them both.

Steve would do whatever it took to keep Rosalyn and their baby safe. And would pray she would give him another chance.

Chapter Sixteen

They believed her. She wasn't exactly sure when it happened, but Rosalyn knew Agents Hatton and Han believed her.

The gorgeous blonde who'd first approached her in the offices before Steve stopped her came into the room. She had a tray of food—some soup and crackers—and water and coffee.

"We thought you might want something to eat. And Steve mentioned you like coffee."

"Steve sent you in here with food and drink? I thought he wanted me thrown under the jail."

The woman set the tray down in front of Rosalyn, then went to stand beside Brandon's chair. He hooked a casual arm around her hips. What a striking couple those two made.

She smiled gently at Rosalyn. "Sometimes it's difficult to see things that are right in front of you when there are feelings involved. I'm sure that's true for Steve."

"I think Steve made it quite obvious he has no feelings for me when he arrested me a few hours ago."

The woman smiled. "Sometimes men are a little bit

slower in recognizing their own feelings." The woman looked over at Brandon and a moment of tenderness passed between them. Obviously at some point Brandon had been a little slow in recognizing his feelings for the woman. Although obviously not anymore.

"I'm Andrea Gordon, by the way." Andrea looked back up at Rosalyn. "And just for the record, you are not under arrest. You're free to leave at any time, although we would very much like you to stay so we can continue working on the case with you."

"Does Steve Drackett know I'm free to go?"

Andrea nodded. "He's the one who gave the word."

Rosalyn didn't know what to make of that, so she just started eating her food.

The other three agents began looking at the papers on the table.

"Steve found two transmitters on Rosalyn's personal effects. One was on a sweater, one on her bag," Jon said and turned his attention to her. "He found those after the fire at the hotel, right?"

Rosalyn nodded. "While we were at the hospital, I think."

"And you went immediately to the superstore and changed out of everything?"

"Yes, the only thing I took with me out of that store that I had brought in was this notebook." She pointed at the one on the table.

Jon looked through it. "It's highly unlikely that there's any sort of transmitter in here, but let's get it scanned just in case." He walked out of the room with it.

Brandon sat back in his chair, taking a cracker Rosalyn offered him from her tray. "Let's say he got the transmitters on you at the very beginning. That he broke into your house and put one on every piece of clothing you had. That would be excessive and expensive, but this is obviously no garden-variety stalker we're dealing with here."

"That's how he followed you for the first six months. He knew where you were and could show up there," Andrea continued.

Jon walked back into the room. "Derek's going to take the notebook over to Molly in the lab."

"We're trying to figure out the transmitter pattern," Brandon told him. "I'm running with the possibility that he put trackers on everything she owned at the beginning."

"Okay," Jon said. "Possible. And scary."

Rosalyn had to agree.

Brandon continued. "When we get your notebook back, we'll double-check for patterns to see if there's any consistency, but maybe he was working around his own schedule. He has a job that requires him to be in an office at least part of the time. That's why some weeks you had notes multiple days in a row, and sometimes you didn't hear from him for a while."

Jon nodded. "That would suggest someone with a career. We can see if weekends were more active with the notes—that might help confirm."

Rosalyn looked at them. "I don't understand. You're saying the Watcher is just a normal guy? Like a businessman or a lawyer or something?" The thought made her feel a little ill.

Andrea reached over and touched her hand. "A lot

of times minds of pure evil can be dressed in very professional packages."

Brandon shrugged. "Times you thought he was toying with you by leaving you alone, making you think you'd gotten away? Maybe he just had something in his schedule that required his attention and he couldn't get to you that day."

"And it is highly likely that the Watcher is from your hometown of Mobile, since that's where it all started. Not only that, but that you know him or met him briefly." Jon grimaced.

Rosalyn shuddered, glad she was almost done with her food. She wouldn't have been able to eat another bite after thinking about this. "I was an accountant. I met with clients all the time."

"We'll check into that right away," Jon said. "Clients you've met with, coworkers."

"But really, it could be anyone. Someone I met at the grocery store or while waiting for the elevator."

Rosalyn saw the compassion in Andrea's eyes. "Yes, unfortunately."

The thought that she might recognize the Watcher's face when they caught him made her want to be physically ill. Every person she'd known was suspect.

But for the first time, Rosalyn actually had hope that they—this Omega Sector team—might really catch him. Before today her only hope had been she might be able to outrun him at some point. Get somewhere he couldn't find her. But there hadn't been much chance of that with the baby coming.

Jon, Brandon and Andrea were discussing particular aspects of the Watcher when the door to the room opened and Steve walked in.

They just stared at each other for a long time. Apology was clear all over his face.

But even with his arm in the sling and the stiffness in his frame—pain from being hit with that telescopic baton thing—Rosalyn found she wasn't quite ready to let this go just yet.

Steve eventually stepped away from the door.

"All right, I've cleared conference room 1 for us to use. I think we'll all be more comfortable there."

Everybody stood and began packing up their notes, still talking about the Watcher they were trying to profile.

"Rosalyn and I will meet you up there in a few minutes."

They all shuffled out quickly after that. Rosalyn remained in her chair. Steve came and sat across from her.

"I overreacted. Made a mistake."

She cocked her head to the side. "You thought I tried to have you killed."

"You made a suspicious phone call and a few hours later someone took a swing at my head with a metal rod. That seemed pretty dubious at the time."

"I told you I called the Ammonses." Her volume began to rise.

His did too. "You also told me the day before that the Ammonses didn't have a phone. It seemed like an inconsistency in your story. You know who tends to have inconsistencies in their stories? Liars and criminals."

Rosalyn rolled her eyes. "I called their café. They have a phone there."

His eyes narrowed. "I know that *now*. But you didn't tell me that."

Rosalyn stood, bracing her hands on the table and leaning toward him. "Because you didn't ask. Because you were convinced I was up to no good. That I was playing you."

"Damn it, Rosalyn, I'm trained to look for suspicious patterns. To see bad things before they happen."

"And that's what I was, right? A bad thing."

"No, it's just—"

She slammed her hand down on the table. "You put handcuffs on me like I was some common criminal that might try to run at any second. You didn't ask. You didn't give me a chance to explain."

"Rosalyn—"

"We made love last night. And today you were convinced I was trying to have you killed. I guess that tells me how you really feel about me."

He stood then. "No, it wasn't like that. I had to force myself to try to look at you objectively."

He reached out toward her, but she snatched herself back. When Steve touched her, she couldn't think straight. Her attraction to him overpowered everything else. She didn't want that now. Maybe never wanted it again.

She rubbed her eyes. She was tired, not just from today but from everything. The only thing good going for her now was the fact that everyone here believed her. The agents seemed ready and willing to put their resources and brainpower into figuring out who the

Watcher was and what Rosalyn could do about it. It was more than she'd had in a long time.

"You know what? Just take me to the conference room. The faster we can get this situation resolved, the sooner I can get myself out of your life."

Because Steve obviously didn't want her there.

STEVE DIDN'T MAKE a lot of tactical errors. Nor did he make many errors in judgment. His job and the lives of the people on his team, not to mention those of the American public in general, depended on it.

But he'd done both with Rosalyn.

They walked to the conference room together in silence. Not the comfortable kind.

She was mad. He didn't blame her.

But she was right. They needed to concentrate on figuring out all they could about the Watcher. Not because Steve wanted Rosalyn out of his life—he'd be damned if he was going to let that happen—but because obviously the Watcher had escalated in violence over the past few days.

Steve would do whatever was necessary to keep Rosalyn and the baby safe. Even if she didn't want anything to do with him right now.

He held the door open for her as they entered the conference room. Jon, Brandon and Andrea were already there. Roman Weber, a member of Omega's SWAT team, had joined them.

One entire wall of the conference room was made up of an electronic whiteboard. Brandon and Jon had already started making a timeline on it. Everything they wrote could be saved onto a computer file to be used later.

"Molly brought Rosalyn's notebook back over from the lab," Andrea said as they walked in. "Nothing suspicious about it."

Steve nodded, not surprised.

Brandon turned to them from the whiteboard. "Basically, we have two inconsistencies that need to be addressed before we can go much further. First, why didn't the Watcher have any contact with you for the six months you were at the Ammonses' in Ellijay? What was different? Something in your life or something in his?"

"I don't know." Rosalyn shrugged as she sat down at the table.

"How did you meet them?" Andrea asked.

"I took a bus from Pensacola as far as the amount of money I had would take me." She glanced over at Steve, then looked away quickly. "That ended up being Ellijay.

"The Ammonses own a small café in town. They've lived there all their lives. They live right on top of the café, although I know Mr. Ammons also has a fishing cabin somewhere." Rosalyn smiled. "I got off the bus, went in to eat and felt like I never really left there again until I went to meet my sister in Pensacola."

Her smile faded into a flinch at the mention of her sister.

"Anyway, I asked Mrs. Ammons if I could make some cash washing dishes or whatever. They're not big fans of the government, so they didn't mind paying me cash under the table."

Jon smiled. "I like them already."

She shrugged, shaking her head with a smile. "The Ammonses are odd. Definitely keep to themselves and don't want people, especially the government, in their business. But they took me in. Let me wash dishes, then started letting me wait tables. When they found out I was sleeping out back under the café's overhang—"

"What?" The word was out of Steve's mouth before he could catch it. But the thought of her homeless, pregnant, sleeping outside.

"Honestly, it wasn't so bad. And it was just for a few days."

Steve's fist clenched but he didn't say anything further.

"Anyway, they invited me to live with them, and that was that. I pretty much never left their property. I worked, then went upstairs. For the first couple of weeks I would run downstairs every morning to see if there was a note from the Watcher."

"And nothing? Ever?" Brandon asked.

"No. Never. I just began thinking of the house as my force field." She scoffed at herself. "Stupid, I know."

Andrea walked over and touched Rosalyn on the shoulder. "No, not stupid at all. No one would blame you for staying somewhere where you felt safe. Where, for all intents and purposes, you *were* safe."

"Why did you leave?" Jon asked.

"The baby." Rosalyn put a hand on her stomach. "Soon it wasn't just going to be me anymore. The Ammonses are in their seventies. I knew I needed to have a backup plan in case..." She trailed off, then finally picked back up. "In case something happened to me."

In case the Watcher killed her. She didn't say it but everyone in the room knew what she meant.

"So you contacted your sister," Andrea prompted when Rosalyn didn't go on.

She nodded. "I asked Lindsey to meet me in Pensacola. I was going to go back to the hotel and see if they would give me Steve's name. Or, if there was some sort of privacy law, see if they would at least contact him on my behalf."

Until that moment Steve hadn't realized he'd held a hardness inside himself against her about that. He'd silently, subconsciously, assumed she'd never planned to tell him about the baby. But she had. He took a step toward her, catching her eyes with his.

"I didn't know who you were," she continued, looking at him. "And I definitely didn't know about all this—" she gestured around the room with her arm "—but I knew the baby had a better chance with you than with me."

He wanted to move closer. To pick her up and plop her down on his lap. To promise her it was all going to be all right. To apologize for being an idiot earlier today.

Andrea looked over at him, sympathy in her eyes. She could clearly read his pain, his concern. Steve didn't care if it was noticeable to everyone.

"And Steve was there identifying what he thought was your body," Jon said.

"With all your sister's drug troubles, I'm surprised her prints weren't on file. But yours were," Steve said. "At least from juvie."

Rosalyn rolled her eyes. "That's when we were sixteen and Lindsey shoplifted. Left me to take the blame."

It explained a lot.

"Okay." Brandon got them back on track. "And once you were in Pensacola, you were immediately contacted by the Watcher again."

Rosalyn's lips pursed as she nodded.

"We know your clothes had the transmitters. Maybe they were short-range and the Watcher couldn't pick them up from that far away," Jon mused.

"Possible, but Rosalyn also traveled nearly as far when she was in Dallas and Memphis and he found her there." Brandon turned back toward the whiteboard.

It was time to take action. Steve turned to Roman. "I need you to get to Ellijay. Talk to the Ammonses, scope out the situation. See why the Watcher might have left Rosalyn alone while she was there."

Roman headed for the door. "You got it, boss. One-horse towns are my favorite." He winked at everyone as he walked by. "I'll call as soon as I have info."

Brandon nodded. "Good. Having solid intel on the Ammonses will help. The other big inconsistency is how the Watcher found you here in Colorado, after you'd removed all the bugs."

Steve ran a hand over his face. "I could've sworn we weren't followed. I was actively watching the entire time." He looked over at Rosalyn and shrugged. "But today hasn't been my finest day when it comes to judgment calls."

Jon had been looking at Rosalyn's notebook but now

looked up to address everyone. "I think we all have to agree. We're either missing something big, or the Watcher isn't just one person."

Chapter Seventeen

The thought that she had one psychopathic stalker had been bad enough. Jon Hatton's idea that it might actually be more than one person had been enough to put Rosalyn into a panic.

She hadn't said anything, had just tried to keep it all together while all the discussion continued on around her. They'd sent someone out for pizza, and Rosalyn had done her best to eat, but it had been difficult.

Eventually she'd put a hand on Steve's arm. Once he'd gotten a good look at her, he'd immediately announced he was taking her home.

His home.

He called Derek Waterman and another SWAT member she hadn't met yet named Liam Goetz. They were tasked with making sure no one followed them to Steve's house. Liam joked and flirted with her, when he wasn't showing her pictures of his newborn twins, while Steve personally inspected the Omega vehicle they'd be using. Evidently it had already been swept thoroughly for bugs, but he wanted to double-check.

They drove around for more than an hour. Derek went to Steve's house and checked it out for them.

They even switched vehicles halfway through their journey. There was no way anyone could've followed them. Hell, Rosalyn was in the car and she hardly knew where they were.

"I couldn't find my way back to your building now if my life depended on it." She had long since closed her eyes, but having them open wouldn't have helped anyway.

"Believe it or not, my house is only a few miles away from the office. We're just taking the scenic route."

"I don't think anyone could've followed us."

Steve grimaced. "I thought the same was true earlier today, but I was wrong. But both Derek and Liam have given us the all clear. So I'm certain no one has followed us now. Plus, we'll have a guard in a car outside the house watching for anyone."

"Derek?"

"No, someone else. Derek will want to get home to his wife and their daughter."

"Yeah, Liam was showing me pictures of his twins and his daughter, Tallinn."

Steve smiled. "Yes, he and his wife, Vanessa, adopted her after a human-trafficking case last year. And the twins…they're just exhausting. Keeps Vanessa and Liam busy."

Rosalyn realized how little she knew about the man she was about to have a baby with. She opened her eyes. "How about you? Do you have any kids? You were married once right?"

"Yes. Melanie. She died in a car accident twelve years ago. But no, we didn't have any kids."

"I'm sorry about your wife." Rosalyn wondered if Steve still loved her.

"Don't take this the wrong way, but you two would've liked each other. Both of you are smart and strong." His smile was pensive, but not sad.

"Do you still love her?" The words were out before she could bite off her tongue. Damn it. "Never mind. You don't have to answer that."

"No, it's okay. I'll always love Melanie—she was a huge part of my life." He looked over at her before returning his gaze to the road. "But no, I'm not in love with her anymore. Not pining after her. As a matter of fact, she'd probably lay into me for taking this long to get serious about someone."

Was that what they were? Serious?

"Do you mean us?"

"You're the only person I'm having a baby with."

"You arrested me earlier today, for heaven's sake."

He grimaced. "I was trying to do the right thing. To keep some perspective. My perspective has been blown to hell since the day you ran into that bar in Pensacola trying to get out of the rain."

"Because I stole from you?"

"No. I couldn't care less about the money. Because you got under my skin the way no one else has."

He pulled the car into a driveway of a small house, then used his phone to activate a code that opened the garage door.

She turned to look at him more fully.

"I did?" She had figured he'd be a little irritated at her running off with his cash, then would never think about her again.

He pressed the button to shut the garage door and turned off the car but still stared straight ahead with his hand on the wheel. "Why do you think I happened to be in Pensacola to identify your body? I had the Pensacola police report sent to my desk every day."

"To look for me? Because you thought I would be arrested?"

"I figured if you were looking for businessmen as marks to steal from, you would eventually get caught."

After her behavior in Florida, she really couldn't blame him for that conclusion, although it still sat heavy in her heart. "And you wanted to press charges too."

"That's what I told myself." He finally looked at her. "But really it was so I could find you again, rescue you from the terrible path I thought you were walking down and bring you back here. Set you straight."

"You sound like a parole officer."

He continued as if she hadn't spoken, his eyes softening. "And then once you were more settled, with a good job and happy with your life, I planned to court you properly. To go out on dates and get to know you."

"Oh."

"Because there has not been one single day that I haven't thought of you. I'll admit, I wasn't always happy with you. But I also have to admit that my plan, once I found you again, was to make sure we were together. Even when I thought you were a petty criminal."

"But you don't think I'm one anymore?"

He reached over and tucked a strand of hair behind her ear. "No."

She asked the question she'd been afraid to ask. "And you believe me when I say the baby is yours?"

"Yes." His hand slid into her hair and pulled her closer. "And I'm going to do whatever it takes to keep you and the baby safe."

He closed the distance between their lips. Soft, this time, full of promise but not demand. His thumb brushed along her jaw, sending a rush of sensation racing across her skin. She leaned in closer but stopped when she felt the oddest sensation in her belly.

She jumped back from Steve. "Whoa." She put both hands on her stomach.

"What? Are you okay? Is something wrong?"

She smiled. "I'm fine. He just kicked. Like, kicked *really* hard."

She grabbed his hand not in the sling and put it on her stomach under her hand. They waited a moment, and then she felt it again.

Steve's eyes grew wide. "I felt that."

Rosalyn's smile felt so big that it might split her face. "I know! He must be a soccer player or something."

"Have you felt him move before?"

"I think so, but I thought it was indigestion or something. Never anything this strong."

They waited a few minutes more, but evidently their little soccer player had gotten tired. Both Rosalyn and Steve were still grinning as he helped her out of the car and led her into the house.

In the midst of all the heartbreak and chaos of the last two days, feeling their baby move so lively inside her made everything seem like it was going to be okay.

But that didn't stop her from being tired. Steve

showed her around as they talked. He stopped and turned to her when they got to the kitchen.

"I don't have much food." He grimaced. "Honestly, I don't usually come here very often during the week. There's a small apartment within the Omega complex I use. Or just crash on the couch in my office. But I could have an agent deliver us something."

"No, I'm fine tonight. Although I know I'll be hungry in the morning." She was always hungry first thing in the morning, but at least she didn't wake up sick anymore like she had in the first few months.

"I've got waffles and toaster pastries."

"Do the important people you work with know you eat Pop-Tarts for breakfast?"

He winked at her. "Please don't tell."

"Would it ruin your big, bad reputation?"

"No." He rolled his eyes. "They would all just want me to bring them some every day."

Rosalyn's laugh turned into a huge yawn.

Steve walked over and slid his good arm around her shoulder. "I guess that answers my question about whether you're ready for sleep or not."

He led her up the stairs to a bedroom. "This is my room. You can sleep here and I'll sleep in the guest room."

She grabbed his arm as he turned to go. "No, stay here with me."

"Rosalyn, are you sure? What I did today…" His head dropped.

"A little overdramatic to be sure, Director." She put a finger under his chin and lifted until they were looking at each other. "But the situation is complicated. If nothing else, I can definitely agree with that. So don't worry about it. We have a big enough enemy to fight without fighting each other."

"Then I would very much love to sleep in that bed with you, where I can hold you and know you and the baby are safe."

She pressed herself up against him and smiled. "Well, I hope not *just* hold…"

TRUE TO HIS WORD, Steve was still wrapped around Rosalyn when she woke up the next morning. Despite all her naughty intentions, she had fallen asleep not a minute after her head hit the pillow.

She eased herself away from Steve and out of the bed so she could use the bathroom and go make some breakfast. Actually, the infamous toaster pastries sounded just about perfect right now, although she still had to snicker a little bit.

She was dressed in one of Steve's T-shirts, a soft gray one that fell to her knees even over her extended belly. She never wanted to get out of it. But it would probably look a little weird if she wore it back to the Omega offices.

Rosalyn made her way down the stairs and into the kitchen, trying to rub sleep out of her eyes. She easily found the breakfast food in Steve's pantry—he hadn't been kidding when he said he didn't have much food here—and started decaf coffee. She ate the first Pop-Tart right out of the toaster to ease her growling stomach, then poured herself some coffee.

Hopefully they would make progress today. Real

progress. If anybody could, it was Steve's team. They were trained and obviously good at what they did.

She grabbed a plate of the breakfast food whose name was not to be spoken and another cup of coffee to take up to Steve. They'd have to leave soon, but maybe she could talk him into a little naughtiness before then.

She stepped out of the kitchen into the front hall and froze.

An envelope sat there on the ground, a garish white on Steve's dark hardwood floors. It had been slid under the front door at some point—she had no idea when. She could see her name on the front in bold letters.

Just like all the others she'd received over the past year.

The coffee cups slipped through her numb fingers and crashed to the floor, shattering. Rosalyn felt the drops of hot coffee burn her bare legs and feet almost from a distance.

She couldn't take her eyes off the envelope.

The Watcher had found her again.

Chapter Eighteen

Steve heard the shattering cups and jumped out of bed. He instantly realized Rosalyn wasn't in the room with him. Habit had him grabbing his sidearm before running toward the stairs.

"Rosalyn?"

He saw her standing there, perfectly still. Two cups lay broken at her feet.

"Are you okay? Don't move. You might cut yourself. What happened?"

Now that he knew she was safe, his adrenaline slowed just a little bit. He set his gun on the hallway table and walked toward her.

She'd dropped the coffee cups, but it didn't look like she was cut or burned.

"Are you all right?" he asked again. "I don't see any cuts."

When he looked up and saw her face, his concern came rushing back. She stood devoid of all color, fists pressed to the sides of her head. She was looking at him, trying to say something.

Glass be damned, he walked all the way to her.

"What, sweetheart? What's wrong? Is it the baby?"

He put his hand on her belly. She lowered her hands and he looked down to see her pointing to something on the floor.

"It's him," she whispered. "I know it's him. He found me."

It was a letter. Steve muttered the foulest expletive he knew. How the hell had the Watcher found them here? Ignoring the ache in his arm, Steve reached down and scooped Rosalyn up and carried her over to the stairs.

"Stay right here, okay?"

She nodded, but he wasn't sure she was processing anything he said. She just stared at the envelope on the ground, face ashen.

Steve got his weapon and did a sweep of the house to make sure no one had entered unawares, then called Derek.

"My house has been compromised," Steve said before Derek could even get a greeting in.

Derek's expletive matched Steve's.

"There's a letter here on my floor. Has been slid under the door. The house is secure now." Steve looked over to where Rosalyn sat huddled on the stairs, arms around her knees, rocking herself back and forth. "Who was on patrol last night?"

"Wilson. I'll call you back in two minutes." Derek disconnected the call.

Steve wanted to go over and open the letter. Read it. But more than that he wanted the forensics team to be able to get off any possible information. He walked over to stand by Rosalyn, rubbing her hair gently. He wished he could pick her up and carry her away but knew they had to deal with this while they could.

True to his word, Derek called back in a little over a minute. His voice was grim. "Wilson hasn't reported in for the last three hours and is not answering his phone now."

"Damn it." That was not a good sign.

"You should have agents at your door in three to four minutes. Liam is on his way, ETA ten minutes. I called Brandon and Andrea too. I figured Andrea might be good for Rosalyn."

"Thanks, Derek."

He could hear Derek's muted talking to someone before he came back on the line. "Molly and I are coming too. She wants to check out the scene herself. She says not to touch anything."

"Okay."

"Just hold tight, boss. We're on our way."

THIRTY MINUTES LATER his house was a circus.

He'd gotten Rosalyn back upstairs before anyone arrived. Helped her wash off the coffee that had spilled on her legs and they both got dressed.

She still hadn't said much. Still had no color in her face. But she was holding it together. That was all he could ask for.

Agent Wilson was dead. Had been shot at close range in his car. Initial estimates put his death at around 3:00 a.m.

Molly Humphries-Waterman and her forensic lab team were doing their job all over his front porch, Agent Wilson's car and around the letter itself.

When Brandon and Andrea got there, Steve sent her straight up to his room to where Rosalyn still sat on the bed.

The rest of his inner team—Derek, Jon, Liam and Brandon—were with Steve in the kitchen. Those were the men he trusted most in the world.

"We need to get Rosalyn moved to Omega," Jon said. "At least we know there that she'll be safe. That he can't get to her."

Brandon nodded. "I agree. There's something we missed, obviously. Some way he's finding Rosalyn's location."

"Because they sure as hell weren't followed." Liam leaned his large frame against the fridge. "I can guarantee that."

Steve agreed. There was no way someone could've followed them last night without their being aware of it.

"I don't want to be the bad guy here," Derek said. "But, Steve, yesterday you were sure Rosalyn had contacted the Watcher. Are you sure something like that didn't happen again?"

Steve wasn't going back down that road. "Yes, I'm sure. However he's finding her, it's not because she's telling him."

Derek held out his hands in surrender. "All right, don't kill me. All I'm saying is sometimes the simplest answer is the most likely one."

"Well, start looking for complex answers because Rosalyn isn't helping the Watcher." If they had seen her face when she'd found that letter, they wouldn't question it either. Steve would give everything he had to never see that look on Rosalyn's face ever again.

Jon jumped in before things got out of hand. "We need to get Rosalyn back to HQ. You too, Steve. We'll work out the hows and whys from there. And I have some other cases I've found that I think might have an interesting tie to what's happening to Rosalyn."

"Steve, I'm going to open the letter now," Molly called out from the hallway. "I've gotten all the forensic evidence I can from the floor around it and the outside of the envelope."

They all moved into the hallway.

Molly looked up, shaking her head. "I had hoped he had licked the envelope. That would've been our best shot at DNA."

"He never licks the envelope." Rosalyn's voice was tight at the top of the stairs. "Not once. He's too smart for that."

"I was going to read the note." Molly looked up at Rosalyn. "Is that okay?"

Rosalyn nodded.

Molly opened the envelope and her eyes flew to Steve. This had to be bad.

"Go ahead," he murmured.

"'I can't wait to meet your baby. Maybe he'll decide to come live with me. But I'll get rid of Dad first.'"

Rosalyn let out a sob and held on to the banister for support. Steve took the stairs two at a time to get to her, then pulled her hard to his chest. He could feel shudders racking her small frame.

"He'll kill you. He'll take the baby."

"No," he whispered in her ear. "Do you hear me? That maniac will never touch our child. I promise you that. And I can take care of myself."

"Not all the time, you can't. He'll wear you down. That's what he does." Her quiet sobs broke his heart.

He held her close, fury streaming through his blood. He looked down the stairs at Liam and Derek.

"I want to get her back to HQ, now."

Within minutes they were on their way. They left the forensic team and coroner's office representatives, as well as members of the SWAT team. Derek stayed to oversee everything but really to keep an eye on his wife if the Watcher decided to come back for any reason.

Everyone else made a caravan to get Rosalyn back to Omega. Liam was in the car in front of Steve, Jon in the car behind. Weapons hot in case there was any problem. Rosalyn sat in the backseat in Steve's car. Andrea was beside her, arm around her shoulder. Brandon was on the other side.

Every time he caught a glance at Rosalyn's face in the rearview mirror, his heart sank a little more. She was pale to the point of gray, her lips pinched until they were colorless. Her blue eyes, usually so full of life, were dull, lifeless.

Like she had given up.

Steve felt marginally better as they pulled into Omega and he got her into the building. The Watcher's violence seemed to be escalating, and now he was using guns. Rosalyn would be staying inside the Omega compound until they caught the Watcher.

They moved quickly past the security guard, Steve biting his tongue when Rosalyn once again set off the metal detector. The guard ran the wand up the front and back of her body but found nothing.

This was ridiculous. "Get those things looked at," he barked to the guard. The man nodded quickly.

He slipped his arm around Rosalyn, keeping her close to his side as they walked down the hall.

"I need to write this note in my notebook. It's important for me to keep an accurate record. Detective Johnson said so."

Rosalyn's voice sounded unnatural. Distant. Steve shot a concerned look over at Andrea.

"Sure, honey." Andrea rubbed Rosalyn's arm. "Your notebook is in the conference room. I'll help you write it down."

When they got to the room, Jon grabbed Steve's arm. "Brandon and I found something interesting last night after you left."

"Okay."

Brandon and Jon both turned to look at the two women, who were settling in at the conference room table. Jon shook his head. "I'm not sure if it's something we should say in front of Rosalyn. Especially given her fragile state right now."

"Okay, let's go into my office. You can run it by me and then we can decide whether to tell Rosalyn. Although I don't want to keep secrets from her if it's going to affect her safety. More information is better in this case."

Brandon nodded. "I think we both agree. It's some other cases we found that are interesting."

As soon as they were in Steve's office, Brandon pulled out four files. He opened one and laid down a picture of a young woman.

"This is the one I remembered. It's from two years

ago." Brandon's genius mind didn't forget much of anything. It had helped them on cases more than once. "Her
name was Tracy Solheim. From Jackson, Mississippi."

Steve picked up the file and looked over it. "Says
she committed suicide."

Brandon nodded. "She did. She was twenty-one.
But for six months before she killed herself she told
multiple people, her family, friends, even the police,
that she had a stalker. Said she was receiving notes."

"Nobody believed her," Jon continued. "Tracy had
a history of emotional trauma. Did a lot of weird stuff
to get attention over the years. Police reports did say
she had notes but that none of them were threatening
in any way."

Steve shrugged. "Okay, there are some similarities
there. But not enough to convince me it's the same
guy."

Brandon nodded. "I agree. But look at these three
others. One's from Tampa, one's from Birmingham,
Alabama, and one's from New Orleans."

"I'm assuming the point is the radius to Mobile,
Alabama, Rosalyn's hometown."

"It's almost a semicircle," Jon said. "And within
the last six years there's been a woman who has committed suicide in all those cities. All white females
within twenty to twenty-five years of age. All who
complained to family and at least once to the police
about receiving 'strange' notes. In all the cases nothing was done to help them, because they were deemed
nonthreatening."

Brandon pulled out a piece of paper. "This is what
clinched it for me. One of the officers from the New

Orleans case at least wrote down in his official report what some of the notes said."

Brandon had blown them up so they were each on a separate sheet of paper.

The park was nice today, wasn't it?

I would've chosen the red sweater, but the blue one looks nice too.

Did you enjoy dinner with your friends? I was hoping you'd get the shrimp rather than the chicken.

"Those are all similar in tone to some of the notes Rosalyn has quoted in her notebook."

Brandon nodded. "Exactly. And also, innocent enough to not be taken seriously by the police."

Steve sat down in the seat next to the table and leaned back. "Okay, let's assume this is the same guy. So what happened? The Watcher killed them? I thought you said they were suicide."

"Yes, all confirmed suicide." Brandon sat in the other chair. "We think that's his MO, Steve. He drives these women away from their families, away from their loved ones. He isolates them. He's smart enough not to threaten them in the notes, so nothing can be done with the police."

"To what end? He's obviously not living out any fantasies with these women." That was almost always part of a violent stalker's MO—having the women with him. "He's not killing them, right?"

"He's a serial killer, Steve." Jon braced himself on the table with both arms. "Every bit as much as ones that we profile. But instead of using a certain weapon or certain ritual, he pushes and pushes until they do it themselves. That *is* his ritual."

It was so sick and yet made so much sense at the same time.

A serial killer who didn't actually kill his victims. Drove them to killing themselves by isolating them from everyone they loved, by terrorizing them until they felt they had no other choice.

It took a special sort of evil to inflict emotional trauma of that magnitude.

Steve realized the Watcher could've killed Rosalyn at any time. She'd been alone, undefended, for months before she met him and months afterward. The Watcher hadn't tried to harm her. It was only within the last few days that he'd turned violent toward her.

And actually, he really hadn't turned violent toward *her*. True, he'd killed Rosalyn's sister, but probably because he found out it was Lindsey and not Rosalyn. He'd also been trying to kill Steve, not Rosalyn; she'd just been near collateral damage.

Brandon cleared his throat, dragging Steve's attention back into the room. "If you think about it, the fact that Rosalyn is still alive is a testament to her strength. We're still gathering information about these other women, but so far it seems that none of them lasted as long as Rosalyn has."

Steve stood. "Because she was alone a long time before the Watcher found her."

"She doesn't have family?" Brandon's brow wrinkled. "That would go against our profile."

"No, she has family. Just none of them have ever been there for her. She has, in essence, been alone her whole life." Steve began restacking the files. "Let's go tell Rosalyn what we've found. I think it will definitely help, not hurt. At least give her an understanding of what's going on."

Yeah, she'd been alone. But she damn sure wasn't anymore.

Chapter Nineteen

Steve had been correct—telling Rosalyn about Jon and Brandon's theory had been the right thing to do. She felt sad for the other women and angry that the Watcher seemed to be getting away with a horrible crime without anyone even knowing. But mostly she was relieved to finally understand what was happening.

"So he was trying to get me to kill myself." She was sitting across the table from him, next to Andrea. Her voice was still soft but at least she didn't look as fragile as she had before. "I almost did, you know. That night I met you."

"He wanted you to feel that way," Steve said.

"Yes," Brandon agreed. "That's his pattern. From what we can tell, he's very methodical about what he does. Almost like this is some sort of experiment to him. He wants to see how far he can push each woman before she breaks."

Jon nodded. "He's smart. Knows about law enforcement. His notes are never threatening and don't mention anything that would raise a red flag with police."

"Like what?" Rosalyn asked.

"Anything that would show obsession. 'We'll be together forever' sort of stuff. Instead the Watcher mentions normal everyday occurrences. Meals. Activities. Something a friend would mention casually, not someone obsessed."

Steve sat down in a chair across from Rosalyn. "Because he's not obsessed."

Brandon nodded. "Exactly. He's scientific. Experimental. He's not obsessed with the women themselves, just what sort of reactions he can get from them."

"And he doesn't actually harm them himself," Brandon continued. "But he uses tools of psychological terror instead—isolation, fear, imbalance. Then it's just a matter of time before they crack."

"You didn't," Steve told her.

A single tear escaped and rolled slowly down the side of her cheek. "I almost did. If I hadn't met you that night…"

He leaned forward, closer to her. "But you did meet me, not that I was of much help at the time. And if you hadn't, you still would've made it through. You're one of the strongest people I've ever met."

Her smile was breathtaking.

She now knew the Watcher's endgame—her taking her own life—and she was bound and determined not to give it to him. It was all Steve could do not to pull her up into his arms right there in the conference room in front of everyone. She was amazing.

And she was his. She might not realize it, but he had no intention of letting her out of his sight even after this was over. The baby was part of that, true, but he wasn't the only part. Steve wanted Rosalyn—

with all her strength, beauty, radiance—in his life. If she would have him.

"The Watcher doesn't hurt the women," Steve finally said, "but he's obviously not above violence. We've got a dead agent and Rosalyn has a dead sister that proves that. He's a killer."

"Yes, absolutely." Brandon nodded. "But killing the others are him manipulating variables in his equation. A means to an end. I don't think he's killing because he likes it. He's killing to further the reaction in his victims. To isolate them further."

"Everything's different now," Rosalyn looked around the room. "He hasn't got me isolated anymore. But he threatened the baby, Steve."

"That's his way of trying to continue his manipulation of you." Steve squeezed her hand. "There's no way he can get to you here. We'll put protective custody around your mom."

"The Ammonses too. In Georgia," Rosalyn whispered.

Steve nodded. "Roman should be checking in soon. He was meeting with them this morning."

"We've still got a lot of holes," Jon said. "The same ones Brandon was mentioning last night. Mainly, why didn't you hear from the Watcher for the six months you were in Georgia, and how he keeps knowing where you are, even though there aren't any more tracking devices on your clothing. There's no way he should've been able to find you at Steve's house last night."

"I swear I didn't tell him where I was," Rosalyn was quick to interject.

"No one thinks you did," Andrea murmured, leaning closer to Rosalyn.

Steve nodded quickly. "No one is idiot enough to think you're involved."

She raised an eyebrow at him.

He shrugged, grinning sheepishly. "At least not today."

She rolled her eyes. Steve was so happy to see her more lively that he couldn't be the least bit irritated.

When he'd seen the note that threatened their baby… Renewed rage caused Steve's fists to clench. He would make this right no matter what it took.

"We're still looking for other cases," Jon said. "Because of the intensity of his crimes, we're pretty sure he can only stalk one woman at a time, maybe two at the most. None of the cases overlap. There are probably others but we haven't found them yet. And we're still gathering info on the cases we have found."

A call beeped through to the conference room's phone. Steve pressed the speaker button.

"Roman Weber is holding for you, Steve," Cynthia told him. "He's in Ellijay, Georgia."

"Good. Maybe he can provide some answers. Put him through."

"Hey." Roman's voice came through clearly. "Remind me next time you want me to go to some tiny town in Georgia to make you send someone else."

Steve caught the slightest hint of a smile on Rosalyn's face.

"Roman, I have you on speaker in the conference room. Everyone's here."

"I talked to the Ammonses this morning. Like Rosalyn said, they're good people. Just don't trust the government much. Their son died in the military, years ago, but I think they were probably pretty skeptical before that."

"Okay. Did you find anything of interest?"

"I tell you what, these people are more than ready for a TEOTWAWKI event. They've got a cellar full of food, water purifiers, ammunition. You name it."

Rosalyn looked confused. "What does *TEOTWAWKI* mean?"

"The end of the world as we know it," Jon explained. "A lot of survivalists use the term."

"They're definitely off the grid. No computers, only one phone. The whole town is prepared for a zombie apocalypse or whatever, but the Ammonses are definitely the most paranoid."

"Did you talk to them yourself?" Steve asked.

"Yes, they said to give you their best, Rosalyn. And to let you know you are welcome back at any time."

Rosalyn smiled. "If you see them again, send my best too. I know they're not very talkative."

"That's for sure. Steve, in all their survivor gear— and believe me, it's extensive—they have some jamming devices. They didn't want the government listening in on them in any way. This wouldn't stop a lot of the higher-end devices we have now, but it would've protected them from the basics."

And there they had it. One mystery solved. Steve looked at Rosalyn across the table. "And their equipment would have interfered with transmissions of all kinds."

"No doubt. I thought you would find that interesting,

given the transmission devices you found on Rosalyn's clothes."

"Great, Roman," Steve said. "I need you to stay there and keep an eye on the Ammonses. If you're right about everything, there shouldn't be a problem. We think we have a profile on the killer. Doesn't look like he'll be coming your way, but just in case."

"Got it, boss."

Roman gave a little more information before hanging up, promising to keep a watchful eye for anything unusual.

"Well, that solves question one of the two. The Watcher couldn't find you while you were at the Ammonses' because the equipment they were using to block the government from hearing them—not that the government is listening to a couple in their seventies who have never broken the law—also kept the Watcher from being able to hear or find you."

He could see Rosalyn's relief at one more piece of the puzzle falling into place.

"Thank God." She leaned back in her chair. "I was afraid he'd just been toying with me. That he was going to hurt the Ammonses in some way, even though I never mentioned him to them."

"Looks like the Watcher may not know about them at all. Their government paranoia saved them from a serial killer." Steve reached over and grabbed her hand again. He didn't care if anyone else knew about his feelings for Rosalyn. It's not like he'd done such a good job hiding them up to now.

They all took a break to eat lunch. Steve walked with Rosalyn to the small cafeteria in the building. He wanted to make sure she wasn't missing any meals she couldn't afford to miss. He saw her hands suddenly fly to her belly and a little smile cross her face. He knew the baby had kicked again.

It just made him all the more determined to keep them safe.

But to do that they had to figure out how the Watcher was finding them now.

Back in the conference after lunch, they pored over the case files, comparing what little dates and specific information they had to Rosalyn's much more in-depth notebook. Jon and Brandon had already left, Jon to Tampa, Brandon to New Orleans, to see if they could gather more intel from talking to the victims' families and the local police.

They wouldn't give the families all the details in the cases, especially since right now it was only a theory, but they would let them know that there had been others who had suffered similar fates. Maybe there would be something—or someone—else the family members could remember.

Andrea worked with Joe Matarazzo to see if they could find any ties between the other four victims and Rosalyn. They'd shown Rosalyn all the women's pictures, but she hadn't recognized any of them.

Steve couldn't stay with Rosalyn the entire day like he wanted to. He had to deal with Doug Wilson's death; the tragic job of notifying the family belonged to him. He also had to catch up the local PD with what had happened at his house this morning.

He wanted Rosalyn's case to be the only thing he had to work on, but it couldn't be.

When he got back to the conference room at nearly nine o'clock that evening, she was still poring over her notes with Andrea and Joe.

"Time for everyone to go home," he announced. "We'll pick up fresh tomorrow."

Joe nodded before hugging both women. Steve wasn't offended or threatened. Joe was a people person to his very core.

"Tomorrow, boss," he said on his way out.

"Tell Laura I said hello." Steve and Laura, Joe's bride, had become close since they both were almost burned alive by a psychopath a few months ago.

"I'm sure she's going to want you to come to dinner with your new girlfriend." Joe said it in an exaggerated stage whisper, winking at Steve.

Steve's eyes met Rosalyn's. She was shaking her head at Joe's antics, as they all tended to do.

"I'll see you guys tomorrow too," Andrea said as she put her blazer back on. She hugged Rosalyn. "We'll start again first thing. Welcome to real-life police work. It takes time."

Rosalyn's frustration colored all her features as she looked down at the case files and papers spread out all over the table. It wasn't messy but it was chaotic.

He slipped an arm around her shoulders and pulled her to his side. "Andrea's right, you know. It takes time."

She eased against him but rubbed her face with her hands. "We've gone over so much my brain hurts. And I don't know that we're any closer to catching the Watcher."

"We are. Every day we put together more of the puzzle pieces. Soon we'll have a good view overall."

"I can't stay here forever. He has me just as much trapped here as he did when he had me on the run before."

He grabbed her by both shoulders so they could look eye to eye.

"No. You're not alone here. You have people who will do whatever it takes to keep you safe. We will catch him, Rosalyn."

She shrugged. "I hope so. Everyone has lives they need to get on with. They can't spend all their time just on this one case."

He pulled her to his chest and felt her arms wrap around his waist.

"You let me worry about that. Working cases, hunting down people who hurt others? That's what we do here. We find the patterns nobody else sees. And we're damn good at our job."

"Okay." She nodded her head against his chest.

"We'll catch him." He brought his lips down to her forehead. "I will do whatever it takes to make sure you and our baby are safe. I promise you that."

It was a promise he had every intention of keeping.

Chapter Twenty

Rosalyn awoke to sounds of voices in the small living room area of the Omega Sector apartment. Evidently the apartment was used by experts who came to help with cases or by agents who needed a night's rest and didn't want to go to their homes.

Or for people who were being hunted by psychopaths.

The apartment was within the compound but outside the main section of offices. Members of the SWAT team, angry over the death of an Omega agent, were taking turns guarding the door. Ashton Fitzgerald had been there when she and Steve had arrived.

Rosalyn had fallen to sleep knowing the Watcher couldn't find her here. Or at least couldn't get to her.

But she had dreamed that he sat right outside the gate. In a lawn chair. Drinking coffee and reading a newspaper. His face was hidden from her in some sort of unnatural darkness, but she could clearly see a giant knife sitting on a small table by his side.

Just waiting for her to exit Omega so he could kill her.

Worse than that, the bodies of everyone she'd come

to know and care about at Omega Sector—Jon, Brandon, Andrea, Derek, Joe—lay around him. Murdered.

Steve's body sat propped up closer to the Watcher, blood staining his T-shirt. Steve's green eyes were open, lifeless, staring out blankly.

Rosalyn took a step outside the gate. The Watcher folded his paper and stood.

"I was beginning to think you'd never come out of there," he said, his voice sounding like it was coming through one of those modulator things. "But I had fun with your friends since you were so busy protecting yourself."

She watched in horror as he kicked Steve's body over and rushed toward her.

"I'm so excited to meet the baby!"

She'd awakened sobbing right before he reached her.

Steve had held her in the bed as she fought him at first—caught in the terror of her dream—then as she sobbed.

"You're all going to die because of me. Because I'm hiding and the Watcher wants to keep his sick game moving forward."

"Nobody else is going to die. We are all on high alert and everyone can handle themselves."

He'd stroked her hair and held her close to his chest, murmuring soft words of comfort and encouragement. But she still couldn't fall back asleep until the light of dawn crept up through the small window.

She heard the deep timbre of Steve's voice right away and soon recognized the other voices to be Derek and Molly Waterman. Maybe Molly had found something when analyzing the crime scene at Steve's house yesterday. Rosalyn got dressed and went out into the small living room. She didn't have any makeup to put on even if she could have been bothered to do so.

Steve immediately crossed to her and kissed her on her forehead.

"You okay?" He led her over to the small kitchen island so she could have something to eat and some coffee. "I'll make you eggs and toast."

"Thank you. Rough dreams, but yeah, I'm okay now." She turned to Molly and Derek. "Good morning. Anything new?"

Molly surprised her by coming over to give her a hug. It had been a long time since she'd had friends, really anyone besides Steve, who cared about her. She returned Molly's hug, trying not to be as awkward as she felt.

"We didn't find anything useful at Steve's house. Like you said about the other notes, there was no usable DNA available."

Rosalyn swallowed and nodded. She hadn't really expected them to find anything. "I'm not surprised. I had hoped maybe a professional would find something I had overlooked all these times."

Molly shook her head. "There was nothing to be found, not by you, not by anyone. I'm sure that was true for the other notes, as well."

Rosalyn felt a little bit better.

"But Jon found a transmitter on an article of clothing of one of the other deceased victims. He's bringing it back here so I can analyze it."

Steve looked over from where he was cooking at the stove. "Our primary focus with your case as of now is figuring out how the Watcher has found you after we removed the trackers in Pensacola."

"Being able to look at a functional transmitter will help me," Molly said. "I might be able to pinpoint where it was made."

Steve fed not only Rosalyn but Derek and Molly breakfast. Molly and Derek told humorous stories of Molly's own pregnancy—their daughter had been born five months ago—and some of Derek's outrageous behavior in the delivery room.

Evidently the big, bad SWAT agent who towered over his petite wife had been reduced to "less than useless"—Molly's words—while their child made her entry into the world.

"It was time to go to the hospital, and he got lost." Molly rolled her eyes. "The man navigated his way through a Colombian jungle once to rescue me and he couldn't figure out how to get to a hospital eight miles away."

Derek nearly choked on his piece of toast. "I made one wrong turn. That is not the same as getting lost."

She slapped him on the back to help with his coughing. "Of course, honey." She turned to Rosalyn. "He was lost," Molly said in an exaggerated sigh.

Steve laughed.

"Just you wait." Derek stabbed some of his eggs, glaring at Steve. "Your time is coming. I'm going to follow you around with a camera."

The normal conversation, the joking, even the glares,

made Rosalyn feel better. Made life seem a little more normal.

But then the vision of the Watcher in her dream came back.

If the Watcher killed Molly and Derek, their daughter would be an orphan. Rosalyn fought to keep down the food she'd just eaten.

Steve moved closer to her. "Whatever you're thinking right now, stop," he whispered in her ear as Derek and Molly gathered her papers so they could all leave.

"But…"

Steve tilted her chin up. "I know it feels this way to you, but the Watcher is not the baddest bad guy we've ever faced. Isn't that right, Derek?"

"Not even in the top ten," Derek confirmed.

"That man is not going to let anything happen to Molly, so don't even let that enter your mind."

"Nope." Derek confirmed again, reaching down to wrap both arms around his wife's hips and lift her so he could kiss her. "Never again."

"And I'm not going to let anything happen to you."

They got the rest of what they would need for the day and the four of them walked out the door and down the hall. Rosalyn tried to hold on to the good feeling she'd had for a few minutes, but it was lost in the weight of what was happening.

They had to go through the security section again as they entered the main offices. Everyone made it through the metal detector without it going off but Rosalyn. Again. Always her luck.

The poor guy looked as though he feared for his

job when he used the wand on Rosalyn and she set it off once more.

"Eastburn, I thought I told you to get that wand checked." Steve spoke through his teeth with forced restraint.

"Yes, sir, this is a new wand. There shouldn't be any problem with it."

"So, you're suggesting that Ms. Mellinger has a weapon in her mouth?" That was where the wand kept beeping.

"No, sir. I'm not sure what is wrong."

"You ever have problems in airports or anything?" Steve asked her.

Rosalyn shook her head. "I haven't been in one for a few years, but no, not that I recall."

Molly put the files she'd been carrying down and walked over to Steve and Rosalyn. "You've set off the metal detector every time you've come through?"

"Yes." Rosalyn shrugged. "Well, the first time I was in handcuffs, so I'm pretty sure that did it. Yesterday we were assuming it was just a defective wand."

Molly, Derek and Steve were all giving each other looks.

"What?" Rosalyn asked.

Steve tossed some keys to Derek, who put them in his pocket. Steve took the wand from the guard and scanned Derek. It beeped when it got to his pocket, signifying the presence of the keys.

Without Steve asking, Derek took the keys out of his pocket and handed them to Molly. Steve scanned Derek again, with no beeps this time.

"Scanner seems to work correctly," Derek said. They all turned and looked at Rosalyn.

"What?" she asked again.

"I need you to come with me over to the lab," Molly said.

"Why?" Rosalyn had no idea what was going on.

"We need to take an X-ray of your mouth. Your teeth in particular. I think we've just discovered how the Watcher keeps finding you."

ONCE MOLLY MADE her announcement, everyone flurried into action. Rosalyn wasn't quite sure what to do except go along with it.

"The X-ray equipment in the lab is not really for use on a human," Molly stated as she walked with Steve and Rosalyn toward the lab. Derek had gone to research transmitters.

"Is it safe for the baby?" Steve asked. "I won't risk any harm to Rosalyn or the baby just for quicker results. If we need to get her to a hospital, we can make that work safely."

"No X-ray machine is great for any human. It's radiation. But it's a small amount for a very short time. And we'll use a lead covering." Molly turned to Rosalyn and took her hand. "Under the same circumstances, I would've allowed the X-ray when I was pregnant. That's the best assurance I can give you."

Rosalyn nodded. It was enough.

Molly's comfort inside her lab was evident. She slipped on a white coat and began giving orders and answering questions the moment she arrived. Obviously how things occurred here every day.

Molly led them into a smaller room with an X-ray machine. "We're fortunate. We got the X-ray as part of the new lab."

Rosalyn looked over at Steve as Molly set up the machine so it could be used on her rather than objects.

"New lab?"

Steve nodded. "About eighteen months ago a terrorist group bombed the lab to try to hide some evidence concerning a bigger crime. We rebuilt a newer, better one."

"I'm glad you weren't in here when it blew, Molly."

"Me too. We did lose one tech, though." Rosalyn saw the glance between Molly and Steve. There was more to this story than they were saying. She was about to ask when Molly brought her over to sit on a step stool.

She arranged the X-ray machine while Rosalyn held her head in an awkward position. Like Molly had said, the machine wasn't meant for humans. But in the end, they got what they wanted. Ten minutes later they were sitting around Molly's computer as the X-ray image came up.

"There." Molly pointed to one of Rosalyn's teeth from the X-ray.

"My tooth?"

"No. It's a crown. And beyond that, it's a transmitting and locating device. It's how the Watcher has been finding you."

Chapter Twenty-One

They were out in the hall talking about her. As soon as Molly announced about the transmitter, Steve and Molly had immediately stopped talking. It took Rosalyn a minute to understand why.

They were afraid the Watcher could hear everything they were saying.

Steve wrote her a note explaining that, but Rosalyn had already figured out that he and Molly weren't just being rude.

Meanwhile, Rosalyn was fighting the urge to find some sort of pliers and yank the crown out of her jaw.

The Watcher had a transmitter *inside* her body. Rosalyn laughed out loud, although she could recognize the hysteria that tinged it.

All these weeks when she thought the Watcher was inside her head she'd been literally right.

She glanced around for pliers again. Yeah, it would hurt, but the pain might be worth knowing he was out of her thoughts once and for all. But she couldn't find anything in the lab.

Steve and Molly came back in about ten minutes later.

"It's okay—we can talk." Steve came to stand in front of her, putting his hands on her shoulders and rubbing them gently.

"But can't he hear us? The transmitter?" Rosalyn fought to keep her voice even.

"No. Not here at Omega. We use a similar jamming device as the Ammonses use in Georgia. We want to make sure criminals are not privy to our private conversations."

Molly looked up from where she had sat down at her computer. "And ours are on a much greater scale and more sophisticated than the jammers in Georgia. Anything you say here is safe."

Steve wrapped an arm around her shoulder. "Let's go up to the conference room. We need to get Jon and Brandon on a conference call and figure out our next step."

"I want to get it out as soon as possible," she told both of them. "Fortunately, I couldn't find a pair of pliers while you were in the hallway talking or I might have already taken care of it myself."

"Absolutely," Steve agreed. "I want that thing out of you just as much, believe me."

"It's still a crown. It's cemented in," Molly reminded them. "A dentist will be much less painful and ready for any emergency."

She and Steve were both deep in their own thoughts as they made it back to the conference room. He had Brandon and Jon on the line within minutes, explaining what they'd found.

"That makes so much sense," Brandon said. "The

reason why he could find Rosalyn at Steve's house but can't find her at Omega."

"Yes," Steve agreed. "Molly and I already double-checked. Omega's frequency jammer is keeping the signal from being broadcast any farther than the building."

"So he probably has no idea where you are, Rosalyn," Jon said.

"That's right," Steve agreed. "And even if he somehow followed her, there's no way he can get in."

She felt safe, but she still wanted the thing out of her mouth.

"More important," Brandon said, "this gives us a big clue as to who the Watcher is."

Steve turned to her. "Your dentist, Rosalyn. There's no way that transmitter could've been put in the crown by accident. Whoever did your dental work is most likely the Watcher."

"Fits the profile," Jon agreed. "Intelligent. Professional. My personal bet had been on some sort of doctor, but I guess a dentist is close enough. Plus, he would've had days he could devote to following you and days he couldn't, thus the gap in notes sometimes."

Of course. Rosalyn felt a little stupid that she hadn't thought of that immediately.

"I'm going to bet you had that done about a year ago?" Brandon asked.

"Yes." Rosalyn sat down in one of the conference room chairs. "I don't like going to the dentist. So I found one who would put me under general anesthesia to do the root canal."

She looked at Steve. "Actually, my sister was the

one who told me about him. I think he practices all
over the Southeast. Gunson was his last name. I don't
remember his first."

Steve reached down and kissed her on the forehead.
"That's enough. We'll get him now."

CHRISTOPHER GUNSON DIDN'T know it, but his days as a
free man were numbered.

Even without the first name it hadn't taken long for
them to find him. His primary practice was based out
of Mobile, but he also did work in New Orleans.

It said so right there on his website. The website
also explained that he understood the fear people had
of dentists, that the fear wasn't unreasonable. That he
would rather work with patients by whatever means
necessary—including general anesthesia for procedures—than for them not to have dental care at all.

It was easy to see how he drew patients in. And then,
when they were out cold for their procedures, he could
easily place a transmitter and tracking device like he
had in Rosalyn's mouth.

Brandon was on his way to Gunson's New Orleans
office right now. Jon was flying from Tampa to Mobile to investigate the practice there.

Steve didn't expect them to find the man at either
site, because he was sure Gunson was still here in Colorado. He might not know where Rosalyn was exactly,
since he couldn't track her or listen to her while she
was in the Omega building, but Steve had no doubt he
would be waiting to make a move as soon as she wasn't
in their protection.

They hadn't found a good picture of Gunson on his

website. The most recent picture they had was taken of him ten years ago at a dental convention in Las Vegas.

In the picture he was in his late thirties, already balding and pretty thick around the middle. Steve imagined the ten years since hadn't been kind. He wondered if that was the reason Gunson stalked women. If it gave him a sense of power he didn't otherwise have in real life.

Maybe he wasn't so different from the average stalker, after all.

Rosalyn was holding it together, but barely. Every time he looked over at her, she was rubbing her jaw where the transmitter was. She wanted it out and he didn't blame her. But they couldn't do it here. And right now it was more important that they make their move on Gunson, before he realized they were onto him.

Once the transmitter was gone from her mouth, Gunson would know his identity was blown.

So as long as Rosalyn wasn't in a panic, they needed to leave it in. At least for a few more hours.

Steve wished he could distract her. Take her back upstairs to the apartment and let her rest. He knew she hadn't slept very well last night.

But he couldn't. He was coordinating with both the New Orleans and Mobile Police Departments to provide back up when Brandon and Jon arrived. They needed to make sure nobody got a call in to Gunson once they raided the offices. They had to collect as much information as they could without clueing in Gunson.

A few hours later Steve received the call. Brandon and the New Orleans police had moved in on Gunson's office. Gunson had surprised everyone by actually being there, in his office, with patients. Definitely not in Colorado. The locals took him into custody and allowed Brandon to use their facilities to interrogate him and were providing Omega with the live feed of the questioning.

As soon as Steve saw the man through the monitor—and Steve had been right; the ten years hadn't been kind to him—crying, before Brandon even asked a question, Steve knew this wasn't the Watcher.

But still he hoped.

Rosalyn sat next to him watching the screen too.

"Yes," she whispered. "That's Dr. Gunson. He's really the Watcher?"

"Let's see what Brandon can find out."

Gunson had already been read his rights but hadn't insisted on an attorney. Probably not a smart move on his part.

Also another clue that he probably wasn't the killer. Steve grimaced.

But if anybody had to be in there questioning him, Brandon Han was the perfect person. His ability to get inside the minds of criminals was unparalleled. Brandon might not be able to get a confession, but he would definitely walk out of there with a pretty damn educated guess about Gunson's involvement.

Andrea came running into the room. "Brandon's about to interview Gunson?"

"Yeah." Steve gestured to the seat beside Rosalyn. "Join us, please. Give us your opinion."

They all tuned in to the screen.

"Can you tell me why you're crying, Dr. Gunson?" Brandon's voice was even, nonthreatening.

"I didn't want to do it."

Rosalyn strained closer to the screen.

"Didn't want to do what, Christopher? Is it okay if I call you that? But I don't mind calling you Dr. Gunson, if that's what you prefer. A title of respect."

"That's my man," Andrea murmured. "He always knows the best route to take."

And in this case showing regard to a person feeling dejected was that route.

"Christopher is fine. Or Chris."

"Okay, Chris. Tell me what you didn't want to do."

"I had gotten into financial trouble. Done too much online betting. Lost too much. I was about to lose my house. My practice. Everything."

The crimes against Rosalyn hadn't been of any financial gain, the opposite, in fact. He would probably lose money being away from his practice to follow the women.

Brandon had to know that, but he didn't let it show. Instead he nodded. "So you did something you shouldn't."

"The transmitters. I knew they were wrong."

Steve heard Rosalyn's soft gasp at Gunson's admission.

Gunson sat back in his seat, defeated. At least he wasn't crying anymore. "I really don't know much. I didn't want to know what he was studying. I didn't want to know how it worked or anything about the transmitters themselves."

"Someone paid you to put transmitters in dental work."

"He's not the Watcher," Rosalyn murmured.

Steve squeezed her shoulder, keeping his frustration at bay. He'd wanted this to be over. Wanted Rosalyn to be able to walk out of here completely free of the Watcher.

That wasn't going to happen today unless Gunson had a lot more info than he was letting on.

"Who paid you, Chris?" Brandon leaned in toward the other man.

"I don't know. I never met him face-to-face. About six years ago I was really in deep with some loan sharks. They were going to break my fingers."

Gunson looked at Brandon as if that explained everything. Brandon gestured for him to continue.

"So when a man approached me and said he was doing some unorthodox experimentation and needed me to put some transmitters into crowns, I finally broke down and did it."

"How many transmitters have you put in in those six years, Chris?"

"I don't know."

"He's lying about that," Andrea said. "Everything else he's been telling the truth about. But about this he's lying."

"How do you know he's lying?" Rosalyn asked.

"The way he looked down and to the left."

"I didn't even see him look anywhere." Rosalyn leaned closer to the screen.

"Andrea is very good at what she does, sweetheart. Don't feel bad—I didn't see it either."

"Brandon did," Andrea murmured. "I can tell."

Brandon leaned in toward Gunson. "Chris, this is only going to work if we're honest with each other. I think you know how many transmitters you put in patients' mouths. That's not something you would forget."

"Twenty-nine," Gunson finally responded. "All women. Over six years. He paid me $10,000 for each one."

Rosalyn sat ramrod straight and Steve sucked a breath through his teeth. Twenty-nine women had transmitters in their teeth. So far, including Rosalyn, they knew of five. And four of them were dead.

They watched as Brandon showed the pictures of the dead women. Gunson remembered each. Brandon didn't tell him the women were dead, a good call since the dentist seemed to be holding on by a thin thread anyway.

Brandon confirmed that Gunson had been in town the last forty-eight hours. The man gave a detailed report of what he'd done and with whom. Brandon would follow up, of course, but there was no doubt in Steve's mind.

Christopher Gunson wasn't the Watcher. He was pathetic and would be going to jail, but he wasn't the Watcher.

He could tell Rosalyn knew it too. When she looked back at him, devastation was clearly written across her face.

The worst news hit them at the very end. Brandon asked for information about the other patients. These women, even if they had never been contacted by the

Watcher, even if their transmitters weren't live, needed to know what had happened to them.

Gunson looked ashamed as he explained that once the procedure had been done, he had given the patient records over to the man in order to receive payments. Although Gunson recognized the pictures of the women Brandon had shown him, he could not provide the names or any information about the other women he'd performed the procedure on.

They still had no idea who the Watcher was. All they knew was that he had two dozen other victims to whom he could turn his attention at any time.

If he hadn't already.

Chapter Twenty-Two

Rosalyn dreamed of the Watcher again that night.

He was still waiting outside the fence of Omega, tossing something small up in the air and then catching it as it came back down. Rosalyn didn't have to be able to see it to know it was a transmitter.

All the Omega agents lay dead around him again. Rosalyn tried not to look at them, knowing she'd never make it if she did.

Make it where? Away from the Watcher? She could go now. He wouldn't be able to follow her.

But now not only did the Watcher have all the Omega agents, he had twenty-eight women tied up in chairs. Blindfolded. Helpless.

Four were obviously dead.

He walked up and down the line of the other women as if he was trying to decide who to choose next.

Rosalyn woke up sobbing again.

"Hey, it's okay."

Steve. He was here, holding her again like he had last night.

"He's going to kill those women. There are twenty-four other women and he's going to kill them. Or get them to kill themselves."

Steve pulled her closer. "We'll stop him."

"How? Dr. Gunson doesn't have any idea who he is."

"We know his pattern now. His MO. We'll catch him, Rosalyn. This is what we do."

"But more women will die first."

Steve was silent for a moment. "Not necessarily. We'll do whatever it takes to keep that from happening."

Rosalyn twisted around, forcing Steve onto his back so she could see his face in the dim light of the moon through the small window. "I'm your best shot at keeping that from happening."

"Why do you say that?"

"If we leave the transmitter in my mouth, we can use it to catch him."

"No. I know how much that thing bothers you. It bothers me too. I don't want him having the means of finding you." He pulled her closer to his side and put his lips against her forehead. "The dentist is coming in the morning. The transmitter comes out. We'll see if it can be salvaged and still used, but your part ends there."

She snuggled into his side. It felt good to have someone care about her. To have someone she could lean on literally and figuratively.

"Go back to sleep," he whispered.

Rosalyn's eyes drifted closed but she knew she would still see the Watcher's other victims when sleep claimed her.

THEY HAD DEEMED it safer to bring a dentist in rather than have Rosalyn go out where she could be tracked.

Once they had the transmitter out of her mouth, Steve hoped to be able to use it to trick the Watcher in some way. To trap him.

Molly had offered one of the rooms in her lab for the dentist to do his work. Rosalyn was less than thrilled with dentists in general—thus how she'd gotten into this mess in the first place—and the thought of one working on her while she sat in a reclinable office chair did not reassure her.

But she wanted the transmitter out. Wanted to know for sure her baby was safe.

She took one look in the room where the dentist was setting up and knew she couldn't do it. But not because of her fear of the dentist.

Because she knew if she had this transmitter taken out of her tooth now, she wouldn't be able to help stop the Watcher.

"Everything okay?" Molly stepped up to her as Rosalyn stood paralyzed in the door. "I know this looks a little rough. But you won't be able to feel anything once he gets you numb."

"I can't do it."

She felt Molly's hand rubbing her back. "Dr. Mitchell is an excellent dentist, I promise you. It won't hurt."

"No, it's not because of the dentist. Believe me, I want this thing out of me enough to probably let him go at me with no numbing at all. It's the Watcher. This is our best link to him. To stopping him."

Molly nodded. "That's another reason we chose Dr. Mitchell. He's one of the most likely people to be able to get the transmitter out intact."

"The Watcher listens to me with the transmitter,

right? I mean, it tells him where I am, but he also physically hears my voice."

"Yes, from what I can tell from the X-ray."

"So if we take it out of my mouth, he's going to know something's different, right? He's going to be able to tell."

"Rosalyn…"

"If I get this removed, I'm making myself safe, but we'll lose our best chance of catching him."

Molly shook her head. "We'll find another way of catching him. You don't need to risk your life. Risk your mental health."

But Rosalyn had already made up her mind. "I'm not going to let another woman go through what I've gone through. Not if it's in my power to stop him."

Molly spent a few more minutes making sure that was what Rosalyn really wanted, but Rosalyn knew it was. She couldn't live with herself if more women got hurt.

She wanted to take this bastard down.

Molly escorted Rosalyn back to the conference room. Steve was there. Jon and Brandon had made their way back from the interviews in Mobile and New Orleans. Derek and Ashton Fitzgerald from SWAT were there also.

They were coming up with a plan. Everyone stopped talking when she and Molly entered.

Steve rushed to her. "Hey, are you done already? That took a lot less time than I th—"

"I decided not to do it," she told him.

Steve grabbed her arm gently and backed her up so they could have a more private conversation in the hall. "Last night we agreed for you to get the transmitter out."

Rosalyn looked down at his arm where it gripped her shoulder. He'd rolled up his sleeves as he was working and she could see the bruises from when the Watcher had hit him at the gas station.

"I can't let him hurt someone else."

"We will stop him. That's our job, Rosalyn. Not yours."

"No." She gently kissed his wrist, then ducked under his arm and into the conference room.

She crossed to the head of the table. "The best shot we have of catching him is if the transmitter is still in my mouth and we use me to set him up."

Steve wasn't willing to let it go. He came and stood beside her. "We already have a plan. We'll use an agent of your general build and coloring—probably Lillian here—" he pointed to a woman at the table "—to impersonate you. We'll give the transmitter to her and put her somewhere, he'll follow it and we'll catch him."

Derek nodded, supporting Steve. "Using a trained agent rather than you is a better tactical position for us."

Rosalyn shook her head. "That's assuming the dentist can get the transmitter out unharmed, which is no guarantee."

"Dr. Mitchell is one of the best oral surgeons in the state," Steve said.

Rosalyn rolled her eyes. "And I'm sure he's had lots of practice taking transmitters out of crowns, because that happens so often. No matter how good he is at normal dental stuff, he's never done anything like this before. You can't deny it's a huge risk."

Steve crossed his arms over his chest. "It's an acceptable one."

Everyone was looking at her now. "Even if we get the transmitter out safely, the Watcher is still going to know something is different. He can hear my voice. Has months of practice listening. He'll know if my voice is different."

Derek looked at Molly, "Can anything be done after the removal of the transmitter to make it sound like it's still in?"

"I can manipulate it somewhat, but it would just be a guess. I agree with Rosalyn about the sound. After all the time he's spent listening to her, he would notice a difference."

"I agree," Jon said. "Part of the thrill for the Watcher is probably listening in to the women. He wants to think of it all as just a science experiment that he's controlling, but listening probably gives him some measure of sexual thrill."

"And he would definitely be aware of changes," Brandon agreed. "He knows not only the sound of Rosalyn's voice but the pitch and the patterns."

Rosalyn couldn't help the shudder that ran through her.

"It's probably part of how he's known what buttons to press to get the biggest reactions out of his victims," Brandon continued. "He studied their voice patterns to see what caused the stress and then preyed on that."

Rosalyn nodded, trying not to lose her nerve. "So we all agree that taking it out is not the best thing to do."

Everyone around the table began talking at once. There was no clear consensus about the best plan.

Steve held up a hand to quiet everyone. He turned to Derek. "Derek, you and Ashton and the rest of SWAT will be heading up most of the sting. What's your opinion?"

Derek leaned back in his chair. "It's never my first choice to put a civilian in the line of fire. A pregnant one makes the situation even more complicated."

Rosalyn refused to be cast aside because of what *might* happen. "But…"

Derek held up his hand in a gesture that encouraged her to let him finish. "But I agree with what you're saying about the transmitter. The Watcher knows your voice. Changes now might spook him."

"We can use you to give all the verbal cues," Ashton said from his place beside Derek. "Then use a replacement agent in the actual location where we plan to arrest him."

Steve looked over at Derek. "You agree?"

Derek shrugged and nodded. "I understand you wanting to keep Rosalyn completely out of this, boss, truly I do. But she's right. Using her is our best bet at catching this guy before he hurts someone else. And if we use Ashton's plan, the risk to Rosalyn is minimal."

Rosalyn reached over and touched Steve's arm, bringing his attention to her. "I want to do this. I *need* to do this."

"And I need to keep you safe. Keep the baby safe."

"We will be safe. You'll be there to protect us every step of the way."

She knew Steve understood. Knew he knew this was the best plan. But she could also understand his hesitancy.

"Fine." He turned back to everyone. "But we don't leave here until we have a plan with no holes. And time is of the essence. Rosalyn has been out of the Watcher's ear for over two and a half days. If we wait too much longer, we'll lose him for good."

Rosalyn knew if that happened, they might never find him again.

Chapter Twenty-Three

"I'll keep hunting him, Rosalyn. We know he's here in the Colorado Springs area because of the note at my house. But I don't think you should leave."

"I don't want to leave you, Steve. We just found each other again. But I have to. We can't be together."

Even knowing the words were fake—an act of theater put on for the Watcher's benefit—Steve didn't like them.

They were about a mile away from the Omega offices. Nothing blocked the transmitter now. The Watcher should be able to hear everything they were saying.

Rosalyn sat inside a café. In the very back corner in a booth. She was huddled down near the table as if she was cold, but really she'd been told to keep her head down in case the Watcher decided to change his MO and take a shot at her.

There were three exits in this café—a front door, a window in the bathroom and the back delivery door. Every person in the building, from the waitstaff to the cooks to the customers, were Omega Sector employees. Not all were active agents, but all were trusted.

Steve wasn't sure exactly how they'd gotten the café

completely emptied in the three hours since they'd finished their planning in the conference room. Steve had
asked Joe for a favor, something he'd never asked Joe
in the six years he'd known him. He'd asked Joe to use
his money and connections to find them a building
to pull this off in a ridiculously short amount of time.

Joe hadn't even blinked an eye. He'd called Deacon Crandall, Joe's sort of jack-of-all-trades, and next
thing Steve knew, they had a café that could be used for
the next week for anything Omega needed. Maybe Joe
had used some of his millions of dollars and bought or
rented the place; maybe he had just smiled prettily for
the owner; who knew? Joe had a way with people. And
Deacon was just a man who got stuff done.

Steve wanted to control as many circumstances as he
possibly could. He already had a bad feeling in his gut
about this situation. But maybe he would have that in
any situation that might jeopardize a pregnant civilian.

The building was surrounded by four snipers. Ashton Fitzgerald, by far the best long-range shooter Steve
had ever known, had the restaurant in his sights. He
wouldn't let anything happen to Rosalyn there.

Steve couldn't be in the café with her. This had to
be a telephone call between them for it to work. They
didn't plan on it being long enough for the Watcher to
get a bead on her location right now. Just enough to
get him here tomorrow, when they'd be ready for him.
Steve was watching the entire scene from multiple camera angles at the home base inside Omega. But still he
itched to be there with Rosalyn. Didn't like having her
so far out of his reach.

But he trusted his team.

"You don't need to leave." Steve continued their scripted conversation. "I'll track him down. Just give me more time."

"I can't risk you, Steve. He almost killed you on the motorcycle. If you hadn't turned in time—"

The emotion in Rosalyn's voice was real. And he could see it on her face in the monitor.

"But I did. And I'm okay."

"But how long before the Watcher tries again? I can't take the chance. I have to go."

"No, Rosalyn, just tell me where you are. Where you've been for the past two days."

This was part of the plan. To assure the Watcher they didn't know about the transmitter in her tooth. To make sure Omega wasn't part of his thought process.

"Just at a hotel."

"You're not safe at a hotel. He might find you."

"I'm not safe at your house either, Steve. He found me there."

Steve pulled from his own frustration at not being there next to Rosalyn and put it in his tone. "I can protect you. The Colorado Springs Police Department can protect you."

Steve and Rosalyn realized that they had never talked about Omega outside the Omega building itself. Therefore, the Watcher would not know Steve worked for the multifaceted law enforcement agency. They would convince him Steve was just a member of Colorado Springs PD.

A lone member with no real backup.

"Did you tell your bosses there about the Watcher?" Steve waited a beat. "Yes."

He could see Rosalyn stir her coffee on the screen. "They didn't believe you, did they?"

"Look, just tell me where you are."

"I can't right now, Steve."

Jon pointed at his watch. They needed to wrap this up. Not give the Watcher enough time to find her today. It had to be tomorrow, when they were ready.

"When are you leaving?"

"Tomorrow. I'm taking a bus. That worked before and the Watcher didn't find me for a long time. I'm hoping that will work again."

"Okay, well, just meet me for breakfast or coffee or something before you go, okay? I just want to see you. To feel the baby kick one more time. You might have him before I can catch the Watcher."

"Okay, fine. My bus leaves at 9:45 a.m. tomorrow."

"Good. Let's meet at eight."

"Fine. There's a little café I'll meet you at." Rosalyn gave him the name and directions to the place she was at now.

"I'll see you tomorrow, sweetheart."

"Be careful, Steve. I don't want anything to happen to you."

Then she clicked the off button.

Steve tapped his communication button to Derek's earpiece. "Okay, get her out of there."

Derek was wearing an apron, posing as a cook in the back. He could see the entire seating area from where he stood.

"Roger that. Everyone in here is still Omega."

Steve watched on the screen as Derek nodded to Lillian, a SWAT team member no less deadly just because she stood barely over five feet tall. She brought Rosalyn a bill. "Here's your check, ma'am."

"Thank you." Rosalyn made a wincing sound as if she was in pain.

"Are you okay?"

"Just my tooth. Something's wrong. But I hate going to the dentist, you know?"

Hopefully the Watcher would buy that there was something wrong with the transmitter. It would force him to move up any timetable he had. To come after Rosalyn tomorrow even if he wasn't planning to. To make a mistake.

"I hope you feel better." Lillian touched the check. "I can take that whenever you're ready."

"Thank you."

That was the agreed-upon code that it was time for Rosalyn to leave. Steve watched as she got up and went out the front door and around to a car in the side parking lot. The camera lost her then, but he knew from there she would drive, as if she was looking for a tail.

Just like she always had done before she'd known how the Watcher was following her. Four different Omega vehicles would be following her, piggybacking off each other so they wouldn't get made. Once they gave her the signal that she was clear, she would drive immediately to Omega, where the transmitter would once again be jammed.

The Watcher would think he'd lost her again for whatever reason. Maybe it was the mountains, or maybe the transmitter itself was faulty—after all, he hadn't had a signal from her the entire time she'd lived with the Ammonses. But hopefully he wouldn't decide to dig too far into it tonight.

But Steve didn't feel like he could draw a complete breath until Rosalyn made it safely back through the gates of Omega. As soon as a member of SWAT brought her up to the offices, Steve pulled her to him, breathing in the scent of her hair.

"How do you think it went? Do you think he bought it?" she asked.

"I hope so."

Jon walked out of the control room. "You did great, Rosalyn. If he doesn't buy it, it's definitely not because of anything you did or didn't do."

She looked up at Steve. "I just want this to be over with."

He kissed her forehead. "Tomorrow it will be."

But Steve knew that even the most well-thought-out plans, the no-holes plans, could sometimes fail.

THE NEXT MORNING all the Omega Sector employees were back at the café. They opened the restaurant at 7:00 a.m. as if they had been doing it for years.

Derek was in the back again as a cook. Jon was in the command room, but it was a van parked around the corner rather than at Omega. He would be calling the shots today, having the bird's-eye view of everything.

Steve had a different role to play: concerned lover. It didn't require much acting on his part.

Steve would arrive at 7:45 a.m. Rosalyn would come in at 7:55 a.m., say something briefly to him, then excuse herself to go to the restroom.

From there, she would be taken out the back door and directly to Omega HQ. Steve categorically refused to risk her life by having her in the middle of a sting operation.

And the operation was huge. Not only were the dozen employees and customers in the restaurant Omega agents, but there were SWAT agents all around the building, and most of the people outside were theirs too. The lady walking the dog. The jogger a few blocks over whose route happened to go by the café a few times.

Others. All watching the café. Anyone who entered would be tagged: faces captured on camera, fingerprints collected and filed. Anyone who could possibly be the Watcher—so any male under the age of sixty—would be followed and/or tracked.

Steve had decided to use the Watcher's own means against him. Lillian was still playing the waitress. Her petite form belied the fact that she could kill a person in a dozen ways with her tiny bare hands. She would make sure that anyone who could possibly be the Watcher got a transmitter put on him.

It was a complex operation, but complex was what Omega did.

And it was showtime.

He parked his car, trying to make this all as normal as possible, and walked in the front entrance. Lillian greeted him with a perky "Good morning" and told him to sit wherever he wanted to.

He chose the booth near the corner and sat with his back to the wall so he could see the door. Just like he would do in any given restaurant. At least he didn't have to pretend that he wasn't law enforcement.

The place was relatively empty outside the people working for Omega. There was an older couple at one table and a young mother with her toddler at one of the booths. They would all be checked out but none of them were viable suspects.

The building had been thoroughly swept for explosives—at this point Steve didn't put it past the Watcher to just take out the whole place. They'd also been sure to search the closets and attics and crawl spaces. After what happened earlier this year—a psychopath deciding to reside in an agent's attic until the time was right for a kidnapping—they'd all learned their lesson.

Now all Steve could do was wait and watch. And pray that nothing tipped off the Watcher. It wouldn't take much.

Five minutes later a man came in, their first real possible suspect. He was tall, sort of bulky, wearing business attire. Jon's voice came on in Steve's ear.

"We've got him. Got a good shot of his face. Running it now to see if he shows up in any of our facial-recognition software."

"He's got a briefcase," Steve murmured behind his hand.

"Roger that."

A briefcase could carry explosives or a weapon.

"Infrared on the briefcase suggests no explosives," Aidan Killock, SWAT's explosives expert, said through the earpiece. He was in a different van outside.

The man was getting a coffee and muffin to go.

"Tag him anyway, Lillian."

He saw her nod briefly before she came around the counter and stood before the man.

"Here," she said, reaching up and messing with the back of his collar. "That was folded up a little, but now it's perfect."

"Thank you." The man seemed relieved and flattered to have received such attention from someone with Lillian's looks.

And the transmitter in his collar would allow them to track him.

"We've got him," Jon said. "He's not showing up in any of our facial software."

"I don't think that's him. Build isn't right for the guy who came at me on the motorcycle."

But Steve knew they would follow him anyway.

Business began to pick up as a number of people entered, some couples but a few single guys. Steve had to trust his team to do their jobs, because right at 7:55 a.m. Rosalyn walked in the door.

She waved to him and he stood and hugged her as if he hadn't seen her in two days rather than just the hour it had been.

"Are you hungry?" he asked her as they sat down at the booth.

"I'm always hungry."

This, again, was part of the script they had worked out last night. The Watcher had to be listening.

"What do you feel like?"

"Something soft. I have a bad toothache."

Lillian came over and took their order. Steve asked Rosalyn how she was feeling and if the baby had moved again.

He wanted Rosalyn out of there. The more crowded it got in the café, the more tense Steve became.

There were three men in the café right now who could possibly be the Watcher. One in particular looked nervous. But then again, Steve didn't think the Watcher would look nervous.

Something wasn't right.

Steve brought his hand up to his mouth and turned his head to the side. "I'm sending Rosalyn out now."

"Are you sure it's not too soon?" Jon asked.

"I don't care. There are too many unknown variables."

"Roger that. The car is waiting."

Rosalyn didn't have an earpiece in case the transmitter also picked up on what was being said to her.

Steve nodded at her. She nodded back, knowing it was time to go. She reached over and grabbed his hand, squeezing it. He winked at her.

"I've got to go to the restroom."

"Okay."

She stood and walked to the back. The agent in the car reported a few minutes later that he safely had Rosalyn and they were headed back to HQ.

Whatever happened now, at least Rosalyn was safe. He breathed a sigh of relief.

It was short-lived, as a man—the nervous one he saw earlier—sat down in the booth across from him.

He pulled at a gun and pointed it straight at Steve.

"I don't think we've met. I'm the Watcher."

Chapter Twenty-Four

A cascade of emotions flooded Steve.

Rage that this bastard had terrorized Rosalyn for so long. And other women too, to the point of them killing themselves.

Relief that Rosalyn was gone, safe. Out of his clutches. She'd never be in this man's clutches again.

Surprise. This wasn't what he'd thought the Watcher would look like. He wasn't sure exactly what he'd thought the Watcher would look like, but it wasn't unkempt and sweaty like this man. But how did you put a face to a monster?

Either their plan had worked perfectly and the Watcher had grossly underestimated who Steve was and what sort of weight he carried in law enforcement, or the man had nerves of steel. He'd just pulled a gun on a cop in broad daylight with dozens of witnesses.

Or perhaps his intent had always been to kill Steve and he didn't care who saw.

Over the man's shoulder Steve could already see Lillian and the other Omega agents escorting the patrons out of the restaurant.

"Don't let any of them go," Steve said into his communication device. He didn't care if the man across from him knew he had backup. Let him worry.

"We're getting everyone's info. Why don't you worry about the guy pointing a gun at you."

"I'm assuming Ashton has him in his sights."

"Roger that, boss," Ashton's voice came through his ear. "But you'll be scrubbing brain matter off yourself for a long time."

Steve was tempted to tell him to take the shot. He had a gun, was pointing it at Steve, might turn and start shooting innocent people any moment. It would be considered an unfortunate but necessary kill.

Steve wasn't even sure he'd consider it that unfortunate.

But something wasn't right. Since his one sentence introducing himself, the man hadn't said anything. His hands were shaking. He was sweating.

"Nervous?" Steve asked.

The man nodded. "I'm the Watcher."

"Yeah, you said that." Steve took a sip of the cup of coffee Lillian had given him while Rosalyn was here, more to put the other man at ease than anything else. "Don't you have anything else you want to say to me? You know we have the place surrounded, don't you?"

"I am the Watcher." The man was sweating and the gun in his hand was shaking.

"Jon, you got an opinion of what's going on here?"

"Obviously the guy is highly stressed. I don't know, Steve. If I had to guess, I would say this isn't him. But then why is he pointing a gun at you?"

Tears squeezed out of the man's eyes. "I am the Watcher."

Steve gestured to Lillian to come over and plucked a

pen out of her pocket. The Watcher continued to point the gun at Steve, not paying attention to Lillian.

Because he thought she wasn't a threat or for another reason entirely?

Like being given instructions to keep the gun pointed on Steve.

"What's your name?" Steve asked the man.

"I am the Watcher."

"How about I arrest you and we figure out your name once you're in custody."

The gun shook more, but the man didn't pull the trigger.

Steve wrote on the napkin. *Are you being forced?*

He spun the napkin and pushed it over where the man could read it. Tears poured out of the man's eyes as he nodded. He reached up and flipped his collar.

It was a transmitter just like he'd found on Rosalyn's clothes.

The Watcher was using this man as a patsy.

"All right, look, let's just talk this out. Okay?"

The man nodded that he understood. Steve wrote on the napkin. *Can he see you?*

The man shook his head no. Steve gestured for him to put down the gun. After a few moments he did so.

"You know I'm police, right?"

"I am the Watcher."

Evidently that was all the man was allowed to say. Steve grabbed another napkin. *Where is the man who did this?*

At my house. Will kill my wife and kids.

"Look, just put the gun down. It's me you want. I don't want anyone else to get hurt by accident." *Address?*

The man wrote it. Then, *I have to kill you or he will kill them.*

Jon's voice sounded in his ear. "I've got the address, Steve, and we have agents en route to the guy's house. They'll go in silently."

Steve picked up the gun and handed it to Lillian.

"You have to put the gun down. If you were going to shoot me, you would've done it by—"

Lillian shot the gun over his head into the wall.

"Oh my God, that guy just shot that guy. He's got a gun!" she screamed at the top of her voice.

"Hey, he's running away—" Derek yelled out, helping along the charade.

Steve reached out and grabbed the transmitter from the guy's collar. He dropped it to the ground and stomped on it.

"Any others?" he mouthed.

The man shook his head, confusion plain in his eyes.

"We've got law enforcement en route to your house," Steve told the man. "What's your name?"

"Donny Showalter. He told me I had to come in here and shoot you. He told me all I could say was that we hadn't met and that I was the Watcher." The guy put his face in his hands. "I have to get to my house."

"How far do you live from here?"

"Only a few blocks."

"Steve, our agents are there," Jon told him. "We have eyes inside. The family is tied up but no one is hurt."

He relayed the information to the man, who promptly deflated on the table in relief.

"Is anybody there with them?" Steve waited for the information to be relayed back to him.

A few minutes later Jon was back in his ear. "Steve, the wife says the guy who tied them up left right after Donny did."

He'd been around here. Maybe in the coffeehouse or directly outside. Seeing what happened. Probably hoping they would kill Donny and cause even more chaos.

"Is my family really okay? I need to see them."

"I'll have them call you in just a minute, okay?"

Donny nodded.

"Can you tell me anything about the man who put you up to this? What he looked like?"

"No. He broke into our house this morning while we were having breakfast. He was wearing a mask."

Damn it. The Watcher had been smarter than they thought. He'd been making sure this wasn't a setup, and if he was anywhere in the vicinity, he would know that Steve was much more deeply entrenched in law enforcement than just some sort of beat cop.

Taking him by surprise was no longer an option.

"Steve." Jon's voice was more somber than he'd ever heard it.

"Go, Jon." He pressed the earpiece farther in his ear so he could hear over the chaos going on around him.

"I just got word from HQ. Travis Loveridge and Rosalyn never checked in. They found the car about a half mile from HQ. Loveridge is dead. Rosalyn is missing."

ROSALYN HAD AGENT Loveridge's blood all over her. Her arms, her neck, her hands. She couldn't get it off.

Of course, dried blood was the least of her problems.

She stared at the man driving the car. "I remember

you. You're Lindsey's psychologist from when she was a teenager. Dr. Zinger."

"Zenger." He turned and smiled at her. Like they were old friends or something. Like he hadn't walked up to the car while they were stopped at a red light and shot the agent driving. Like he hadn't been stalking and terrorizing her for the better part of a year.

Rosalyn shrank back against the car door. He hadn't touched her at all, except to catch her when he drugged her and tied her hands, but she didn't want to take a chance.

She was barely holding it together. If he touched her, she might start screaming and never stop.

"Lindsey liked you," she whispered. "Thought you were so handsome."

Rosalyn remembered. They'd been eighteen. Lindsey had been in trouble again and sent to group counseling this time. When Rosalyn had come home from college for a semester break, she'd asked her sister how things were going.

Rosalyn hadn't been encouraged when all her sister would talk about was how hot the counselor was rather than showing any interest in truly kicking her drug habit.

He was handsome, if Rosalyn could distance herself enough from the terror. Clean-cut, short brown hair. Good physique. But all Rosalyn saw was the monster.

"You killed her," Rosalyn whispered.

He shrugged, not looking at her. "If it helps, she never knew it was me."

It didn't help at all.

Rosalyn's hands were tied with some sort of zip tie. "Where are you taking me?"

"We have to get out of Colorado, of course. Your boyfriend is already dead—I sent a friend of mine in to shoot him. Since Steve didn't know who I was, I'm sure he won't care that it wasn't me who actually killed him."

Rosalyn stared and could hear her breath sawing in and out of her nose and mouth. Was he telling the truth? Was Steve really dead?

"I wasn't exactly sure how the whole café scenario was going to play out. But when I saw you leave out the back door, I knew it had been some sort of setup. How did you know I would be there?"

Rosalyn tried to get her panic under control. She had to keep the fact that Omega Sector was onto him a secret. "We didn't. I guess Steve was doing stuff just in case. I was hitching a ride from that guy to the bus station. You didn't have to kill him."

Zenger's eyes were narrowed as he turned to look at her. She wasn't sure if he was buying her story. "Hitch-hiking is dangerous."

She bit back a hysterical laugh. "Ended up being much more dangerous for him."

She looked out the window again. They were on the interstate. There was no way she could jump out of the car now and survive.

She refused to believe him when he said Steve was dead. Zenger hadn't been there; he'd been too busy killing that poor agent who'd been with her. There was no way he could know for sure Steve had actually died. Maybe the shot hadn't killed him.

Steve was alive and would be coming for her. He and

Jon and Brandon…they would figure out who Zenger was; they would find him.

Steve would rescue her. He wouldn't leave her and the baby in the hands of this madman.

She had to hold on to that or there was no way she would survive.

They sat in silence for miles.

"Where are we going?" she asked again finally.

"Back to familiar ground. I'm from Mobile too, you know. I have a nice little place where you can stay."

"And do what?" She couldn't keep the revulsion out of her voice, not that she tried.

He laughed, a friendly sound under any other circumstances. "Rosalyn, I'm not like that at all. I don't plan to force myself on you in any way. That's beneath me."

"But killing people isn't?"

He sighed. "I don't kill out of choice or some sort of sport. Honestly. It brings me no pleasure."

"Then why kill at all?"

"For the research. This is all for science, Rosalyn."

Oh God, Jon and Brandon had been right all along with their profile. That gave Rosalyn hope that they would be able to follow through and find her.

"Science?"

"I am a psychologist. I help people. The data I'm collecting about isolation will be used to help disturbed people for decades to come."

He honestly believed it.

"Isolation?"

"Yes, yes, that's what all of this has been about. I take young women and divide them from everyone in their life. I prey upon their worst fears and then see what they do to cope. How long they can last."

She wondered if he would tell her, if she asked, about the tracking devices. About the dentist and the one in her tooth. But she didn't want to tip her hand.

"What happens to them when they can't last any longer?"

Zenger shook his head sadly. "Unfortunately, they commit suicide. It's a regrettable side effect of this research. But don't you understand? The loss is acceptable for the greater good. I am on the forefront of research that every mental-health-care professional would love to be a part of."

If it hadn't been absolutely sickening, Zenger's zeal for his work would almost have been commendable.

"Was that what you wanted with me? For me to kill myself?"

"You, my dear, you have been the longest-lasting subject in my research." He glanced at her again. "And to think, you weren't supposed to be my original subject."

"Lindsey was."

"Exactly. But I realized that the drug abuse made Lindsey a poor test subject. You were much stronger, more resilient. I just had to wait for the right time."

She assumed that meant wait until she went to the dentist. The dentist that Lindsey had suggested. Had suggested because a doctor mentioned it to her.

Zenger had been that doctor. Had helped orchestrate the entire thing from the beginning.

"I'm sure your pregnancy has played an important

role in your resilience. You don't want to die. You want to live for your baby."

Maybe she could get him to understand that. Make him think that she could understand the importance of his research so he would let her go.

"Yes. The baby is an unforeseen variable with me, I'm sure." Rosalyn nodded. "It must mean I can't fit into the conceived categories and corrupt your data analysis."

He nodded, obviously glad she understood. "I forgot you majored in accounting. So you are familiar with data and experimentation."

"Yes. You're obviously the expert, but I do have some knowledge. I know the baby changes things."

"You're absolutely right. He does. I had to really think about what needed to be done when I found out you were pregnant."

"Dr. Zenger, now that you've explained it to me, I see how important your research is. Like you said, the baby changes things for me. I can never be truly isolated from people when I have a little person growing inside me."

"That's exactly right, Rosalyn. I'm so happy you understand."

"So you'll let me go? You know I will never tell anyone about your research. Unless you want me to, of course."

She meant it with every fiber of her being. If she could get out of this with both her and the baby unharmed, she would do whatever Zenger wanted.

Steve would hunt him down to the ends of the earth, but Rosalyn would stay out of it.

"No, I can't let you go, Rosalyn. I'm sorry."

She tried not to let the disappointment crush her. She needed to reason with him. "But what about the baby? Like you said, I don't fit any categories anymore. I'm not useful for your research."

"Rosalyn, you were an outlier even before the baby. I'm not sure you would've ever been statistically useful."

"Then why are you taking me to Mobile?"

"I'll keep you there until you have the baby. Then, unfortunately, I'll have to kill you. Like you said, you're not useful for my research anymore."

"What about the baby?"

"Oh, he will give me a lifetime worth of data. Just think of what I'll be able to do."

Suddenly there wasn't enough air in the car. Rosalyn reached for the handle of the door. She didn't care that they were on the interstate. She couldn't stay in this car a moment longer. She would have to take her chances with jumping.

Zenger swung the car toward the shoulder, slowing rapidly, grabbing her arm tightly to keep her from jumping out.

She fought him. Slowing was what she wanted him to do. It gave her a better chance to survive.

"Stop, Rosalyn."

She kept fighting.

He pulled the car to a stop, both of them slamming forward as he hit the brakes hard. Now he had both hands to hold her with.

She didn't care if she had to stay here and fight him for the rest of her life. She was not going to let him drive her somewhere where he could keep her baby and do experiments on him.

She felt a sharp sting on the side of her neck. It took only a few moments before all her movements began to feel slushy.

"No…" she whispered. She felt tears leak out of her eyes, but her arms were too heavy to wipe them.

"You fought the good fight. Now go to sleep."

She tried not to, but in just moments the darkness pulled her under.

Chapter Twenty-Five

Steve did what he did best: worked the problem.

He did not focus on the fact a psychopath had Rosa-lyn in his clutches. Did not focus on the fact that they had no idea where said psychopath was taking her or how they would find her. That they still had no idea what the Watcher looked like or where he was from.

Because if he focused on those things, the fear and agony would overwhelm him.

He'd known helplessness when Melanie had died; it had ripped a hole in his heart.

But he knew he wouldn't survive if Rosalyn didn't make it.

He kept that all pushed aside because it would do nothing to help them find her now.

Travis Loveridge was dead. Evidently the Watcher had walked up to their car while they were stopped at a red light and shot him point-blank in the head. There had been witnesses, but no one had been able to see the Watcher's face. They'd seen him pick up a woman—an unconscious woman with long black hair—and carry her to his car parked at the side of the street.

A gray sedan. There were thousands of them on the roads. They were checking, but so far a dead end.

They'd pulled up the feed from the traffic camera, but it had been pointing in the wrong direction. Another dead end.

Brandon was interviewing Gavin from the café and his wife. Molly's lab crew was checking for forensics at the house. But so far…

Steve was studying computerized maps. Working on the assumption that the Watcher was taking Rosalyn out of Colorado. He assumed back to Mobile.

But it was too far to make it in one day. Steve knew from personal experience a week ago going the opposite way. He had every Omega person who could be spared making calls to hotels along the interstate heading south.

Steve personally had called the state and highway patrols for New Mexico, Kansas and Texas. He wanted them to understand the direness of the situation; he didn't want it to be just be another report that came across their desks.

It was all long shots, but Steve would keep taking long shots until one of them paid off. It was getting late now. Dark. The thought of her alone with the Watcher overnight…

Derek put a hand on Steve's shoulder. "How are you holding up?"

Steve wiped a hand across his face. What could he say?

That panic was crawling up his spine, threatening to take over not only his whole body but the whole world?

How would anyone understand that?

"She's alive, Steve. When the panic starts to overwhelm you, you push it back down with the thought that until we know definitely otherwise, Rosalyn and the baby are both alive."

Maybe someone could understand that.

Derek could. Hadn't Steve seen the very agony in his own eyes in Derek's eighteen months ago when a sadistic bastard had kidnapped Molly?

Derek had moved heaven and earth to get her back. Steve had helped. He prayed he would get his own happily-ever-after with Rosalyn and their child.

"I thought she was dead once, Derek. And that was before I knew what she meant to me. I'll be damned if I'll let her die again not knowing I love her."

Molly walked through the door. "You're not going to have to."

Both men turned to her. "What do you mean?"

"I've found the frequency the Watcher was using to track Rosalyn from a transmitter Jon and Brandon brought back from other victims. The transmitters were still live."

"What?" Derek asked.

"I don't know if the Watcher was trying to keep tabs on the families or what. But I was able to use them to find other transmitters. Actually, I've found *all* the women—since he used the same frequency for all the transmitters."

"How do we know which one is Rosalyn?"

She ran over to the computer and brought up a navigation system on the screen.

"I'm going to assume she's the one halfway between

here and Mobile." She pointed to a red dot near Oklahoma City.

Oklahoma City was less than six hundred miles. They could've made it there if the Watcher drove at a rapid pace.

He would've been moving at a rapid pace.

Derek kissed Molly and ran for the door. "The team and I will meet you at the helicopter in ten minutes," he called back to Steve.

Molly touched Steve's arm as he moved toward the door and handed him a small GPS screen. "You're going to need this. Outside Oklahoma City is the best I can do from this far away. As you get closer, this monitor will provide more details."

Steve kissed her forehead. "Thank you, Molly."

She shrugged. "You once broke all the rules and gave Derek a plane to come after me. If you hadn't, I wouldn't be here now." She pushed him. "Go get your girl."

TRUE TO MOLLY'S WORD, the GPS continued to become more detailed the closer they got to Oklahoma.

The transmission wasn't in Oklahoma City at all; it was in Guymon, a much smaller town northwest of the city.

At some point the Watcher had gotten off the main interstates, which had been a smart move on his part.

"Boss, there's no actual helicopter landing site big enough for us in Guymon. But we've been given permission to land on the high school field." Lillian was flying the helicopter. One of her many skills.

"Good." Steve spoke into the headset he and the five members of the SWAT team were wearing.

As they got closer, Steve was able to pinpoint Rosalyn's location. A hotel about two miles south of the high school. Steve provided the info to Lillian, who relayed it to the local police, who would also be providing them transportation to the hotel. They landed a few minutes later.

The local deputies were there with a county van to take the SWAT team and Steve to the location. Steve could tell the team was ready.

There wasn't anybody he would want at his back more than these men—and this woman—right here.

"You guys…" He looked at Derek, then at Lillian. He needed to express how important Rosalyn was to him.

"No need to say it, boss," Derek told him. "We'll get her out, safely."

They were less than a minute out when the news came over the van's CB unit.

"We've got reports of shots fired at the Best Holiday hotel on Thirty-Second Street."

That was the hotel where Rosalyn's tracker had stopped.

Steve's curse was foul. The van squealed into the hotel parking lot and Steve and the team poured out the back door before it even stopped moving.

The place was surrounded by cop cars, officers using their vehicles for cover, weapons drawn.

Steve rushed up to the officer in charge, a kid, probably in his mid-twenties. Doubtful he had any experience with this sort of situation. "I'm Steve Drackett, head of the Critical Response Division of Omega Sector. I need your name and a rundown of the situation."

"Keith Holloway, sir. Evidently a man was bringing in his exhausted pregnant wife, who'd been very sick. He was half carrying her, according to one witness. But then she started screaming that he was kidnapping her and he pulled out a gun. Shot the clerk."

"How long have you been out here?" he asked Holloway.

"Less than two minutes, sir."

Steve looked over at Ashton. "Got any ideas for a distance shot?"

Ashton was already putting his distance scope on his rifle. "It will be hard without knowing where Rosalyn is."

"I'm going in to draw him out. As soon as you can get a good shot, you take it."

"Steve—" Derek put an arm out as Steve stood up.

"He's trapped. He knows it. Getting out with Rosalyn will be nearly impossible. He'll cut his losses and shoot her as a distraction. And he knows the longer he stays, the less chance he'll have to get away."

"He'll shoot you."

The other members of the team were taking out their rifles too. None of them were as good a shot as Ashton, but that didn't matter now.

Steve looked at them. "I'll draw him out. You take him down."

Mind made up, he walked quickly to the front door and went through. A little bell chimed as he did.

"Leave right now or I will kill her!" Steve couldn't see anyone but could tell they were behind the counter.

"I think it's time we meet face-to-face, Watcher."

He heard Rosalyn's sob but didn't know if it was from pain or relief.

"Who are you?"

"You sent someone to kill me today. That didn't work out."

"Steve Drackett? How did you find me?" His tone was incredulous.

Steve took another step closer. He needed to draw the man out. "The same way you've been finding Rosalyn all these months. And the other women. We know about the transmitters in the teeth. It's over."

"Do you know what you've done?" He stood up now but kept Rosalyn right in front of him, his gun to her head. No one would be able to get a clean shot.

And Rosalyn was glassy-eyed, pale and covered in blood. The Watcher seemed to be half propping her up.

Steve forced himself to stay focused.

"You've ruined my research. My life's work! You have no idea what good I was doing for the world." He was frantic, voice high-pitched, hysterical.

"All I want is Rosalyn." Steve kept his arms out in front of him but shifted his weight to the balls of his feet. He was going to make a move that would draw the Watcher's attention and gun to him.

"No. She's already promised me her baby. She understands my research and knows how important it is."

Now. He had to do it now.

But Rosalyn beat him to it. Her eyes rolled up in the back of her head and she slid to the floor.

The Watcher couldn't hold her up and turned his gun on Steve.

Glass shattered all around him and the Watcher flew back and onto the ground, dead, shot six times. Every single member of the SWAT team had taken him out.

Steve jumped over the desk counter and picked up Rosalyn's still form. There was more blood on her now. Had she been shot? His hands were so shaky he couldn't get a pulse.

Derek and Lillian made their way to him first. He was rocking Rosalyn in his arms but couldn't get her to wake up.

"She's bleeding," he told Derek. "She's hurt."

Lillian put two fingers at Rosalyn's throat. "She's alive, Steve. I think she's been drugged."

All he could see was the blood. "But she's bleeding."

He felt Derek's hand on his shoulder, pressing hard.

"You're bleeding, boss. Bastard got a shot off at you before we took him down."

Steve didn't care. As long as Rosalyn was alive, the baby was okay, Steve didn't care about himself. He pulled her close to him, uncaring of the pain, certain he was never going to let her go ever again.

Chapter Twenty-Six

"You're going to get fired if you keep taking all this time off work, you know," Rosalyn told Steve as they walked through the sands of Pensacola beach a month later.

He smiled at her and pulled her closer to his side. "I have ten years' worth of vacation time saved up. I'm not going to get fired."

"So you brought me back here to the scene of the crime, literally and figuratively."

She was glad. The drugs Zenger had given her had slowed both her and the baby's heart rates to dangerously low levels. She'd been unconscious for two days. But that had probably been for the best since Steve had been shot while rescuing her.

He'd gone into surgery and they'd removed the bullet, but there had been some pretty significant damage done to his shoulder. It would require quite a bit of rehab to get it back to full motion again.

While she was unconscious, since the drug Zenger gave her worked similarly to a general anesthetic, Steve had convinced the doctor of the medical necessity of

having the crown with the transmitter removed and replaced with just a plain old regular crown.

Rosalyn had been thrilled to hear it, even though
the Watcher was dead and it didn't matter anymore.

The Watcher was truly gone. Rosalyn had explained who he was, and with the technology Molly
had cracked, they had let the other women know what
had happened to them so they could get the transmitters removed.

Of course, it was too late for the four women they
knew of who had committed suicide and a fifth one
whose case they hadn't discovered yet.

But Rosalyn had made it. She was still so thankful she'd met Steve at this beach—now seven months
ago—because otherwise she wasn't sure that she
would've.

He was everything to her.

Rosalyn had been alone most of her life, even when
she'd been surrounded by her family. This past month
she'd been shown what a family was really meant to
be. People willing to stand with you, protect you, put
their lives on the line for you.

Family was something that had nothing to do with
blood and DNA and everything to do with love. She
knew no matter what happened between her and
Steve, the baby she carried would have a family who
loved him. The people in Omega already did.

She knew Steve loved the baby. She just wished she
knew how he felt about *her*. Even though she'd lived
in his house the last month, they still hadn't talked
about the future.

"I'm not really good at romance," he murmured.

She shook her head. "Says the man taking me on a stroll on the beach as the sun is setting. I think you're doing okay."

"There's something I've been wanting to ask you since the first night we met."

"Oh yeah, what's that?"

"Will you have dinner with me?"

"What?" She laughed.

"I want to take you out to dinner and on dates. I want to court you and show you how much you mean to me. I want to show you that you can trust me with your secrets. You can trust me with your heart."

"Steve, if this is about the baby…"

"No." He turned so they were face-to-face. "All of that has nothing to do with the baby. It's what I've wanted to say to you since the first minute you walked into that tiki bar when I could tell you were capital-*T* trouble."

He smiled at her. "I'm excited and terrified about the baby, as all new fathers should be. But you're the one I want, Rosalyn. Always. I will ask you to marry me tomorrow. But today, I just want to take you out. Will you have dinner with me?"

She reached her arms around his waist and pulled him to her.

"Yes. To both."

And right there in the sand where everything had almost ended, her new life began.

* * * * *

APB: BABY

JULIE MILLER

For my husband, Scott E. Miller.
I'm so proud of you for writing your stories
and getting them published.
(Welcome to the joys and headaches
of being an author.)

Prologue

Dr. Niall Watson would rather be at the crime lab conducting an autopsy instead of standing at the altar, babysitting his brothers.

But saying no to his baby sister on the day of her wedding wasn't an option. Putting on the groomsman's suit and facing the crowd of smiles and tears that filled the church was as much a gift to Olivia and her fiancé as the sterling silver tableware he'd bought at the online department store where they'd registered. If Olivia, the youngest of the four Watson siblings, and the only sister, asked him to keep older brother Duff and younger brother Keir in line today, then Niall would do it. It was a brilliant strategy on her part, he silently admitted. Not only would their rowdier brothers be kept in check, but asking the favor of him was sure to keep Niall engaged in the ceremony. It was smart to give him a specific task to focus on so his mind didn't wander back to the dead body he'd analyzed yesterday morning at the lab in southeast Kansas City, and the follow-up notes he wanted to log in, or to the facts on a drowning victim he wanted to double-check before turning his findings over to the detectives supervising those particular cases.

As a third-generation cop in a close-knit family of law enforcement professionals, it was practically impossible not to be filled with investigative curiosity, or to have dedication and responsibility running through his veins. When it came to work and family, at any rate. And for Niall, there was nothing else. Work filled his life, and the Watson family filled his heart.

Except when they were screwing around—like Duff beside him, running his finger beneath the starched collar of his white shirt and grumbling something about Valentine's Day curses while he fiddled with the knot on his cherry-red tie. Or Keir, chattering up the aisle behind Niall, saying something outrageous enough to the bridesmaid he was escorting to make her giggle. Then Keir patted her hand on his arm and turned to wink at Millie, the family housekeeper-cook they'd all grown up with, as he passed the silver-haired woman in the second pew. The older woman blushed, and Keir blew her a kiss.

Niall adjusted the dark frames of his glasses and nailed Keir with a look warning him to let go of the bridesmaid, stop working the room and assume his place beside him as one of Gabe's groomsmen, already.

"Natalie is married to Liv's partner, you know." The tallest of the three brothers, Niall dropped his chin to whisper under his breath.

"Relax, charm-school dropout." Keir clapped Niall on the shoulder of the black tuxedo he wore, grinning as he stepped up beside him. "Young or old, married or not—it never hurts to be friendly."

Olivia might be the youngest of the four siblings, all third-generation law enforcement who served their city proudly. And she might be the only woman in the tight-knit Watson family since their mother's murder when Niall had barely been a teen. But there was no question that Liv ran the show. Despite Duff's tough-guy grousing or Keir's clever charm or Niall's own reserved, logical prowess, Olivia Mary Watson—soon to be Olivia Knight—had each of them, including their widowed father and grandfather, wrapped around her pretty little finger. If she asked Niall to keep their headstrong Irish family in line today, then he would do exactly that.

With Keir set for the moment, Niall angled his position toward the groom and best man Duff. He didn't need to adjust his glasses to see the bulge at the small of Duff's back beneath the tailored black jacket. Niall's nostrils flared with a patience-inducing breath before he whispered, "Seriously? Are you packing today?"

Duff's overbuilt shoulders shifted as he turned to whisper a response. "Hey. You wear your glasses every day, Poindexter. I wear my gun."

"I wasn't aware that you knew what the term *Poindexter* meant."

"I'm smarter than I look" was Duff's terse response.

Keir chuckled. "He'd have to be."

Duff's muscular shoulders shifted. "So help me, baby brother, if you give me any grief today, I will lay you out flat."

"Zip it. Both of you." Niall knew that he was quickly losing control of his two charges. He scowled at Keir. "You, mind your manners." When Duff went after the collar hugging his muscular neck again, Niall leaned in. "And you stop fidgeting like a little kid."

A curious look from the minister waiting behind

them quieted all three brothers for the moment. With everything ready for their sister's walk down the aisle, the processional music started. Niall scanned the rest of the crowd as they rose to their feet. Their grandfather Seamus Watson hooked his cane over the railing as he stood in the front row. He winked one blue eye at Niall before pulling out his handkerchief and turning toward the aisle to dab at the tears he didn't want anybody to see.

And then Olivia and their father, Thomas Watson, appeared in the archway at the end of the aisle. A fist of rare sentimentality squeezed around Niall's heart.

His father was a relatively tall, stocky man. His black tuxedo and red vest and tie—an homage to the date, February 14—matched Niall's own attire. Niall knew a familiar moment of pride and respect as his father limped down the aisle, his shoulders erect despite the injury that had ended his career at KCPD at far too young an age. Other than the peppering of gray in Thomas's dark brown hair, Niall saw the same face when he looked into the mirror every morning.

But that wasn't what had him nodding his head in admiration.

His sister, that tough tomboy turned top-notch detective, the girl who'd never let three older brothers get the best of her, had grown up. Draped in ivory and sparkles, her face framed by the Irish lace veil handed down through their mother's side of the family, Olivia Watson was a beauty. Dark hair, blue eyes like his. But feminine, radiant. Her gaze locked on to Gabe at the altar, and she smiled. Niall hadn't seen a glimpse of his mother like that in twenty years.

"Dude," Duff muttered. He nudged the groom beside him. "Gabe, you are one lucky son of a—"

"Duff." Niall remembered his charge at the last moment and stopped his older brother from swearing in church.

Gabe sounded a bit awestruck himself as Olivia walked down the aisle. "I know."

"You'd better treat her right," Duff growled on a whisper.

Niall watched his brother's shoulders puff up. "We've already had this conversation, Duff. I'm convinced he loves her."

Gabe never took his eyes off Olivia as he inclined his head to whisper, "He does."

Keir, of course, wasn't about to be left out of the hushed conversation. "Anyway, Liv's made her choice. You think any one of us could change her mind? I'd be scared to try."

The minister hushed the lot of them as father and bride approached.

"Ah, hell," Duff muttered, looking up at the ceiling. He blinked rapidly, pinching his nose. The big guy was tearing up. "This is not happening to me."

"She looks the way I remember Mom," Keir said in a curiously soft voice.

Finally, the gravity of the day was sinking in and their focus was where it should be. Niall tapped Duff's elbow. "Do you have a handkerchief?"

"The rings are tied up in it."

"Here." Niall slipped his own white handkerchief to Duff, who quickly dabbed at his face. He nodded what passed for a thank-you and stuffed the cotton square into his pocket, steeling his jaw against the flare of emotion.

When Olivia arrived at the altar, she kissed their father, catching him in a tight hug before smiling at all three brothers. Duff sniffled again. Keir gave her a thumbs-up. Niall nodded approvingly. Olivia handed her bouquet off to her matron of honor, Ginny Rafferty-Taylor, and took Gabe's hand to face the minister.

The rest of the ceremony continued with everyone on their best behavior until the minister pronounced Gabe and Olivia husband and wife and announced, "You may now kiss the bride."

"Love you," Olivia whispered.

Gabe kissed her again. "Love you more."

"I now present Mr. and Mrs. Gabriel Knight."

Niall pondered the pomp and circumstance of this particular Valentine's Day as the guests applauded and the recessional music started. Logically, he knew the words Liv and Gabe had spoken and what they meant. But a part of him struggled to comprehend exactly how this sappy sort of pageantry equated to happiness and lifelong devotion. It was all a bit wearing, really. But if this was what Olivia wanted, he'd support her whole-heartedly and do whatever was necessary to make it happen.

Following Duff to the center of the aisle, Niall extended his arm to escort bridesmaid Katie Rinaldi down the marble steps. Despite his red-rimmed eyes, Thomas Watson smiled at each of his children. Niall smiled back.

Until he caught the glimpse of movement in the balcony at the back of the church. A figure in black emerged from the shadows beside a carved limestone buttress framing a row of organ pipes.

In a nanosecond frozen in time, a dozen observations blipped through Niall's mind. The organist played away upstairs, unaware of the intruder only a few yards from his position. The figure wore a ski mask and a long black coat. Clearly not a guest. Not church staff. The pews were filled with almost two hundred potential targets, many of them off-duty and retired police officers. His new brother-in-law had made more enemies than friends with his cutting-edge editorials. What did he want? Why was he here? Didn't have to be a cop hater with some kind of vendetta. Could be some crazy with nothing more in mind than making a deadly statement about a lost love or perceived injustice or mental illness.

The gleam of polished wood reflected the colored light streaming in through the balcony's stained-glass windows as the shooter pulled a rifle from his long cloak. Mauser hunting rifle. Five eight-millimeter rounds. He carried a second weapon, a semiautomatic pistol, strapped to his belt. That was enough firepower to do plenty of damage. Enough to kill far too many people.

Time righted itself as the analytical part of Niall's brain shut down and the years of training as a cop and medical officer kicked in. *Move!* Niall shoved Katie to one side and reached for his father as the shooter took aim.

"Gun!" he shouted, pointing to the balcony as his fingers closed around the sleeve of Thomas Watson's jacket. "Get down!"

The *slap, slap, slap* of gunshots exploded through

the church. The organ music clashed on a toxic chord and went silent. Wood splintered and flew like shrapnel. A vase at the altar shattered. Flower petals and explosions of marble dust rained in the air.

"Everybody down!" Duff ordered, drawing the pistol from the small of his back. He dropped to one knee on the opposite side of the aisle and raised his weapon. "Drop it!"

"I'm calling SWAT." Keir ducked between two pews, pulling his phone from his jacket as he hugged his arms around Natalie Fensom and Millie Leighter.

Niall saw Gabe Knight slam his arms around Liv and pull her to the marble floor beneath his body. Guests shouted names of loved ones. A child cried out in fear, and a mother hastened to comfort him. Warnings not to panic, not to run, blended together with the screams and tromping footfalls of people doing just that.

"I've got no shot," Duff yelled, pushing to a crouching position as the shooter dropped his spent rifle and pulled his pistol. Niall heard Keir's succinct voice reporting to dispatch. With a nod from Katie that she was all right and assurance that her husband was circling around the outside aisle to get to her, Niall climbed to his knees to assess the casualties. He caught a glimpse of Duff and a couple of other officers zigzagging down the aisle through the next hail of bullets and charging out the back of the sanctuary. "Get down and stay put!"

Niall squeezed his father's arm. He was okay. He glanced back at the minister crouched behind the pulpit. He hadn't been hit, either. The man in the balcony shouted no manifesto, made no threat. He emptied his gun into the sanctuary, grabbed his rifle and scrambled up the stairs toward the balcony exit. He was making a lot of noise and doing a lot of damage and generating a lot of terror. But despite the chaos, he wasn't hitting anyone. What kind of maniac set off this degree of panic without having a specific—

"Niall!" His grandfather's cane clattered against the marble tiles. Niall was already peeling off his jacket and wadding it up to use as a compress as Thomas Watson cradled the eighty-year-old man in his arms and gently lowered him to the floor. "Help me, son. Dad's been shot."

Chapter One

Niall stepped off the elevator in his condominium building to the sound of a baby crying.

His dragging feet halted as the doors closed behind him, his nostrils flaring as he inhaled a deep, weary breath, pulled the phone from his ear and checked his watch. Two in the morning.

Great. Just great. He had nothing against babies—he knew many of them grew into very fine adults. But he'd been awake going on twenty hours now, had been debriefed six ways to Sunday by cops and family and medical staff alike, hadn't even had a chance to change his ruined fancy clothes, and was already feeling sleep deprived by switching off his typical nocturnal work schedule to be there for Liv's wedding. No way was he going to catch a couple hours of much-needed shut-eye before he headed back to the hospital later this morning.

He put the phone back to his ear and finished the conversation with Duff. "You know we can't investigate this shooting personally. There's a huge conflict of interest since the victim is family."

"Then I'm going to find out which detectives caught the case and make sure they keep us in the loop."

"You do that. And I'll keep track of any evidence that comes through the lab."

"We'll find this guy." Duff's pronouncement was certain. "Get some sleep, Niall."

"You, too." Niall disconnected the call, knowing he couldn't comply with his older brother's directive.

But it wasn't the pitiful noise of the infant's wails, nor the decibel level of distress that solid walls could only mute, that would keep him awake.

His brain's refusal to let a question go unanswered was going to prevent his thoughts from quieting until he could solve the mystery of where that crying baby had come from and to whom the child belonged. As if the events of the day—with his grandfather lying in intensive care and an unidentified shooter on the loose in Kansas City—weren't enough to keep him from sleeping, now a desperately unhappy infant and Niall's own curiosity over the unexpected sound were probably going to eat up whatever downtime he had left tonight. Cursing that intellectual compulsion, Niall rolled his kinked-up neck muscles and started down the hallway.

Considering three of the six condos on this floor were empty, a retired couple in their seventies lived in one at the far end of the hall and Lucy McKane, who lived across the hall from his place, was a single like himself, the crying baby posed a definite mystery. Perhaps the Logans were babysitting one of the many grandchildren they liked to talk about. Either that or Lucy McKane had company tonight. Could she be watching a friend's child? Dating a single dad who'd brought along a young chaperone? Letting a well-kept secret finally reveal itself?

Although they'd shared several early-morning and late-night chats, he and Lucy had never gotten much beyond introductions and polite conversations about the weather and brands of detergent. Just because he hadn't seen a ring on her finger didn't mean she wasn't attached to someone. And even though he struggled with interpersonal relationships, he wasn't so clueless as to think she had to be married or seeing someone in order to get pregnant.

So the crying baby was most likely hers.

Good. Mystery solved. Niall pulled his keys from his pocket as he approached his door. Sleep might just happen.

Or not.

The flash of something red and shiny in the carpet stopped Niall in the hallway between their two doors. He stooped down to retrieve a minuscule shard of what looked like red glass. Another mystery? Didn't building maintenance vacuum out here five days a week? This was a recent deposit and too small to identify the source. A broken bottle? Stained glass? The baby wailed through the door off to his right, and Niall turned his head. He hadn't solved anything at all.

Forget the broken glass. Where and when did Lucy McKane get a baby?

He'd never seen her coming home from a date before, much less in the company of a man with a child. And he was certain he hadn't noticed a baby bump on her. Although she could have been hiding a pregnancy, either intentionally or not. He generally ran into her in the elevator when she was wearing bulky hand-knit sweaters or her winter coat, or in the gym downstairs, where she sported oversize T-shirts with one silly or motivational message or another. And then there were those late-night visits in the basement laundry room, where there'd been clothes baskets and tables between them to mask her belly. Now that he thought about it, Lucy McKane wore a lot of loose-fitting clothes. Her fashion choices tended to emphasize her generous breasts and camouflage the rest of her figure. He supposed she could have been carrying a baby one of those late nights when they'd discussed fabric softener versus dryer sheets, and he simply hadn't realized it.

If that was the case, though, why hadn't he seen the child or heard it crying before tonight? The woman liked to talk. Wouldn't she have announced the arrival of her child?

Maybe he'd rethink other options. It was the wee hours after Valentine's Day. She could be watching the child for a friend out on an overnight date. But why hadn't Lucy gone out for Valentine's Day? The woman was pretty in an unconventional kind of way, if one liked a cascade of dark curls that were rarely tamed, green eyes that were slightly almond shaped and the apple cheeks and a pert little nose that would make her look eternally young. She made friends easily enough, judging by her ability to draw even someone like him into random conversations. And she was certainly well-spoken—at least when it came to washing clothes and inclement weather, gossip about the building's residents and the news of the day. So why wasn't a woman like that taken? Where was *her* date?

And why was he kneeling here in a stained, wrinkled tuxedo and eyes that burned with fatigue, analyzing the situation at all? He needed sleep, desperately. Otherwise, his mind wouldn't be wandering like this.

"Let it go, Watson," he chided himself, pushing to his feet.

Niall turned to the door marked 8C and inserted his key into the lock. At least he could clearly pinpoint the source of the sound now. The noise of the unhappy baby from behind Lucy McKane's door was jarring to his weary senses. He was used to coming home in shrouded silence when his swing shift at the medical examiner's office ended. Most of the residents in the building were asleep by then. He respected their need for quiet as much as he craved it himself. He never even turned on the radio or TV. He'd brew a pot of decaf and sit down with a book or his reading device until he could shut down his thoughts from the evening and turn in for a few hours of sleep. Sending a telepathic brain wave to the woman across the hall to calm her child and allow them all some peace, he went inside and closed the door behind him.

After hanging up his coat in the front closet, Niall switched on lamps and headed straight to the wet bar, where he tossed the sliver of glass onto the counter, unhooked the top button of his shirt and poured himself a shot of whiskey. Sparing a glance for the crimson smears that stained his jacket sleeve and shirt cuffs, he raised his glass to the man he'd left sleeping in the ICU at Saint Luke's Hospital. Only when his younger brother had come in to spell him for a few hours after Keir and Duff had hauled Liv and her new husband, Gabe, off to a fancy hotel where they could spend their wedding night—in lieu of the honeymoon they'd postponed—

had Niall left Seamus Watson's side. "This one's for you, Grandpa."

Niall swallowed the pungent liquor in one gulp, savoring the fire burning down his gullet and chasing away the chill of a wintry night and air-conditioned hospital rooms that clung to every cell of his body. It had been beyond a rough day. His grandfather was a tough old bird, and Niall had been able to stanch the bleeding and stabilize him at the church well enough to keep shock from setting in. He'd ridden with the paramedics to the hospital, and they had done their job well, as had the ER staff. But the eighty-year-old man had needed surgery to repair the bleeders from the bullet that had fractured his skull and remove the tiny bone fragments that had come dangerously close to entering his brainpan and killing him.

Although the attending surgeon and neurologist insisted Seamus was now guardedly stable and needed to sleep, the traumatic brain injury had done significant damage. Either due to the wound itself, or a resulting stroke, he'd lost the use of his left arm and leg, had difficulty speaking and limited vision in his left eye. Seamus was comfortable for now, but age and trauma had taken a toll on his body and he had a long road to recovery ahead of him. And as Niall had asked questions of the doctors and hovered around the nurses and orderlies while they worked, he couldn't help but replay those minutes at the end of the wedding over and over in his head.

Had Seamus Watson been the shooter's intended target? And since the old man seemed determined to live, would the shooter be coming back to finish the job?

Was Grandpa safe? Or was his dear, funny, smarter-than-the-rest-of-them-put-together grandfather a tragic victim of collateral damage?

If so, who had the man with all those bullets really been after? Why plan the attack at the church? Was the Valentine's Day date significant? Was his goal to disrupt the wedding, make a statement against KCPD, or simply to create chaos and validate his own sense of power? Even though others had been hurt by minor shrapnel wounds, and one man had suffered a mild heart attack triggered by the stress of the situation, the number of professionally trained guests had kept the panic to a minimum. So who was the shooter? Duff said he'd chased the perp up onto the roof, but then the man had disappeared before Duff or any of the other officers in pursuit could reach him. What kind of man planned his escape so thoroughly, yet failed to hit anyone besides the Watson patriarch? And if Seamus was the intended target, what was the point of all the extra damage and drama?

And could Niall have stopped the tragedy completely if he'd spotted the man in the shadows a few seconds sooner? He scratched his fingers through the short hair that already stood up in spikes atop his head after a day of repeating the same unconscious habit. Niall prided himself on noting details. But today he'd missed the most important clue of his life until it was too late.

His brothers would be looking into Seamus's old case files and tracking down any enemies that their grandfather might have made in his career on the force, despite his retirement fifteen years earlier. Duff and Keir would be following up any clues found by the officers investigating the case that could lead to the shooter's identity and capture. Frustratingly, Niall's involvement with finding answers was done—unless one of his brothers came up with some forensic evidence he could process at the lab. And even then, Niall's expertise was autopsy work. He'd be doing little more than calling in favors to speed the process and following up with his coworkers at the crime lab. Although it galled him to take a backseat in the investigation, logic indicated he'd better serve the family by taking point on his grandfather's care and recovery so his brothers could focus on tracking down the would-be assassin.

Niall picked up the Bushmills to pour himself a second glass, but the muted cries of the baby across the hall reminded him that he wasn't the only one dealing with hardship tonight, and he returned the bottle to the cabinet. He wanted to have a clear head in the morning when he returned to the hospital for a follow-up report on his grandfather. He could already feel his body surrendering to the tide of fatigue, and despite his unsettling thoughts, he loathed the idea of dulling his intellect before he found the answers he needed. So he set the glass in the sink and moved into the kitchen to start a small pot of decaf.

While the machine hissed and bubbled, he shrugged out of the soiled black tuxedo jacket and draped it over the back of a chair. After pulling out the rented tie he'd folded up into a pocket and laying it over the coat, he went to work unbuttoning the cherry-red vest he wore. Typically, he didn't wear his gun unless he was out in the field at a crime scene. But with his family threatened and too many questions left unanswered, he'd had

Duff unlock it from the glove compartment of Niall's SUV and bring it to the hospital, where he'd strapped it on. Niall halted in the middle of unhooking his belt to remove it, opting instead to roll up his sleeves and leave himself armed. Until he understood exactly what was going on, it would be smart to keep that protection close at hand.

Whether it was the gun's protection, the resumption of his nightly routine or the discordant noise from across the hall receding, Niall braced his hands against the edge of the sink to stretch his back and drop his chin, letting his eyes close as the tension in him gave way to weariness.

The distant baby's cries shortened like staccato notes, as if the child was running out of the breath or energy to maintain the loud wails. Maybe Miss McKane was finally having some success in quieting the infant. Despite how much she liked to talk, she seemed like a capable sort of woman. Sensible, too. She carried her keys on a ring with a small pepper spray canister in her hand each time he saw her walking to or from her car in the parking lot. She wore a red stocking hat on her dark curly hair when the weather was cold and wet to conserve body heat. She sorted her jeans and towels from her whites and colors. Okay, so maybe she wasn't completely practical. Why did a woman need so many different types of underwear, anyway? Cotton briefs, silky long johns, lacy bras in white and tan and assorted pastels, animal prints…

Niall's eyes popped open when he realized he was thinking about Lucy McKane's underwear. And not folded up in her laundry basket or tucked away in a dresser drawer, either.

Good grief. Imagining his neighbor's pale skin outlined in that tan-and-black leopard-print duo he'd found so curiously distracting tossed on top of her folding pile was hardly appropriate. Exhaustion must be playing tricks on him. Pushing away from the sink, Niall clasped his glasses at either temple and adjusted the frames on his face, as if the action could refocus the wayward detour of his thoughts. It was irritating that he could be so easily distracted by curves and cotton or shards of glass or mystery babies who were none of his business when he wanted to concentrate on studying the events before, during and after the shooting at the wedding. Perhaps he should have skipped the shot of whiskey and gone straight for the steaming decaf he poured into a mug.

He added a glug of half-and-half from the fridge and carried the fragrant brew to the bookshelf in the living room, where he pulled out a medical volume to look up some of the details relating to his grandfather's condition. He savored the reviving smell of the coffee before taking a drink and settling into the recliner beside the floor lamp.

Niall had barely turned the first page when the infant across the hall found his second wind and bellowed with a high-pitched shriek that nearly startled him into spilling his drink.

Enough. Was the child sick? Had he completely misjudged Lucy McKane's competence? Niall set his book and mug on the table beside him and pushed to his feet. Maybe the muted noise of a baby crying didn't bother anybody else. Maybe no one else could hear the child's distress. He was so used to the building being quiet at this hour that maybe he was particularly sensitive to the muffled sounds. And maybe he'd come so close to losing someone he loved today that he just didn't have the patience to deal with a neighbor who couldn't respect his need for a little peace and quiet and time to regroup.

In just a few strides he was out the door and across the hall, knocking on Lucy McKane's front door. When there was no immediate response, he knocked harder. "Miss McKane? Do you know how late it is? Some of us are trying to sleep." Well, he hadn't been. But it wasn't as though he could if he even wanted to with that plaintive racket filtering through the walls. "Miss McKane?"

Niall propped his hands at his waist, waiting several seconds before knocking again. "Miss McKane?" Why didn't the woman answer her door? She couldn't be asleep with the baby crying like that, could she? In a heartbeat, Niall's irritation morphed into concern at the lack of any response. That could explain the infant's distress. Maybe Lucy McKane *couldn't* help the child. He flattened his palm against the painted steel and pounded again. "Miss McKane? It's Niall Watson from across the hall. Are you in there? Is everything all right?"

He reached down to jiggle the knob, but the cold metal twisted easily in his hand and the door creaked open a couple of inches.

Niall's suspicion radar went on instant alert. What woman who lived alone in the city didn't keep her door locked?

"Miss McKane?" he called out. But his only response

was the even louder decibel level of the crying baby. He squinted the scratches on the knob into focus and quickly pulled his phone from his pocket to snap a picture. A familiar glint of red glass wedged between the frame and catch for the dead bolt higher up caught his eye. The tiny shattered orb looked like the source of the shard he'd found in the carpet.

Finally. Answers. But he didn't like them.

There were deeper gouges in the wood trim around it, indicating that both locks had been forced. His brain must have been half-asleep not to have suspected earlier that something was seriously wrong. Niall snapped a second picture. "Miss McKane? Are you all right?"

For a few seconds, the concerns of his Hippocratic oath warred with the procedure drilled into him by his police training. His brother Duff would muscle his way in without hesitation, while Keir would have a judge on speed dial, arranging an entry warrant. Niall weighed his options. The baby was crying and Lucy wasn't answering. His concern for the occupants' safety was reason enough to enter a potentially dangerous situation despite risking any kind of legalities. Tonight he'd forgo caution and follow his older brother's example.

"Hold tight, little one," he whispered, unstrapping his holster and pulling the service weapon from his belt. Although he was more used to handling a scalpel than a Glock, as a member of the KCPD crime lab, he'd been trained and certified to use the gun.

He held it surely as he nudged open the broken door. "Miss McKane? It's Niall Watson with the KCPD crime lab. I'm concerned for your safety. I'm coming in."

The mournful wails of a baby crying itself into exhaustion instantly grew louder on this side of the walls separating their living spaces. He backed against the door, closing it behind him as he cradled the gun between both hands. A dim light in the kitchen provided the only illumination in the condo that mirrored the layout of his own place. Allowing his vision to adjust to the dim outlines of furniture and doorways, Niall waited before advancing into the main room. He checked the closet and powder room near the entryway before moving through the living and dining rooms. Empty. No sign of Lucy McKane anywhere. No blood or signs of an accident or struggle of any sort, either. In fact, the only things that seemed out of place were the bundles of yarn, patterns and knitting needles that had been dumped out of their basket onto the coffee table and strewn across the sofa cushions and area rug.

He found the baby in the kitchen, fastened into a carrier that sat on the peninsula countertop, with nothing more than the glow of an automatic night-light beside the stove to keep him company. A half-formed panel of gray knitted wool hung from the baby's toes, as if he'd once been covered with it but had thrashed it aside.

Niall flipped on the light switch and circled around the peninsula, plucking the makeshift blanket off and laying it on the counter. "You're a tiny thing to be making all that noise. You all alone in here? Do you know where your mama is?"

The kid's red face lolled toward Niall's hushed voice. It shook and batted its little fists before cranking up to wail again. Niall didn't need to take a second whiff to ascertain at least one reason why the baby was so unhappy. But a quick visual sweep didn't reveal any sign of a diaper bag or anything to change it into besides the yellow outfit it wore. Had Lucy McKane left the child alone to go make a supply run?

Niall moved the gun down to his side and touched the baby's face. Feverish. Was the kid sick? Or was that what this ceaseless crying did to someone who was maybe only a week or so old?

The infant's cries sputtered into silent gasps as Niall splayed his fingers over its heaving chest. Not unlike his grandfather's earlier that day, the baby's heart was racing. A quick check farther down answered another question for him. "You okay, little man?"

How long had he been left unattended like this?

And where was Lucy? There was no sign of her in the kitchen, either, despite the dirty dishes in the sink and what looked like a congealed glob of cookie dough in the stand mixer beside it. It seemed as though she'd left in the middle of baking a dessert. Why hadn't she completed the task? Where had she gone? What had called her away? And, he thought, with a distinct note of irritation filtering into his thought process, why hadn't she taken the baby with her?

"Hold on." Niall's gaze was drawn to a screwdriver on the counter that didn't look like any piece of cooking equipment he'd ever seen his late mother or Millie Leighter use.

After a couple of silent sobs vibrated through the infant's delicate chest, Niall pulled his hand away. Tuning out the recommencing wail, he opened two drawers before he found a plastic bag and used it to pick up the tool. The handle was an absurd shade of pink with shiny baubles glued around each end of the grip. He rolled it in his hand until he found what he suspected he might—an empty space in the circle of fake stones. Niall glanced back through the darkened apartment. The bead stuck in the frame of her door suddenly made sense. But even if his neighbor had lost her key and had to break into her own place, she'd turn on the lights once she got in. There'd be signs of her being here. And she'd damn well take care of the baby.

Unless she wasn't the one who'd broken in.

"Don't go anywhere," he ordered needlessly. Wrapping the screwdriver securely in the bag, Niall slipped it into his pocket and clasped the gun between his hands again. "I'll be right back."

A quick inspection through the bedroom and en suite showed no sign of Lucy McKane there, either. He didn't see her purse anywhere, and her winter coat and accoutrements were missing from the front closet. There was no baby paraphernalia in any of the rooms.

Had she been kidnapped? What kind of kidnapper would leave evidence like the screwdriver behind? Had she been robbed? Nothing here seemed disturbed beyond the topsy-turvy knitting basket, and anything of typical value to a thief—her flat-screen TV, a laptop computer—was still here.

More unanswered questions. Niall's concern reverted to irritation.

This child had been abandoned. Lucy McKane was gone, and the woman had a lot of explaining to do.

Niall was surprisingly disappointed to learn that she was the type of woman to leave an infant alone to run errands or enjoy a date. She was a free spirit, certainly, with her friendly smile and ease at striking up conversations with neighbors she barely knew and ownership of far too many pairs of panties. But she'd told him she was a social worker, for pity's sake. He wouldn't have pegged her to be so self-absorbed and reckless as to leave a child in an unlocked apartment—to leave the child, period. *If* she'd left by choice.

With the mandate of both his badge and his medical degree, and three generations of protecting those who couldn't protect themselves bred into him, Niall could not walk out that door and abandon this baby himself. So, understanding as much about children as his medical books could teach, he tucked his gun into its holster, pulled his phone from his pocket and picked up the baby in its carrier. He spared a glance at the soft wood around the deadbolt catch, debating whether or not he should retrieve the decorative bead jammed there or report Lucy as a missing person. Making the crying infant his first priority, Niall closed the door behind him and carried the baby into his apartment before dialing the most knowledgeable parent he knew.

The phone picked up on the third ring. "Niall?"

"Dad." He set the carrier on the island in his own kitchen and opened a drawer to pull out two clean dish towels. A quick glance at his watch indicated that perhaps he should have thought this through better. "Did I wake you?"

"It's three in the morning, son. Of course you did." Thomas Watson pushed the grogginess from his voice. "Are you still at the hospital? Has there been a change in Dad's condition?"

"No. The doctors are keeping Grandpa lightly sedated. Keir will stay with him until one of us relieves him in the morning."

"Thank God one of my boys is a doctor and that you were there to give him the treatment he needed immediately. We should be giving thanks that he survived and no one else was seriously injured. But knowing that the bastard who shot him is still…" Thomas Watson's tone changed from dark frustration to curious surprise. "Do I hear a baby crying?"

Niall strode through his apartment, retrieving a towel and washcloth along with the first-aid kit and a clean white T-shirt from his dresser. "Yes. Keir will contact me if there is any change in Grandpa's condition. I told Grandpa one or all of us would be by to see him in the morning, that the family would be there for him 24/7. I'm not sure he heard me, though."

"Dad heard you, I'm sure." Niall could hear his father moving now, a sure sign that the former cop turned investigative consultant was on his feet and ready for Niall to continue. "Now go back to the other thing. Why do you have a baby?"

Niall had returned to the kitchen to run warm water in the sink. "Can I ask you a favor?"

"Of course, son."

"Dad, I need newborn diapers, bottles and formula. A clean set of clothes and some kind of coat or blanket or whatever babies need when it's cold. A car seat, too, if you can get your hands on one at this time of night. I'll reimburse you for everything, of course." Niall put the phone on speaker and spread a thick towel out on the counter, pausing for a moment to assess the locking mechanism before unhooking the baby and lifting him from the carrier. "Good Lord, you don't weigh a thing."

"The baby, Niall." That tone in his father's voice had always commanded an answer. "Is there something you need to tell me?"

"It's the neighbor's kid," Niall explained. "I'd get the items myself, but I don't have a car seat and can't leave him alone. Oh, get something for diaper rash, too. He needs a bath. I can use a clean dish towel to cover him up until you get here, although I don't have any safety pins. Do you think medical tape would work to hold a makeshift diaper on him until you arrive?"

"You're babysitting? I never thought I'd see the day—"

"Just bring me the stuff, Dad."

Another hour passed before Thomas Watson arrived with several bags of supplies. His father groused about bottles looking different from the time Olivia had been the last infant in the house and how there were far too many choices for a feeding regimen. But between the two of them, they got the baby diapered, fed and dressed in a footed sleeper that fit him much better than Niall's long T-shirt. At first, Niall was concerned about the infant falling asleep before finishing his first bottle. But he roused enough for Thomas to coax a healthy burp out of him before drinking a little more and crashing again. Niall was relieved to feel the baby's temperature return to normal and suspected the feverish state had been pure stress manifesting itself.

The infant boy was sleeping in Thomas Watson's lap as the older man dozed in the recliner, and Niall was reviewing a chapter on pediatric medicine when he heard the ding of the elevator at the end of the hallway. He closed the book and set it on the coffee table, urging his waking father to stay put while he went to the door.

He heard Lucy McKane's hushed voice mumbling something as she approached and then a much louder, "Oh, my God. I've had a break-in."

Niall swung open his door and approached the back of the dark-haired woman standing motionless before her apartment door. She had turned silent, but he knew exactly what to say. "Miss McKane? You and I need to talk."

Chapter Two

"The man wasn't following me," Lucy chanted under her breath for the umpteenth time since parking her car downstairs. She stepped off the elevator into the shadowed hallway, trying to convince herself that the drunken ape who'd offered to rock her world down on Carmody Street wasn't the driver of the silver sports car she'd spotted in her rearview mirror less than a block from her condominium building a few minutes earlier. "He wasn't following me."

Maybe if she hadn't spotted a similar car veering in and out of the lane behind her on Highway 71, she wouldn't be so paranoid. Maybe if her voice mail at work didn't have a message from her ex-boyfriend Roger that was equal parts slime and threat and booze.

"Guess what, sweet thing. I'm out. And I'm coming to see you."

Maybe if it wasn't so late, maybe if she'd felt safe in that run-down part of Kansas City, maybe if she wasn't so certain that something terrible had happened to Diana Kozlow, her former foster daughter, who'd called her out of the blue yesterday after more than a year of no contact—maybe if the twenty-year-old would answer her stupid phone any one of the dozen times Lucy had tried to call her back—she wouldn't feel so helpless or alone or afraid.

Fortunately, the silver car had driven past when she'd turned in to the gated parking garage. But the paranoia and a serious need to wash the man's grimy hands off her clothes and skin remained. "He was *not* following me."

She glanced down at the blurred picture she'd snapped through her rear window the second time the silver roadster had passed a car and slipped into the lane behind her on 71. Her pulse pounded furiously in her ears as she slipped the finger of her glove between her teeth and pulled it off her right hand to try and enlarge the picture and get a better look at the driver or read a possible license plate. Useless. No way could she prove the Neanderthal or Roger or anyone else had followed her after leaving the rattrap apartment building on Carmody, which was the last address she had for Diana. Not that it had been a productive visit. The super had refused to speak to her, and the only resident who would answer her questions about Diana was an elderly woman who couldn't remember a young brunette woman living in the building, and didn't recognize her from the old high school photo Lucy had shown her. Ape man had been willing to tell her anything—in exchange for stepping into the alley with him for a free grope.

None of which boded well for the life Diana had forged for herself after aging out of the foster system and leaving Lucy's home. Lucy swiped her finger across the cell screen to pull up the high school photo of the dark-haired beauty she'd thought would be family—or at least a close friend—forever. "Oh, sweetie, what have you gotten yourself into?" she muttered around the red wool clasped between her teeth.

She glanced back at the elevator door, remembered the key card required to get into the building lobby.

"Okay. The creeper didn't follow me," she stated with as much conviction as she could muster. "And I will find you, Diana."

She was simply going to have to get a few hours' sleep and think this through and start her search again tomorrow. Except...

Lucy pulled up short when she reached the door to 8D. The late-night chill that had iced her skin seeped quickly through the layers of clothing she wore.

"Oh, my God. I've had a break-in."

So much for feeling secure.

The wood around the locks on her apartment door was scratched and broken. The steel door itself drifted open with barely a touch of her hand. Lucy retreated half a step and pulled up the keypad on her phone to call the police. After two previous calls about Diana's failure to show up for lunch or return her calls, they were probably going to think she was a nutcase to call a third time in fewer than twenty-four hours.

"Miss McKane? You and I need to talk."

Lucy's fear erupted in a startled yelp at the succinct announcement. She swung around with her elbow at the man's deep voice behind her, instinctively protecting herself.

Instead of her elbow connecting with the man's solar plexus, five long fingers clamped like a vise around her wrist and she was pushed up against the wall by a tall, lanky body. Her phone popped loose from her slippery grip and bounced across the carpet at her feet. Her heart thumped in her chest at the wall of heat trapping her there, and the loose glove she'd held between her teeth was caught between her heaving breasts and the broad expanse of a white tuxedo shirt. What the devil? Diana was missing, and she had no idea why her tall, lanky neighbor was glowering down at her through those Clark Kent glasses he wore.

"Wow," she gasped, as the frissons of fear evaporated once she recognized him. No one else roamed the hallways this time of night except for him. She should have known better. "Sorry I took a swing at you, Dr. Watson." She couldn't even summon the giggly response she usually had when she said his name and conjured up thoughts of medical sidekicks and brainy British detectives. Not when she was embarrassingly aware of his hard runner's body pressed against hers. Nothing to giggle about there. The full-body contact lasted another awkward moment. "I didn't hurt you, did I?"

"Of course not." Once he seemed certain she recognized him as a friend and didn't have to defend himself, Niall Watson released his grip on her arm and stepped away, leaving a distinct chill in place of that surprising male heat that had pinned her to the wall. "I shouldn't have startled you."

"I thought you...were someone else."

"Who? Were you expecting someone?"

"I, um…" She wasn't about to explain her paranoid suspicions about ape man or Roger and the silver car, so she covered her rattled state by stooping down to retrieve her glove and phone. "Sorry if I woke you. I've had a break-in. I thought this was supposed to be a secure building in a safe neighborhood, but I guess there's no place that's truly safe if someone is determined to get to you. That's probably why I swung first. A girl has to take care of herself, you know. I'd better call the police."

Niall Watson's long fingers reached her phone first. He scooped it up and tapped the screen clear. "A 911 call won't be necessary."

Frowning at his high-handedness, Lucy tilted her face up. "Why not?" She was halfway to making eye contact when she saw the crimson spots staining his rolled-up sleeve. She stuffed her loose glove into her pocket, along with her phone, and touched her fingertip to the red stains on the wrinkled white cotton clinging to his long, muscular forearm. There were more droplets of blood on the other sleeve, too. Irritation vanished, and she piled concern for him onto the fears that had already worn her ragged today.

"Are you hurt? Did you stop the intruder?" She grasped his wrist in her hand, much the same way he'd manhandled her, and twisted it to find the wound. Despite the tempting awareness at his toasty-warm skin beneath her chilled fingers, she was more interested in learning what had happened. She knew he was affiliated with the police. Had he stepped in to prevent a burglar from ransacking her place? Had Roger followed his release from prison with a road trip to Kansas City? Had Diana shown up while she was searching the city for her? Now she looked up and met those narrowed cobalt eyes. "Have you already called for help? Do I need to take you to the hospital?"

A dark eyebrow arched above the rim of his glasses

before he glanced down to see the source of her concern. Blinking away his apparent confusion, he pulled out of her grip to splay his fingers at his waist. "This isn't my blood."

"Then whose…?" His stance drew her attention to the holster strapped to his belt. Had she ever seen Niall Watson wearing a gun before? His badge, yes. But she'd never seen the erudite professional looking armed and dangerous the way he did tonight. Had he just come from a crime scene? "You wore a tuxedo to work?" Wait. Not his blood. That meant… A stone of dread plummeted into Lucy's stomach. Was that Diana's blood? "Oh, God." Before he could say anything, she spun around and shoved open the door to her apartment. "Diana?" Niall Watson was a doctor. But he wasn't hurt. That meant someone else was. "Diana? Are you here?"

She called out again for some sign that the young woman she'd been searching the city for all day and night had somehow shown up here.

The vise clamped over her wrist again and pulled her back to the door. "Miss McKane."

"Let go of me." She yanked her arm free and charged toward the mess on the couch. "Diana?" She paused a moment to sift through the pile of unraveling yarn and interrupted projects before snatching up the overturned basket and inspecting the insides. Lucy always kept a twenty or two hidden beneath her work. The only other person who knew where she stockpiled for a rainy day was Diana. "She was here. She took the cash," she whispered, her sense of dread growing exponentially.

"So it *was* a robbery?"

She startled at the deep voice beside her. "What? No. I would gladly give her the money."

"Give who the money?"

"Diana?" Lucy tossed the basket onto the couch and took off for the light in the kitchen.

But she hadn't taken two steps before Niall Watson's arm cinched around her waist and pulled her back against his chest. "Miss McKane. There's nothing for you to see here. I need you to come with me."

She gasped at the unexpected contact with a muscled torso and the surprising warmth that seemed to surround her instantly and seep through the layers of coat and clothing she wore. "Nothing? I have to..." For a split second, her fingers tightened their grip around the arm at her waist, needing his strength. She'd had a bad feeling all day. Diana Kozlow hadn't shown up for a long-overdue lunch and gab session. And then that phone call...

If the answer was here—even one she didn't want to be true—Lucy had to see for herself. With a renewed sense of urgency, she pushed the doctor's arm and body heat away and turned. "You need to stop grabbing me, Doctor. I appreciate your concern, but I have to—"

She shoved at his chest, but he released her waist only to seize her by the shoulders. He squeezed enough to give her a little shake and hunched his face down to hers. "Lucy. If you would please listen."

Lucy? Her struggles stilled as she assessed the stern expression stamped on his chiseled features. When had her taciturn neighbor ever addressed her as anything but a polite *Miss McKane*? That couldn't be good. The tight grip on her upper arms and the piercing intensity of those blue eyes looking straight at her weren't any kind of reassurance, either. She curled her fingers into the wrinkled cotton of his shirt and nodded, preparing herself for the news she didn't want to hear. "What's wrong? What's happened? Did you see a young woman here? Is she…" Lucy swallowed hard. "Is she okay?"

He eased his grip and straightened, raking one hand through his short muss of espresso-colored hair as he inhaled a deep breath. But he kept the other hand on her arm as if he suspected she might bolt again. "If you would come with me." He pulled her back into the hallway and closed the door to her condo behind them. "I need to ask you some questions."

Now he wanted to talk? After all those friendly overtures she'd made to her seriously hunky and completely-oblivious-to-a-lady-dropping-a-hint neighbor, tonight of all nights was when he wanted to have a private conversation with her? Somehow she doubted that he'd finally clued in on the crush she had on him. Preparing herself for a worst-case scenario, Lucy planted her feet before blithely following him into his condo. "Just tell me. Did you find a dead body in there? You told me you were a medical examiner during one of our elevator rides together when I first moved in. That's when I told you I was a social worker—that I've seen some pretty awful things, too. But my bodies weren't dead like yours. Just damaged in one way or another." Her mouth was rambling ahead of her brain. "I'm sorry. But you can tell me. Is this a crime scene? Is that why I can't go in there?" She touched the blood on his sleeve again. Although it was dry, its presence was disturbing. "Is this Diana's? Don't feel you have to spare my feelings. I've been sick out of my mind with worry all day. I just need a straight answer about what's happened. I can deal with anything—I'm good at that—as long as I know what I'm facing."

"You can deal with anything?" He angled his head to the side and his eyes narrowed, as if her plaintive assertion baffled him. Then he shook his head. "There is no dead body," he answered starkly. "I don't know who Diana is. This blood is my grandfather's. He was shot yesterday afternoon at my sister's wedding."

"Shot? Oh, my God." Lucy's fingers danced over the ticklish hair of his forearm, wanting to act on her instinct to touch, to comfort, to fix the hurts of the world. "Is he okay? I mean, clearly he isn't. Getting shot is really bad. I'm sorry. Is he going to be all right?" His brusque answers explained the remnants of the James Bond getup, as well as the stains on what had once been a neatly ironed shirt. But what any of that had to do with the break-in or her or possibly Diana, she hadn't a clue. Lucy curled her fingers around the strap of her shoulder bag and retreated a step. "You don't need to worry about my problems. You should be with your family."

"Miss McKane." They were back to that now, hmm? "I'm sorry if the blood upset you—I haven't had time to change since coming home from the hospital." He scraped his palm over the dark stubble dotting his chin and jaw before sliding his fingers over his hair and literally scratching his head. "I can see I haven't explained myself very well. Your sympathy is appreciated but misplaced. My grandfather's condition is serious, but please, before you go off on another tangent, would you come inside? I do have a problem that concerns you specifically." He glanced toward the end of the hallway. "And I don't think we should have that conversation here."

She remembered the retired couple down the hall and nodded. "The Logans. I suppose it would be rude to wake them at this hour."

A man with a wounded grandfather, a gun and a badge, and an inexplicable sense of urgency could take precedence for a few minutes over her suspicions and the futile desperation that might even be unfounded. Lucy hadn't seen Diana Kozlow in months. Perhaps she'd read too much into the telephone message at the office this morning. She was probably chasing ghosts, thinking that Diana had really needed her. Roger Campbell hadn't needed her for anything more than sex and a punching board. The only reason her own mother had needed her was to ensure her own meal ticket. How many times did she have to repeat that codependent mistake?

Inhaling a deep breath, Lucy pulled off her left glove and cap and stuffed them into her pockets, too, as Niall opened the door for her to precede him. "So what concerns me specifically besides a busted front door…" She tried to smooth her staticky curls behind her ears. "Oh, hello."

At this late hour, she was surprised to see another man—a stockier version of Niall Watson, with a peppering of silver in his short dark hair—rising stiffly from a recliner as she stepped into the living room.

She extended her hand because she was that kind of friendly. "I'm Lucy McKane from across the hall. Sorry to visit so late, but Dr. Watson invited me…" The older man angled his body to face her, and she saw the blanket with tiny green and yellow animals draped over his arm. "You have a baby."

"Can't put anything past you," the tall man teased in a hushed voice, in deference to the tiny infant sleeping contentedly against his chest. "Thomas Watson." He easily cradled the child in one arm to shake her hand. "I raised three boys and a girl of my own, so I've had some practice. I'm Niall's father."

"I could tell by the family resemblance. Nice to meet you. You seem to be a natural." Lucy stepped closer to tuck the loose blanket back around the tiny child's head. The newborn's scent was a heady mix of gentle soap and something slightly more medicinal. A tightly guarded longing stirred inside her, and she wanted to brush aside the wisp of dark brown hair that fell across the infant's forehead. She wisely curled her fingers into her palm and smiled instead. "And this is…?"

Niall's crisp voice sounded behind her. "I was hoping you could tell us."

Lucy swiveled her head up to his as he moved in beside her. "I don't understand. Isn't the baby yours?" She glanced at Niall's father. He was older, yes, but by her quick assessment, still a virile man. "My apologies. The baby is yours."

"No, ma'am."

The older man grinned, but Niall looked anything but amused when he reached across her to adjust the blanket she'd tidied a moment earlier. "*I* broke into your apartment, Miss McKane."

"You? To steal twenty dollars? Why on earth would you do that?"

"I wasn't the first intruder. I found a screwdriver that had apparently been used to break into your place." He pulled a tiny gem from his pocket and held it up between his thumb and forefinger, twisting it until she could see the fracture in the clear red glass. "I believe this came off it."

"A screwdriver?" Lucy clutched at her purse strap, the bittersweet joy of seeing the baby momentarily forgotten. Diana *was* in trouble. "A pink one with glitter on the handle?"

He picked up a bag marked with numbers and the scratch of his signature from the coffee table and folded the excess plastic out of the way so she could see the contents inside. "This one."

"Oh, my God." Lucy plucked the screwdriver from his open palm and turned it over in her hand. The room swayed at the instant recognition. Diana hadn't wanted jewelry or dolls for birthdays and Christmas. She'd been a tomboy and tough-kid wannabe from their first meeting. Diana had wanted a basketball and running shoes and a toolbox, although she'd seemed pleased with the bling on this particular set. Lucy blinked away the tears that scratched at her eyes and tilted her face to Niall's. "Where did you get this?"

"Is it yours?"

"Answer my question."

"Answer mine."

"Niall," Thomas gently chided.

A deep, resolute sigh expanded Niall Watson's chest before he propped his hands at his waist again in that vaguely superior stance that emphasized both his height and the width of his shoulders. If it wasn't for his glasses and the spiky muss of his hair that desperately needed a comb, she might have suspected he had an ego to go with all that intellect. "Apparently, someone jimmied the locks on your door several hours before I got home, and I suspect they used that tool to do it. I let myself in when I heard this child crying in distress. I thought, perhaps, you weren't being responsible—"

"With a child?" He thought…that she… Lucy didn't know whether to cry or smack him. "I would never. My job is to protect children."

"I know that." Her burst of defensive anger eased as he continued his account.

"But then I suspected that you might be in some kind of distress yourself. I entered the premises to make sure you were all right." He plucked the screwdriver from her fingers and returned it to the table along with the shattered bead and another bag that appeared to be holding the beginnings of the gray scarf she'd been knitting for a coworker. She could see now that the markings meant he'd labeled them all as evidence. "I found it on your kitchen counter beside the baby. I brought him here since there didn't seem to be anyone else watching him. We've given him food, clean clothes and a bath. Other than a nasty case of diaper rash, he seems to be healthy."

That explained the medicinal smell. "It's a boy?" She turned back to the older man cradling the sleeping infant. "He was in my apartment? All alone?"

"I believe that's what I've been saying." Niall Watson could sound as irritated with her as he wanted. He'd saved this child, and for that, she would be forever grateful.

Lucy pressed her fingers to her mouth to hold back

the tears that wanted to fall. Tears that wouldn't do anyone any good. Diana's cryptic phone message that had sent Lucy on a wild hunt all over Kansas City finally made sense. "That's what she wanted to show me. I had no idea. The baby is what she wanted me to take care of. But why wouldn't she stay, too?"

"What are you talking about, Miss McKane?"

"I have a favor to ask, Lucy. I don't know who else to call. I need to show you something, and I need you to keep it safe."

"Why didn't she tell me?" Lucy whispered. She couldn't help but reach out to stroke her finger across the infant's cheek. His skin was as velvety soft as it looked, and she was instantly in love. "You precious little boy."

"Do you know who is responsible for this child?" Niall asked.

"Possibly." Lifting her gaze to Niall's father, Lucy held out her hands. "May I?"

"Of course."

Lucy sighed with a mixture of longing and regret as the baby's sweet weight filled her arms and settled against her. "He's so tiny. How old do you think he is?"

"I'd say a week. Two, tops," Niall answered from behind her. "Obviously, pediatrics isn't my area of expertise, but I know enough to handle the basics. I still think he needs to see a pediatric specialist to ensure a clean bill of health. Now what can you tell us about his parents?" Niall stepped aside as she circled the coffee table and sat on the edge of his sofa to hold the baby more securely. She heard a huff of what could be resignation a second before the cushion beside her sank with his weight. When she tumbled toward her tall neighbor at her shifting perch, his hands shot out to balance her shoulder and cradle her forearm that held the baby. "Easy. Don't let go of him."

"I couldn't."

Niall's hand remained beneath her arm, making sure of her hold on the infant. His chest pressed against Lucy's shoulder, and for a split second she was overcome by the normalcy of the family she'd never known and would never have. A mother, a father, a child they shared together. The yearning inside her was almost painful.

Blinking rapidly to dispel the impossible image of the brainy doctor cop and her creating a perfect little baby together, Lucy scooted away to break the contact between her and Niall Watson, although she could still feel that crazily addictive warmth he radiated. "What's his name?" she asked, craving the information as much as she needed to put space between her and her errant fantasies.

"He didn't come with an ID," Niall answered. "He didn't come with anything. Not even a fresh diaper. If you could answer at least some of my questions—"

"Son." The older Watson chided the tone in Niall's voice and offered her a smile. "I nicknamed him Tommy. But that's just a family name I was using so we could call him something besides 'little munchkin.' We were hoping you'd be able to fill in the blanks for us. But I take it you're not the mother."

His green eyes were kind, but Lucy still felt the sting of truth. "No. I… I can't have children of my own."

"I'm sorry. You seem like a natural with Tommy, too."

His kind words enabled her to smile back. "Thank you." But a glance up to the man seated beside her indicated that answers were the only thing that was going to soften that empirical focus zeroed in on her. He was this baby's champion, and nothing short of the entire truth was going to satisfy him. "I think... Tommy..." She stroked her fingertip over his tiny lips, and they instinctively moved to latch on, even though he was asleep. "I have no idea who the father is. But I think he belongs to my foster daughter, Diana Kozlow."

Niall's posture relaxed a fraction, although that stern focus remained. "The woman whose name you kept calling out."

Lucy nodded. "Technically, she's my former foster daughter. Diana was with me for six years until she aged out of the system. She's twenty now. We kept in touch for a year or so. But I lost contact with her after that. She changed her number, changed her job. I had no idea she'd gotten pregnant." She nodded toward the screwdriver on the coffee table. "I gave that to her in a tool set one Christmas. I guess she broke into my apartment to leave the baby with me. Probably took the twenty I had stashed in my knitting basket. She called me out of the blue yesterday—said she had some*thing* she wanted to show me. I invited her for lunch today, but she never came. I tried calling the number she used, but the phone went straight to voice mail."

She rocked back and forth, ever so subtly, soothing the infant as he began to stir. "I went to my office to look up her most recent address and phone number to make sure I had it right—and discovered she'd left me a pretty disturbing message on my answering machine there. I've been out looking for her ever since. One of the neighbors at the last address where I knew her to live said Diana had a boyfriend move in with her about six months ago. She never knew his name, so that was a dead end. Shortly after that they moved to Carmody Street, she thought—"

"Carmody?" The elder Watson muttered a curse under his breath. "That's not a good part of town. You didn't go there to look for her by yourself, did you? At the police department, we call that part of town no-man's-land."

"I can believe it." The two men exchanged a grim look. "No one there recognized Diana, and they couldn't tell me the boyfriend's name, either. I wasn't sure where to look after that. How does a young woman just…disappear?" Lucy's thoughts drifted to all the morbid possibilities that had driven her to search for Diana. "Why wouldn't she keep Tommy with her? Why wouldn't she stay at my place with him if she was in trouble?"

"*If* she's the mother," Niall cautioned. "We'd have to blood-type him and run DNA on both mother and son to be certain."

A DNA test couldn't tell Lucy what she already knew in her heart. "He looks like her—the shape of his face, the thick dark hair. What color are his eyes?"

Thomas shrugged. "You know, I don't remem—"

"Brown," Niall answered.

Lucy glanced up when he reached around her to tuck in the tiny fist that had pushed free of the blanket. She didn't mind Niall's unvarnished tone quite so much this time. He'd put his clinical eye for detail to work on doing whatever was best for this baby. "Diana has brown eyes."

Niall's startling blue gaze shifted to hers for a moment before he blinked and rose from the couch. He paced to the kitchen archway before turning to ask, "Did you save that message?"

Lucy nodded.

The two men exchanged a suspicious sort of glance before Thomas picked up a notepad and pen from the table beside the recliner. Niall adjusted his glasses on the bridge of his nose before splaying his fingers at his waist and facing her. "Maybe you'd better tell me more about your friend Diana. And why you thought she might be dead."

Chapter Three

Lucy added another round of quarters to the clothes dryer. "Oops. Sorry, munchkin."

She quickly apologized for the loud mechanical noise and leaned over the infant fastened into the carrier sitting on top of the dryer. But she needn't have worried. Tommy was still asleep, his tiny body swaying slightly with the jiggle of the dryer. She smiled, resisting the urge to kiss one of those round apple cheeks, lest she wake him again. He'd fussed and bellowed for nearly an hour upstairs before she remembered the advice she'd once heard from a coworker about tricks to help stubborn babies fall asleep and got the idea to bring Tommy and all his new clothes and supplies down to the basement laundry room to wash them.

Instead of disturbing him again, she opted to pull a blanket dotted with red, blue and yellow trucks from the basket of baby clothes she'd just unloaded and drape the cotton knit over him, securing him in a warm cocoon. Then she picked up the basket and set it on the neighboring dryer to start folding the rest of the light-colored sleepers and towels and undershirts. She was handling more than one problem here. She'd removed the noisy baby from Niall Watson's apartment so the enigmatic doctor could get some much-needed sleep. Since she had no chair to rock the baby in, she'd found the next best thing down here in the laundry room. And at this time of the morning, before the residents stirred to get ready for church or work, she'd found a quiet place for herself to think without being distracted by hunky neighbors with grabby hands and hard bodies, or caring for the needs of a newborn with too little sleep herself, or worrying about the unanswered calls and cryptic clues surrounding her foster daughter's disappearance.

When the second load of darker clothes was done in twenty minutes or so, she'd take Tommy back up to Niall Watson's apartment and sneak back in without waking him. Then she'd have another hour or two to curl up on his stiff leather couch and try not to notice how much the smell of it reminded her of the man himself. Crushes were terrible things when they were one-sided like this. Niall Watson, ME, was a good catch, according to her mother's standards—not that she credited Alberta McKane for giving her any useful set of values to judge a man by. But he was as dependable as he was curiously aloof, and that was a quality Lucy valued more than several framed degrees or the amount of money a man made. She vowed to be a good friend to her socially awkward neighbor, but she didn't have to torture her dreams with the vivid memory of his body flattened against hers as he pinned her to the wall. If he was a different man he'd have kissed her then. And chances are, she would have responded to that kiss with a purely female instinct.

But Niall Watson wasn't that man. He had a set of

rules he lived by, an order of right and wrong he believed in. He wasn't a smooth talker. He wasn't much
of a talker, period. But, awkward body contact aside, he
treated her with respect. He put Tommy's and his family's needs above anything he and his hormones might
feel. And that made him so much more attractive to
her than anything her mother could have envisioned.

Stress, fatigue, the rhythmic sound of the dryer and
the warmth of the insulated laundry area were beginning to have the same hypnotic effect on Lucy as they
did on Tommy. After several big blinks, her thoughts
drifted and her hands came to rest in the pile of warm
cotton garments. Her chin was dropping toward her
chest when hushed voices entered her dreams. "Down
here."

"Are you sure?"

"If her car's outside, but she's not at her place, then
yes."

"This is a mistake."

"I just have to know—"

"Get out of here."

Lucy snapped her head up at the slam of a heavy
door from somewhere above her. The muffle of words
weren't inside her head. They were as real as the terse,
angry exchange of voices bouncing off the concrete-
block walls outside the laundry room. She touched the
gentle rise and fall of Tommy's small chest, reassuring
herself that he was safe, while she blinked the grogginess from her eyes and reoriented herself to the waking world. "Hello? Is someone there?"

"I know you're here," came a heavily accented voice.
"You can't take what is mine."

Lucy thought she heard a bell. Someone getting off the elevator?

Or on it. "Move. Don't let him see you. Go!"

"Where is she?" the louder voice shouted. "You know what I want."

Lucy whirled around to the vicious argument, wondering if she was still half-asleep since she couldn't make out all the words.

"You stay away from her."

"You mind your own business."

Then she heard a grunt and a gasp plainly enough, before running feet stomped up the stairs.

"Diana?" Had she heard a woman's voice in the middle of all that? Or only dreamed it? Lucy fingered the phone in her jeans pocket. But the sounds of the argument were fading and she didn't want to panic the good doctor upstairs unnecessarily by waking him from a sound sleep.

"You stay away from her."

Oh, no. "Stay away from *me*?" Maybe Niall was already awake and dealing with some kind of trouble that she'd missed. What if someone *had* followed her to their apartment building and her neighbor had come downstairs to confront him? "Niall?"

If he got hurt, it would be her fault for getting him into this mess.

After ensuring that Tommy was still sleeping, Lucy ventured out into the hallway. It was empty now. Nothing but concrete walls and utility lights. Had the two parties she'd overheard arguing split up? The elevator was moving on the higher floors of the building, and whomever she'd heard run up the stairs had exited either out the side entrance to the parking lot or into the building's lobby. "Niall? Is that you? Who was—"

Lucy jumped at the loud thump against the steel door at the top of the stairs. Outside. They'd taken what could only be a fight, judging by the low-voiced curses and rattling door, out to the parking lot. "Niall!"

Lucy charged up the stairs, pulling her key card from her jeans and hurrying out the door to the harsh sounds of a revving engine and tires squealing to find traction along the pavement. She saw the silhouette of a man racing between the cars. "Niall? Hey! Don't hurt him!"

She glanced toward the front entrance as one of the glass doors swung open. Was help coming? Or more trouble? She should call 911. She reached for her phone.

But when she saw the running figure lurch as if some invisible force had jerked him back a step, she sprinted forward to help. "Stop!"

There were two men trading blows out there. One had ambushed the other.

"Lucy!" The warning barely registered as her feet hit the pavement. She glimpsed the man hitting the ground a split second before a pair of headlights flashed on their high beams and blinded her.

Forced to turn away, she stumbled back a step. She thought she heard another car door open. She knew she heard the terrible sound of a transmission grinding too quickly through its gears. The headlights grew bigger, like a nocturnal predator bearing down on her. The lights filled up her vision. The roar of the engine deafened her. The heat of the powerful car distorted the chill of the early February morning.

"Lucy!"

Two arms slammed around her body and lifted her out of harm's way. She hit the hard earth with a jolt and tumbled, rolling two or three times until she wound up flat on her back with Niall Watson's long body pinning her to the ground.

She noted the flash of a silver sports car speeding past, bouncing over the curb into the street and disappearing into the night before the strong thigh pressed between her legs and the muscled chest crushing her breasts and the hot gasps of Niall's deep breaths against her neck even registered. "I knew that car was following me…" Lucy's triumphant words trailed away in a painful gurgle as the pain of that tackle bloomed through her chest. "Oh, man. That hurts."

"Not as much as getting mowed down by that Camaro would have." She flattened her palms against his shoulders and tried to push, but he only rose up onto his elbows on either side of her, leaving their hips locked together. He glared down at her through those dark frames. "What were you thinking? Didn't you see him driving right at you?"

"I thought you were hurt." She sucked in a deeper breath and found more voice as the ache in her lungs eased. "There was a fight outside the laundry room. He knocked the other man down. I thought it was you."

"It wasn't."

"Duh." Her breath returned in shallow gasps. "What are you doing here, anyway?"

"Saving you, apparently."

"You're supposed to be asleep."

"You're supposed to be in my apartment."

Lucy was blatantly aware of cold ground and damp

clothes and the black KCPD T-shirt that left little of that sleekly muscled torso to her imagination now. But Niall flattened himself right back on top of her when another vehicle engine roared to life in the parking lot. She found herself flat on her back a second time, pinned beneath Niall's body as the second car raced past.

Only after it turned into the street and sped away after the silver Camaro did Niall raise his head again. "Do you recognize that vehicle, too?"

Lucy shook her head. She hadn't even gotten a look at it. A fat lot of help she was. As her body warmed in places it shouldn't, Lucy gave him another push. "You can get off me now."

Without even so much as a *sorry for invading your personal space and making your brain short-circuit again*, Niall rolled to his feet and extended a hand to help her stand up beside him. While she brushed at the mud on her knees and bottom, he bent down to pick up her key card and phone and pressed them into her hands. "Are you hurt?"

"No."

Despite her answer, he turned her hands over and inspected the muddy smear on her elbow. "What are you doing out here at this time of the blessed a.m.?"

Lucy plucked away the dead bits of grass that clung to the scruff of his beard and hair. "Are *you* hurt?"

"Lucy," he prompted, dismissing her concern. "Give me an answer."

She pulled away and shrugged, wondering how long she was going to feel that stiff catch in her chest, and how much of it had to do with hitting the ground so hard and how much had to do with learning Niall's shape in a far-too-intimate way. "I heard voices. Someone was fighting on the basement stairs, and they ran out. One of them got on the elevator, maybe. I was half-asleep."

"Where's the baby?"

"Tommy." Her blood chilling at what a doofus she was turning out to be at this whole instant-motherhood thing, Lucy ran back to the side exit. She slid her key card into the lock and pulled the door open.

Niall was right behind her. "I woke up, and you and Tommy were gone." That explained the bare feet and pseudo pajamas he was wearing. "I saw the sacks with all his clothes had disappeared, too. When you weren't in your apartment, either, I came down to look for you. Then I heard the engine outside. For a second I thought—"

"What? That I'd run off and taken the baby?" She hurried down the steps. Niall followed right behind her. "I would never do that. You're just as important to him as I am." The door to the laundry room had closed, and she quickly accessed it with her key card while Niall glanced up at the numbers lighting up on the elevator behind them. But he caught the door and followed her in as she hurried to the baby carrier still rocking on top of the clothes dryer. Her breath rushed out with relief when she saw those sweet brown eyes tracking their movement across the room. "Thank goodness. He's fine. He was being so fussy. I fed him and changed him and still couldn't get him to stop crying, and you said you hadn't slept in forty-eight hours. So I remembered a trick that one of the older women in my office said worked for her kids when they wouldn't sleep. Besides, all these new things need to be washed before he can wear them."

"You left him here alone?"

"I must have dozed off myself until I heard the argument out in the hallway." Lucy unhooked the straps on the carrier and reached for Tommy. "There you are, sweetie. See? He's fine. Wide-awake again, hmm—"

"Wait." Niall's hand on her arm startled her. "Don't touch him."

She glanced up to the narrow-eyed scrutiny behind his glasses. "What's wrong?"

"How long were you gone?"

"I don't know. A few minutes, maybe…" And then she zeroed in on what had put Niall on alert. There was a lipstick mark on Tommy's forehead. Without asking, the scientist beside her captured Lucy's chin and tilted it up to run his thumb over her mouth with a friction that tingled across her lips and made her tremble from head to toe.

Despite her body's traitorous response to his firm touch, it wasn't meant to be a caress. Niall released her and held the tip of his thumb beside the mark on Tommy's forehead. The gloss she wore was rosy pink. The color on Tommy's skin was a tannish coral.

"Oh, my God." She *had* heard a woman's voice earlier. Another woman had been in here when Tommy was alone. That whole fight must have been a distraction—a way to get Lucy to leave while another woman sneaked into the laundry room. She'd kissed the baby while Lucy had been chasing shadows and dodging cars.

"Someone was here," Niall pronounced.

Not someone.

"Diana." Lucy quickly glanced around, realizing what she should have seen when she'd unhooked

Tommy from his carrier. The clean, warm blanket she'd covered him with was missing. "She took the blanket I put over him. She was right here."

And now the young woman was gone.

Again.

Chapter Four

Niall clipped his badge onto the belt of his jeans, debated about leaving his gun locked inside its metal box, then decided to strap it on. If Diana Kozlow was in serious trouble, as Lucy claimed—and the twenty-year-old hadn't simply punked out on the responsibility and expense of caring for a baby—then he'd do well to be prepared for any contingency that could come back to harm Tommy or Lucy.

It wasn't just his civic-minded sense of duty that prompted him to take a proactive role in guarding the security of his building and neighbors—too many unanswered questions surrounding the baby still nagged at him. Before he'd left, Thomas Watson had suggested Niall keep an eye open for further suspicious activity around the building. Certainly, alleged fights and a silver Camaro nearly running down Lucy—either intentionally or as collateral damage in a speedy getaway from the second driver—qualified as suspicious.

He couldn't tell yet if that woman was simply a magnet for trouble or if she was truly embroiled in a legitimate missing-person case. Niall trusted his dad's gut warning him that something felt seriously wrong here as much as he trusted his own assessment of the clues surrounding Tommy, the violation of Lucy's apartment and those two near misses in the parking lot last night. The break-in had been an act of desperation, not planning. The mark of lipstick on Tommy's forehead that didn't match Lucy's dark pink color indicated a kiss. From a guilt-ridden mother reluctant to say goodbye to a baby she couldn't take care of on her own? Or a frightened young woman who saw no other option to keep her son safe than to abandon him to her most trusted friend?

But safe from what? Or whom?

If he hadn't been reliving the nightmare of the shooting at his sister's wedding and woken himself up to clear his head, he wouldn't have discovered Lucy and Tommy missing from his living room. He wouldn't have gone looking for them and seen his pretty neighbor blinded by the car barreling toward her. He wouldn't have known that gut-wrenching sense of helpless inadequacy knowing that someone out there was a step ahead of him, luckier—if not smarter—than he was when it came to taking care of an impulsive woman and an innocent child.

And Niall needed to be able to take care of Lucy and Tommy. He hadn't spotted the shooter soon enough. He hadn't prevented his grandfather from stroking out. And unless a dead body showed up on his autopsy table, there wasn't a damn thing he could do to help his family figure out who had targeted Seamus in the first place. But watching over Lucy and Tommy was something he could do. Helping them find Diana Kozlow and the other answers they needed was the challenge that would keep him busy and his mind occupied. Helping them was the worthwhile difference he *could* make.

Besides, there was something about a tiny baby who quieted at the sound of his voice or the touch of his hand that awakened something so alien inside Niall that he'd almost forgotten the words his mother had once spoken to him as a child. He'd been bewailing going to a new school after moving across Kansas City. Athletic Duff and outgoing Keir had made new friends easily enough. But gangly, bookish Niall, who'd inherited his mother's shy genes, had spent the first few weeks of fourth grade feeling utterly alone. She'd climbed up into the tree house where he'd been hiding out to share a hug and some loving wisdom. *"There are certain people in this world, Niall, that we are destined to have a special connection to. You don't need a lot of friends. Just one or two who understand you. Who'll have your back. Who need you to be their friend, too."*

Perhaps she'd been referring to his brothers and sister sharing that kind of closeness with him. But the very next day, he'd met another new student on the playground, and the two of them had become good friends who'd gone through middle school and high school together. Although they'd taken separate college and career paths, he and Jack Riggins still kept in touch.

The moment he'd picked up Tommy, Niall had felt a similar, irrational connection being made. Tommy liked him. Tommy needed him to be his friend. Whether as a doctor or rescuer or simply as an authoritative presence to quiet his tears, Niall Watson intended to be there for Tommy Kozlow—or whatever the little boy's name turned out to be.

Tommy's real identity was only one of several questions Niall intended to find answers to today. As soon as he checked in with his grandfather at the hospital and reported any medical updates to his family, he wanted to assess Diana Kozlow's fitness as a parent, determine whether the danger Lucy suspected was genuine and track down the missing mother. And, if Diana wouldn't share the father's name, or a birth certificate couldn't be found, Niall planned to work out the legalities between guardianship and what was in the child's best interest and obtain permission to draw some of Tommy's blood to run his DNA to locate the boy's father. Lucy had already put the paperwork into motion to secure temporary foster placement of the baby with her. Her permission would be enough to run Tommy's DNA and give him his real name, so there was that conversation on his agenda today, as well.

That should be plenty to keep him busy until he reported back to work at the lab tonight.

Prepared with a plan for the next several hours, Niall ran a comb through his damp hair and picked up his mug of cold decaf off the dresser before heading out into the living room, where he'd left Lucy and Tommy sleeping a couple hours earlier.

His structured day quickly hit its first glitch when he saw that the lamp beside the sofa was on and his guests were both wide-awake. Niall stopped, his eyes narrowing on the crown of Lucy McKane's dark curls as she leaned over the baby in her lap. Nerve endings in his chest and thighs awakened with a mysterious sense memory, recalling the impression of soft curves pressing against his harder angles during that tussle in the hallway and that tumble across the grass last night. He was equally fascinated by her hands. Royal blue yarn dangled from her fingers as she deftly twisted knots onto the slender pair of knitting needles she worked. The glossy kinks of her hair bobbed against her shoulders and over the curves of the mud-stained sweater she still wore as she played peekaboo with Tommy.

She knit several stitches, then clutched her work to her chest and teased Tommy with an "I see you" that made his little fists pump with delight. The baby gurgled and cooed when she brushed his nose and shook her hair against his fingers. Then he calmed when she went back to knitting and obscured her face again.

Niall studied the interchange twice before Lucy looked up and smiled. "You know, you can stare at the details for so long that you miss the bigger picture."

He hadn't missed a thing. Abandoned baby. A woman who was proving more intriguing to study than she should be, making herself at home on his couch. Apparently, despite his insistence that her apartment wouldn't be safe for her and Tommy until maintenance could come and replace her locks, she'd sneaked inside a second time. "Excuse me?"

Lucy cupped the half-formed cap she'd been knitting over Tommy's head before tying it off and pointing to the wet bar. "Diaper. You don't smell that? Our little friend here has been very busy since I gave him his last bottle. I left the changing pad over there and didn't want to risk moving him in case he made a mess on your nice leather sofa. Your place isn't exactly babyproofed."

Niall glanced at the stockpile of supplies his father had brought over and crossed the room to get the things she needed. "The sofa has no sentimental value. It can be cleaned. You should have called me if you needed help with the baby."

"You were in the shower."

He returned to the couch, nodding toward the basket of knitting supplies she'd retrieved from her apartment. "Longer than I thought, apparently. You went back to your place. After that incident in the laundry room last night, I thought we'd agreed that you'd stay put."

"No. You suggested it. I promised to be careful," she clarified. "Tommy was sound asleep on the pallet we made for him, so I figured it'd be fine to go across the hall to gather up my knitting. I like to keep my hands busy. Especially when there's a lot on my mind." She thanked him for the supplies and set up a changing station beside her before moving Tommy onto the pad and dropping down to her knees in front of the couch. "I didn't want to wake you because, well, I already woke you once, and I could tell you needed to sleep." She turned her face up to his and winked. "You still look tired, if you ask me."

"I didn't." Niall picked up the soiled diaper and carried it to the kitchen trash. "I'm used to keeping odd hours. I'm fine."

"No, you're not," she insisted, strapping a fresh diaper into place. "How can it be with everything you've had to deal with in the past forty-eight hours or so? I imagine your job is pretty stressful, but I'm guessing your weekends don't always include a wedding, your grandfather going into the hospital, and the wacky neighbor lady and a baby taking refuge in your living room."

Wacky? His analysis of Lucy McKane had included terms like *caring, vibrant, sensual.* Although *garrulous, stubborn* and *unpredictable* were certainly apt descriptors, too.

Niall shook his head, puzzled by how easily his thoughts seemed to derail around this woman. Perhaps the shower and shave hadn't revived him as much as he'd hoped and he needed to switch to caffeinated coffee to unfog his brain. The important point here was that she'd taken another unnecessary risk, negating the whole purpose of him insisting she and Tommy take refuge in his apartment. He picked up a new outfit from the laundry she'd folded and carried it to the couch. "What if the intruders had come back?"

"You mean Diana? Then I would have brought her here and helped her, too."

She was making assumptions that couldn't yet be proved. "What if Diana had nothing to do with breaking into your apartment? What if hers wasn't the woman's voice you heard last night?"

"Who else would kiss—"

"What if someone took advantage of her connection to you, borrowed her toolbox and broke in to surrender a baby without any legal hassles?"

"And knew where I hid some extra cash?"

Fine. If Lucy was so certain Tommy was Diana's son, he had a reasonable argument for that, too. "What if the threat that prompted Diana to abandon Tommy in the first place followed her to your apartment? What if those men you heard last night had come back for you? To finish something they'd started? You could have been seriously hurt."

Her fingers stopped. Everything about her seemed to pause for a split second before Lucy shook her head, spilling her hair over the neckline of her sweater. As quickly as she'd frozen, she went right back to changing the baby, lifting Tommy to position the new sleeper beneath his back. "I appreciate your concern. But I was only gone a few minutes—long enough to clean up the cookie dough spoiling in the kitchen and gather up my knitting. If I'd sensed anything was wrong, I would have come straight back. Nothing happened."

"This time." Niall adjusted his glasses, averting both his gaze and the unexpected flare of curiosity about her reaction to the suggestion that she, and not Tommy or Diana, was the one in danger. Was it wrong of him to want to push her to reveal just what had caused her to hesitate like that? And he wondered if she knew she had a long tendril of hair caught in the nubby tweed of her sweater. He could easily reach down and free the strand for her. When he'd knocked her out of the way of that speeding car last night, he'd inadvertently discovered that her hair was as silky as it looked. That the ends were cool to the touch and the length of it was as strongly resilient as the woman herself. His fingers itched to tangle in those curly locks again, to re-create the chance touch and confirm his observations. Niall blinked away the thought. *That* wasn't on the agenda for today. She was changing Tommy's diaper, for pity's sake, not seducing him. "Lucy, I need to know that you're taking this seriously. I believe Tommy was in grave danger yesterday. That means you could be, too. I need you to be able to take care of him so that I can conduct my investigation."

"So that we can conduct *our* investigation," she corrected, as if he had misspoken. Lifting Tommy into her arms, she stood, cradling the infant against her chest and gazing down into his attentive brown eyes. "I appreciate more than you know that you and your father promised to help me find Diana and reunite her with her son. I'm grateful that you offered to let us stay with you until maintenance can replace the locks on my door. I wouldn't have felt safe there."

"You weren't. You still aren't."

She looked up at him then. "I'm grateful that you probably saved me from my own impulsiveness last night. But don't think for one moment that I don't know how serious this situation is. If Tommy and I are in danger, then Diana must be facing something worse. If she has anything to do with those men I heard arguing last night, then I know she is. I know her better than anyone. At least, I used to. You need my help."

"And if I don't accept it, you'll go off searching the city for her on your own again, won't you."

Lucy's expression brightened with a wry smile. "Now *that* is an accurate conclusion, Dr. Watson."

Not understanding the giggle that followed, Niall simply nodded, conceding the wisdom of having someone with inside information on Diana Kozlow to guide his investigation so he could either confirm or rule out Lucy's belief that Tommy was her foster daughter's baby. It pleased him, too, to know that Lucy would have temporary custody of Tommy as a foster parent, keeping the little boy close by so that Niall could keep watch over him, too. "So we agree to work as a team. For Tommy's sake."

"For Tommy's sake." She took a step closer, and Niall inhaled the scents of baby powder and something slightly more exotic that didn't have anything to do with the infant she was pushing into his arms. "Since I've convinced you that we're on the same side now, would you feel comfortable watching him for about ten minutes? That's all the time I'll need to freshen up and change so we're ready to go." Her fingers caught for a moment between Tommy and the placket of his shirt, and even through the pressed cotton, Niall's stomach muscles clenched at the imprint of her knuckles brushing against his skin. But she pulled away to drape a burp rag over his shoulder, apparently unaware of his physiological reactions to her touch and scent. "You still want to drive us to my office to pick up a bassinet and some other supplies?" she asked, gathering up her boots and purse and sweater coat.

"*I'm* the one with a car seat, so yes, I'm driving." Niall shook off his weary brain's inability to focus and shifted Tommy to one arm, catching the door as she stepped into the hallway. "I want to listen to that message from your foster daughter, too, before I bring you back here." He entered her living room right behind her, frowning at how easy it had been for her to push open the damaged door. He plowed into her before realizing she had stopped. "What are you doing?"

Her hands went straight to Tommy, even as she stumbled back a step. "What are *you* doing?" she asked. She released her grip once she seemed assured that there was no chance of him dropping the baby.

Niall looked over the top of her head to scan the empty, seemingly undisturbed living room. "I want to check your apartment before allowing you to remain here for any length of time on your own."

She nodded her understanding of his intention and crossed to a lamp to flip it on and fill the room with light. She opened the powder-room door so he could see it was clear, as well. "Your dad said we have to wait twenty-four hours to file an official missing-person case on Diana with KCPD. I'm glad you both agreed that we could start looking for answers sooner."

He followed her to the kitchen and saw that, other than the dishes she'd washed, it, too, showed no signs of the intruder returning. "Tommy needs his mother. If we can locate her and reunite them—"

"And make sure she's okay—"

"—and ensure she's competent enough and able to care for him—"

"Competent?" Lucy planted her feet, and Niall nearly knocked her flying again. But she put up a hand with a huff of exasperation, and it was Niall who retreated a step this time. "Diana would never abandon Tommy unless something was terribly wrong and she thought it was for the best. People like her and me, we have issues about family. When you've never had one, once you get one...you protect it with everything you have in you. I have to believe that, whatever's wrong, she left Tommy here in order to protect him."

"Then why come back for him? If that was her in the laundry room last night."

"Her instinct may be to protect him, but giving up the family you love, especially your brand-new child... I can't imagine how hard that would be. I don't know if I could be strong enough to say goodbye to this little one." Lucy reached out to stroke Tommy's hair as if she'd already convinced herself that Tommy was her family now. A conclusion founded purely on emotions, no doubt.

Niall—and the law in the state of Missouri—required more incontrovertible proof. "You told Dad your mother was still alive when he was taking down your personal history, asking about other people Diana might have contacted. You have family."

"Trust me, I don't. Family are people who love you unconditionally. People you can trust and rely on. The man who sired me left before I was ever born, and my mother and I have been estranged since I emancipated myself at seventeen. She's not a part of my life anymore. She never will be again."

"What happened?"

Lucy curled her fingers into her hand and turned down the hallway. "Any number of things from not always having a place to live to the revolving door of men she *did* try to make a home with. But my breaking point was when we had a difference of opinion about my boyfriend." Although she laughed, Niall was certain there was no humor in that wry sound. "It's not what you think. I wasn't some kind of teenage rebel wanting to date a bad boy. In fact, she did everything she could to encourage me to keep the guy I was trying to get away from."

"Get away from?" Niall wondered at the fist of suspicion that hit him as squarely as discovering a clue on his autopsy table. "Why? What did he do to you?"

When she faced him this time, her eyes had dulled to a mossy shade of green. "Funny. My mother was more upset about what I'd done to him." Niall waited for her to elaborate. Lucy didn't disappoint. "Roger was Falls City's golden boy—you know how it is in a small town—the high school's star quarterback, Daddy runs the manufacturing plant that employs most of the town. But Roger and I weren't a good fit."

"How so?"

"No question is too personal for you, is it?" Her typically direct gaze dropped to the middle button of his shirt. Instead of giving an immediate answer, Lucy pulled a towel from the linen closet and hugged it to her chest before turning and tilting her gaze back up to his. "All that mattered to my mother was that Roger was rich. He was going to take over the family business one day. And if he was interested in me, then no matter how awful that relationship was I needed to suck it up and…" She paused midsentence to lean in and press a kiss to Tommy's temple as the baby dozed in his arms. Niall felt that wistful caress as though her mouth had made the connection against his own skin. Before he could question his empathetic response, Lucy shook her head and headed into the bathroom to set the towel on the edge of the sink. "I realized I was just a tool for her. It was easier than I expected to leave her and move to Kansas City. I've been on my own ever since. With the exception of Diana, of course. There's no blood between us, but she's family more than my mother ever was."

Niall considered the vehemence of her statement, detecting not one trace of melancholy or regret as he followed her into the small room. "And Roger?"

Her slender shoulders sagged briefly before she

straightened. "Testified against him. Sent him to prison instead of college."

"For what?"

Her eyes met his in the mirror. "No more questions right now, okay?"

Niall needed a last name. He intended to follow up on this Roger lowlife and decide if he had anything to do with Tommy's abandonment—or even if he could be the child's father. But he'd follow up on a different tack until Lucy opened up again. "I'd give anything to see my mother again."

"I have a feeling you were raised very differently than I was. Your father is funny and kind, and I believe he truly cares about Tommy and Diana, and maybe even me. The way he told me all about your brothers and sister and his dad?" She turned, sitting her hip back on the counter of the sink. She was smiling again, and for some reason, seeing the soft curve of her lips seemed to take some of the edge off the concern that wasn't entirely professional. "I could tell that Thomas is really proud of each of you. And clearly, he loves you and supports you. It's not every son or daughter who has a parent who drops everything in the middle of the night to do some emergency shopping for them. Even when you're a grown-up. You're lucky."

Niall concurred. "I know."

A genuine laugh echoed off the tile walls. "You are one of a kind, Doctor. You see everything in black-and-white, don't you? Sometimes I envy your ability to ignore your emotions."

Funny, he'd been thinking he'd better understand his reactions to her and that mysterious Roger devil he'd never met if he could turn off the emotional responses she seemed to evoke in him and take the time to analyze whether it was fatigue, the sense of duty he was raised with—or the fact he hadn't interacted this closely with a woman on a personal basis since some time back in med school—that was clouding his perceptions.

Lucy curled her finger into Tommy's tiny hand and tucked it in beside Niall's arm. "I'm sorry about your mother. If a man like your dad loved her, I'm sure she was someone special."

"She was."

"Diana never met my mother. I wouldn't let Alberta McKane get close to anyone I cared about. The woman is toxic." A chilly palm print marked Niall's shoulder as she pushed him out the door into the hallway. "Now go. I still need ten minutes."

Lucy was dressed in jeans and a Kansas City Royals sweatshirt and was ready to go in nine. Since she was motivated to work and Tommy was content to watch them do so, it made sense to set aside his curiosity about Lucy McKane's past and focus on the very present problem of locating Diana Kozlow and identifying Tommy's birth parents and possibly the man who had nearly run down Lucy with his fancy car.

Niall loaded a bassinet and stroller into the back of his SUV while Lucy packed a new diaper bag with items they'd picked up en route to her office at Family Services. They stopped to feed Tommy four more ounces of formula before he fell asleep on Lucy's shoulder. Only then did the dark-haired woman with the riot of silky curls tumbling over her shoulders sit down at the pod of four desks surrounding a power pole and play the messages on her answering machine.

After the first beep, a man's voice, possibly slurred by alcohol, came on the line. *"Hey, Luce, it's me. I know I screwed up. I need to see you, sweet thing. I just want to apologize. Make things right between us. Please don't—"*

Lucy's cheeks reddened and she punched the button, cutting off the rest of the drawling message. "Ignore him."

"Is that a client?"

He wondered if she would ever tell him a lie to escape answering one of his questions. "Roger Campbell. High school ex. Somehow he's gotten my work number. I guess it's not tricky. We're a state institution listed in the phone book. He must have asked the main desk to transfer his call to my extension."

"Could he have your personal information, too? Does he know where you live? If you testified against him—"

She shook off his questions and pulled up the next message on the machine. Not a lie. But not an answer, either. "Here's the recording I want you to listen to."

"Lucy? It's Diana. I won't be able to make it for lunch. I know that doesn't makes sense after calling you yesterday when I hadn't called you at all for a while and I changed my number and... I'm sorry. I have so much to tell you, but...there's really no time right now." The younger woman's voice was already hurried and breathless, but now it dropped to such a soft whisper that Niall sat on the edge of the desk and leaned in to hear it over the muted mechanical noises grinding in the background. *"Something's come up and I have to*

*take care of it. I thought I could handle it myself, but...
I have a favor to ask, and I don't know who else to call.
I need to give you something, and I need you to keep it
safe while I..."* There was a sniffle and a hushed gasp.
Diana was crying. Niall looked across the desk to discover Lucy's eyes tearing up, as well. *"We're family,
right? I need you to have my back even though I don't
deserve it. I really made a mess this time. But I can fix
it... I have to fix it..."*

There was another sob, and Lucy's fingers began
a slow massage up and down Tommy's back. A quick
gasp ended the weeping on the answering machine.
The muffled shout of someone calling through a door
or wall triggered the sound of quick footsteps. *"I have
to go. I'll get there as soon as I can, but I can't stay.
I'll explain everything when there's more time. You're
the only one I can count on. Please."* Then, in a louder
voice, Diana added, *"I'm here. Yes, I'm alone. Who
would I be talking to? Just hold your—"*

He heard a muffled commotion at the end of the message, as if Diana had been hiding the phone in her purse
or pocket before she finished disconnecting the call.
Even with Niall's limited imagination, it was impossible to miss the distinct sounds of the young woman's
distress.

Niall had never seen the stoic expression lining Lucy's
face before as she pressed a button to save the message.
"I waited at my apartment for her to bring me this mysterious *thing*, and when she didn't show up, I went looking for her. Of course, I didn't know where to go. I went
to the hair salon where she used to work, but they said
she hadn't been there in ages. I tried her old apartment.

The boyfriend I knew said she'd moved out months earlier. Then I went to the place on Carmody Street. I hit a dead end. How does a twenty-year-old drop out of sight like that?"

"And you tried the cell phone number she called you from? You said her voice mail was completely full?"

Lucy nodded. "I'm right to be worried, aren't I? Tommy is the *something* she wanted me to keep safe. And it sounded to me as if she didn't want anyone on her end of the conversation to listen in." When Lucy rolled the chair away from her desk and stood, Niall did the same. "I didn't recognize the other voice, but it sounded like a man, don't you think? I couldn't make out what he was saying, though. Just like that argument last night."

"Because the man wasn't speaking English." Niall had been listening to more than just the recorded words. "Does she know a foreign language? Would she have understood the man?"

"She took Spanish in high school. That wasn't Spanish. I know enough of that to at least identify it."

It would require a bit of research, but Niall was thinking the words had been something more Russian or Germanic. They'd been angry words. And Diana Kozlow had definitely been afraid. Even though he expected it to be archived, he wanted to read through Diana's Family Services file to see if there was any friend or reference or job connection that might link her to a man with a foreign accent.

After staring at him expectantly for a few moments, Lucy swiped away her tears and made efficient work of strapping Tommy into his carrier and covering him with a blanket. She replaced the cap on his bottle and folded the burp rag to tuck into the diaper bag. "What are you thinking, Niall?"

Although Diana had been vague in her request and had never mentioned a baby or Tommy's real name, he could see that Lucy believed the younger woman and this child had been in terrible danger. For the moment, Niall agreed. Certainly, Carmody Street was no place for a young woman with a baby to take refuge. He reached out and stopped Lucy's hand from zipping the bag shut. "You can't go back to the apartment by yourself until we know more." And he damn sure didn't want her there by herself until he'd run a background check on Roger Campbell. "I need to analyze that recording at the crime lab. I have a friend who's a sound engineer there who owes me a favor. I'll call him, and we'll go there after the hospital."

Her gaze darted up to meet his, and he felt her skin warming beneath his touch before she turned her hand to squeeze his fingers then pull away to finish packing. "But we've already been too much of an imposition. You need to go by Saint Luke's to visit your grandfather and spend time with your family. I've already kept you from them longer than you planned this morning. I can grab the car seat and call a cab so you don't even have to drive us. Tommy and I will be fine—as long as you don't mind us staying in your apartment. Maintenance said there was a chance they could get someone to see to my locks today."

"And they also said it could be Monday morning." No. Tommy needed Dr. Niall Watson of the KCPD crime lab to be his friend right now. And no matter how independent she claimed to be, Lucy needed a friend, too. Right now that friend was going to be him. Niall shrugged into his black KCPD jacket and picked up the sweater coat she'd draped over the back of her chair. "I work quickly and methodically, Lucy. I will find the answers you and Tommy need. But I can't do that when I'm not able to focus. And having half the city between you and me when we don't know what all this means or if you and Tommy are in any kind of danger—"

"Are you saying I'm a distraction?"

Nothing but. Confused about whether that was some type of flirtatious remark or whether she was simply seeking clarification, Niall chose not to answer. Instead, he handed her the sweater and picked up Tommy in his carrier. "Get his things and let's go."

Chapter Five

"I'm so sorry to hear about your foster daughter. If Niall says he'll find her, he will. I've never known that boy not to solve a puzzle. Don't give up hope."

"I won't." Lucy tried to imagine how different her life might have been if she'd had Millie Leighter for a grandmother or a sweet spinster aunt or even just a friend growing up in Falls City. With Tommy charmingly blowing bubbles and taking an instant liking to the plump silver-haired woman, too, Lucy had spent the last hour in the fifth-floor lobby waiting area at Saint Luke's Hospital getting to know the fellow knitter along with a little Watson family history.

Millie had been hired by Thomas Watson when Niall had barely been a teenager, after the murder of Mary Watson. Seamus had come to live with the family then, too, to help give the stunned, grieving children and their father a sense of normalcy and security. By turns touched and then genuinely amused, Lucy listened to Millie's stories about Duff's penchant for making trips to the emergency room, Niall's awkward shyness, Keir's vivid imagination and Olivia's ability to keep the brothers who were twice her size in line. But all the while

Lucy kept remembering flashes of her own childhood and teen years, when her mother had sent her out to beg for coins so they could buy dinner. Or later, when her mother would send her to the park to play to keep her away from the trailer they sometimes lived in while Alberta slept with the crooked local sheriff to stave off getting arrested for shoplifting. Millie's humorous rendition of the New Year's celebration when Seamus had reheated a bunch of leftover pizza and she'd had to come home from her vacation to take care of an entire family stuck in the bathroom with food poisoning made Lucy laugh at the miserable story. But she couldn't help but feel the sting of useless jealousy.

She had no such loving anecdotes to share about growing up, no dear friend she'd been able to call when she really needed someone. She'd gotten herself to the hospital that night Roger Campbell had beaten her so badly. And the only reason her mother had come to visit her after the emergency surgery that had nearly gutted her was to advise her to accept Roger's apology and take him back.

It was almost impossible for her to imagine being part of a family as close and supportive as Niall's, despite the tragedies the Watsons had faced. But she could very well imagine her being a friend to a generous woman like Millie Leighter.

"Oh, my. Little Tommy's dropped off again." Millie glanced up as the elevator dinged across from the carpeted waiting area. An orderly rolled a noisy cart of lunch trays into the hallway, trading a greeting with the clerk at the floor's main desk. "I'm surprised all this hustle and bustle hasn't kept him awake."

Lucy smiled at the tiny bundle of baby nestled against Millie's chest. "Are you getting tired of holding him?"

"Not on your life."

"He's content. I'm sure he enjoyed your stories as much as I did."

Millie's cheeks warmed with a blush. "Pish-posh. You're a dear for letting me rattle on so."

"It fills the time while we're waiting to hear about Seamus. I know I can talk ninety miles a minute when I'm nervous or worried about something."

"I don't believe that." The older woman smiled. "You're trapped here with me because Niall didn't leave you a way to get home. But I thank you for listening." Millie's smile faded. "I live in a house with police officers, and I know their work is dangerous. I've been through a lot with them—kept the ship running through good times and tough ones, so to speak. But I've never been in the middle of a shooting myself, and I'm not handling this very well. I'll never forget the awful sound of all those guns firing, and the screams, and…watching Seamus crumple to the floor like that. There was so much blood. I thought… I was certain…"

Lucy reached across the gap between their chairs to comfort the other woman. "I can't imagine what it must have been like to be there."

Millie sniffled away the tears that threatened to spill over. She patted Lucy's hand before pulling up the cotton blanket Tommy was swaddled in to shield his face from the hospital's bright lights. "New life like this is always the best antidote for a horrific experience like that. And so is friendly conversation. Now why don't you tell me something about you. What were you like as a little girl?"

Not Lucy's favorite topic of conversation. She sat back in the cushioned chair, running through the short list of memories she was willing to share. "Well… I had a next-door neighbor who taught me how to knit when I was in the fourth grade. I made everybody I knew a pot holder for Christmas that year. They got scarves the year after that."

"And now you're creating intricate patterns like those beautiful socks you're wearing. The curved needles give me fits. I invariably drop a stitch. If you have any hints—" A door opened down the hallway and Lucy turned as the older woman straightened in her seat to look across the carpeted waiting area. "There are Thomas and the boys. I wonder if they have any news."

Duff came out of the room first. "That guy disappeared like a freakin' magician. One minute I'm running after him on the roof, and then poof—he jumps onto the next building and he's gone."

Keir Watson followed. "He probably had help to make his getaway."

Lucy sat up straighter when Niall appeared. The three brothers gathered in the hallway, close enough for her to eavesdrop on their conversation. "Then I'm guessing he's not a crazy. Most shooters like that work solo. They're expecting notoriety after the fact and don't care if they get caught or not. I've got a couple of guys at the lab combing social media to see if there's any kind of suicide note or manifesto posted. This guy had a purpose for being there."

"To take down Grandpa?" Keir asked.

Duff swore under his breath. "To take down some-one. Either he's a lousy shot and Grandpa is collateral damage—"

"Or he hit exactly who he was aiming for," Niall concluded.

Thomas Watson entered the hallway after his sons. "And the man with the best shot at telling us why he was targeted can't talk."

The raised male voices were instantly shushed by a middle-aged woman sporting green scrubs and a honey-brown ponytail. She shut the door behind her and moved past them, speaking as if she expected the four men to follow her. "I thought the doctor made it very clear, Mr. Watson. No more than two visitors in the room at the same time. And only for a few minutes. And I find you all in there grilling him for information? You'll tire your father out."

Thomas lengthened his rolling stride to catch up to the nurse's quick steps. "But he wants to see us. We have decisions to make about his care, and I want his input."

"Input?" The nurse stopped in the waiting area, un-fazed by the circle of Watson men towering around her. "You asked him one question about hiring me, then went right back to your investigation. Seamus can't speak, and having him squeeze your hand so often to indicate yes and no is taxing on his fine-motor muscles and the neural transmitters he needs to slowly learn how to master all over again. You saw how agitated he was."

"We were reassuring him that we're staying on top of KCPD's investigation into his getting shot," Thomas explained. "He's a retired cop. He needs to hear that."

The nurse seemed unimpressed by his argument. "He needs to rest."

Millie stood with the baby. "Is Seamus all right?"

Thomas propped his hands at his waist, echoing the stance Lucy had seen Niall use so many times. "I think *frustrated* is the word for it, Millie. Clearly, his ideas and stubbornness are intact, but he's struggling to communicate what he means."

The nurse, whose name badge read Jane Boyle, RN, tilted her face up to admonish Thomas. "Small steps, Mr. Watson. Your father needs to take small steps if he's going to recover fully. And if you intend to hire me, then we'll follow the doctor's orders and do exactly as I say with my patient. And that means no interrogations."

Niall's older brother, Duff, crossed his massive arms beside their father. "We haven't signed on the dotted line yet, lady."

Millie's voice sounded much older than it had just a few moments earlier. "You're hiring someone to take care of Seamus when he comes home?"

Thomas nodded. "Dr. Koelus said Dad needs round-the-clock care for a couple of weeks and physical therapy for some time beyond that. He recommended Ms. Boyle here. She's a private nurse with PT experience. But we're trying to decide if she and Seamus are compatible. Hell, we're trying to decide if she and I are compatible. If she's staying at the house…"

Millie's blue gaze darted over to Lucy, and she turned her head to whisper, "I think Tommy needs to be changed. Do you mind if I take him to the ladies' room?"

"Of course not. Do you want me to take him?"

"Don't be silly, dear. I can manage."

"Thank…you?" Although her nose hadn't detected any telltale odor, Lucy deferred to the older woman's experience. But when she handed her the diaper bag, Lucy read something else in Millie's eyes before she scurried away down the corridor. Of all the family meetings she'd imagined being a part of, they'd never included taking any member for granted. Perhaps worry and fatigue had clouded Niall's keen powers of observation. Or maybe it was a guy thing that all four men were oblivious to what was so painfully clear to Lucy.

Before Lucy could mention Millie's distress, Jane Boyle dismissed herself from the conversation. "I select my assignments very carefully, Mr. Watson. If I don't feel good about the patient's home environment, then I don't take the job."

"Home environment?" Thomas pointed a finger at the nurse. "Are you questioning my—"

"I'll be in Dr. Koelus's office for another ten minutes if you want to continue the interview. Then I'll be looking for my next potential assignment."

The younger brother, Keir, was a shorter, twenty-twenty version of Niall. He eased a low whistle between his teeth as the nurse brushed past him to turn the corner into the crossing hallway leading to the doctor's office. "You get a load of that lady? She's full of herself, isn't she?"

Duff needed a shave and something to take the edge off the wary tension surrounding him. "The fact that she didn't succumb to your questionable charm is the only thing she's got going for her."

"Hey, I get along great with older women. Isn't that

right, Millie? Millie?" Keir turned to discover Lucy's new friend had disappeared. "Where did she go?"

"Is Tommy all right?" Niall asked, noting the baby's absence.

Lucy tilted her chin to see concerned looks on the faces of all four men. But it was Niall's probing gaze she answered. "The baby is fine. None of you have any clue to what just happened, do you? Millie cares about Seamus—she thinks of your family as her own."

Keir's blue eyes narrowed. "She *is* part of the family."

Lucy shrugged. "She might even have extra feelings for your grandfather."

"Extra?" Niall adjusted his glasses on the bridge of his nose, demanding clarification.

"I think she's sweet on him. Or whatever it is that a woman in her seventies feels for an eighty-year-old man."

Duff scrubbed his fingers over the stubble of his beard. "She's got the hots for Grandpa?"

Thomas silenced him with a look and urged Lucy to continue.

"She certainly cares about him." Lucy gestured down the main hall to the room where Seamus Watson lay just a few doors away. "She hasn't even been allowed in to see him yet because, strictly speaking, she's not a relative."

"Of course she's family." Thomas shook his head as if her statement didn't make sense. "The two of them have lived in the same house for twenty years. I've been so preoccupied with Dad, convincing Olivia and Gabe to take some sort of honeymoon, and trying to make sense of the whole damn shooting—"

"You're not in this alone, Dad. We all dropped the ball." Niall reached over to squeeze his father's shoulder. But he was looking to Lucy for an answer. "How do we make it right?"

Lucy wasn't sure it was her place to interfere, but she was starting to get used to explaining people and emotions to her intellectual neighbor. "She's always taken care of all of you, right? I think she's hurt because you're hiring someone else to do her job."

Thomas muttered a rueful apology under his breath. "Ms. Boyle is a registered nurse. She'll be Dad's caretaker and physical therapist. I don't expect her to do anything else. And I'm certainly not kicking Millie out of the house."

"Don't tell me. Tell her. Let her know she's welcome, that she's important to each of you, that you still need her…even if it is just to cook and clean, or to spell the nurse when she needs a break. And she probably wants to be close to Seamus. She's feeling like there's nothing she can do to help right now."

Duff swore under his breath. "I can relate to that."

Thomas agreed. "We all can."

Lucy startled when Keir leaned over to kiss her cheek before thumping Niall's arm and leaving the carpeted waiting area. "Thank you. You know, I like that Niall's finally got a real live girlfriend."

"Oh, I'm not—"

"Excuse me?" Niall frowned at his brother's teasing assertion.

Keir ignored both protests and headed down the hallway. "I was beginning to think Dr. Frankenstein was going to have to build one in that lab of his."

"Where are you going?" Thomas asked.

"To find Millie. I'll take her to lunch and make amends, while you and Duff and that battle-ax Boyle make arrangements to take Grandpa home and get him set up." He turned, backing down the hallway without missing a step. "You *are* hiring her, right? I mean, who else is going to put up with his guff? She stood up to all of us, didn't she? Not an easy task, is it, Luce? You said what we needed to hear."

"I was just pointing out—" Keir winked at Lucy and then turned, including her in that sideways compliment before planting himself outside the ladies' restroom.

"You need to learn to keep your mouth shut, Lucy Claire McKane. No man on this planet likes a woman who doesn't know when to zip it. Now you go right back to the Campbells' house and apologize to Roger."

"But Mama, he slapped me."

"Well, he wouldn't if you ever learned to stop talkin' when it's not your business. How he treats his own dog isn't your affair. And put on them tight jeans I got you before you go back to see him. Those curves will help him see how sorry he is for mistreatin' ya. He's a Campbell—the best ticket out of this two-bit town we're ever gonna get."

Lucy squeezed her eyes shut against the bile rising in her gullet at the remembered incident. She'd never learned to keep her opinions to herself. And while, ide-alistically, she never regretted standing up for someone in need, she had learned to regret speaking those opin-ions without thinking through the consequences first.

Dropping her head, Lucy crossed back to the chair where she'd sat to go through her purse, ostensibly looking for something to busy her hands with until she could bury the painful flashback in her memories and concentrate on the present again—and how best to apologize to the Watsons for butting into their family business when they already had plenty on their plate to worry about.

With some sort of tacit agreement reached, Duff and Thomas followed Nurse Boyle around the corner to Dr. Koelus's office while Keir called someone on his cell phone and paced back and forth at the far end of the hall. Lucy pulled a tube of lip balm from her cosmetic bag and ran it around her mouth before she realized Niall was still standing behind her shoulder, staring down at her. She recognized that look, as though she was a specimen under a microscope he wanted to understand.

She dropped the lip balm back into her purse and turned, chin tipped up to meet his studious gaze. "What?" she asked, hearing a defensive edge to her tone she instantly wished she could take back. That only made him curious to ask more questions.

"You're avoiding me. Did Keir embarrass you with the girlfriend comment? He's a relentless teaser."

Those blue eyes were perfectly serious. Bless his stoic heart. The man could earn a medical degree and help solve crimes for the police department, but he still had no clue about the crush she'd had on him since their first meeting in the laundry room. Keir might have tuned in to her interest in his older brother, but she wasn't about to explain that attraction to Niall and risk the alliance they'd made for Tommy's and Diana's sakes. She also wasn't about to embarrass herself with any more details about her past than she'd shared with him earlier, either. "Don't worry. I know you and I are just friends. I hope I didn't overstep the boundaries of our agreement by butting in to your personal family business. Perhaps I didn't choose the best time to mention my suspicions about Millie."

He nodded, although what Niall was agreeing to, she couldn't be sure. "Keir was right about one thing. You have a real talent for reading people. You understand the subtleties of emotion in a way I never will."

"That's not true. I know you rely on that brain of yours, but you have good instincts, too." Lucy tucked a stray curl behind her ear and smiled up at him. "You knew where to find me last night when I needed you. And look at the bond between you and Tommy. You know when he needs you, too. I think he's already forming an emotional attachment to you. He senses you care about him."

Niall's gaze followed the movement of her hand. And then he surprised her by capturing one of the strands of hair that had curled beneath the neckline of her sweatshirt between two fingers and freeing it. She tried to dismiss the way he held on to the curl, arranging it just so behind her shoulder. It was probably just a scientist's impulse to have everything in a neat and tidy order, but her pulse was having other ideas. "I'm a calm presence, that's all. I'm guessing he's had a lot of upheaval in his young life."

Upheaval, yes. She could relate. With Lucy's pulse leaping at his curiously intimate touch, her words held double meaning. "Some people find security in that sort of quiet confidence."

"I hope he knows one day what a champion you are for him." As he pulled away, Niall paused, brushing away the imaginary mark his brother's lips had left on her cheek.

If the tangle of his fingers in her hair hadn't been unsettling enough, the warm stroke of his thumb across her cool skin made her remember that pragmatic touch in front of the clothes dryer last night, and she shivered. Her words came out in an embarrassingly breathy stumble. "You are, too. A champion, I mean."

Niall's fingers splayed along the line of her jaw, his thumb lingering against the apple of her cheek. When his eyes narrowed behind his glasses and the distance between their heights disappeared, Lucy caught her breath in a gasp that was pure anticipation.

Lucy's awareness of the world around her—the bustle of hospital workers, the constant beeps and whirrs of medical equipment, and the medicinal smells wafting through the chilly air—shrank to the subtle pressure of Niall's warm mouth curving over hers. Her palm found a button at the middle of his shirt and settled there, balancing her as she tipped her head back to move her lips beneath his. They shared a quiet, deep kiss that heated Lucy's blood all the way down to her toes.

She wasn't sure when her heels left the floor or when her fingers curled into the crisp cotton of his shirt, or even when her tongue boldly reached out to touch his. But Lucy was blatantly aware of her world shifting on its axis, of a two-year-old fantasy coming to life—of something stirring inside her that felt as dangerous as it was desirable. Niall Watson was kissing her. It was sweet and patient and thorough and perfect, made all the more sexy by how clueless he was of his masculine appeal. His mouth was an irresistible combination of tender purpose and firm demand. And that crazy heat he exuded that drew her like a moth to a flame—

An abrupt chill filled the air around her when Niall pulled his mouth from hers. His chest expanded against her hand as he drew in a deep breath and slowly exhaled. But his blue eyes remained locked on hers. "Was that all right? Your pupils dilated. Did I misread the signal you were sending? Or did I just interpret it the way I wanted to?"

"The signal? No. You read me just fine." Lucy pulled away from the tempting warmth radiating through the Oxford cloth she'd crinkled beneath her hand. She wished she wasn't blocked by the chair behind her or she'd put some serious distance between them while she gathered her wits. *Did I misread the signal?* "Was that an experiment to test your people-reading skills?"

"An experiment?" He shook his head. "I wanted to thank you. Millie means a lot to me—to all of us."

"Oh. Of course. Glad I could help." Lucy managed a smile, salvaging some pride at the knowledge that her first, and most likely only, kiss with Niall Watson hadn't been in the name of science. Still, that tender exploration wasn't any admission of a mutual attraction. He'd intended to express his gratitude while she'd taken another step toward falling in love with the man. He probably thought her traitorous pupils and the goose bumps that prickled beneath the warm fingers still resting against her neck were some sort of involuntary response to the cold, filtered air inside the hospital. "I kind of specialize in creating healthy family relationships. It's the least I could do after all you're doing to help Tommy and Diana."

"Lucy—"

He opened his handsome mouth to say something more, but Thomas Watson appeared around the corner and called for his son to join them. "Niall. I'd like your two cents on this, too. Sorry. Am I interrupting?"

Lucy sidled away the moment Niall turned to his father's bemused smile. "What do you need, Dad?"

"I thought you'd have a better idea of where we can fit all of Dad's medical equipment. There's more room in the guest suite, but if we have to accommodate Ms. Boyle for a few weeks, then she'll want a private bathroom—"

"You'd better go." Lucy gave Niall a nudge toward his father. "It's important."

He glanced over the jut of his shoulder at her. "So is this. I think there's been some kind of misunderstanding between us."

"Not at all. You said thank you, and I said you're welcome." They were friends, allies—and she was grateful for that. But a few minutes apart would allow her to clear her head of any of the misguided fantasies that were still firing through her imagination. "Looks like we might be at the hospital a little longer. Could I borrow your keys and get my knitting bag out of your car? It'll help me pass the time. Tommy will be fine with Millie until I get back."

After a momentary pause, he reached into the pocket of his jeans and handed them over. "Straight there and back, all right? If you overhear any arguments, call me before you go investigate on your own."

"I won't be gone more than ten minutes. Then I'll come back and spell Millie with the baby."

"Ten minutes," he clarified.

"Okay." She uttered the promise in as conversational a tone as she could muster, not wanting him to suspect just how eager she was to put some thought-clearing distance between them.

He didn't release the keys once she'd wrapped her fingers around them, holding on without actually touching her. "I haven't forgotten about Tommy and Diana. We'll go to the lab right after this."

"I know." She could never question his commitment to finding answers.

Lucy pocketed his keys and hurried to the elevator, knowing Niall continued to study her retreat, probably trying to make sense of her passionate response to a simple thank-you kiss. But she refused to look back and let him see the confusion and embarrassment that was no doubt evident on her face. Last night he'd touched her, more than once. They'd traded some full-body contact that had ignited more than a distant fantasy. And now he'd kissed her. With any other man—like that drunk in the disreputable neighborhood the police had dubbed no-man's-land—she'd think he was into her. But Niall Watson didn't quite understand the intricacies of attraction—and these increasingly intimate interactions that were wreaking havoc on her heart and hormones were nothing more than gratitude and practical necessities to Niall.

When the elevator opened, Lucy dashed inside and pushed the button for the lobby. When she did dare to look back across the hallway, she saw that she was still the object of Niall's piercing scrutiny. It wasn't until she held up ten fingers right before the doors shut that he finally turned away to Dr. Koelus's office. And it wasn't until she broke contact with those blue eyes that she was finally able to release a deep sigh of relief.

The elevator descended, and with each floor, a little more common sense returned. She was foolish for letting her feelings for Niall simmer into anything more than a stupid crush. Maybe these weren't real feelings, anyway. It made sense for a woman with her background to idolize a man who was the complete opposite of a volatile glory seeker like Roger Campbell, to be drawn to a man to whom family was so obviously important. But that didn't mean she was falling in love with the quiet mystery man across the hall. She had far more important things to worry about than her love life, anyway. Like finding Diana. Making sure Tommy felt safe and nurtured. Even just finishing the blue cap she was knitting for him.

When Lucy stepped outside the hospital's sliding glass doors, she was hit by a sharp blast of damp wind that cut through her sweatshirt and camisole, reminding her that she'd been in such a hurry to escape before Niall started grilling her with questions she didn't want to answer, that she'd left without her sweater coat. Spring was trying to come to Kansas City, but it wasn't here yet. Although the temperature was well above freezing, the drab day did little to perk up her spirits. She crossed her arms in front of her and surveyed the dingy landscape of sooty snow melting against the curb and the muddy mess of brown grass surrounding a few denuded trees. Even the evergreen shrubs had a grayish cast that reflected the low, overcast sky.

Maybe the promised rain would wash away the last dregs of winter and she wouldn't worry quite so much about Diana being out in this. Was money the reason she'd left Tommy with her? There'd been nothing with the infant but the clothes on his back. She and Niall and Thomas Watson had bought or borrowed everything Tommy could need. But did Diana have a warm coat to wear? A safe place to stay out of the weather? Food to eat? Did she know how much Lucy ached to see her foster daughter's beautiful smile and hug her in her arms again?

Warmth of a different kind trickled down Lucy's cheek and she quickly wiped the tear away. Crying wouldn't do Diana or Tommy any good. And she certainly didn't need to embarrass herself any further by standing here in front of a big city hospital crying her eyes out, especially after that humiliating lapse in judgment with Niall upstairs.

Shaking off both the cold and the negativity of her fatigue-fueled thoughts, Lucy crossed the driveway and followed the sidewalk around to Saint Luke's visitors' parking lot. She found Niall's SUV easily enough and slung the long strap of her knitting bag over her shoulder and across her chest before locking it again.

Glimpsing a distorted movement reflecting off the side window, she shut the back door and swung around. She slowly released the breath that had locked up in her chest and nodded to the older couple walking past the rear bumper. Of course. It was probably them that she'd seen, reflecting at a weird angle as they approached and then passed Niall's SUV. After that close call outside their condominium building last night, she was probably being extra paranoid about silver cars and parking lots. Still, it was hard to shake the sense that there was something unseen just beyond the corner of her eye, something that she was missing.

A shiver skittered down her spine that had nothing to do with the penetrating breeze. Had she imagined the car following her? Or simply confused another resident's new vehicle with something similar she'd seen down in no-man's-land? Holding the strap of her knitting bag in both fists, she walked to the rear of the SUV and looked up and down the lane of parked cars. Was someone watching her? She seemed to have a sixth sense for when Niall was studying her, and she lifted her gaze to the hospital's fifth floor. Was he spying on her from the waiting-area windows, making sure she didn't disappear before all the mysteries swirling through that brilliant head of his could be solved? Lucy frowned. All the glass on the front of the building reflected the sea of clouds, making it impossible to tell if anyone inside was overly curious about her. Best to get moving and go back inside.

Although she felt fairly certain that neither Roger nor the drunk from the aptly named no-man's-land Thomas Watson had described would have any clue how to track her to this part of the city, she still found herself looking at all the cars she passed as she hurried across the parking lot. She was specifically looking for a silver sports car, but it was daunting to see exactly how many gray and silver vehicles there were in the parking lot, and impossible to know whether any of the people walk-

ing in and out of Saint Luke's main doors belonged
to one of those cars or if anyone, seen or unseen, was
watching her.

The uneasy suspicion remained when she reentered
the hospital's lobby and moved through the main visitors' area to the bank of elevators. Maybe it was just
the chill of the dreary February air staying with her.
Maybe that's why she'd felt someone's eyes on her—
they'd thought she was a fool for venturing outside without mittens or a cap or even so much as an umbrella to
ward off the coming rain.

The elevator doors opened, and Lucy watched with
an envious tug on her heart as a nurse pushed out a
wheelchair with a new mom holding her baby while the
dad and a big brother and sister followed them with bal-
loons and flowers and a basket of gifts. And though she
managed a smile and "Congratulations" to the expand-
ing family, Lucy's arms tightened around her middle.
That was never going to happen for her. Roger Campbell and her mother had seen to that. Despite her good
fight to remain optimistic, a gloom as chilly and blah
as the weather outside settled around her shoulders.

Once the elevator was clear, Lucy stepped inside.
She had five floors to push the past out of her head and
fix a legitimate smile on her face for Niall and Tommy
and Millie and the Watsons and the rest of the world
she intended to take on until she located Diana and reunited her with Tommy. She retreated to the back rail
as two men converged on the waiting elevator, giving
them space to come in. But the younger man darted past
the gentleman carrying a bouquet of flowers, pushing
a button as he slipped inside.

"Hey, I think that guy wanted—" The young man pushed the close button with rapid-fire repetition, nearly catching the other man's outstretched hand between the sliding doors before he wisely pulled back to wait for the next car. "Okay."

Guess you're in a hurry.

Lucy arched an eyebrow at his rudeness and kept her distance from the preoccupied man. With his back to her and the collar of his leather jacket turned up, masking all but the top of his coal-black hair, she could only speculate whether fear for a loved one's health or excitement over a new birth or simply being self-centered were what drove him to get to where he needed to go so quickly. She couldn't even see around him to find out what floor number he'd pushed. But he certainly smelled good—if one liked the scents of Italian cooking that filled the elevator. He must be a chef or come from a family who—

"You were downtown yesterday, asking about Diana Kozlow?"

Lucy's wandering thoughts smashed into the steel door of reality. Her gaze shot to his upturned collar and her heart raced with a wary excitement. "You know Diana? Can you help me?" She took a step forward but quickly retreated to the far corner of the car when he shifted his back to her, not only to keep his face hidden, but to expose the sheath of a long knife, strapped to the waist of his dark jeans. "Where can I find her?"

"You need to stop asking questions." His accent, a mix of guttural consonants and rolling *r*'s, reminded her of the argument outside her laundry room and the answering machine message at her office.

"Were you at my building last night? Was Diana with you?" Was he the man Diana had sounded so afraid of on the answering machine? Had he hurt her? Had he threatened her with that knife? Hell, he wasn't that much taller than Lucy, but he was muscular enough to do damage with his bare hands.

His only answer was a terse "Shut up. You're only making it worse."

"Making what worse?" She desperately wanted him to answer. "Who are you? Is Diana okay? Where is she?" One answer. Any answer. She was beginning to understand Niall's obsession with resolving loose ends. "Please. She's like a daughter to me. I just need to see her and know she's okay. Can you help me? I need to talk to her."

His shoulders hunched inside his jacket, and he exhaled an audible groan of what—impatience? Frustration? "What about the baby?"

He knew about the baby? "Tommy is hers, isn't he?"

"Tommy?" The man angled his face partway toward hers, although she still couldn't make out much more than olive skin with beads of sweat making the black strands of hair stick to his forehead.

"Tell me the baby's real name. What does Diana call him?"

"Is he safe? He is well?" Was that a wistful note in his cryptic words?

He cared about Tommy. He *knew* Tommy. "Yes. Didn't you see him last night? I think Diana did. He needs his mother. Can you take me to her?"

"Tommy is a good name. Whatever you do, don't let

that baby out of your sight. And don't let him anywhere near Diana again."

Again? Diana *was* the woman who'd left the lipstick kiss on Tommy's forehead. "How can I? I don't know where she is. What's going on? Did you break into my apartment? Wait. What kind of car do you drive?" The elevator slowed its ascent and stopped with a soft bounce. She glanced up. Fourth floor. He was getting off without telling her anything except veiled threats that made her even more afraid for Diana. "Please. Is she okay?" He slipped between the sliding doors before they were fully open. Forgetting the knife and the muscles, she lunged forward and grabbed his arm to stop him. "I just want to talk—"

He winced and muttered a foreign curse before he jerked free of her grip and shoved her back into the elevator. Lucy barely caught a glimpse of dark eyes and sharp cheekbones before he reached back in to push the door-close button.

"Hey. Hey!" She clipped her elbow on the steel railing, sending a tingle of momentary numbness down to her fingertips, before landing on her bottom. But she ignored the bruising pain and scrambled to the control panel to reverse the command. She caught the door as it stopped, then opened again, narrowing her gaze on the bloody palm print sliding out of sight between the elevator and outside wall.

Confused shock stopped her for a moment. That was *her* palm print. The blood was on *her* hand.

But she wasn't bleeding.

The mysterious man was injured.

And he was getting away.

"Hey, stop!" The staff and visitors walking the hall paused and turned as she rushed out. "Come back!"

"Miss?" A black man wearing a white lab coat over his tie and dress slacks put a hand on her arm. "Are you all right?"

She twisted away, taking a step one direction, then the opposite, looking for a leather coat. "Did you see a man get off the elevator? A dark-haired man?"

The woman beside him also wore a lab coat and carried a tablet computer. "Are you hurt?"

"I'm fine. There was a man in the elevator. He must have been running."

"This is Dr. McBride," the woman introduced her companion. "Do you need him to look at that hand?"

"No." Lucy flashed a smile and dismissed their concern. "This is his blood. I have to find him."

"Him?"

"Did you see—" An elevator beeped beside the one she'd exited. "Do you know if that's going up or down?"

The woman shrugged an apology as Dr. McBride asked, "What's the man's name?"

"I have no idea. I've never met him before."

The doctor crossed to the nurses' station and ordered them to notify security about the injured man.

"Do you need to wash up?" his assistant offered.

"No. I need to find…" Lucy's gaze zeroed in on the door marked Stairway gently closing and took off at a run. "Excuse me."

She pushed open the door and stopped on the concrete landing, glancing up and down, adjusting her hearing to the sudden quiet compared to the noises and voices out on the hospital floor. There. Footsteps running down the stairs.

"Wait!" she shouted, hurrying down the steel and concrete stairs. "I need your help."

Lucy wasn't an athlete by any stretch of the imagination, but she'd walked miles on the treadmill in the gym back in her building, so she pushed herself to move faster and catch the man before he exited the hospital. She slung her bag behind her back and balanced her hand against the railing, leaving her bloody mark as she spun around one landing and the next. She was nearly breathless, as much from desperation as from her sprint down four flights, when she burst through the stairwell exit onto the sidewalk outside.

"Where…" So many cars. Too many people. Too many bushes and trees.

Lucy almost headed over to the main entrance to see if the man who'd given her the cryptic warning had taken a turn somewhere and come out into the main lobby. But then she saw the small red blob seeping into the sidewalk a few feet away. She jogged out to the edge of the driveway, spotted another blood droplet on the opposite curb and hurried across into the main parking lot. There. A spot on the fender of someone's car. Another one on the white arrow marking the turn lane to the exit. She wasn't aware of the gray sky anymore, was barely aware of the damp chill in the air as she hurried behind the bloody trail. She was nearly to the road at the far end of the parking lot when the path she was following ended.

"No." Her nostrils flared as she took a deep breath to slow her panic. "You're my best lead." She scanned the grassy brown berm for one more clue to finding the man, praying she hadn't reached a dead end. "Help me. Help…"

Lucy looked up and saw an orangey-red pickup truck, its noisy engine idling and sending out plumes of stinky exhaust as it waited to turn onto the hilly road that ran in front of Saint Luke's. She saw the driver, staring at her through the window.

Dark hair. Brown eyes. Sad brown eyes.

Lucy's heart leaped in her chest. "Diana!"

The how and the why didn't matter. Overwhelming relief gave her a second wind. Lucy charged up the hill.

"Diana!" The young woman splayed her fingers against the glass, turning away and shaking her head. Was that a wave goodbye? "No. Wait!"

She saw the blur of movement between two parked cars a second too late.

"I said to leave us alone!"

She caught a glimpse of shiny gray steel before something hard struck her in the temple, spinning the world around her. Lucy crumpled to her hands and knees as the man in the leather jacket charged past her.

Her jeans and sweatshirt were soaking up the moisture from the grass by the time she heard the squeal of tires against the pavement and her world faded from gray to black.

Chapter Six

Niall would allow Lucy ten minutes to come back from her errand.

At eleven minutes, he excused himself from the meeting with his father and Jane Boyle, which had somehow devolved into a discussion about overstepping personal boundaries and who'd be in charge of what once she moved in to care for Seamus. Leaving the two of them to butt heads, Niall went back to the waiting area, looking for dark curls and a knitting bag but finding neither. Adjusting his glasses on the bridge of his nose, he scanned up and down the hallway. No Lucy. Something was wrong.

Although he still hadn't figured out why she'd pulled away from that kiss—and hadn't even had time to fully process the impulse that had prompted him to put his fingers in her hair and taste every inch of her rosy lips in the first place when a verbal thank-you would have sufficed perfectly well—there were two things he knew for certain about Lucy McKane: she was a woman of her many words, and she didn't want to be away from Tommy any longer than was necessary. If she'd promised to be right back, she should be here by now. She would be with the baby.

While assessing his options and formulating a plan, Niall rubbed his palm on the thigh of his jeans, trying to erase the memory of Lucy's silky curls twisting around his fingers as if they'd grabbed hold of him with the same enthusiasm her grip against his chest had. He needed to concentrate on the clues around him and figure out his best plan of action. Realizing her purse and cell phone were still sitting there in the chair where she'd left them, and that calling her wasn't an option, he quickly moved on to plan B.

Spying Keir and Millie conversing outside the ladies' room, Niall strode down the hallway to join them. "Is Lucy in there?"

Millie shifted back and forth on her feet, rocking the cooing infant on her shoulder. "No. Tommy and I were the only ones in there. I haven't seen Lucy since we left."

"Keir, have you seen her?" Niall wondered at the little gut punch of satisfaction when Tommy shifted his alert brown eyes to him at the sound of his voice.

"No, bro." Keir gave him a playful punch on the arm. "Aw, come on. I liked her. You haven't scared her off already, have you?" His teasing grin quickly faded when he didn't get a rise out of Niall. "Hey, just kidding. Is something wrong?"

Niall couldn't wait here and play negotiator while his father and Ms. Boyle tried to reach a compromise. And he sure as hell didn't have time to be responsible for keeping Duff's mouth shut in there to prevent a serious rift between the family and the woman they needed to see to their grandfather's recovery. Instead, he took Millie's arm and walked her toward Seamus's room. "Are you okay watching Tommy a little longer?"

"Of course. What's happened, Niall?"

"Lucy went out to the car. She should have been back by now."

"She said she thought someone had been following her the past couple of days. Do you think he found her?"

"What?" Niall stopped and looked down into Millie's crinkled blue eyes. "Who's following her?"

"She didn't know. Someone in a silver car."

"Ah, hell. There was a car like that at our building last night. Silver Camaro. Nearly ran her over."

Millie wrapped her hand around the back of Tommy's head, as if she didn't want him to hear this surprising tidbit of news. "She said she spotted it downtown when she was looking for her foster daughter and then again about a block from your building. She didn't mention anything about last night."

"Probably because she didn't want to upset you," Keir suggested. "But if this guy has located where she lives and saw you two leaving this morning—"

"He could have tracked us to her office and then the hospital." Niall raked his fingers through his hair, berating himself for making such a rookie mistake. "I wasn't even looking for something like that."

"When you work a crime, you're used to the people being dead, not chasing after you," Keir pointed out. "It's been a long time since your academy training."

"That's no excuse."

"Maybe it's her foster daughter, trying to make contact again," Millie suggested.

Niall doubted it. "Or the creep trying to hurt Diana and Tommy."

Keir was the detective here. He pulled out his phone. "I can do a search for silver Camaros in Kansas City. If you're thinking about tracking one down without a license plate or even make and model, though, it'll be a long shot. Maybe we can narrow down the search grid to certain neighborhoods."

Niall nodded and resumed walking. He wondered why Lucy hadn't mentioned seeing the Camaro more than once when she'd seemed so open about everything else, including some disturbing hints regarding her past. If someone had been following her, that could explain her instinct to punch first and ask questions later, or run outside to confront whoever was tailing her.

When they reached room number 5017, he pushed open the door and ushered them inside. He dropped the diaper bag on a chair and crossed to the bed where Seamus Watson lay. The old man's bright blue eyes tracking Niall's movements were the only color in his wan face. "Grandpa, I brought someone to keep you company." He leaned over and kissed Seamus's forehead beside the layers of gauze that covered the bullet hole and surgical incision there. "I have to go to work. Millie's going to introduce you to little Tommy. He belongs to a friend. He's..." He palmed the small, warm head resting on Millie's shoulder. Tommy's eyes looked up at him, too. "...a baby."

Seamus's eyes opened as wide as the stroke would let him, and his lips fluttered with a remembered task. Clearly, there was a question there.

But Niall didn't have time to answer. He headed for

the door before he lost his focus again. With Lucy's penchant for being led by her instincts and emotions and not thinking things through, she could be in real trouble. "Millie will explain."

Keir stopped him at the door. "You want backup?"

"No." They still had no leads on their grandfather's shooting—whether it was an accidental hit, or if somebody would be coming back to finish the job. And he couldn't focus on two mysteries that hit so close to home at the same time. "I need to know these people are safe."

Keir pulled back the front of his jacket, tapping his belt beside the badge and sidearm holstered there. "They will be. I'll find out what I can about the car."

With a nod, Niall strode from the room. When he got on the elevator, he was more certain than ever that something was terribly wrong. A crimson palm print, half the size of his own, stared at him from the closed steel door. He inhaled a deep breath to counteract the rush of unaccustomed anger that heated his blood. It wasn't necessarily Lucy's. The blood didn't mean she was hurt. His gaze dropped to the number-four button and the smudge of a bloody fingerprint marking it. It was too big to come from the hand that marked the door.

There'd been two people on this elevator. A man and a woman. And at least one of them was seriously injured.

Ah, hell. Niall pushed the button, stopping the elevator at the next floor. When the doors opened, he stepped out. "Lucy?"

A quick visual sweep of the people moving on the fourth floor revealed no curly-haired brunette. But two security guards were converging on the nurses' station.

Niall held up his badge as he approached the doctor standing there. "Have you seen a dark-haired woman? Thirtyish? Wearing a Royals sweatshirt?"

The other man turned from the guards he was giving a report to. "She was here a few minutes ago. She said there was an injured man on the elevator. Last I saw she was heading—"

Niall didn't need to hear the rest. A second scan picked up the elongated blood drops on the tiles leading to the stairwell exit. Directional spatter. Whoever had been injured on the elevator was running—away from someone or after someone, he couldn't tell. Logic indicated that one of them had to be Lucy.

The blood left a clear trail down the stairs. Too much of a trail. Niall took the stairs at a jog, skipping two steps at a time, burning inside at the idea any drop of it could be Lucy's.

He found another bloody print on the door handle leading outside and pushed it open. "Lucy?"

A half dozen people on the front sidewalk turned at his shout. Not her. None of them were her.

A sprinkling of rain spotted his glasses. He looked through the drops to zero in on the next bloodstain on the opposite curb. Even with the growing intensity of the rain, thinning the spot into rivulets that washed away in the gutter, he could tell that the blood marks were getting bigger, more circular. Whoever was injured was slowing down, succumbing to his or her wound. The instinct to run to his truck and grab his kit to preserve some of the blood so he could ID its owner blipped into his brain and out just as quickly when he saw four or five people converging at the far edge of the parking lot.

Good Samaritans running to help.

Help whom?

"Lucy? Lucy!" Niall stretched his long legs into a run, zigzagging between parked cars until he saw the woman on her hands and knees wearing muddy clothes and the people helping her to her feet. When she turned to thank one, he got a clear glimpse of the sticky red substance matting the hair beside that warm, velvety cheek. Niall had his badge in his hand by the time he reached the group and moved them aside. "KCPD crime lab. I'm a doctor."

"Niall." Lucy reached out her hands and tumbled into him as the others stepped back. He caught her in his arms and sat her down on the curb. Why was she smiling? Was she delirious? How bad was that head wound? "I saw her. I saw Diana. She was right here. She's alive."

"I'm tired of seeing you muddy and beat up. Where are you hurt? What happened?"

She was urging him to retreat as much as clinging to his arm for support. "We're getting wet. Where's your car? If we don't hurry we'll lose her again—"

"Stop talking." He quickly assessed her injuries, pushing her back onto her bottom and kneeling beside her when she tried to use him to stand again. The blood on her hand was washing away as the skies opened up and the rain began to fall in sheets around them. No cut or scrape there. But she winced as he pushed the damp curls away from her temple and saw the ugly gash in her hairline where the skin had split open. He pulled a white handkerchief from his back pocket and pressed it against the wound.

"Ow. Damn it, Niall, you need to listen to me."

"Can you see this?" He held up a finger in front of her face and moved it from side to side, watching her green eyes track the movement.

"Of course I can. There's nothing wrong with my eyesight. I *saw* Diana. She was right there." Since there was no obvious indication of a concussion, Niall shifted his attention, running his hand along her shoulders, elbows, hands, knees, ensuring there were no other injuries needing immediate attention. "Let me up. I'm soaked to the skin. We have to do something. Have you heard a word I've said?"

Niall was obliquely aware of a break in the rain hitting the top of his head as Duff ran up beside him. "Oh, hell. Is she all right?" A quick glance up to his big brother asked for an explanation and thanked him at the same time. Duff understood. "Keir called me. Said there might be a problem. What do you need?"

"Have you got a handkerchief on you?" Duff pulled a blue bandanna from his pocket. Niall wrapped it around the cuff of Lucy's sweatshirt and tied it off, trying to preserve some of the blood that had soaked in there. Since she had no injury to her hand or wrist, he suspected it would match the bloody fingerprint in the elevator and possibly give him a name for the culprit who had cracked her head open. "Look for a silver Camaro. Someone's been following her."

Lucy shook her head, dislodging the compress that stuck to the wound at her temple and moaning at the sudden movement. "No, Diana drove away in a red pickup truck. I mean, yes, there was a car yesterday. And last night. But just now...they turned north. Diana and the man from the elevator. They left together."

"What man?" Duff asked, pulling out his notepad and pen.

"He warned me not to try to find Diana. But I did. They were here together."

"Can you describe him?"

"He was bleeding." That made sense. Lucy's blood was redder, fresher, than the mess he'd found inside. Niall plucked up the soiled handkerchief from the shelf of her breasts. It was already getting too wet to do much good as a compress, so he used it to dab at the bruising and swelling so he could get a clearer look at the wound there. "He warned me not to try to find her. But she was here. She saw me...and then he..." She pushed Niall's hands away. "It's hard to think when you're doing that."

"I need to see how badly you're hurt."

"It's not my blood."

He held up the blood-soaked handkerchief. "The hell it isn't!"

"Easy, Niall." Duff rested his big hand on Niall's shoulder and knelt down beside him to talk to Lucy. "Can you give me a description of the truck?"

Lucy's wide eyes had locked on to Niall's at his irrational outburst. But she blinked away the raindrops glistening on her dark lashes and turned to Duff. "Faded red. Rusted around the wheel wells. Small. But I never saw a license plate. I didn't think to read it at the time, but it had words and a logo on the side of the door— like a business name."

Duff jotted down the information while Niall tried

to ignore the irony of Lucy's calm recitation of facts when he'd been the one distracted by his emotional reactions. "And the guy?" Duff asked.

"Black hair. Black leather jacket and jeans. Mediterranean looking. He smelled like a restaurant, if that helps."

Duff pushed to his feet and turned to the people who'd gathered around to make sure Lucy was all right. "Did anybody else see the truck or the man who hit her?"

He took statements from a couple of bystanders who'd stayed to make sure she was all right. But Niall had collected his thoughts enough to understand they had little to add beyond confirming the details Lucy had shared. "Your perp has lost a lot of blood, too. He couldn't risk coming to this hospital, but he'll have to go somewhere for treatment soon or you'll be looking for a dead body."

"I'll put a call out to notify area hospitals and clinics. I'll check in when I know something." Duff pulled out his phone and punched in a number as Niall pulled Lucy to her feet. "You'll get her to the ER?" Niall nodded. "Sorry this happened, Luce. Stay strong. We'll find him. And don't let this guy scare ya too much."

Duff jogged away while Niall wrapped an arm around Lucy's waist and pulled her to his side, shielding her from the rain while keeping her close enough to hold the compress to her temple. "Let's get you inside."

Although the man in him was certainly aware of her sweetly rounded curves pressed against his body, the doctor in him was concerned about the chill he felt through the wet clothing where denim and cotton rubbed together. He tried to quicken her pace, but he had to shorten his stride when he felt her fingers dancing at the right side of his waist looking for a place to hold on to for balance. Finally, she slipped her cold thumb beneath the waistband of his jeans and latched on to a belt loop. "You know, sometimes I forget you're a cop as well as an ME. With your gun there, I'm not sure where to put my hand."

"You hang on anywhere you can. I've got you."

Three more steps, then a hesitation to blink the rain from her eyes, then another step. "Why would your brother think I'm scared of you? I'm not, you know. I mean, I get frustrated..." She tried to laugh, but the sound ended up more like a groan and she stopped, laying her hand over his on her forehead. "Okay, I guess I am hurt."

"Could we keep moving?" he suggested.

They made it past the next row of cars before she stopped again. "Wait a minute. Where's Tommy? Is he okay? That man knew about him. He said not to let Tommy out of my sight. And I don't even know where he is."

"Tommy's fine. He's with Keir and Millie. He's meeting Grandpa. He'll be safe with them." She smiled, and he took a little more of her weight and pulled her into step beside him again.

"That's sweet. And Millie got to see Seamus. A visit like that will make all three of them feel better. Thank you for listening. And taking the time to come help me. Again. I know I said I'd be right back, but I couldn't pass up the chance to learn something about Diana. Oh, wow. You don't even have your jacket. You're getting so wet."

Chatty woman. Sometimes, he enjoyed the melodic sound of her voice filling up the silences he was far too accustomed to. But was there anyone she wasn't going to mention before she started taking care of herself? Or was the rambling an indication of some undetected head trauma?

Barely missing a step, he reached down behind her knees and swung her up into his arms, knitting bag and all. "Too much talking and not enough walking."

"Put me down."

He ignored the protest of her hands pressing against his chest and quickened his pace, carrying her straight to the hospital's main entrance. They could reach the ER through the lobby. "Put your arm around my neck and keep pressure on that wound."

Instead of obeying his instructions, she squiggled against him, trying to free herself from his grasp. "I can't afford to be an invalid, Niall. You do realize that I'm the only family Diana has. I mean, we can't exactly count Tommy when it comes to helping out. We're not like your family where your dad and your brothers and Millie and all your lab and cop friends jump in and help out. It's just me. I *have* to be there for her."

So what was he in all this? Who was ignoring the breast squeezed against his chest and the rain smearing his glasses to keep her from bleeding until she fell unconscious? Who'd rescued Tommy from hours alone without food or attention, or torn a hole in his UCM sweatpants saving her from that speeding car last night? Who'd agreed to team up with her for the baby's sake? How was she alone? "I swear to God, woman, if you don't stop talking, I'm going to kiss you again, just to keep you quiet."

"What? I...oh." Her struggles against him ceased. "Yes, Dr. Watson. Sorry to inconvenience you." Her arm crept around his neck, and she moved the wet compress back to her temple. "Shutting up now."

The receptionist at the front desk was on her feet to meet them. An orderly with a wheelchair joined him halfway down the long hallway that led into the emergency wing. Niall was aware that Lucy had stopped talking, doing exactly as he'd asked, except to give brief answers to the medical staff attending her. With her skin so pale and her eyes refusing to make contact with his, Niall made the decision not to prompt her into conversation, partly because he didn't want to upset her further and partly because he had no idea what he had done to make her shut down in the first place. Well, he had a good idea that he'd let his frustrations get the better of him and he'd said the wrong thing.

But was she mad at him? Hurt? Tired? Did she not see he was doing what needed to be done in order to keep her safe so that she *could* be there for both Diana and Tommy?

Niall gave a quick account of his assessment and what he'd done to treat Lucy's injury to the attending staff, then phoned his brothers to report on Lucy's condition and find out, as he'd expected, that there simply wasn't enough information yet to pinpoint the owner of either the silver car or the rusted red pickup. Was that why she had her nose out of joint—that he'd had someone to call on for help in a difficult situation? Didn't she understand that his family was helping her, too? And why, why, why did Lucy McKane get in his head like this and fill it up with so many unanswered questions?

He desperately needed to lose himself in the provable logic of his work and restore the equilibrium inside him. While Duff and Keir continued to make calls, Niall put on a dry shirt from his go bag and got his ME kit from the SUV to take pictures and secure blood samples before the hospital cleaning staff disinfected the elevator and stairwell. Whatever evidence might be outside had already been compromised by the rain, so he focused his attention on the evidence he *could* collect.

Lucy sat propped up on an examination table in one of the ER bays, wearing a hospital gown and shivering beneath the heated blanket draped over her lap when Niall returned nearly an hour later. He stood back for several seconds, watching her study her own toes wiggling fretfully beneath the edge of the blanket while an intern on the stool beside her tied off another stitch in her scalp. Did the woman have an inability to truly be still? Or was that her way of coping with the pain and discomfort she must be feeling?

The younger man acknowledged Niall as soon as he set his kit down on a chair just inside the curtain. "You were right about there not being a concussion, Dr. Watson. Looks like whatever he hit her with was small and the injury was localized."

The edema surrounding the wound gave a clear impression of the instrument used in the attack. Aware of Lucy's green eyes shifting from her purple-polished toenails to his every movement, Niall pulled his camera from his kit and snapped a few pictures before the intern put in the last two stitches. He enlarged the image on the camera screen. "Looks like a weapon about an inch wide, with a distinctive ridge pattern to it."

After tying off the last stitch, the intern placed his suture kit on a rolling stainless steel tray and ripped open a package of gauze with his sterile gloves. "Maybe the butt of a gun?"

Lucy tugged on Niall's wrist, pulling the camera down so that she could look at the image, too. "Or the handle of a knife?"

No comment on the puffy swelling beside her right eye or the gray-and-violet bruise that marred her pale skin? She was an expert on wound markings now? Niall adjusted his glasses on the bridge of his nose. "It's not a cut. Blunt-force trauma split the skin open."

She opened her mouth to explain her comment, but the doctor was giving her directions to care for the wound. "When the anesthetic wears off, you're going to be pretty sore. It's okay to use an ice pack for the swelling, but don't let the stitches get wet. And no aspirin or ibuprofen for twenty-four hours or so." Young Dr. Shaughnessy, according to his name badge, peeled off his gloves and tossed them onto the tray as he rolled it over to the counter, where he typed something on to his laptop. "Since your tetanus shot is current, I think we can forgo the antibiotics. But if you do see any signs of an infection setting in, give us a call or contact your personal physician."

"I'll monitor her recovery," Niall assured the younger man.

With a nod, the intern picked up a plastic bag and handed it to Niall. "We bagged her clothes like you requested. I wouldn't leave them in there too long or they'll start to mildew. I took the liberty of labeling it and signing my name to preserve the chain of custody. I start my forensic rotation next month," he added with a slightly boyish enthusiasm.

"Thanks." Niall scanned the sealed bag and quickly scrawled his name beneath John Shaughnessy's. A pointed glare from Lucy seemed to indicate that something more needed to be said. She was still putting someone else before her own well-being. Niall frowned, but acquiesced to the silent demand. "Good luck with that."

"Thank you, sir. I might run into you at the ME's office then. Here's a clean set of scrubs you can change into." Dr. Shaughnessy handed that bag to Lucy. "Take your time, ma'am. Unfortunately, we're having a run of business this afternoon. I'd better go get my next assignment. Have a good one."

"Thanks, John." Before the curtains had even closed behind the intern, Lucy was squiggling off the edge of the table. "I've been here way too long. I keep thinking about how everything would be different if I'd just gotten Diana to talk to me."

When her toes hit the floor, she swayed and Niall reached across the table to steady her. But she put her hand up to keep him away.

"It's a bump on the head and a couple of stitches." Technically, Niall had counted seven. But if she still wanted to keep some distance between them the way she had after that kiss upstairs and battle of wills outside, he'd respect the patient's wish. After he retreated a step, she dumped out the bag with the scrubs onto the exam table and pulled out a pair of white cotton socks.

"I've just been off my feet too long. I need to get the circulation going again. Not to mention that it's freezing in here. I think my blood stopped flowing half an hour ago."

When she bent over to slide the first sock on, the gown split open at the back and gave him a clear view of her underwear clinging to the curves of her hips and bottom. He remembered those panties from the laundry she'd been folding late one night. They were a pretty lavender color, a few shades lighter than the polish on her toes, and Niall's groin tightened with an unexpected response that was as potent as it was ill timed. Niall politely turned away from the tempting sight. He needed something to focus on besides the way Lucy McKane was transforming his well-ordered world into a topsy-turvy mess.

"Tell me about the knife," he stated, maybe a little more harshly than he intended. "Tell me everything."

After a moment's hesitation, Lucy went back to dressing and Niall went back to being a medical examiner with ties to KCPD's crime lab. He heard about the silver car that she'd seen in no-man's-land and again just a block from their condo building—and yes, she thought it could be the same car that had nearly run her down last night. She told him about the brute in the elevator and the long knife he'd carried that could explain the distinct pattern of her head wound. When Niall thought he had his physiological and emotional reactions well in check again, he pulled a narrow file from his kit and scraped the dried blood from beneath her fingernails and labeled it as evidence. In the back of his mind, he kept thinking how much easier it was to process a dead body in the lab than to deal with the scents of rain and blood and antiseptic on a living person. On a friend. On a woman who was the most alive person he'd ever dealt with.

On Lucy McKane.

Niall shook his head, warding off the uncharacteristic anger that simmered in his veins when he snapped a picture of the ugly bruise on her elbow and she told him how she'd followed the trail of blood the same way he had to track down the man who'd assaulted her and warned her to mind her own business. But when she raised her arms to slip into the pink scrub top, his temper boiled over. "Hold it."

Lucy froze at the sharpness in his voice and instinctively hugged the top to her waist. "What now?"

It wasn't the smooth curves of her lavender bra that had caught his attention, but the fist-size bruise turning all shades of purple framed between her breasts that had him circling around the exam table to stand directly in front of her. "Did he do that to you, too?"

A rosy blush dotted her cheeks as she tilted her face up to his. She turned away and lifted the shirt up over her head again before answering. "I suppose so. On the elevator when he shoved me back inside to get away."

Niall raised his camera. "I'd better get a shot of that, too."

She whirled around on him. "I am not a crime scene!"

"It's what I know how to do, Lucy. It's how I can help." Okay, so maybe going on seventy-two hours with hardly any sleep was giving him a short fuse he'd never had before, but the tear she swiped off her cheek and the soft gasp of pain wasn't helping him clear his head, either. "Apparently, I can't keep you from getting hurt, but I can analyze the size of his hand and the weapon he carries. If I can get a clean sample of his blood off you and your clothes, maybe I can identify him. If I get DNA and he's in the system, I can send Duff and Keir to arrest him, and he won't be able to hurt you or threaten Tommy and Diana anymore."

"And if he's not?"

Niall slipped his fingers into his hair and scratched at the frustration jamming his thoughts. "I'm not up to that part of the plan yet."

"What plan is that?"

He threw out his hands and glared down at her. "The one where I keep you and Tommy safe and stuff like this doesn't happen."

Had that outburst really just come from him?

A gentle touch to his jaw snapped him out of his roiling thoughts. Lucy's lips were almost smiling when she reached up to stroke the spiky strands of hair off his forehead. He calmed at her tender caress. "I'll be okay, Niall. I've been hurt worse than this."

"Is that supposed to make me feel better?" There. He'd admitted it out loud. Maybe he'd just admitted it to himself. He was *feeling*. The visual of Lucy's injury and the touch of her hand made him feel emotions that were unexpected, and clearly more powerful than he was equipped to handle.

Yet with a smile he craved as much as her touch, she seemed to take every mood swing in stride. "You know, I was processed like this when I was seventeen. Back in Falls City."

"Processed? You were assaulted?" Parts of his brain

were starting to click again. She'd mentioned something about her past earlier. "By the boyfriend your mother wanted you to stay with?"

She nodded, but he didn't miss the way her lips pressed together in a taut imitation of a smile, or the way her hands slipped across her belly and she hugged herself.

"Roger Campbell. He got pissed off when I refused to have sex with him. Apparently, my mother had promised him that I would. It was her solution for getting him to take me back, I suppose." Opening up a dead body never made Niall feel physically ill the way Lucy's matter-of-fact recitation of the crime against her did. "It was a shaky relationship to begin with. I didn't want to take a step I couldn't turn back from. To be honest, I didn't want to end up like Alberta—so dependent on a man to take care of her that she didn't care what it cost her." Her shoulders lifted with a weary sigh. "It cost me too much, anyway. That's why I can't have kids, you know. He broke a couple of ribs, damaged my…" She rubbed her hand across her flat belly. "I had to have emergency surgery."

Every one of Duff's rich vocabulary of curses raced through Niall's head. But only two words came out. "I'm sorry."

For a lot of things. Lucy was a natural caregiver. She should have scads of children and dozens of relatives to share her life with. That this woman should have been so used, so hurt by the people who were supposed to love her, gave him a clearer understanding of her obsession with tracking down her foster daughter and saving her. He'd redouble his efforts, as well. Maybe then she'd believe that she was not alone in her quest to do whatever was best for Tommy.

"It's not the memory, you know. It happened. Life goes on. Roger went to prison and I moved to Kansas City. But I didn't want to ever be in an ER again, feeling so useless, like there's not a single thing I can do to help myself. Especially when I know there's someone I *can* help. Someone who needs me. I want to go see Tommy and make sure he's all right. At least I could be taking care of him right now. That would be something useful I could do to help Diana. It's important to feel useful, isn't it?" Lucy paused for a moment. "Oh. And the lightbulb just went on. I think I understand where you're coming from now." She reached for the hem of the scrub shirt. "Take your picture."

Niall curved his grip around both her hands, stopping her. She wasn't a DB on an exam table at the lab. She was a living, breathing, beautiful woman with fears and goals and needs he should be addressing instead of falling back on the procedures and science that only made him feel comfortable and in control—not necessarily better.

Her fingers trembled within his grasp, drawing his attention to her icy skin and the sea of goose bumps sweeping up both forearms. Instead of taking the photo, he put away the camera and pulled his ME's jacket from his kit. It was little more than a windbreaker with a knit cotton lining, but he slipped it over her shoulders anyway, wanting to shelter her—no, needing to protect her—from at least one thing in this world that had or could ever hurt her.

"You are the coldest woman I've ever met." When she

arched a questioning eyebrow, he realized how that must have sounded. "Temperature-wise. Not personality-wise. Not at all. You know, cold hands, warm…"

"No wonder your brothers tease you. You're such a straight man, Niall." Her expression had changed from accusation to a full-blown grin, and he felt the muscles around his own mouth relaxing. "That's a wonderful compliment. Thank you." She slid her arms into the sleeves and rolled up the cuffs to expose her hands. "This does feel better. I swear, you're as warm to the touch as I am cold all the time." This time, she was the one to draw back in embarrassment.

Niall chuckled and pulled the collar of the jacket together at her neck. "It's nice to know I *can* offer something you appreciate."

She curled her fingers around his wrists, keeping them linked together. "I appreciate everything you're doing for me—for us—Diana and Tommy and me. I just need you to remember this is a team effort. You don't get to say whether or not I help. I'm going to."

"Understood. But you are a steep learning curve, woman." He dropped his forehead to rest against hers, carefully avoiding her injury. "And I just need you to understand that, in your efforts to save the world—"

"Just my little part of it."

Niall conceded the point, but not the entire negotiation. Her little part of the world seemed to be a far too dangerous one for his liking. "I need you and Tommy to stay in one piece."

Lucy tilted her green eyes beneath his, looking straight up into his probing gaze. "Speaking of Tommy—I know he's only a couple of weeks old, but

I think babies can sense separation. He's already lost contact with his mother. I don't want to be gone so long that he thinks we've left him, too."

He could feel her trembling, an indication that the hospital's cold air was still affecting her. Cupping his hands over her shoulders, Niall rubbed up and down her arms, instilling what warmth he could before reluctantly raising his head and breaking contact with her. "I don't want that, either. Let's go upstairs and check in with him. I want to find out what Dad decided about Grandpa, too."

"And then we'll go to the lab?"

Niall gathered the evidence bags he'd labeled and stowed them inside his kit. "I think I'd better take you home so you can rest. You'll at least want to put on some of your own things."

A hand on his arm stopped his work. "I need answers more than I need sleep or clean clothes. I can watch Tommy, and we'll stay out of your way while you work. I have a seriously bad feeling that there's a clock ticking somewhere in Diana's life. That she doesn't have a lot of time. I need to know why she was with that man. Maybe the blood you found *will* tell us who he is. Diana said I was the only person she could count on. I need to know why she keeps running away from me instead of allowing me to help."

Taking Lucy and Tommy to the lab with him wasn't the wisest course of action. With them there it would be a challenge to focus on all the tests he needed to start running. But it was what Lucy wanted.

"Okay."

She picked up his camera and handed it to him, help-

ing him finish packing. "Oh, and never *threaten* to kiss
me again, okay, smart guy? I know relationships are
a challenge for you. At least, I think that's what I'm
learning about you. Don't overthink it when you're attracted to someone. If you're afraid for me or worried
about Tommy or your grandfather and you have that raw
feeling inside that you don't quite understand, finding a
logical explanation won't make it go away. All that does
is distance you from your real feelings. If you want to
kiss me, go for it. Don't make it some little scientific
experiment and don't do it to shut me up. Either kiss me
because you think there might be a special connection
between us or don't do it at all."

And with that intriguing little life lesson hanging in
the air for him to analyze, Lucy walked out of the ER,
leaving Niall to gather up his equipment and follow.

Chapter Seven

Answers were not to be found at the crime lab.

Lucy watched while Niall made phone calls and ran tests and accessed computers, but apparently forensic science, while it worked miracles in many ways, moved at a much slower pace than she expected. Results were coming in due time, Niall promised. But his patient attention to detail made her feel as if she was suffering from ADHD. Or perhaps, with Tommy asleep and Niall running tests and consulting with the CSIs and lab technologists in the building, while Lucy had nothing to do but pace, she only felt useless and isolated and not able to do one small thing to help find Diana. Even knitting was out of the question, since everything in her bag had gotten soaked with the rain and would need time to dry out before she could finish Tommy's cap or start any other project.

New locks for Lucy's front door couldn't be found, either, at least not until the entire door frame could be replaced. Which meant another night of sleeping on Niall's couch, fixing breakfast together, changing the dressing on her stitches, reminding Niall to put his books away and get some rest. She enjoyed a sur-

prise visit from Duff and Keir with a pizza, loving how
Niall murdered all three of them in the most competi-
tive game of penny-ante poker she'd ever played. The
next day she enjoyed the tour of Thomas Watson's big
two-story house even more when they went over to
help move furniture, install a ramp, and share a big
pot of Millie's chili and cornbread around a long farm-
house table. She and Niall took turns feeding, diapering
and playing with Tommy and wrestling him away from
pseudo uncles and wannabe grandparents.

It was forty-eight hours of the family life she'd always dreamed of—and she had to constantly remind
herself that it wasn't real. Lucy and Niall were just
friends. Neighbors. Two concerned adults who'd joined
forces to care for and protect an abandoned child.

Domestic bliss this wasn't. Not really. It hurt to discover herself feeling so at home with Niall's boister-
ous family, knowing all the while their laughter and
friendship and support was just a temporary gift. It hurt
even more to realize how easily her attraction to her
handsome, geeky neighbor had grown into something
deeper. She was becoming as addicted to Niall's quiet
strength as Tommy was, and Niall's fierce devotion to
a cause—her cause—gave her a sense of security and
importance she'd never felt before.

What an idiot. She'd fallen in love with the brilliant
doctor next door. And since love wasn't something that
could be examined under a microscope or explained in
twenty questions, she knew that Niall was sweetly clueless to the depth of her feelings for him. As for what
he might feel for her? Since he scarcely acknowledged
his feelings about much beyond his work and family,

that was as much of a mystery as locating Diana and identifying the young man who'd threatened her in the elevator, then assaulted her when she'd refused to heed his warning. What logical benefit could she offer the inimitable Dr. Watson, anyway? Despite their friendship, Niall would probably want someone a little more staid and respectable, someone who didn't butt her nose into things and leave chaos in her wake. As much as he loved his family, he probably wanted someone who could give him that, too—lots of little shy brainiacs who would quietly change the world one day. Nothing like setting herself up for heartbreak.

So it was an easy decision to go back to work on Tuesday, returning her life to some sense of the independent normalcy she was used to. Since she and Niall worked opposite shifts, they'd agreed that she would take Tommy to the office with her. Either because he was still worried about her head injury or because he didn't want her and Tommy to be on their own and unprotected for any length of time, or some combination of both reasons, Niall insisted on driving her and the baby to her office. After dropping them off in the morning, the infant could nap comfortably in one of the family visitation rooms while she caught up on her caseload. And with Niall putting in so many extra hours at the lab and with his family, he could return home and have the day to catch up on some much-needed sleep before reporting in for his regular shift.

Lucy cradled Tommy against her shoulder, turning her nose to the unique scents of baby wash and formula burps as she sang a little ditty and danced around the tiny room, lulling him to sleep. *This* would be hard to lose, too. It was selfish to wish Tommy was *her* son, that fate would finally be kind enough to gift her with a child she loved this much. But Diana had been her child, too, for a time, until the law and the lure of a new boyfriend and an exciting career had made it easier than it should have been to lose contact and drift apart. Lucy still loved Diana and felt that inexplicable maternal urge to protect her just as fiercely as the helpless infant in her arms.

So despite the all-too-human envy in her heart, Lucy wanted Diana to be reunited with her son and for both of them to continue to be a part of her life. She'd be the mother Tommy needed until she could lay the precious baby in his real mother's arms. That would be happiness enough for her. Lucy pressed a kiss to Tommy's soft hair as pointless tears made her eyes feel gritty. "I love you, you little munchkin," she promised. "I will always do whatever is best for you."

A soft knock on the door interrupted the mush fest. Kim, one of Lucy's coworkers, opened the door to the private room and stuck her nose inside. "Hey, Lucy, your two o'clock is here."

Lucy turned with a frown. "I didn't know I had a two o'clock. Did Mrs. Weaver reschedule again?"

"Nope. It's a guy. I didn't recognize him. If he's a client, he's new."

"New?" Lucy instinctively hugged Tommy closer, thinking of dark-haired men wielding knives and warning her to stop caring about finding Diana. "Is he wearing a leather jacket? Does he have black hair?"

Her friend with the short straight hair and freckles

laughed. "Um, no. Try tall and blond. And he looks like he could bench press my car."

"Oh, no." Lucy felt the blood drain from her head down to her toes. She didn't have to see the man to identify him. Too many phone calls begging for forgiveness these past few days practically confirmed it. Her dread was quickly replaced by a flood of anger. "Here. I need you to watch Tommy. Keep him in here, out of sight."

She handed Tommy over to the other woman and apologized when his eyes opened and he stirred into wakefulness again.

"Is something wrong?" Kim asked, adjusting her grip to hold Tommy more securely. "I didn't mean to upset you. Do you know this guy?"

"Unfortunately."

"Sorry. I already told him I'd come get you, so he knows you're here." Kim juggled to keep hold of both the baby and the blanket Lucy had covered him with. "Otherwise I would have made up an excuse. I thought he was cute. You know, in a bad boy kind of way. Thought maybe he was a cop with news about Diana and that you'd want to see him."

Lucy caught the blanket and tossed it over the edge of the bassinet she'd set up in the small room. A smidgen of hope tried to take hold that Kim could be right, but Lucy pushed it aside. The description was too accurate to be anyone but Roger. "Never be taken in by a pretty face, Kim."

"Huh?"

Ignoring the question in her friend's tone, Lucy smoothed her skirt over the tights she wore and tilted her chin above the collar of her turtleneck before closing the door and marching down the hallway. She didn't need this visit. Not today. Not ever. But maybe Roger Campbell could put some unanswered questions to rest, and she could weed out a few of the facts regarding recent troubling events that might not have anything to do with Diana.

A fist of recognition robbed her of breath for a moment when she saw the familiar face that had once haunted her nightmares. Roger Campbell stood from the chair where he sat beside her desk and pulled off the ball cap he wore. "Luce. It's good to see you."

The feeling wasn't mutual. His hair was ridiculously short, his face a little more careworn than she remembered from that last day in court and a new tattoo on his forearm marked his time in prison. A black-and-blue circle beneath one eye made her think he'd had a recent run-in with someone's fist. But the playful wink from the uninjured eye reminded her he thought he was still big, bad, I-own-this-town Roger Campbell.

"Say your apology and get out here." She picked up a pen from the calendar on her desk. "Do I need to sign off on something for your parole officer? That you apologized to your victim?"

He chuckled and sat without any invitation to do so. "Luce, this isn't about my parole. This is important to me, personally. I learned a lot about earning forgiveness in prison. I've taken more anger-management courses than you can imagine. I know I hurt you. But I've made peace with what I've done, and I'll never let it happen again. I'm a different man."

Lucy tossed the pen onto her desk and propped her hands at her waist. "Yeah, well, I'm the same woman.

Damaged beyond repair because of you. I didn't want anything to do with you then, and I don't want anything to do with you now."

"Look, I know I made it so you can't have babies. I remember you testifying about that in court, so I know that's important to you. But I'm gonna make up for that."

"Make up…" The nerve. The ego. She shook her head in disbelief. "You can't."

"This is for you as much as me. You have to forgive me."

"No, I don't." When she realized the sharpness in her voice was drawing the attention of others at the sea of workstations across the room, Lucy pulled out her chair and sat. She lowered her volume if not the frostiness of her tone. "I mean, maybe I already have—there's no sense letting you have that kind of power over me. But I'll never forget. I'll never trust you. Plus, I've moved on. Falls City isn't part of my life anymore. My mother isn't. You aren't. I've made a life for myself here in Kansas City. A pretty decent one. And I don't want you to be any part of it. I don't wish you any harm, Roger. I just want you to go away."

"Stubborn as ever, aren't you, sweet thing. Is there someone else?"

"Why? Are you jealous?" She turned her chair toward him, growing a little more wary when he didn't answer. "Come on, Roger. You don't really have feelings for me. I don't even think you did back when we were dating. Those were teenage hormones running amok, your sense of entitlement and ungodly pressure from your father that made you—"

"A bastard?" He studied the ball cap he twirled between his fingers as he worked through that admission. Then his nostrils flared with a deep breath, and he nodded to the bandage on her forehead. "Does he treat you right? This guy you're with now?"

"How he treats me is none of your business. Nothing about me is any of your business." Although the relationship she was defending didn't exist, there was a tall, dark-haired ME in her heart that no one from her past would ever be allowed to malign. Lucy got up and headed toward the building's front exit. "I'll show you to the door."

She heard the chair creaking behind her as he got up to follow. "Luce, if he's hurt you, I can—"

The fact that he would dare to touch her incensed her fight-or-flight response. Lucy smacked his hand away.

She waved aside the security guard who stood at the front desk. She could deal with this. Lucy McKane could deal with anything, right? She had to. Pushing open the glass front door, she stepped outside onto the concrete stoop. The brisk wind whipped her hair across her face and cut right through her clothes to make her shiver. Maybe Roger *had* developed a conscience while serving his sentence, but alleviating any regrets he might have or assisting with the atonement he wanted to make wasn't her responsibility. "You can do nothing for me. Except leave." She crossed her arms against the chilly breeze and moved to the top of the steps leading down to the parking lot. "I want to see you get into your car and drive away."

"Look, I know guys in prison who are so obsessed

with their girlfriend—or kid or wife or whatever—that they killed the very person they loved. I don't want to see that happen to you."

"You're the only man who ever beat me up and left me for dead, Roger. Goodbye."

"Look, Luce, I'm only trying to make amends." He actually thought there was something he could do to make up for robbing her of her ability to bear children? "I saw a guy lurking around your building the other night. Had words with him. I could tell he didn't belong there. I just want to know it's not him who did that to you."

Lucy's eyes widened. "You know where I live?"

"I knew where you worked, and I followed you home one day last week. I've been keeping an eye on you ever since."

And he was worried about some other guy stalking her? "Never do that again or I'll call the police."

"If it is him who hurt you, that ain't right. Look, I learned some skills in prison I'm not proud of, but if you need me to have another conversation with this guy, I can make him stop."

"Another..." Lucy grabbed the cold steel railing and leaned against it. "My life is none of your business."

He shrugged his big shoulders, apparently impervious to the wind and her outrage. "I sat outside for a few hours, hoping to catch you coming or going. I fell asleep in my car. Woke up to see you running after that guy from the other night. Thought maybe you two had had a fight. I tried to have a conversation with him. He wasn't interested in listening." Roger tapped his cheek. "That's how I got this. By the time I was back on my feet, I saw you with that guy with the glasses and figured…"

"Wait. Go back." Lucy put up her hand to stop his rambling. "You saw him?"

"Yeah. Tall guy with glasses and no shoes. He was bookin' it across the yard."

"No. The driver of the silver car. The man I was chasing. Can you describe him?"

"Black hair. Eyes so dark they looked black, too. Cussed at me in some language I didn't understand. He's not from around here."

Wind wasn't what chilled her blood now. "Did you see a dark-haired woman with him? Younger than me?"

"No."

"Was the man injured? Did you see any blood on him?"

He shook his head. Lucy needed a better witness than Roger Campbell. Had he seen the man who'd attacked her or not?

"Can you tell me what kind of car he drove?"

This time Roger nodded, his frown suggesting that she was missing the point. "Look, he was nosing around your car before he went into the building. When he came back out, I stood up for you. At least until he pulled a knife on me. Hell, I even followed him out to Independence, until I lost him somewhere along Truman Road. You gotta give me credit for that. I'll make him go away if that's what you want."

"So you hit a guy. He hit you back. I don't need that

kind of protection, Roger. I need answers. If you can't tell me anything else, tell me about the car."

He shrugged. "Silver Chevy Camaro 2LS. Recent model. Two door."

"Did you see the license plate? Do you remember it?"

"Didn't think to look. I was busy trying to get out of his way before he ran me over." Lucy was already pulling her cell phone from the pocket of her skirt when Roger reached over to squeeze her shoulder. "What kind of trouble are you in?"

She shrugged off his touch. "Nothing I need your help with. Apology accepted. Please don't try to do me any favors anymore." Maybe that silver car hadn't been racing toward her. Maybe the driver had been speeding to get away from Roger. But she'd seen that car before, and the driver must want something from her. "Go back to Falls City, Roger. Don't contact me again or I'll call the police. Just get in your car and drive away."

He considered her request for a moment, then put his black ball cap back on his nearly shaved head and trudged on down the steps. "Whatever you say. I'm just sayin' I know trouble when I see it—"

"Goodbye, Roger."

Lucy stood there to verify that one, Roger was indeed leaving, and two, that it wasn't in any silver car. Learning that Roger knew where she and Tommy were living, and that someone else, perhaps even more sinister than the bully Roger Campbell had been, also knew her home address, shook the ground under her feet. There were too many threats hiding in the fringes of her life, and thus far, she hadn't been able to pinpoint one of them. Roger hadn't given her much of a lead, but it was something.

She pulled up the numbers on her phone and called Niall.

He picked up after one ring. "Lucy?"

A single word in that deep, resonant tone shouldn't be enough to soothe her troubled heart. But it did. "Did I wake you?"

"What's wrong? Are you all right? Is Tommy?" She heard movement in the background. Was he searching for his glasses on the nightstand? Unlocking his gun from the metal box in his closet or doing whatever the man did when he thought there was an emergency?

Her mouth curved with a wry grin as she headed back into the building. "Why do you assume that something is wrong? Am I that much of a train wreck?" When he didn't answer, Lucy paused in the lobby, the embarrassing truth heating her cheeks. She started talking, needing to fill the silence. "Okay, fine. I just had a visit from Roger Campbell."

The noises in the background stopped. "The man who put you in the hospital? The man harassing you on your answering machine at work?"

So her brainy savior had pieced all that together, too. "Yes. That's him. He wanted to apologize for hurting me."

"Do you need me there to get rid of him? A guy on parole doesn't want to see a man with a badge."

"No. I managed that myself. But thanks for asking." She hurried through the maze of desks toward the back hallway and the room where Kim was watching Tommy for her. "Besides, you're supposed to be sleeping."

"I was going over a DNA report from the lab on my laptop."

"DNA?"

"Tommy's blood sample matched the DNA we got off the screwdriver used to break into your apartment. Diana Kozlow's. She's his mother."

Lucy pushed open the door to find Kim singing a country song to Tommy. She smiled as the baby batted at her friend's moving lips, fascinated by the movement and sound. Diana loved music like that, too. Well, maybe a different genre. She was just as curious about the world around her. At least, she had been when she'd lived with Lucy. She couldn't imagine loving that little squirt any more than she already did. But her heart swelled at Niall's words. "You're not telling me anything I didn't already know."

"Yeah, well, now I know it, too. I said I'd be there at five to pick you up when you got off work. If Campbell's not a problem, why did you call me?"

To hear his voice. To let his coolly rational strength remind her that she wasn't the victim of her mother's machinations or the evils of Falls City anymore. To remind herself that she wasn't alone in her quest to find the truth—that she had an ally she could depend on without question—albeit a temporary one. But she couldn't tell him any of that. The big galoot probably wouldn't understand.

Lucy winked at Kim and quietly closed the door to finish the conversation. "I have a lead on finding Diana. Or at least on identifying the man who attacked me at the hospital."

"From Roger Campbell?"

"Yes. He... I think he was one of the men fighting outside the laundry room this past weekend. He said he's keeping me safe, making up for what he did to me." Was there any other humiliating, sordid, painful element from her past that she hadn't confessed to this good man? "Niall, I don't want *his* protection."

"I'm on my way."

NIALL DIDN'T LET Lucy out of his sight for the next five hours. The research he'd done on Roger Campbell led him to the conclusion that he didn't want the man anywhere near her, even if he could provide missing information on their investigation. Not only had the teenage Campbell kicked and beaten Lucy severely enough to break ribs and cause enough internal hemorrhaging to destroy her ovaries and necessitate the removal of her spleen—the crime for which he'd been sentenced—but he'd been involved with more aggravated assaults in prison, extending his time. Niall couldn't believe that Roger Campbell's motives now were altruistic. Too much violence, too many people who didn't value her for the unique treasure she was, had touched Lucy's life already. He couldn't allow it to touch her again. Not for Lucy's sake. Not for Tommy's. Not for his own.

Now, cocooned inside his apartment by the starry night outside, Niall watched her giving Tommy a bath in a small inclined tub in the kitchen sink. He was considering calling in sick and letting someone else take his shift at the lab because it made him crazy to think of her and Tommy alone here, having to face the threat of Roger Campbell's unwanted surveillance along with the possibility of the man who'd struck her hard enough to require stitches coming back to take his intimidation tactics to a deadlier level.

He no longer had doubts that Diana Kozlow was in serious danger. Whatever mess the young woman had gotten herself into had now touched her baby's life and Lucy's. He had no answers yet, either. And for Niall, that was equally unacceptable.

He glanced over at the clock on the stove, knowing he had to head to work in just a few minutes. But leaving behind a giggling baby with suds on his tummy and a woman with a matching dollop of bubbles on her left cheek didn't feel right. The autopsy lab was hardly the place to invite a woman and child to spend the night. And though there was a cot in his office to catch a nap during extra-long shifts, he couldn't confine them there as if they were under house arrest, either.

Keir was working on tracking down the silver car Lucy had described in detail. Duff was following up on the shooting at the church, running a long-shot check on the spent casings the CSI team had recovered in the organ loft. Maybe he could find the shop where they'd been purchased and track down the identity, or at least an image from a security camera, of the shooter. His father and Millie were busy reorganizing the house to accommodate Seamus and his wheelchair, as well as the arrival of the nurse they'd hired, Jane Boyle, and all her equipment, when the two of them moved in the following week.

Although a carpenter from the building's maintenance crew had worked on rebuilding the door frame leading into Lucy's apartment this afternoon, Niall wasn't prepared to let her move back across the hall with

Tommy until the job had been completed. He wasn't ready to let her and Tommy leave, period, not when he knew she was impulsive enough to follow a lead on her own if Diana Kozlow should call. Lucy didn't seem to believe that he considered them to be a team, and that that meant they should pursue any leads together. She didn't seem to understand his need for her to stop chasing bad guys who wanted to run her down with cars or bash in her head. He didn't know how to make her understand how it upset the balance of his life when he heard things like her meeting up with the man who had once assaulted her.

He needed her here. Safe. Close enough to see and hear. Close enough to breathe in the exotic scent of her shampoo. Close enough to touch.

Decision made, Niall pushed away from the counter where he'd been leaning and picked up a diaper to cover Tommy's bare bottom as Lucy lifted him from the sink. She laid Tommy on a hooded towel and dried him while Niall anchored the diaper into place before the baby watered either one of them.

Once Lucy had Tommy swaddled in her arms, Niall reached out and brushed the smear of bubbles off her cool cheek and wiped his finger on the towel at Tommy's back. "How long do you think it'll take you to pack an overnight bag for the two of you?"

He noted the blush warming her cheek where he'd touched her, and his blood simmered with an answering heat. She tilted her eyes up to his, and Niall wondered if she knew just how many shades of moss and jade and even a hint of steel were reflected there. "Are we going somewhere?"

"I can't leave you two here alone. I'll call Dad, see if it's all right to drop you off at his place."

"You don't have to bother him. We'll be fine."

He sifted his fingers into the hair behind her ear. "*I* won't be. Too many people know how to find you now. I need to know someone I trust is keeping an eye on you around the clock." With the pad of his thumb he brushed a few wayward curls away from her temple before leaning in to press a kiss to the edge of the gauze bandage there. Tommy turned his face toward Niall's voice and wobbled against Lucy's chest, either startled or excited by him coming so close. Although he trusted Lucy to keep a sure grip on the baby, Niall splayed his hand across Tommy's back. "Easy there, munchkin."

He could feel Lucy trembling, too. Her eyes shone like emeralds beneath his scrutiny of her reaction to the simple contact. But there was nothing simple about the heat stirring inside him. Niall dipped his head a fraction of an inch and her pupils dilated, darkening her eyes. He moved even closer, and a ripple of contractions shimmered down her throat as she swallowed. Niall's heart thundered in his chest, nearly drowning out her soft gasp of anticipation that clutched at something inside him and ripped it open. Niall closed the distance between them.

Her lips parted beneath his, and he hungrily took advantage to sweep his tongue inside her mouth and lay claim to her soft heat and reaching, eager response. Niall tightened his fingers in her hair with one hand and palmed her hip with the other. He turned her, pushing her back against the counter, crowding his thighs against hers to soothe the ache swelling behind his zip-

per. He slipped his hand beneath the nubby wool of her
sweater and clawed at the layer of cotton undershirt she
wore until he could slide his fingers beneath that, too,
to find the cool skin along the waist of her jeans.

Squeezing her generous curves between his hand
and thighs, Niall angled her head back into the basket
of his fingers and kissed her harder, deeper. His chest
butted against the hug of her arms around the baby, and
the earthy sensuality of mother and child ignited something protective, possessive inside him. He captured the
rosy, tempting swell of Lucy's bottom lip between his
own, then opened his mouth over hers again, matching each breathy sound of pleasure she uttered with a
needy gasp of his own.

The coo of a baby and tiny fingers batting against
his chin returned Niall to his senses. With a deep sigh
that was a mix of frustration and satisfaction, he pulled
his hands from her hair and clothes and moved them to
the baby. He caught Lucy's lips once more, then kissed
her again. Each peck was less frantic, more tender, as
he eased himself through the withdrawal of ending the
incendiary physical contact. Finally, he angled his hips
away from hers and retreated a step, pressing the last
kiss to the top of Tommy's head as the curious infant
clung to the scruff of his evening beard and squiggled
with excitement at the sensation, which probably tickled his sensitive palm. "You want to be in on the action, too, hmm?"

Lucy's lips were swollen and pink from the same
sandpapery rasp as they curved with a shaky smile before she stepped aside and turned her back to him. She
set Tommy in the bouncy seat on the counter before

reaching behind her to straighten the shirt he'd untucked and smooth her purple tweed sweater down over the curvy flare of the hip that was branded into his hand. "Niall, you didn't have to do that. I'll go to Thomas's for the night. I'd love to visit with your dad and Millie again, if I won't be in the way. You don't have to persuade me with a kiss."

"Persuade?" He took her by the elbow and turned her to face him again, his eyes assessing the relatively blank expression on her face. "You said when I felt raw and unsettled inside that I could kiss you."

"I meant—"

"You said never threaten to kiss you, to just do it."

Her cheeks colored with a blush, bringing the animation he was used to seeing back into her face again. "I did say that, didn't I?" She reached up to comb her fingers through that glorious muss of hair. "I forgot for a second how well you listen. Did it help you feel better?"

"Yes." Releasing her, Niall drew in a deep breath, trying to cool the fire Lucy McKane stoked inside him. He felt as though there was something unfinished between them, and he wasn't quite sure how to verbalize it. "And no. I'm more concerned about how it made you feel. I don't want to scare you off or make you uncomfortable. But then your response is so natural, so…combustible— it feeds something inside me." He scratched his fingers through his own hair before adjusting his glasses at the temples. Her frowning eyes following his every movement didn't tell him where he was going wrong in this conversation. "I know that there are rules about men and women and…and we don't have time to explore that right now."

"You worry too much about rules and logic." She reached up to stroke the hair off his forehead. Niall felt that tender caress and her returning smile all the way down to his bones. "There are some things in this world that can't be fully explained—like a mother's bond with her child or what makes one person attracted to another. Sometimes you just need physical contact to feel better. We all do. I'm not quite sure how you manage it, but you damn sure know how to kiss, Doctor. Sweeps a girl right off her feet." He liked those words, too, and was glad he wasn't the only one left a little off-kilter each time they touched. "I just need you to understand your motives if this…attraction…develops into something more than a friendly alliance. I need you to be fully aware of what you're getting with me, so that neither one of us gets hurt."

"What I'm getting with you?" That sounded like some kind of warning. "I'm not like Campbell. I have no intention of hurting you. I don't understand."

"I know." She touched that springy spike of hair again. "I'm not about to put words into your mouth or try to tell you what you're feeling. But if anyone can figure it out, you can." She pulled away to pick up Tommy and push him into Niall's hands. "If you'll get Tommy dressed, I'll go pack a bag for us."

The lights of the city turned streets into a foggy twilight as Niall wound his SUV through the back roads south of Kauffman and Arrowhead Stadiums until he could catch Blue Ridge Cutoff and take a straight shot to the two-story white home where he and his brothers and sister had grown up. He stepped on the brake, slowing behind the last dregs of rush-hour traffic, and waited to make a turn.

While he waited, he glanced over at Lucy in the passenger seat, nodding and drumming her fingers against the armrest in time with the tune playing through her head. Or maybe it was nervous energy. She hadn't really explained herself to his satisfaction after that kiss in the kitchen, so he couldn't be sure what ideas were going through that quirky mind of hers. She wouldn't surrender herself so completely to an embrace like that if she didn't feel something for him, would she?

Lifting his gaze to the rearview mirror, he glimpsed the royal blue knitted cap peeking above the top of the car seat, where Tommy dozed in the back. It seemed he understood the baby's needs and moods better than he did the woman beside him. Niall hated to trust what most people called instincts, but something inside him was telling him that he was on the verge of finding something—or losing it—if he couldn't figure out a better way to communicate his thoughts clearly to Lucy.

He understood right and wrong, yes and no, justice and crime. He understood fear and anger—had known both growing up when he'd lost his mother or when one of his brothers or sister had gotten hurt in the line of duty, or when he'd seen his grandfather fall at the church shooting. But this fascination with Lucy, this overwhelming urge to protect her, to find answers for her—that irrational desire to touch her and listen to her ramble and see her smile—he needed to put a name to it and understand it before he said or did one wrong thing too many and he pushed her out of his life or, God forbid, someone took her from him.

"You're staring again, Dr. Watson." She giggled and the soft sound made him smile, even though her amusement with his name continued to confuse him. "Better watch the road."

"It's a red light."

"Well, it's about to change."

Not yet, it hadn't. "Why do you find my name so funny?"

"Dr. Watson?" She was still grinning. "It's the irony. The revered Dr. Watson makes me think of the Sherlock Holmes mysteries I read in school. But you are so much more Holmes, with your intellectual prowess and manners and lack of empathy for lesser mortals like me, than you are the earthy sidekick doctor."

"Lack of empathy? I feel things."

"Of course you do. It's clear how much you love your family and your work." She glanced back over the seat. "How much you care about Tommy and making sure he has a good, safe life." By the time she turned her wistful expression to him again, the light had changed, and he had to concentrate on moving with the flow of traffic. "But you're always thinking so many steps ahead of everyone else in the room that you sometimes miss what's going on right in the moment. I always thought Dr. Watson was sort of the Everyman for Holmes. He understood the witnesses in the cases they worked on together and, to my way of thinking, translated the world for him. You know, he took what Holmes was thinking and expressed it in a way the other characters and readers understood. In turn, he took what others said or did and helped Sherlock Holmes understand their emotions and motivations." She nestled back in her seat. "I feel like I'm Watson to your Holmes. You've got the wrong name for your character. And that's why it's funny."

Niall turned the SUV onto Forty-Third Street, organizing his thoughts before commenting. "You *do* translate the world for me. I see things differently when I see them through your eyes. I'm learning through you— things that don't come from books. I admit that I'm more comfortable talking procedure with other cops or talking about a dead body into a digital recorder than I am conversing with…"

"Real live people?" He glanced over to see her sympathetic smile and, after a moment, nodded. "Niall Watson, I think you're a little bit shy. You live in your head most of the time."

The woman was as intuitive as his mother had once been. "And you live in your heart."

Lucy's lips parted, then closed again as she turned aside to look out the passenger window. "That gets me into trouble sometimes."

Definitely. But it also enabled her to smile often and laugh out loud and feel joy and passion and even sorrow to a degree he sometimes envied. He slowed as they neared a stop sign. "Don't ever change."

Her head whipped around to face him as his phone buzzed in his pocket. "You say the oddest things sometimes."

Niall felt himself grinning as he reached into his pocket. "Translate it, okay?"

The call was from Keir. Niall instantly put on his

work face. This could be something about Grandpa Seamus or the follow-up he'd asked his brother to run on Roger Campbell and the owner of the silver Camaro. He handed the phone to Lucy. "Answer that and put it on speaker for me, will you?"

She tugged her glove off between her teeth and swiped the screen. "Hey, Keir. This is Lucy. Niall is driving right now so I'm putting you on speakerphone. Okay?"

"Hey, Lucy. Is he giving you any trouble?"

Niall cut off the teasing before she could answer. "What do you need, little brother?"

"It's work, Niall." The sudden shift in Keir's tone indicated as much. "The lab said you're the ME on call. I've got a DB at Staab Imports over on Truman Road. It's up in the old caves in the bluffs off I-435."

"I know them. Businesses rent the old limestone quarries now for warehousing inventory or running electronic equipment." But Niall had a feeling that the underground caverns being naturally cool and practically impossible to break into had nothing to do with a dead body.

"That's the spot. And I think you'd better bring Lucy along." That put him on alert.

Lucy's gaze sought his across the front seat. "Why?" And then the color drained from her face. "Oh, God. Please tell me it's not Diana."

Niall reached over to squeeze her hand as Keir quickly reassured her. "It's not your friend. Our dead body is a Latino male. There's no ID on him. But there are a couple of things at the scene I need you to see."

Niall looked across to see her blinking away tears.

"You okay with this? Crime scenes aren't pretty. I can have an officer stay with Tommy in the car."

Her grip tightened around his. "I'm okay. If I can help…"

Niall nodded and released her hand to end the call with his brother and turn the SUV around. "We're on our way."

Chapter Eight

Lucy knew she had issues with staying warm. But even with gloves, a knit cap and her sweater coat, this man-made cave cut out of the limestone bluffs rising above Truman Road was downright freezing.

"You're sure you're okay with this?" Niall asked, pulling out the squarish attaché that held his crime-scene kit and a rolled-up package that looked surprisingly as though it might have a body bag inside from the back of his SUV. He tucked the package under the arm where he held the kit before closing the back of the SUV and facing her. "It's not for the faint of heart. Not that anyone would accuse you of being that."

Lucy huddled inside her layers and shivered. "I suppose there's a joke here somewhere about this not being my first crime scene."

He squeezed her shoulder, then rubbed his hand up and down her arm, feeling her reaction to the unheated open space at the mouth of the cave where he'd parked behind two police cars and an unmarked police vehicle. His eyes narrowed, and she suspected he was trying to determine whether her trembling was from the chilly temps or nerves. She wasn't sure she had an answer for him. "I'll be right there with you, the whole time. Keir, too. If it proves to be too much for you, one of us will bring you back to the car and Tommy. I'll leave the engine running so he can stay warm." He nodded toward the compactly built detective leaning against the front fender of the SUV. "In the meantime, Hud—Detective Kramer—will keep a close eye on the baby."

Lucy glanced at the young man in a denim jacket, with work boots crossed at the ankles, chewing on a toothpick while he texted someone on his phone. "Does he know anything about infants?"

"I didn't know much about infants a week ago."

Leave it to Niall to point out the logical reason she shouldn't be worried. Detective Kramer *was* wearing a gun and badge that looked authentic enough. "Are you sure Keir trusts him?"

"They're partners. I know he does. Let's go." Niall looped his camera around his neck and nodded to the detective left to guard the infant in the backseat before heading down the stone driveway in the middle of the high cave. "Hopefully, whatever Keir wants you to identify won't take long."

Lucy hurried her pace to catch up with him. "Is it bad form for me to hold the ME's hand when he's on his way to a crime scene?"

Niall reached over and caught her fingers within his grasp. "It wouldn't matter if it was."

Lucy held on as they walked past the sliding gate that had a broken padlock dangling from one of its steel bars. Deeper inside the cave she noted a serpentine trail of conduits mounted to the squared-off walls and ceiling. Niall explained that they were used to run electricity, water, fresh air exchanges and computer lines deep under the ground to supply the offices, repair shops and storage units housed inside. Lucy had seen the openings in the bluffs several times but had never had a reason to go inside before. It surprised her to see cages and iron bars shielding the businesses after hours, just like the shops on a city street downtown.

"How far back does this go?" she asked as they turned a corner around a limestone post and entered another, wider area that had only one office front next to a pair of garage doors that were large enough to drive a semitruck through. One door stood open, and the lights shining from inside the entrance bathed the whole area in an artificial yellowish light. "Is that really a whole warehouse under the ground?"

"Feeling claustrophobic?"

"A little." She tightened her grip around his hand. He didn't protest her desire to cling to something steady and familiar as they approached the line of yellow tape strung crossways in front of the open garage door. A large commercial fan over each door helped circulate the air deeper inside the bluff. The moving air tickled her nose with a familiar scent. She sniffed again and slowed her steps. "Wait. I recognize that smell."

Then she saw the sign painted on the office window and closed garage door—Staab Imports: Mediterranean Spices & Delicacies.

Lucy stopped in her tracks. "The man in the elevator smelled like that." She supposed a man who smelled like a restaurant could also work for a company that stored and shipped the spices and ingredients a restaurant chef would use. She swiveled her gaze up to Niall. "Does your brother want me to identify the body?"

Niall's grim gaze indicated that was a likely possibility. "We'll take care of this fast and get you out of here while I work."

Lifting her chin to a resolute angle, Lucy followed the tug of Niall's hand.

Keir Watson appeared at the garage opening and lifted the yellow tape when he saw them approach. The hand he shook Niall's with was gloved in sterile blue plastic, and he winked at Lucy. "Thanks for coming. Back here." She could see the stoicism in Niall's posture and expression once he'd released her and knew he was changing from the man she was falling in love with into the city's night-shift expert on analyzing dead bodies. Keir was as efficiently businesslike as she'd ever seen him, too. He led them between two long rows of pallets piled high with bags and crates labeled Sea Salt, Rosemary and Olive Oil. "I called the ME wagon for a pickup, but I wanted you to see this first before the CSIs cleared the scene and sent the body to autopsy. The custodian who discovered the body thinks our vic might have interrupted a robbery. There's a safe in the warehouse's office, and Friday is payday, so it should have money in it. Apparently, these guys deal with a lot of immigrant and low-income labor. They prefer cash instead of maintaining bank accounts."

"But you don't think it's a robbery?" Lucy questioned.

"No, ma'am. The safe hasn't been opened. I've got a call in to the owner to unlock it for us, though, to check the contents."

"We passed the office out front," Niall pointed out. "A thief wouldn't need to enter the warehouse. This is something else." He lifted his camera and paused to take a few pictures of the footprints and scuff marks at the base of one of the pallets. "Looks like an altercation of some kind happened here." He pointed back toward the exit and then in the opposite direction into the makeshift walls of food and spices. Lucy didn't need a medical degree to see the different sizes and designs of shoe imprints in the thin layer of dusty residue on the floor. One track led to the exit while the other followed the path Keir was taking. But how did Niall know the different trails had anything to do with the crime and hadn't simply been left by the people who worked here? He pointed to the partially flattened burlap bag about chest-high in the pile. There was a small hole in one corner and a scattered mound of ground dry oregano at the base. Niall snapped a picture of the dark red stain in the material surrounding the hole. "Make sure one of the CSIs gets a numbered photo of this, and cut out that piece for analysis."

"Got it." Keir jotted the order on his notepad and ushered them on to the scene she was dreading. "I figure whatever started there ended here."

They turned a corner to meet a forklift jammed into a stack of crates filled with broken and leaking bottles.

"Watch your step," Keir warned. "The spilled oil makes the floor slick."

But shaky footing wasn't what caused Lucy to shudder and recoil into Niall's chest. A man was pinned upright between the pallet on the raised forklift and the wall of crates. He stood there, frozen forever in time, with blood pooling above his waist where the empty pallet had caught him. But even that ghastly mess wasn't the most disturbing part of the scene.

Now she understood why Keir had wanted her to come with Niall.

There was a soiled piece of fabric draped over the man's head and chest—a square of white knit cotton dotted with yellow, red and blue trucks.

The baby blanket someone had stolen off Tommy that night in the laundry room.

Keir must have put two and two together and had been waiting to see her reaction to the way the murder victim had been displayed. "So you do recognize it. I thought it matched the description you gave Niall."

Niall switched positions with her, putting his tall body between her and the bloody scene. "You didn't put Lucy through this to identify a stolen baby blanket."

Keir shook his head. "I'm sorry, Luce. The blanket wasn't the only part of this mess that was too familiar for us to ignore." He nodded to the CSI working nearby to remove the blanket and place it in an evidence bag. Keir was talking to his brother now. "This death shows a lot of rage."

"Or an act of desperation." Niall moved to keep her from seeing the dead man as the blanket was removed. "Who uses a forklift to kill a man?"

Lucy sensed where this conversation was going. "Someone who couldn't overpower him on her own?" She was already shaking her head. "Diana didn't do this."

"I need her to see him, Niall." Keir reluctantly asked his brother to step aside.

Standing like an unmoving wall in front of her, Niall explained a few practical details. "Lucy, the victim's eyes are open. His face is bruised and puffy, partly from what appears to be a fight, and partly from the initial stages of postmortem swelling as fluids disperse through the tissues. He won't look like the body of a deceased person you've seen at a funeral."

His facts prepared her, softened the jolt of him stepping aside and giving her a view of the victim's face.

Still, Lucy recoiled, maybe less from the horrible death Niall had described than from the familiar face that had haunted nearly every waking moment these past few days.

Niall stepped between her and the black-haired man in the bloodied leather jacket once more. "Is this the guy who assaulted you at Saint Luke's Hospital? He fits the description you gave Duff."

Lucy nodded. "That's him."

But the situation could only get impossibly worse. Bless his practical, protective heart, Niall couldn't shield her from the other detail that had been hidden beneath the baby blanket. She peered around his shoulder to confirm the truth.

"Please tell me I'm not imagining that." Niall reached for her, but Lucy was already pointing at the dead man's chest. "What is happening? Why? My poor girl."

She gasped and pressed her fist to her mouth, resisting the urge to gag as the rock walls swayed around her. Niall caught her by the shoulders and backed her away from the body. He pushed her clear around the corner and leaned her up against an undamaged stack of crates. He hunched his shoulders to bring his height closer to hers, demanding she focus on him and not the scene they'd left behind. "Deep breaths, sweetheart. Deep breaths."

The endearment he used barely registered. Her mind was too full of the image of that screwdriver with plastic jewels decorating the pink handle plunged into the dead man's heart. It was the mate to the one Niall suspected had been used to break into her apartment the day Tommy had been abandoned there.

"Lucy." Niall's voice was as firm as the grip of his fingers around her chin as he tipped her face up to his. "Don't faint on me. Are you with me?"

"I have never fainted in my life. I'm not about to start now." Anger blended with shock and fear, clearing her head. She twisted her fingers into the front of Niall's jacket and clung to him. "I know what you're thinking. Diana did not do this."

"That's not what I'm thinking right now," he answered quietly.

Those piercing blue eyes revealed nothing but concern as he released her chin to brush a lock of hair off her cheek. Lucy tightened her grip on his jacket and walked right into his chest, pushing aside the camera that hung between them. "Put your arms around me, Niall. Just for a few seconds, okay? I need…"

His arms were already folding around her, anchoring her shaking body against his. His chin came to rest on the crown of her hair, surrounding her with his body. She snuggled into his heat, inhaled his scent, absorbed his strength.

Several endless moments passed until her world righted itself and she could draw in a normal breath. Niall showed no signs of letting go, and she wasn't complaining.

But the comforting embrace lasted only a few seconds longer until Keir cleared his throat beside them. "I hate to do this, you two. But the sooner we can get some questions answered, the sooner Lucy can leave. Do you think the beating or the forklift or the screwdriver killed him?"

With a reluctant nod, Lucy pushed away and tilted her eyes to Niall's. "I won't freak out again. I promise."

"I know you won't. But you stay here. You and Keir can talk and I can work while we figure this out." Niall needed one more nudge to leave her and disappear around the corner of the crime scene.

Keir's dark brows were arched in apology. "So you recognize the screwdriver?"

Lucy nodded, hugging her arms around her waist, already feeling the chill creep into her body again. "It matches the one Niall found in my apartment—from the set I gave Diana a few years back when she still lived with me."

Keir's blue eyes glanced around the corner, no doubt exchanging a pitying, skeptical look with his older brother. His suspicions were wrong. She'd said as much to Niall. She'd say it to anybody. "Diana did not do this. Maybe someone stole her toolbox. Maybe someone is framing her."

Keir pulled back the front of his sports jacket and splayed his hands at his waist, assuming a more brotherly stance, looking less like a detective interviewing a witness. "Maybe it was self-defense. It fits the warning he gave you about staying away and making things worse. If he was hurting her, then it makes sense that she'd want to get Tommy out of the picture."

"No. She couldn't kill anyone."

Niall suddenly reappeared, holding what looked like a meat thermometer and a wallet in his blue-gloved hands. "Would you kill to defend that baby out there? Or to protect yourself from someone like Roger Campbell?"

"That's not the same. I didn't retaliate against Roger."

"You testified against him. Maybe Diana didn't think she'd be able to get away before she had that opportunity."

Keir flipped through the pages of his notepad. "Campbell's the guy from Falls City who went to prison after assaulting you?"

Lucy glared a question at Niall, not sure she wanted every sordid detail about her past shared with his family. "He's the investigator, Lucy. I deal in dead bodies, remember?" But knowledge was power in Niall's book— understanding was the way to make everything fall into place. "Campbell said he wanted to make amends with Lucy. If he knew this guy had hurt her, could he have done this to square the debt with her?"

"Murdering someone is not squaring a debt," she argued.

"You don't think the way a criminal does," Keir suggested. "I'll add him to the list of suspects we want to question." He made the notation in his book, then turned to Niall. "Find any ID on our vic yet?"

Niall opened the wallet in his hand and pulled out

the driver's license to hand him. "Antony Staab." While Keir jotted down the information from the license, Niall continued his preliminary report. "Liver temp says he's been dead about eight hours. But the temperature in here would make the body cool faster, so the time of death might be closer to dinnertime."

"That would explain why no one discovered him until the night custodian reported for duty." Keir jotted down more notes. "We'll narrow down the window of opportunity to, say, 5 to 8 p.m. Don't you think that covering the face indicates a personal connection—not wanting to see a loved one's face? Possibly remorse?"

"It wasn't Diana," Lucy reiterated.

Niall had more gruesome details to report. "In addition to the contusions on his face, his knuckles are pretty scraped up. Looks like there's an older knife wound in his flank. That probably accounted for the blood trail he left at the hospital. He had it bandaged, but there weren't any stitches and signs of infection are evident."

"So this guy was dying, anyway," Keir suggested.

"Possibly. I want to check out these other injuries before I pronounce the cause of death. See what story they tell," Niall says. "Mr. Staab here put up a good fight somewhere along the way."

Lucy had a speculation of her own. "Could he have died of those other injuries? And the screwdriver is an attempt to pin his murder on Diana?"

"Like I said, I'll know more when I open him up."

The high-pitched wail of a baby crying echoed off the cavern walls. An instinctive alarm clenched low in Lucy's belly, and she spun around. When she saw the compact detective carrying Tommy and several bags over his shoulder, she hurried to meet them. "Don't let him see this."

Niall was right there beside her. "Get him out of here, Hud."

Hud Kramer halted inside the garage-door entrance. "I'm stopping right here, ma'am. Sir."

"Is something wrong?" Lucy asked, reaching for the trembling infant and turning him in to her arms. "There, there, sweetie. Mama's here…" She went silent at the slip and pressed a kiss to Tommy's soft wool cap. "Lucy's here, sweetie. What do you need?"

Tommy's little toothless mouth opened wide as he squinched up his face and cried against her ear.

"Easy, bud." Niall moved behind Lucy to catch Tommy's gaze. "You're making a lot of racket for someone your size."

Tommy's cries stuttered and he turned his head to the sound of Niall's voice. But then he cranked up again.

Hud held his hands up in surrender. "The kid started hollering. I tried to give him one of those stuffed toys, but that only helped for a few seconds. I didn't smell anything, but I didn't open him up to check, either." He pulled the diaper bag, plus Lucy's knitting bag and her purse, from his shoulder. "Not sure what the issue is, so I brought everything. I wasn't sure what you needed. Thought maybe I could be more help back here than walking him around the car over and over."

Keir had joined the group, too, and was making faces to distract Tommy, but with little success. "I thought you said you had a half dozen nieces and nephews."

His partner shook his head. "I'm the fun uncle. I play

horsey with them and give them drum sets for Christmas. I don't deal with their personal issues."

"It's too cold in here for him to stay." Niall peeled off a sterile glove and caught one of Tommy's batting fists between his fingers and guided it to the infant's mouth. "Hey, munchkin. What's the sit-rep?"

The instant she heard the sucking noise around his tiny fingers, Lucy diagnosed the problem. "He's hungry."

Niall released Tommy. "He's starting to put on some weight. Maybe he needs to eat more. Or more frequently."

"Hey, Mom and Pop." Keir was grinning as he interrupted them. He thumbed over his shoulder. "Crime scene, remember?"

All too vividly. The baby whimpering around his tiny fist must be feeling as helpless and distressed as Lucy was right now. She glanced up at Niall and the other two men, glad to have something to do. "I'll take him."

"Don't go back to the car by yourself," Niall warned. "The killer could still be close by. And if Campbell's watching, I don't want him to see the two of you alone."

"Even if he's too young to know what's going on, Tommy can't stay here. We'll be fine."

"That's unacceptable."

"Niall—"

"You can use the office right next door, ma'am." Hud Kramer extended a hand toward the entrance, offering a quick compromise. "There's a restroom in there and it's unlocked. Until the owner comes to open the safe, we've eliminated it as part of the crime scene. There are enough cops around here that we'll be able to keep an eye on you and the kid."

Lucy nodded her thanks and hurried as far away from the grisly murder scene as she could get.

The bell over the door startled Lucy and set Tommy off on another crying jag. "Poor guy." Quickly assessing her surroundings, she dropped her bags on top of the gray metal desk in the center of the room and balanced the baby in one arm while she unzipped the diaper bag and pulled out the items she'd need to prepare a bottle. She was learning to juggle things with surprising efficiency, although the job would have gone a lot faster if Detective Kramer had thought to bring Tommy's carrier, too. Since everyone from KCPD seemed to have a job he or she was working on, she didn't want to ask any of them to run to the car to retrieve it. She rubbed her nose against Tommy's, distracting him for a brief moment from his hunger pangs before he cranked up again. "You and me—we can deal with anything, right?"

Once she'd warmed the formula a tad under the hot water tap in the adjoining restroom, Lucy snugged Tommy in the crook of her arm and gave him the bottle. The instant his lips closed around the tip, his crying changed to greedy little grunts of contentment. Lucy kissed away the tears on his cheeks and let him have his fill. While Tommy ate, she walked around the office, mindlessly taking in the neatly arranged awards hung on the walls, as well as the vibrant silk flowers on top of a file cabinet and bedazzled pencil holder on the desk that added a woman's touch to the otherwise austerely masculine room.

Tommy was smiling and full and playing with her

hair by the time Lucy's gaze zeroed in on the familiar handwriting on the calendar beside the pencil holder. She read the lines and notation marking off several weeks in February and March. "Maternity leave."

Maternity leave? Diana's penchant for glittery objects? The handwriting? Being warned to stop looking for her by the dead man found at the same business? "This is your mama's desk."

But Niall would need concrete evidence to prove that her foster daughter had been in this room—that she had a connection to Staab Imports and one of its namesake employees, Antony Staab.

Eager to find anything that might lead her to Diana and clear the young woman of suspicion, Lucy knelt down to pull the changing pad from Tommy's diaper bag and spread it on the area rug beneath the desk. Then she pulled the needles out of her knitting bag and squished the yarn and fabric inside to create a safe spot to lay him down. Once he was content to snuggle with his stuffed toy and watch her move above him, Lucy started searching. She opened drawers and sifted through files and office supplies. She wondered about booting up the computer, but decided to save that as a last resort. Instead, she flipped through the names and numbers in an address book that revealed business associates like grocery stores and restaurants, and foreign names she couldn't pronounce. But there was no record of Diana anywhere.

She tried to open the center drawer next, but it was locked. Remembering her long steel knitting needles, she pulled one from her purse and wedged it between the drawer and desk, twisting and jabbing until something tripped inside and she could slide the drawer open. "Victory."

Setting the needle on top of the desk, she opened it wide to find some loose change and dollar bills, along with a calculator and a tablet computer. She was about to close the drawer again when she spotted the corner of what looked like a blurry photograph poking out from beneath the tablet. But when she pulled the paper free, she discovered the torn-up squares of an ultrasound printout that had been carefully taped back together. Her gaze went straight to the numbers and letters printed at the bottom. *Baby Kozlow.* Proof.

She found another photograph underneath the mended printout. Unlike the grainy ultrasound, the image on this one was crystal clear. "Oh, no. Oh, God no."

It was a photograph of a pregnant Diana standing with the man who'd been so violently murdered in the warehouse. Antony Staab. He had his arm around her shoulders, his straight white teeth beaming against his olive skin. They were dressed up in this photo—suit and tie, maternity dress. Diana stood with her hands cradled beneath her heavy belly. But she wasn't looking at the camera. And she wasn't smiling. Was the dead man the father of her baby? Were the police right? Had Diana surrendered her baby to Lucy to keep him from this man who stole her smile? Had she killed Antony Staab in self-defense? Were those Diana's footprints that Niall had photographed at the scene of that so-called altercation?

She needed to show this to Niall and Keir. Diana worked here, maybe in past tense. But she definitely had a connection to Staab Imports. And now Niall would have a name and a whole dead body he could use to find answers. He could prove to his meticulous satisfaction that Tommy's father was the dead man in the warehouse.

Lucy stuffed the printout and photo into her purse and closed the drawer. But she jumped at the bell ringing above the door and snatched up her knitting needle as if she could defend herself with so simple a weapon.

Her racing heart stuttered a beat, and she stumbled back into the rolling chair when a stocky, black-haired man wearing jeans and a leather jacket stepped into the office. Just like the dead man.

"You... How...?"

"What are you doing in my office?" The man asked the question in a crisp foreign accent. "Who are you? Why are you going through my things?"

"Your things?" He didn't strike her as the flowers and glitz type. But she was shocked enough that she could do little more than parrot his accusatory questions.

"I know they are not yours."

How could a man be alive and dead at the same time? "Who are you?"

He advanced to the opposite edge of the desk, glanced down at the knitting needle she wielded like a sword, then looked back at her. His angular features were harsher, more lined than the quick glimpses she remembered from the hospital.

"I am Mickey Staab. Mikhail. I own this place." Did he know Diana? She'd need more proof to convince Niall, but she was certain these were her foster daughter's things. "I asked, what are you doing here? You are trespassing on private property."

Mickey, not Antony. A brother? Cousin? Her breath unlocked from her chest as a rational explanation kicked in. "I'm Lucy McKane. The police told me to wait in here." She pulled the needle down to her side and summoned her compassion. "There's a dead man in your warehouse. Niall—Dr. Watson, the medical examiner—said his name is Antony Staab. Is he a relative of yours?"

The man's predatory demeanor changed in a heartbeat. The harsh lines beside his eyes softened.

"Anton?" He collapsed in a chair on the far side of the desk. He dropped his face into his hands. He shrugged his shoulders as if in disbelief before he looked up at her again. "He is my brother. *Was* my brother."

"I'm sorry for your loss."

"Anton is dead?"

"Murdered, actually. I'm so sorry, Mr. Staab."

"Murdered? When the police came to my house about someone breaking into the warehouse, I had no idea they meant…" He signed a cross over his head and heart and muttered something in his native language. Then he pushed to his feet. "How? Who did this?"

"That's what the detectives and ME on the scene are trying to figure out."

He paced the small office twice before stopping across from her again. "You're no detective. Why are you here?"

She supposed anger was a normal response to grief, but Lucy wasn't exactly feeling her stubborn, independent self right now. She slid a step toward Tommy, feeling the need to protect as well as the need to be closer to an ally—even one only a few weeks old. "I'm a witness."

"A witness? You saw someone breaking into my warehouse?" His hands curled into fists before he pointed toward the warehouse. "You saw this…killing…happen?"

"I'm not a witness to the murder. But I met the victim. It's a long story." Lucy picked up her purse and stuck the knitting needle inside, checking on Tommy as she stooped down. His arms and legs were stretched with tension, a sure indication that he was probably filling his diaper or hungry again. *Please don't cry, munchkin.* She sent the telepathic plea before she quickly straightened. "Maybe you'd better talk to the police before I say anything I shouldn't."

"Yes, I will talk to them. I know who is responsible." He was pacing again, his cheeks ruddy with temper. "That witch. She was no good. I knew she would be trouble. I told Anton to stay away from her."

Lucy tried not to bristle too much at the insults to the woman she was almost certain was Diana. "The police think there could have been a robbery. There was certainly a fight of some kind."

"A robbery?" The pacing stopped, and he crossed to the safe behind the desk. "She knew the combination. I wouldn't put it past her—"

Tommy cried out from his makeshift bed, and Mickey Staab halted. His dark, nearly black eyes narrowed with a frown as he glanced down at her feet. "You have a baby here?"

"Yes, he's…" Tommy mewled softly, his discontent growing. When Mikhail squatted down as if to touch him, Lucy quickly bent to scoop the infant up into her arms and circle to the far side of the desk. He couldn't belittle the mother and then expect to be all coochie-coo with the child. "His name is Tommy."

"Tommy?"

"Yes."

"A boy? You have a son?" He followed them around the desk, smiling, in awe of the baby he'd discovered, it seemed.

Tommy's fussy cries grew in duration and decibels. Despite Lucy's cooing words and massaging his back, he was probably picking up on the tension she was feeling. "He's very precious to me."

"You are a lucky woman." Mickey Staab palmed the top of Tommy's head, touching without asking. Lucy cringed away. "Who is his father?"

Suddenly, a tall, stern Clark Kent wannabe filled the open doorway. "If you have any questions, you ask me." Lucy exhaled an audible gasp of relief as Niall took Tommy into his arms and angled his shoulder between her and the business owner. She wasn't even jealous that the baby calmed down at the sound of his voice. She was glad to see him, too. "I'm Dr. Niall Watson, KCPD crime lab. Are you Mr. Staab?"

Backing out of her personal space now that Niall was here, the shorter man answered. The momentary joy he'd shown at discovering a baby disappeared beneath a resigned facade. "Yes. The victim is my brother, Anton?"

"That's what his driver's license says." Niall nodded to the door. "There's a Detective Keir Watson in the warehouse. He'll need you to make a positive identification of your brother." He inclined his head toward Hud

Kramer, waiting outside the door. "Detective Kramer will show you where to go."

Mickey Staab hesitated, looking at the baby before giving Niall a curt nod. "You are a lucky man." He leaned to one side to include Lucy. "And a fortunate woman. Congratulations." He was almost out the door when he paused to slide his hands into the pockets of his jacket and face them. "Do you always bring your family to the scene of a murder?"

"We're not exactly—"

Niall cut her off and motioned Hud into the room. "Detective Kramer?"

Hud's grin was friendly enough, but the broad span of his shoulders and muscular arms crossed over his chest indicated he could be very persuasive if he needed to be. "This way, Mr. Staab."

After the two men had disappeared, Niall pushed the door shut and turned Lucy in to his chest. He wrapped his arm around her, holding both her and the baby. "Hud said you were having a conversation with some man he didn't recognize, and I just needed to see that you…" His chest expanded against her cheek with a deep breath. "I thought it might be Roger Campbell paying another unwanted visit. That he'd followed you."

"I'm okay, Niall." She wound her arms around his waist and willingly snuggled close to his strength. "I needed to see you, too."

"Did Staab frighten you?"

Lucy nodded against his chest. "He's understandably upset. And normally, I could deal with that. But he looks just like his brother—like that dead man. For a minute, I thought I was seeing a ghost. The two of them could be twins."

"He's a ringer, all right." She felt his lips stirring against her hairline. "I'm sorry he scared you. Kramer shouldn't have left you alone."

"I'm better now—just hearing your voice, feeling your warmth around me…" Smiling at the fleeting sense of security this man instilled in her, Lucy reached up to touch the baby. "I'm as bad as Tommy. You have the same effect on both of us."

"It'll be another thirty minutes or so before I'm finished with the body. Do you want me to have Hud or one of the other officers drive you back to the apartment?"

"No. I don't want to be that far from you. Besides, someone has to stand up for Diana before everyone around here railroads her into a murder charge."

"There's a difference between exploring all the possibilities and—"

"Wait." Lucy pushed away, remembering her discovery from a few minutes earlier. She scooped up her purse and pulled out the wrinkled printout and photo she'd found. "Look at these. I found them inside the desk. And this is Diana's handwriting on the calendar. I think she must have worked here. And the ultrasound has to be Tommy."

"So she definitely knew Antony Staab."

"I'm sure they drove away from the hospital together in the same truck."

"You were nearly unconscious—"

"No. Look." Enough with the skepticism. She was giving him the facts he wanted. She crossed to the office's front door and pointed to the logo on the window. "This is what I saw on the side of the truck. Staab Imports. We have to find out if their company uses orange-red trucks. And you have to do that blood sample thing on the body so you can prove Antony is the father. And then we can find out who else might have wanted him dead."

"No." Nodding in that sage way of his, Niall joined her at the door and slipped the baby into her arms. "*I* have to find out. You stay here with Tommy. Lock this behind me so you don't have any more surprise guests. I'll have Keir wait to check the safe until after we leave. I'll figure out how all this connects to Diana's disappearance."

"She didn't kill Anton," Lucy insisted.

"Right now, I can't state anything conclusively. But I'm willing to work with that hypothesis."

"Niall?" Slipping her fingers behind his neck, Lucy stretched up on her toes. The moment she touched his lips, his mouth moved over hers in a firm, thorough, far too brief kiss.

"Feeling raw inside?" he asked as she dropped back onto her heels and pulled away.

Lucy smiled, wondering if the smart guy would ever figure out how much she loved him. Whoa. The rawness inside her eased as the revelation filled her. This wasn't just a crush or an alliance. This was way more than friendship or gratitude. "Not so much anymore." Still, the truth was bittersweet. She tried not to wonder if Niall was capable of comprehending that kind of love, much less whether he could ever feel that way about her. "Go. Find the truth. We'll be waiting here for you."

Chapter Nine

Lucy buttoned up a cable-knit cardigan over her jeans and T-shirt and slipped on a warm pair of socks before unwrapping her hair from the towel she'd worn since stepping out of the shower. She hung the dark blue towel up beside Niall's and picked up her wide-tooth comb to carefully pull it through her damp hair. The swelling on her head wound had gone away, although the colorful bruise and stitches in her hairline still made her think she looked a bit like a prizefighter.

She was losing track of the days since Niall had taken her in, and making herself so at home in his bathroom made her feel as though she was living out some kind of domestic dream. Or maybe it was more like living in an alternate universe with a strong, supportive man and a sweet little baby and all the extended family and security that went with it.

Because this wasn't her life. The Watsons and Tommy weren't her family. Niall wasn't her husband or fiancé or even her boyfriend.

She was the eccentric neighbor lady who talked too much and butted into other people's business and couldn't have babies of her own.

Even though her door had been repaired and her locks were secure, Lucy was reluctant to go back to her apartment. She wasn't ready to leave this fantasy life behind. But other than insisting that he wanted to keep an eye on her and Tommy until Diana was found and her link to Antony Staab had been resolved, Niall hadn't asked her to stay. Not for any personal reason.

And somehow, she suspected that blurting out her love for him would either confuse him or scare him away. There was a little part of her, too, that hoped if she never said the words out loud that the handsome cop doctor who'd righted her world time and again couldn't really break her heart when this alliance between them ended.

She watched her face contort with a big yawn. She still had a ways to go to adapt to the long, late hours Niall kept. Although she and Tommy had dozed on and off in his office down at the crime lab while he performed an autopsy on Antony Staab, she was exhausted this morning. She'd called in sick at work, blaming some lingering aftereffects of her injury for her fatigue. Perhaps it was better, though, if they remained ships that passed in the hallway or laundry room in the late hours of the night or early morning. That was the kind of advice her mother had given her.

"Don't you go givin' your heart and time to any man, Lucy, honey. Not until he puts a ring on your finger. Or you'll be paying the rest of your life."

Her mother had been talking about the financial difficulties that had motivated every decision Lucy could remember. But she was far more worried about the emotional toll it would cost her to reveal her feelings to a man who struggled to comprehend the human heart. He'd find a way to dismiss the irrationality of such feelings, or maybe he'd decide there was no logical way a quiet intellectual like him, from a tight family and a good home, could embrace a lasting relationship with a woman like her. Lucy knew that Niall was attracted to her physically—that crazy talent for kissing he had gave that away. But she had enough experience with her mother's peccadilloes to know that sexual attraction didn't equate to emotional commitment and long-term happiness. And Lucy wasn't going to settle for anything less.

Still, he was irresistible. She realized just how far gone she was on Niall Watson when she walked into the living room and found him sitting in the recliner with Tommy. The man needed a shave after his shift at the lab. His rich, dark hair stuck up in unruly spikes above his black-framed glasses. The wrinkled blue Oxford shirt that should have completed the brainy scientist look clung to broad shoulders and strong biceps in a way that was anything but nerdy. The baby was nestled securely in the crook of one arm. Tommy looked up between big blinks to the deep, drowsy timbre of Niall's voice.

"And so your daddy's name was Antony Staab." Niall ran his finger along the page inside the folder he was holding. "These pictures are markers, which is how we visually code DNA to identify people and find out if they're related. This is your code. See them side by side? These patterns show all the alleles you have in common."

Longing aside, Lucy couldn't help but grin as she

picked up the empty bottle and burp rag from the table beside the recliner. "You're reading him a DNA report for a nap-time story? He can barely see colors yet."

"You said he liked hearing the sound of my voice." That she had. "Theoretically, I should be able to read him anything and it would have the same effect."

"Theoretically?"

"Practically, then. We don't have any children's books."

Truth be told, Lucy could listen to him read from a grocery list or phone book and that deep, fluid voice would make her pulse hum. "Point made, Dr. Watson." The big blinks had won. She pointed to the child snoring softly in his arms. "You put him to sleep."

Niall set the report aside and carried Tommy to his bassinet, where he gently placed him and covered him with a blanket. He rested one hand on the butt of the gun he wore holstered at his hip while Lucy looked down at the open report. "So it's true? Antony Staab is Tommy's father?" She read through the summary at the bottom of the page and studied the graphs and statistics she didn't fully understand. "Do you think Diana is all right? Or did she get hurt in that fight with Antony?"

"Somebody's hurt, based on the injuries I saw on his body. He got a few licks in on whoever attacked him. But if she's hurt, Antony Staab isn't responsible. In fact, I may be ready to rule her out as the killer."

"May be?"

"I found traces of her DNA on skin cells inside the victim's jacket."

"I thought you said you were going to rule her out

as a suspect. If you found DNA, doesn't that prove that she was there? If you think she—"

"*Inside* the jacket," he emphasized. Niall crossed the room to retrieve his crime-lab jacket from the entryway closet and came back to drape it around her shoulders, to demonstrate his point.

Lucy huddled inside the jacket as she had that day in the hospital's ER. "She wore his jacket. So she was a friend—or even something more."

"But there was no evidence of her around the stab wound itself. No trace of her on him anywhere except from when she most likely wore his jacket." Niall tossed his jacket onto the sofa and put his hands up between them as if he wanted to start a fight. "If you and I were going to tussle—"

"My skin cells, hair, maybe even my blood would be all over your hands and clothing." He wiggled his fingers, urging her to come closer. "So tell me how you think you can prove she's not guilty of killing this man who once offered her his jacket."

"How big is Diana?"

"About my size. Skinnier. At least she was the last time I saw her. Why?"

Niall grabbed her hand that still held the bottle and raised it to his chest, using her to show how Antony Staab had been killed. "He was already pinned against the crates when he was stabbed. Even being injured like that, since there wasn't any momentum to drive him into the weapon—"

"As if he was lunging toward someone in a fight?" Lucy backed up a few steps and Niall moved toward her raised hand until his chest hit the bottle.

Then he stood still and pushed her hand away to show the difference in using just her forearm to strike the blow. "It would require a lot of strength to plunge that screwdriver all the way into the heart of a stationary victim who was standing upright. The wound track showed the weapon glanced off his clavicle. But there was no second strike, just one powerful thrust that tore through his heart."

Although the forensic details were so unsettling that she needed to stop the reenactment and pull away, Lucy appreciated that his evidence supported what her instincts had been telling her all along. "You don't think Diana would be strong enough to strike a blow like that?"

He followed her into the kitchen while she rinsed out Tommy's bottle and set the parts in the dish drainer. "It's not impossible, but it's unlikely—especially if she's injured."

Hugging her arms around her middle at the sudden chill she felt, Lucy went back into the living room. "I can't stand the thought of her being hurt and frightened and alone."

"You survived it." She felt the warmth of his body come up behind her as she stood over Tommy's bassinet and watched the peacefully sleeping baby. "She will, too."

She closed her eyes against the urge to lean back into his heat and strength. "I don't suppose there's anything in that report that *does* say who murdered Antony."

"Roger Campbell is still a possibility. Staab put you in the ER. He might see killing him as vindication for his crime against you. Duff took a drive down to Falls

City to find him and check out his alibi." She opened her eyes when the warmth disappeared. She turned to see him thumbing through the autopsy report again. "His killer must have worn gloves. I found no transfer of skin cells or blood in the wounds. Usually there is in a fight like that."

"You scraped under my fingernails. Was there anything helpful under Antony's?"

"Environmental residue from the warehouse, and his own blood and tissue."

"I can't imagine how frightened Diana must be." Determined to focus on Niall's belief that Diana wasn't a killer, Lucy joined him, leaning her cheek against his shoulder to look at the report with him. "Would you read to me, Dr. Watson?"

"You've heard all the pertinent details. The rest is technical jargon. Oh." He set down the file and frowned down at her. "Tired? You want me to put you to sleep, too?"

"Your voice doesn't have quite that same effect on me." She reached up to brush that spiky lock of hair off his forehead and ease the concern from his expression. "But I do find it soothing."

"What do you want me to talk about?"

"It doesn't matter, really. Anything. Everything. Whatever you want so long as I get to be a part of the conversation."

He considered her answer for a moment, then unbuckled his belt to remove his gun and holster and carry them into the bedroom, where he set them up on the closet shelf. Just when she thought he was going to ignore her request, he came back into the living room. He caught her hand and sat in the recliner, pulling her onto his lap. "I'm so sorry you have to go through this. The aftermath of violence is something I deal with every day. But this is the first time I've witnessed firsthand the emotional consequences of that violence. I think about Grandpa going down like that with a bullet..." His hands hooked behind her knees, turning her in his lap to face him and holding her there when she would have scooted to a less intimate position beside him. "At least I know he's alive and that he'll get better. I know he's not alone."

Although the sturdy trunks of his thighs and the distinctly masculine shape of him behind his zipper were warming her hip and bottom, she suspected Niall was seeking the intimacy of comfort and conversation, too, and her heart reached out to him, even as her body buzzed with awareness. "Seamus knows all of you care about him. Your family is such a blessing, Niall."

"Diana doesn't have any family but you, does she?"

Lucy shook her head. "None to speak of."

"I wish I had better answers for you. So you could at least know where she is. I hate to see you worried like this. You have such a big heart." He slipped his fingers into her hair, curling one finger, then another into the tendrils there, softly brushing them away from her stitches. He studied the way each lock twisted around his hand until his palm came to rest against her cheek and jaw, and his gaze locked onto hers. "You're not alone, Lucy. I'll stay with you and Tommy as long as you need me."

She tried to smile at the bittersweet promise. Lucy knew he was sincere and that she was lucky to have

Niall in her life. But if he suspected how much she needed the sound of his voice and his strength and heat and clever mind and kisses, would he give her forever?

Tenderly stroking her fingers through that independent lock of silky hair, Lucy wished that every day of her life could include this kind of caring. Niall needed someone to translate the world for him, someone to see beyond the erudite speech and obsessive focus and teach him to recognize his kindness and passion, and allow them to be given back to him. She wanted a family like his. She needed his calming strength and the unquestioned reliability he brought to her chaotic world. She wanted this good man to be *her* good man.

His blue eyes narrowed suspiciously behind his glasses, and she realized she'd been petting him this entire time. "What are you thinking, Miss McKane?"

"How much I want you to kiss me right now."

"That's a good answer."

Lucy felt a blush warming her cheeks. "Why is that, Dr. Watson?"

"I was thinking the same thing. That I could shake this feeling that I'm missing something important and make all those unresolved questions that are nagging at me go away if I could just…" His hand stilled in her hair. "Is this what needing someone feels like?"

Lucy nodded. It was for her, at least. His grip tightened on her thigh and scalp, pulling her into his body as he leaned in and kissed her.

His lips opened urgently over hers, giving her a taste of creamy coffee when their tongues met and danced together. Lucy wound her arms around his neck and tunneled her fingers into his hair, lifting herself into the tender assault of his firm lips. The rasp of his beard stubble against her skin kindled a spark deep inside her. The smooth stroke of his tongue over those sensitized nerve endings fanned the embers into a flame. Each demand of his mouth on hers stoked the need burning inside her.

His hands moved to her waist, lifting her onto his chest as the recliner tipped back. She twisted her hips against his belt buckle to stretch out more fully on top of him. Her breasts pillowed against the hard plane of his chest, and she crawled up higher, whimpering at the friction of her nipples pebbling between them.

Niall moved his lips to her jaw, her earlobe, the sensitive bundle of nerves at the side of her neck. He pushed aside the neckline of her sweater and nibbled on her collarbone. At the same time, he slipped a hand beneath her sweater and T-shirt. He moaned some little words of victory or satisfaction or both when he found the bare skin of her back and splayed the fiery stamp of his hand there. It wasn't fair that he could slide his hand up along her spine and down beneath the waist of her jeans to squeeze her bottom when she couldn't touch bare skin. Determined to explore the same territory on him, Lucy braced a hand on his shoulder and pushed herself up, trying to get at the buttons of his shirt. One. Two. She slipped her hand inside the Oxford cloth to tickle her palm against the crisp curls of hair that dusted his chest, and her fingers teased the male nipple that stood proudly at attention. The muscles beneath her fingers jumped, and Lucy wanted more.

Niall's hand moved inside her shirt to mimic the same action. Her breast was heavy and full as he palmed her through her bra, and Lucy groaned at the frissons of heat stirring her blood from every place he touched her. He pinched the achy nub between his thumb and finger, and she realized those breathy gasps of pleasure were coming from her mouth. She wanted his soothing tongue on the tips of the breasts he explored so thoroughly, with no barriers between his greedy touch and her sensitive skin. She wanted the straining bulge inside his jeans sliding inside her, claiming her body as thoroughly as his hands and mouth had claimed the rest of her.

She sensed he wanted that, too. His hips shifted beneath hers, spreading her legs. Her knee bumped the arm of the chair. He lifted her to center her above him, but she hit the other arm and jiggled the lamp on the table beside the recliner.

"Niall..." There was no place for her to move. No room to make this happen. "Niall—"

In a quick show of strength, he righted the recliner and pushed to his feet, palming her bottom as he commanded, "Legs. Waist. Now."

Lucy happily obliged as he caught her in his arms, locking her feet together behind his waist as he carried her into the bedroom. From the moment they left the recliner until he set her on her feet beside the bed, she got the feeling that there was a clock ticking somewhere, that the rightness of this moment with Niall might pass before she got to live out the fantasy of being loved by this man.

He seemed just as impatient to discover his passionate side, to find solace or to explore the human connection blossoming between them or whatever this was.

His lips kept coming back to hers as they unbuttoned shirts and unsnapped jeans and dropped her sweater to the floor. She pushed his shirt off his shoulders and he reached for the hem of her T-shirt. He whisked the shirt off over her head and stopped, his eyes feasting so hungrily on her breasts that he didn't even have to touch her for the muscles deep inside her womb to pulse. Leaning in to touch his forehead to hers, he skimmed his hands up her arms to slide his thumbs beneath the straps of her bra. "Heaven help me. The leopard print?"

"What?"

He drew one finger along the line of the strap down to the swell of her breast and traced the curved edge of the material into her cleavage and up over the other eager breast, eliciting a sea of goose bumps across her skin. "I've made a very unscientific study on the design and color of underwear that goes through your laundry every week."

His deep, ragged breaths blew warm puffs of air across her skin, and she felt each breath like a physical touch. If he'd been a different man, she'd have thought he was toying with her. But Niall was Niall, and she half suspected that the way he studied her body and analyzed her reactions was part of the arousal process for him.

Lucy tried to capture a rational thought for his sake. "That's a little voyeuristic."

His finger slipped inside a leopard-print cup and the back of his knuckle brushed across the sensitive pearl. Lucy gasped at the bolt of pure longing that arced from that touch to the damp heat between her thighs. She swayed on unsteady feet and braced her hands against his warm chest. "So you like these?"

"Yes. Very much. Take them off."

Lucy laughed at the growly command, loving the rare revelation of impulsive need. As he pushed the straps off her shoulders, she reached for the waistband of his briefs. "You take yours off."

And then it was a race to strip off their remaining clothes and tumble onto the bed together. She giggled at the way his glasses fogged between them when they kissed and reached up to pull them from his nose and set them gently on the nightstand.

His hand was there along with hers, pulling open the drawer and digging around inside, blindly searching while panting against her mouth. "Condom. Need to find a condom."

Lucy pushed him back onto the pillows and straddled his hips, reaching for his eager flesh, ready to be with him completely. "No need. Can't make babies, remember?"

He prodded her opening with a needy groan, but his hands squeezed her thighs, keeping her from settling over him. "That's not fair. You deserve a dozen of them."

"Fair? Maybe not. But that's life. And I'm not letting what's happened to me stop me from living this moment with you. Right here. Right now. I need you, Niall. Inside me. All around me. Setting me on fire with all that body heat."

"Technically, it's your own body heat that's rising and making it—"

"Niall?" She leaned over him, pressing a finger to his lips to shush him.

"Yes?"

"Now is when you need to stop talking. Do you want this to happen?"

He nodded.

"Then kiss me like you mean it."

"I'll do my best." And, oh, his best was crazy wonderful. He rolled her onto her back and moved between her legs, his strong thighs nudging hers apart. His hands fisted in her hair as he slowly pushed his way into her weeping core until they were completely one. He suckled on a tender breast, then stretched the hard weight of his body over hers to reclaim her mouth as he moved inside her.

As his thrusts came faster, more powerfully, Lucy gave herself over to the exquisite pressure building inside her. What he'd denied her a moment earlier, he gave back with generous attention to detail, sliding his thumb between them to the spot where they were tightly linked, bringing her right to the edge and taking her over in a rush of feverish pleasure that washed over her arching body like waves of blissful fire. And while the aftershocks were still pulsing deep inside her, Niall's body tightened over hers. With a groan of pure satisfaction humming against her throat, he released himself inside her.

By the time Lucy came to her senses and her thumping heart settled into a steady beat against Niall's, she was already falling asleep. With her head nestled against the pillow of his shoulder, he pulled the covers over them both. There were no tender words exchanged, no questions asked, no promises made. But it felt as though the man she loved wasn't going anywhere. For a few minutes on an overcast day at the end of February, when the rest of her world was in complete limbo, Lucy felt as though she was a part of something, as if she belonged.

Treasuring the gift of these precious moments together, she snuggled into the circle of Niall's arms, surrounded by his heat, shielded by his strength and saved—for a few minutes, at least—from the fears and vulnerability and loneliness she'd lived with for far too long.

LUCY WOKE UP to the distant sound of chimes playing.

She was drowsy with contentment and deliciously warm in the cocoon of the bed and the furnace spooning behind her. Only half-alert to the sunshine filtering through the blinds at Niall's window, she savored the scent of Niall's soap clinging to the cotton sheets and the earthier scent of the man himself filling her senses. She wanted nothing more than to snuggle in beneath the possessive weight of Niall's arm and leg draped across her waist and thighs.

But moment by moment, the reality of the outside world stole the dream of her blissful morning away from her.

The sun was too bright. It must be afternoon already. She heard Tommy fussing in the other room—not crying yet, but awake and realizing he was hungry or wet or alone. She heard the beep of her phone. Missed call. Then the chimes sounded again.

Lucy pushed Niall's arm aside and sat bolt upright. "My phone."

He was awake, too, tucking the covers around her naked body before swinging his legs off the side of the bed. He stood in all his lean, lanky glory, reaching for his glasses and slipping them on. "Living room. I'll get it."

"No, thanks. I can…" Ignoring her body's traitorous rush of interest in the gallant ME's bare backside, she scrambled off her side of the bed, gasping as the chill of the air hit her warm skin. Lucy crossed her arms over her breasts and shivered. She made a quick search for her clothes and grabbed the first thing she saw—Niall's shirt that she'd tossed over the foot of the bed earlier. Feeling an increasing sense of urgency with every chime of the phone, she slid her arms into the long sleeves and hooked a couple of buttons as she hurried out the door. "Stay put. I'll get it. I need to check on Tommy, anyway."

But he was right behind her moments later in unsnapped jeans and miles of bare chest when she pulled her phone from her purse. He nudged her aside. "You talk. I've got the munchkin."

Lucy didn't recognize the number on her phone. But too much had happened in the past week for her to take the chance on ignoring it. "Hello?"

"Lucy?"

"Diana? Thank God." She braced a hand on Niall's arm to steady herself as relief overwhelmed her. "Are you all right? Are you someplace safe? I know you used to work at Staab Imports. You didn't have anything to do with that horrible murder, did you? I told the police you couldn't have."

"Even though it was my screwdriver stuck in his chest?" Diana sniffled a noisy breath, as if she was fighting back tears. "I'm so sorry to get you involved in this mess. Everything is so screwed up. I need to ask one more favor of..." She hesitated as the baby wrinkled up his face and cried out in earnest when Niall left him lying in the bassinet to eavesdrop on the call. "Is that Dorian? He sounds healthy. Is he?"

"Dorian?"

Diana sniffed again. "Of course. Anton said you were calling him Tommy. I like it. I named him after the lead singer in one of my favorite rock bands. But Tommy's a good name. It makes him sound like a regular, normal kid. And I want that for him—"

The conversation ended with an abrupt gasp. "Diana? Yes. He's healthy. I took him to a pediatrician. Are you still there—"

A different voice cut Lucy off. "I want to hear my son."

The voice sounded familiar. It was thickly accented, deep pitched, and it could have been melodic—if it weren't for the absolute chill she heard behind the tone.

"Who is this?" she asked.

Niall's calming, more familiar voice whispered beside her ear. "Put it on speaker. Keep him talking."

She nodded her understanding and watched as he took a few steps away to call his brother Keir and order a trace on the incoming call.

"Tell me who you are," she demanded. "What have you done to Diana?"

"She does not matter" came the smug answer that frightened, angered and saddened her at the same time. "I am the boy's father."

Niall had evidence to the contrary. Lucy had seen it. "She matters. His father is Antony Staab. And he's dead."

"You lie!" Lucy jerked at the angry voice, flashing back for a split second to the night she'd said no to Roger Campbell.

But Niall's blue eyes, demanding she focus on the call and stay in the moment with him, gave her something to concentrate on. "I saw his dead body," she explained. "I read the medical examiner's report." She hardened herself against the man's curses and Diana's pleas muttering in the background. "I'm guessing you had something to do with his murder. And you tried to pin it on Diana."

Blowing off the accusation she'd just made, the man came back on the line, speaking in a deceptively calm voice. "My son was taken from me. You kidnapped him."

"No. I'm watching him for his mother." Poor Tommy's cries quieted to a mewling sound of frustration when she reached into the bassinet and captured one of his little fists in her fingers and moved it to his mouth to suckle on. "I'm his legal guardian."

"I am his father! He belongs to me. Let me hear him."

She heard Keir's voice coming from Niall's phone. "We got a ping on her phone from a cell tower downtown."

"Narrow it down, little brother. I need an exact location." To Lucy, Niall gave her the sign to draw out the conversation for as long as she could.

Lucy nodded.

"Here." She pulled Tommy's fist from his mouth

and the baby wailed. Lucy put her phone next to the crying baby for several seconds before pulling it back to speak. "Is that what you wanted to hear? I need to change and feed him. Are you willing to do that kind of work to take care of an infant? To be responsible like a real father? Or is he just some prize to you? Now either tell me who you are or put Diana back on the phone." There was a terse command about explaining things and a sharp smack of sound. "Diana? If you hurt her…"

"It's me, Luce. I'm okay." But she wasn't. Diana was crying again. No wonder her foster daughter had wanted to get her baby away from such a dangerous situation. But why wouldn't she save herself, as well? "I thought after I had the baby I could disappear on the streets the way I used to before I came to live with you. You know, when I was a runaway. But I've never met anyone like Mickey before."

"Mickey?" Now the accent made sense. "Mickey Staab?"

"Yes." Diana's voice was rough with tears. "I used to cut his hair, you know. That's how we met. I thought he was handsome and charming. He offered me a job that paid three times what I was making. I thought we were going to live happily ever after. Then I got pregnant and everything changed."

Lucy glanced over at the bassinet. "All he wanted was the baby."

Diana sniffled an agreement and continued. "It's some cultural thing from his country—something about firstborn sons being raised by their fathers. But I couldn't let my baby grow up like that—with all the violence and no regard for others. You taught me how

children should be treated. How I should be treated."
Niall had crossed the room, pinning down some important piece of information with his brother he didn't want anyone to overhear. "He found me. He found us. I was desperate to save Dorian—er, Tommy. And then Anton, sweet, sweet Anton, tried to help me get away. Stupid me. I fell in love with the wrong brother. I wanted to tell you that I didn't kill him. In case we don't get a chance to talk later."

How long did she have to listen to these horrible things Diana had had to deal with before KCPD could find her location and get her out of there? "What do you mean? We will see each other again. I promise you."

Guilt and regret shook in Diana's voice. "Mickey knows I left Tommy at your place. He followed Anton and me to your place the other night and tried to take him from you."

"In the laundry room."

"Keir?" Niall prompted, returning to her side to squeeze her hand. Lucy held on just as tightly.

"Yes. I wanted to see my baby one more time and explain everything to you. But this guy showed up and made everything worse." *Roger Campbell*. "Mickey blamed Anton—said his brother should be helping him get his son back, not helping..." She didn't need to explain whatever crude word Mickey had called her. "He was so angry. There was a horrible fight."

The blood at the hospital. He'd cut his own brother. Mickey Staab was a sick, obsessive man.

And now, without Antony Staab alive to even try to protect her, Diana was completely at his mercy.

Mickey's cruel tone at the other end of the call confirmed as much. "Tell her what I said. Tell her!"

Diana's next words came out in a panicked rush. "Stay away, Lucy. You stay away and don't let my baby anywhere near—"

Lucy heard the sting of a slap and a sharp cry of pain.

Her knees nearly buckled at the helpless rage surging through her. "Diana! You sorry SOB. You keep your hands off her. Diana!"

Niall's arm snaked around her waist, pulling her to his side. She tilted her gaze to his and he nodded. Keir had pinpointed the source of the call and dispatched every available unit to the location. "We're coming for you, Staab."

For a moment, there was only silence at the other end of the line. And then, "You think you have it all figured out, Dr. Smart Cop?"

"I know you killed your brother." Niall's articulate voice held none of its mesmerizing warmth. "It's the only answer that makes sense, Mikhail. Or should I say Mickey? You and Antony are twins. That's why all the DNA at the crime scene showed up as his. You share the same genetic code. That's why I thought he was Tommy's father."

"His name is Dorian," Mickey corrected, his articulation slipping each time his anger flared. "My son's name is Dorian."

"No court of law is ever going to let you be his father. *I* won't let you be his father," Niall warned. "Now let Diana go when the police arrive, and maybe you'll live long enough for Tommy to visit you in prison someday."

"You cannot deny me what is mine." Lucy collapsed

against Niall's strength at the frightened yelp she heard in the background. "The time for conversation is over. Listen very carefully, Miss McKane. I will leave the phone here so all your police friends can find it. But you—and you alone—will bring my son to me at the address I will tell you, and then I will give you this piece of trash you value so highly. If I see any police, Diana will die. If you are a minute late, she will die. If you do not bring me Dorian, you both will die."

Chapter Ten

"Is that the clearest picture we can get?"

Lucy heard Niall's voice over the device in her ear, taking some comfort in the knowledge that he was with her, even if he was stuck in a surveillance van with Keir nearly half a block away on the far side of the Saint Luke's Hospital parking lot. Meanwhile, she was making a grand show of unpacking a stroller and diaper bag from the trunk of her car, taking her time to assemble and stow Tommy's belongings before she retrieved the doll dressed in Tommy's clothing from the carrier in the backseat.

The deception was risky, but no way was she going to let Tommy anywhere near his father, especially after Mickey had murdered the baby's uncle and kidnapped his mother. While she followed the rest of Mickey Staab's directions to the letter, Tommy was safely hidden away at Thomas Watson's house, with Niall's father and Millie Leighter keeping a careful watch over the infant.

"I've got tech working on it," Keir assured him. "And remember, I've got men stationed all around the hospital complex. If Staab's Camaro or anyone matching his description shows up, we're going to know about

it long before he gets to Lucy." Then she realized Keir
was talking to her. "Luce, we've got you on screen. I
need you to do an audio check, too."

She pulled her knitting bag out, keeping appearances
as normal as possible. "Make sure you're getting my
best side."

"This isn't the time to joke," Niall warned. "You
know how easy it is for this meeting to go sideways.
No matter how prepared we are, we can't control all the
parameters. Staab is vicious and unpredictable."

"I know, Niall," she answered, wondering if he even
realized how worried he was about her, and wishing she
knew how to help him recognize and deal with those
burgeoning emotions. "Trust me, I know."

She'd stood up to Roger Campbell in a courtroom
over a decade ago, and she hadn't had backup of any
kind then beyond her attorney. Today she was standing
up to another violent man—but this time she had Niall
Watson, the rest of the Watson clan and a good chunk
of the Kansas City Police Department supporting her.
Meeting Mickey Staab face-to-face again would be far
more dangerous than testifying against Roger had been,
but knowing she had people she could rely on in her
corner this time made it easier somehow.

Niall's brother, on the other hand, appreciated a little
sarcasm to lighten the tension of the situation. "We're
reading you loud and clear, Lucy. We'll keep you posted
as soon as we spot our guy. Are you sure you're still
up for this?"

Keir, who'd worked sting operations like this before, suggested Staab had picked the parking lot at Saint
Luke's Hospital because of the easy access to traffic,

enabling a quick getaway once the hostage exchange was made, and because there were so many innocent bystanders around the busy public hospital who could get caught in the potential line of fire that he rightly assumed the police wouldn't be eager to get into any kind of gun battle with him. And if they cleared the area, then Staab would immediately know they were waiting for him. That left Lucy out there, unprotected and alone to face off against a kidnapper and killer.

"I'm sure." She held her breath as a car backed out of a parking space a few stalls away. She didn't breathe again until it drove past and turned toward the hospital building. No threat there. "But I want to move to a house with a private driveway. I'm sick of parking lots."

Niall surprised her by responding to her nervous prattle. "When this is all said and done, I'll take you to Mackinac Island, Michigan, where they don't have any cars or parking lots."

Lucy looped her knitting bag over her shoulder with her purse and closed the trunk lid. "Is that an invitation, Dr. Watson?"

She didn't giggle when she said his name this time.

He didn't answer the question, either. "Let's get through the next few minutes first."

Right. That would be the smart thing to do. She checked her watch and moved to the back passenger door, unable to delay the inevitable any longer. "And you're sure you've got Roger Campbell out of the picture? I don't want him thinking he's going to come in and save the day and wind up getting someone killed instead."

Niall answered. "Not to worry. Campbell violated his

parole six ways to Sunday by showing up at your office and our building. Duff's got him down at the precinct offices now booking him."

That was one less random factor about this whole setup she could eliminate. "So it's just Mickey Staab we have to worry about."

"Theoretically."

"Theoretically?" Lucy shook her head, unstrapping the doll and covering its face with the blanket she'd wrapped around it. "Is there some other bad guy you want to tell me about?"

But someone on Keir's team had spotted the car. "Be advised. We've got Staab in a silver Camaro approaching your position from the north entrance."

Lucy inhaled a deep breath, spying the all-too-familiar car turning down the lane where she was parked. She was shivering from the inside out. She was scared. Scared for herself and scared for Diana. But she wasn't alone, right? She didn't have to do this alone. "Talk to me, Niall. I need to hear your voice right now. Ask me a question or something."

"We need to talk about what happened this morning."

"What?" This morning? Did he mean making love? Or going over Antony Staab's autopsy report and DNA tests? Or something else entirely? Those weren't exactly topics that she wanted to get mixed up, especially over an open com line where Keir and a bunch of other cops could hear. "I can't talk about that right now. I can't…"

Mickey Staab's car slowed, and Lucy carried the camouflaged doll in her arms to the back of the car. The man who'd terrorized her foster daughter was close enough that she could see his dark eyes. But she didn't spot anyone else in the car with him. "Where's Diana?" she whispered, more afraid of what she didn't see than what she did.

"All right, people, this is it," Keir announced. "Eyes sharp. Nobody moves until I... Niall? Where are you going, bro? Son of..." Keir swore something pithy in her earbud. She heard a metallic slam in the distance. "Be advised. Hold your positions until I give the go to move in. We need eyes on the hostage."

Lucy adjusted the straps of her bags on her shoulders and hugged the doll to her chest as the silver car that had nearly run her down once before stopped in the driving lane only a few feet away. She swallowed hard, steeling herself for the coming confrontation. Mickey shifted the car into Park but left the engine running. She was confused when he leaned across the front seat. Why wasn't he getting out? Did he know there were a dozen cops watching him?

Eyes on the hostage. She couldn't see Diana.

"Where's Diana?" she shouted. She dipped her head to kiss the doll's forehead, keeping her eyes trained on the black-haired driver. "I did what you said. I brought Tommy. Where is she?"

The passenger door opened and a young woman tumbled out onto the asphalt with a barely audible moan.

"Diana!" Lucy lurched forward.

She froze when she saw the bloody knife in Mickey's hand. It was a long, wicked-looking thing like the one his brother had carried. Maybe it was even the same blade the monster had taken off his brother's dead body. Mickey followed Diana out the same door, standing over her as she curled into a fetal position, but crouching low enough that the door and frame of the car protected him from the eyes of any cop who might take a shot at him. He knew this was a setup. He knew he was being targeted. But he was that desperate to be united with his son.

And a desperate man was a dangerous one. "In my home country, women are good for two things. Betraying me is not one of them."

Lucy's eyes burned with tears. "You lousy son of a—"

He pointed the knife at Lucy. "Give me my son."

Lucy inched around the hood of his car, trying to get a clear look at how badly Diana was injured. "Let me help her. Please. Let me get her inside to the ER."

His dark eyes tracked her movement until she came one step too close. He thrust the knife in her direction, warning her to stop. "My son first."

The charade had gone on long enough.

"Here he is." Lucy tossed him the fake baby and grabbed Diana's hand to drag her from beneath the open door.

Even though he was startled enough to catch the doll dressed in Tommy's clothes, as soon as Lucy threw the package, Staab must have guessed the deception. "You bitch!" He dropped the doll and charged around the door into the open.

Lucy heard a chorus of *"Go! Go! Go!"* in her ear and dropped Diana's hand to reach into her bag as he raised the knife to attack.

"You are all lying—"

She jabbed the knitting needle into his arm as hard as she could, ripping open a chunk of skin. But she'd only deflected the blade, and his momentum carried the screaming man into her, knocking her to the ground. Lucy ignored the pain splintering through her shoulder and rolled.

"Move in! Move in!" She was hearing real voices now, echoing the shouts in her ear.

Lucy was on her feet first, but she stumbled over Diana's body before she could get away. Mickey's feet were surer, his stride longer. He latched onto a handful of her hair and jerked her back. A million pinpricks burned like fire across her scalp. That knife was so very close, and help was so very far away.

Lucy heard three loud bangs.

Mickey's grip on her hair went slack, and she dropped to her knees. His dark eyes glanced up to some unseen point behind her. Three spots of crimson bloomed at the front of his jacket, and he fell to the ground, dead.

Lucy scooted away before he landed on her and turned to see Niall holding a gun not ten feet away. His feet were braced apart on the pavement. A wisp of smoke spiraled from the end of the barrel, and she looked beyond the weapon to his steely blue glare.

She'd defy anyone to spy one trace of the nerdy scientist now.

But the heroic impression was fleeting. Niall was already holstering his gun and kicking Mickey Staab's knife away from the dead man's hand as Keir and several other police officers swarmed in.

He didn't say a word but knelt beside her, switching from cop to doctor mode before she could utter a thank-you or ask why he wasn't back in the van where he was supposed to be. He checked her eyes and ran his hands up and down her arms. She winced when he touched the bruise on her shoulder, but the sharp pain woke her from her stupor. "I'm okay." She turned his hands to Diana. "Help her."

"I need a med kit!" Niall yelled the moment he rolled Diana onto her back. She was bleeding from the cut across her belly that Mickey had no doubt inflicted upon her. "Diana?" He peeled off his ME jacket and wadded it up against the gaping wound. "Diana. I'm a doctor. Open your eyes."

Lucy crawled to the other side of her and took her hand, squeezing it between both of hers. "Diana, please, sweetie. It's Lucy. Listen to Niall. Open your eyes if you can."

Diana groaned and blinked her eyes open. But they were dull and unfocused. "Luce?" she slurred through a split lip.

"Yes. It's me. You're safe now. You're safe."

"Tell me…about…my baby." Her breath railed in her chest. "Mickey…he can't end up like Mickey."

Lucy glanced over at Niall, who was doing his best to stanch the wound. When he shook his head, the first tear squeezed between her eyelashes.

She kissed her foster daughter's hand. "He won't. Tommy's fine. Dorian, I mean. He's such a good little boy. Such a healthy eater. And loud. But he's safe. You did it, Diana. You protected your little boy. You kept him safe."

Diana's eyes drifted shut again. But her swollen lip curved into a smile. "Tommy's a good name. Tell him how much I loved him."

"Diana—"

"Tell him."

"I will, sweetie. I will. I promise that he will always know what you did for him."

"I knew you'd have my back." Diana's hand grew heavy in Lucy's grasp. "He couldn't have a better mother than you. Because you were always a mother to me."

"Diana?"

Lucy knew the moment she lost Diana forever. She gently set Diana's hand on her still chest and brushed the dark hair off her forehead to press a kiss there. The rest of the world blurred through her tears—the police, the EMTs on the scene taking over for Niall in a futile effort to revive the dead woman, the cars, everything. A merciless fist squeezed the air out of her chest, and then she was sobbing.

A soothing, deep-pitched voice reached her ears. "Sweetheart, stop."

She knew very little of what happened over the next few minutes, only that Niall's arms were around her. She didn't care about the blood on his hands that were now in her hair. She didn't care about the weeping spectacle she was making of herself. The only thing that mattered was that Niall was here.

Lucy McKane could deal with anything. But not this. Without Niall, she knew she absolutely couldn't deal with this.

Lucy cried a lot over the next few days, a sight that tore Niall up inside every time he saw those red-rimmed eyes and felt the sobs shaking her body.

She'd lost someone she considered a daughter. She'd relived the nightmare that could have been her a decade ago if she hadn't fought and scrapped and kept moving forward with her life. Lucy talked about feeling guilty for losing touch with someone she'd once been so close to and how angry she was that she hadn't been able to find Diana in time to save her.

But Lucy McKane was a kind of strong that Niall had never known before. Yes, she cried. But she also teased his brothers and had long talks with Millie and traded hugs with his father. She was even finding things in common with Niall's sister, now that Liv and Gabe were home from their honeymoon. She laughed with Tommy when he was awake and hummed with contentment when he fell asleep in her arms.

It was an emotional roller-coaster ride that Niall wasn't sure how to help with. But he could offer practical assistance and muscle. He'd stood by her side at Diana's funeral, and now he was helping her move Tommy and her stuff back to her apartment.

He'd almost been too late that afternoon when she'd faced down a killer. He'd felt too far away watching her on a TV screen from a distant van. And though firing his weapon wasn't his first duty as a cop, it had been the only duty that day that had mattered. Mickey Staab was hurting the woman who was more important to him than any other since his mother had died. When he'd raised that knife to gut Lucy the way he had Diana Kozlow, Niall had quickly taken aim and stopped him.

And now, as he set down the bassinet in her bedroom, Niall felt as if time was ticking away from him again, as if living just across the hall from Lucy and Tommy would be too far away. And if he didn't do something about it now, he might lose them forever.

He turned to watch Lucy leaning over the changing table to rub noses with Tommy. She smiled and the baby laughed. After tossing the soiled diaper she'd changed into the disposal bin, she carried him to the bassinet and laid him inside with one of his stuffed toys.

Why did having his own space back, and getting his world back to its predictable routine, feel as though Lucy was leaving him? And why did an irrational thought like that make his chest ache?

He was memorizing the curve of her backside in a pair of jeans when she straightened and faced him. "You're staring again, Niall."

"Am I?" His gaze dropped to the rich green color of her eyes. There was still sadness there, but a shining light, as well, that he couldn't look away from.

"You don't know when you're doing that?" She nudged him out into the hallway and closed the door behind them so Tommy could nap. "I feel like a specimen under a microscope."

"Sorry. I guess I'm a little brainless when I'm around you."

"Brainless? You? Never."

He followed her out to the living room. "There's no logic to it. I can't think straight. I'm disorganized. I can't focus on my work. All I do is react and feel."

"Feeling isn't a bad thing, Niall. What do you feel?"

He raked his fingers through his hair and shook his head, searching for the definitive answer. "Off-kilter. Out of sorts. Like I never want to let either of you out of my arms or out of my sight. I think about you when we're apart. I anticipate when I'll see you again. I'm thinking of Tommy's future and whether or not he'll go to college and how he shouldn't grow up without a mother. I worry that you're not safe or that you're talking some other man's ear off or—"

Lucy shushed him with her finger over his lips and offered him the sweetest smile he'd seen in days. "I love you, too."

"Yeah." He nodded as his heart cracked open inside him and understanding dawned. "Yes. I love you." He tunneled his fingers into her hair and tipped her head back to capture her beautiful mouth in a kiss. Her arms circled his waist, and he pulled her body into his as that eager awareness ignited between them.

Sometime later, when she was curled up in his lap on her couch and he could think clearly again, Niall spoke the new discoveries in his heart. "Lucy McKane, I have a question for you."

She brushed aside the hair that stuck out over his forehead. "You know I love to listen to you talk."

"I'm a patient man, and I'll give you all the time you need."

"To do what?"

"Will you marry me? Can we adopt Tommy together after the six-month waiting period? Can we be a family?"

She grinned. "That's three questions, Dr. Watson."

"See? Completely brainless. I'm new at all this touchy-feely stuff, so be kind. Don't make me beg for an answer."

She tilted her mouth to meet his kiss. "Yes. Yes. And yes."

Epilogue

The unhappy man skimmed through the article he'd already read a dozen times before folding the newspaper and setting it on the corner of his desk. "The *Journal* says that Niall Watson was involved with a shooting outside Saint Luke's Hospital. Internal Affairs vindicated it as necessary force to protect the intended victim. It's not front-page news, but the story is long enough to mention his grandfather being well enough to leave the hospital and move home to continue his recovery."

The man sitting across from him refused to apologize if that was what this late-night meeting was about. "I did what you asked. I ruined the wedding. I got those Watson boys and their daddy all up in arms without any clue about what's going on. And there's no way they can trace anything about that shooting back to you. For all they know, some crazy guy went off his rocker."

"Seamus Watson is supposed to be dead." He pulled open the top right drawer of his desk and fingered the loaded gun he kept there. "When I hire you to do a job, I can't afford to have you fail."

"Then tell me what I can do to make things right.

Reputation is everything in my business. The next job will be on the house."

Satisfied, for the moment, with that arrangement, the man pushed the drawer shut. His employee could live for another day.

The Watson family might not be so lucky.

* * * * *

JOIN THE
MILLS & BOON
BOOKCLUB

* **FREE** delivery direct to your door

* **EXCLUSIVE** offers every month

* **EXCITING** rewards programme

50% OFF
YOUR FIRST
PARCEL

Join today at
Millsandboon.co.uk/Bookclub

MILLS & BOON

HEROES

At Your Service

Experience all the excitement of a
gripping thriller, with an intense romance
at its heart. Resourceful, true-to-life
women and strong, fearless men face
danger and desire - a killer combination!

MILLS & BOON
MEDICAL
Pulse-Racing Passion

Set your pulse racing with dedicated, delectable doctors in the high-pressure world of medicine, where emotions run high and passion, comfort and love are the best medicine.

Medical stories published every month, find them all at:

millsandboon.co.uk

MILLS & BOON

Desire

Indulge in secrets and scandal, intense drama and plenty of sizzling hot action with powerful and passionate heroes who have it all: wealth, status, good looks…everything but the right woman.